I0589394

# FREAKS ANON

*Freaks Anon*, a novel by Matt Darst.

*Monument,* a short story by Matt Darst

Copyright 2016 by Matt Darst, Grand Mal Press. All rights Reserved. Printed in the United States of America. No part of this book or short story may be used or reproduced in any manner whatsoever without written consent except in the case of brief quotations embodied in critical articles or reviews. For information, contact Matt Darst via http://www.mattdarst.com or http://www.grandmalpress.com.

ISBN: 978-0-692-62493-7


Published by Grand Mal Press, Forestdale, MA
http://www.grandmalpress.com

*Freaks Anon,* Copyright 2016Monument, Copyright 2016
Library of Congress Cataloging-in-Publication Data
Matt Darst, Grand Mal Press

Cover by Matt Hale
http://www.MattHaleDesign.com

Connect with Matt Darst
Blog: http://www.mattdarst.com
Like: http://www.facebook.com/FreaksAnon
Dead Things: http://www.deadthingsthenovel.com


p. cm

FIRST EDITION

All proceeds from the sale of this book will be donated to Stand Up To Cancer (SU2C). Private donations can be made at http://do.eifoundation.org/goto/mattdarst

# FREAKS ANON

## by Matt Darst

&

MONUMENT

A dystopian short story by Matt Darst

GRAND MAL

P R E S S

# Acclaim for *Freaks Anon*

"Darst works his magic in horror once again, this time expanding into the realm of superheroes in an exciting mash-up that fans of both comic books and the paranormal are sure to enjoy!"— Stuart Conover, ScienceFiction.com

"I had so much fun reading *Freaks Anon*. Being a huge Alan Moore fan, I'm always hoping to read something intelligent when it comes to superheroes. I crave material like that . . . and with its great writing and believable characters, *Freaks Anon* nails it. It's a fanboy's dream. I once read that you should only keep the books you will read again, and I've tried to live by that. I will definitely keep this book." — Frank Hrin, Fearshop.com Horror Podcast

"As with *Dead Things*, Matt Darst has created another sublime world. *Freaks Anon* is a dark, weird fairy tale of monsters and heroes. Excellent." — Rich Hawkins, Author of *The Last Plague* and *The Last Outpost*

## Acclaim for *Dead Things*
"Matt Darst is a truly original talent. His quick pacing, encyclopedic grasp of literature and history, and spellbinding mix of social commentary and jaw-dropping action make *Dead Things* a first-rate triumph. With a dash of Bradbury, hints of Huxley and Orwell, and heavy dollops of smart pop culture, Darst is taking the zombie novel in a really cool new direction, and you're going to love every page of it. Hang on, if you can, because this guy has written a future history that will rattle every nerve you've got." — Joe McKinney, author of *Dead City* and *Apocalypse of the Dead* and recipient of multiple Bram Stoker Awards

"A first-class zombie story which takes place in a beautifully realized post-apocalyptic world. In many ways a spiritual cousin to Matheson's classic *I am Legend*, this is a fantastic and surprising horror tale. Highly recommended." — David Moody, author of *Them or Us, Autumn,* and *Trust*

"Matthew Darst is a writer who shares my Romero-esque love of zombies. Ever true to the vision of the zombie holocaust brought to us by *Night of the Living Dead*, Darst brings the collapse of civilization up to date. Darst brings us a startling real glimpse of the cause of the zombie contagion." — Iain McKinnon, author of *Domain of the Dead* and *Remains of the Dead*

"Matt Darst . . . writes masterfully in the genre and fine art of zombie horror, and *Dead Things* is the zombie novel for the rest of us. You know . . . the readers who do not really 'get' the deep dark obsession with the ghouls? Well, even if you have a subtle disdain for anything flesh-eating, do yourself a favor and pick up *Dead Things*. It— in a word— is brilliant. The plotline is perfect, the characters flawless and the solution is so simple that it is entirely plausible. Even zombie-purists cannot help but enjoy this book that takes the reader off the beaten path of zombification. A fresh twist creates an a-ha moment that the horror reader is sure to appreciate." — Sylvia Cochran, *The Deepening World of Fiction*

"A fabulous debut novel. Darst excels in creating a unique vision of the aftermath of America after the dead begin to rise. The characters are well written, and I found myself getting emotionally invested. Darst took special care with this book, and it absolutely shows. The zombie action is used with razor sharp efficiency. This is a great read, and I cannot recommend it highly enough." — Chip Fehd, BuyZombie.com

"Darst uses a number of nifty maneuvers to keep this a fresh offering. The dialogue is smart and witty. The science behind the story is very well thought out. Integral to the plot are zombies; however, it is more than a zombie novel. It's a novel about human beings, a novel where the monsters we become are far more frightening than the things shambling from the graves to gnaw on our flesh. A well-written, smartly entertaining debut." —John Boden, Shock Totem Publications (ShockTotem.com)

*This book is dedicated to a real superhero.*
*Mom, I love you with all of my heart.*

# TRACKLISTING

## Side A

1. Ripple
2. Apron Strings
3. Making Plans for Nigel
4. Ugly American Girl
5. Sensoria
6. Disguises
7. Sound of Thunder

## Side B

8. They Said Tomorrow
9. My Death
10. Look Back in Anger
11. Tall Ships
12. Louis Quatorze
13. Nite Flights
14. A Means to an End

## Side C

15. Crazy Wisdom
16. I Liked You Better When You Were Dead
17. Confusion
18. Red Headed Stranger
19. Don't Change
20. One Step Ahead
21. The Endless Sea

## Side D

22. What Goes On
23. The Naked Part
24. Talk about the Past
25. Show of Strength
26. Hero
27. Both Ends Burning
28. Of All the Things We've Made

**Bonus Track**

*Monument*, a Dystopian Short Story

# Track One: Ripple

*Auvergne, France. November 1764.*

Clouds of vapor materialize then retreat. Ghostly apparitions, the cold gives the monster's pants form.

Dusk cedes to night. This is the "hour between dog and wolf." This is the hour between worlds. This is *his* hour.

Winter's come early. A thin veil of newly formed ice masks the churning beneath the surface of the brook. He prowls the bank on all fours, frozen reeds crunching under the thick pads of his paws.

He's just a dozen feet from the creaking waterwheel when the second oil lamp flickers to life.

He stops dead, his lupine body going stiff, his breath silent. He hides among the willows, secreted by lengthening shadows. He shifts his weight to his haunches, slowly rises.

Inside the mill, the silhouette of a woman beckons to a child studying at a desk. The boy stands and moves to join her near the stove. The creature's head cocks, his pointed ears tilting to catch their exchange of words. "*Le dîner est presque prêt.*" Dinner is almost ready.

He inhales deep. Chicken, boiling in onions. Bread.

But there's more, so much more. Masked beneath those broad strokes are subtleties, hidden scents.

In his human form, he could never detect these nuances. But now, his sense of smell is specialized. It is fifty times stronger. A nasal pocket traps odor molecules in a layer of mucous. The cilia of receptor neurons pick up the diffused particles. Signals are transmitted to his olfactory lobe.

The aromas are distinct: sweet, the woman's perfumed skin; sour, milk on the boy's upper lip; salty, the trace of sweat on her neck; and savory, the blood that pulses through their arteries, filling their muscle tissue, powering their organs.

His tongue rolls over his teeth, pausing on the tip of an elongated canine. The umami makes him salivate. Steaming drool escapes from his maw, melting the snow beneath him.

The wolf inside—yes, he has given over his body to *canis lupus lupus* this night—screams at him like a fiend from folklore. *Break down the door, give chase, and tear out their throats.* But his mind, a vestige of his humanity, holds him fixed. It tells the inner wolf to sit, stay. He has—no, *they* have—all night.

Pierre Delmas—husband, father, and the owner of this mill—is in Lorcières. He won't return until well past dawn. Of this, the monster is certain. He confirmed as much with Delmas himself just last week.

❖❖❖

Sipping witbier in a darkened corner of L'Abattus Agneau, the monster watched as Delmas and a dozen farmers quarreled around a beer-soaked oak table at the front of the pub.

"Our grain is rotting at the gates as we speak," Delmas said. "Monsieur Gance, if we do not break this stalemate, the season is lost."

Gance raised a brow and shook his head. "Perhaps lost for those less enterprising."

*Enterprise.* The monster snorted. This man knew nothing of enterprise.

Henri Gance, the youngest of six brothers, was born into richness. His father's massive estate stretched thousands of acres east to west, virtually separating Auvergne from Bourgogne. Before his passing from Consumption last spring, the elder Gance had provided Delmas and others passage to the markets north to sell their grain.

With his death, the vast farm was divided between the brothers, Balkanized like so many other privately held lands in feudal France. Lacking the canals and rivers of England, the bequest necessitated the negotiation of new easements. Five of the six brothers eventually agreed to allow Delmas and his peers passage. However, the sixth, Henri, withheld signature.

"What right do you have to condemn our grains to decay?" an elderly man said, straining to stand. "There are people, woman and children, starving less than a dozen miles away."

"I claim and require no right but birthright, Monsieur Meursault."

Jean Meursault poked a shaking but furious thumb in Gance's direction. "Pure arrogance. Your father was a good man. He would be ashamed if he could see you now."

"You'll be able to convey that message to him yourself any day now, I'm sure, old man," Gance said, eyes on his goblet.

A wide man called Guy Debucourt interceded. "Gentlemen, gentlemen, this bickering achieves nothing. I'm sure we can find common ground."

"Yes," Gance replied, looking up, "that is, as long as your 'common ground' and the grounds of my property are not one and the same."

They debated like this for an hour, the monster barely concealing his smirk behind a stein.

Delmas grew frustrated. "Please, Mr. Gance, listen to reason—"

Gance cut off Delmas with a wave of his hand. "Look, we've been through this before. It is all very easy. I'm happy to provide an easement across my land. In return, all I ask is for reasonable compensation."

"What you've asked for is a third of our grain," Meursault spat. "That's a tax, pure and simple."

Someone behind the old man nodded angrily and echoed him. "You're no king, Gance. You have no right to levy taxes."

"What? And I don't have expenses?" Gance asked, touching his chest in offense.

"Like?" said someone in the throng.

"There is infrastructure to maintain," Gance replied, looking past Meursault. "Plus, more importantly, there's the cost of protection."

"Protection?" another farmer, Frederic Malle, asked. "From what?"

Malle had not noticed that the other farmers had gone quiet. They exchanged nervous glances, confirming a communal but unspoken fear.

The monster laughed from a table away. This perturbed Malle. "From what?" he repeated, brow furrowing. "Highwaymen?"

Malle's inquiry could almost be excused. There was a time, after all, when footpads and mounted robbers lurked the fields and woodlands, preying on the unsuspecting. That is, until last June, when the killings started in Langogne. Criminal activity had since been suspended.

"No," Gance answered with a hush. "Not highwaymen."

"What then?"

No one answered. All remained silent. Until—

"La Bête," the monster said.

Malle gulped. "I see."

*La Bête.* The monster had been called many things by many people. *The Wolf of Chazes. Le Loup de Soissons. The Monster of Besseyre Saint Marie. The Beast of Gévaudan.* Even *The Beast Who is Eating Everybody.* It was the Royal Wolfcatcher, Le **Louvetier Royal,** though, who called the creature, simply, "The Beast."

*The Beast.* It was an abbreviation that inadvertently solidified the monster's status as the country's single and greatest manifestation of evil . . . and the single greatest threat to the monarchy.

Another moment of uncomfortable silence passed before Gance announced his intention to retire for the evening. "Look, gentlemen, I appreciate your time, but it seems no agreement will be had tonight. I bid you *adieu*—"

"Wait," Debucourt interrupted. "Just how many hands will you make available to escort our carts?"

"Nearly a dozen," Gance replied.

Debucourt sighed. "Then I'll agree to your terms."

"Me as well," came another voice.

"Guy," Delmas exclaimed, taking Debucourt by the shoulder. He leaned in. "You can't mean it."

"Mean it I do, Pierre. I can't just abandon our grain. My family has worked too hard. Something is better than nothing, especially with that *thing* running about devouring everything that breathes."

"We can't stand alone on this issue," Delmas implored. "Divided we fall."

Malle interrupted. "I'm afraid I must accept Monsieur Gance's terms as well."

"What?"

"Pierre, people are going to starve—my family among them—if our grain doesn't hit the market. We'll have revolution on our hands."

"I don't care about hypotheticals," Delmas said. "I care about the here and now, about my mill, my family." He turned to Gance. "The King's taxes are already unprecedented. How can we be expected to pay for this as well?"

Gance shook his head. "Those who fear looking in the mirror ascribe fault elsewhere. Don't blame King Louis XV, and don't blame me. If you can't take responsibility for your station, Pierre, maybe you should blame The Wolf."

The monster found this a curious but valid point. There was plenty of blame to pass around: the King, the laws of inheritance, opportunists, the drought. But the beast took particular pride in his role in dragging the region into poverty and famine.

The King regularly conscripted farmhands. They were forced to join his hunting parties. They left their wives and children behind, but dared not ask them to mind the livestock and the pastures. They knew well La Bête punished those who did. They told tales of how the monster preferred the taste of humans to animals. It targeted people, choosing them over cattle roaming the same fields.

"Monsieur Gance," Delmas begged. "Please. Things are dire for my wife and son. There's a lien on the mill, and sickness has struck the cattle. I worry for our newborn calves. We depend on the revenues from each and every grain."

Before Gance could respond, however, another farmer assented to pay. "I'm in, Henri."

And then another. "Me too."

"As am I."

"*Moi aussi.*"

Delmas' cause was lost. He drank deep from his goblet as he watched his summit disintegrate, the farmers capitulating in turn. Even Meursault eventually acquiesced. Slumping in his chair, Delmas ordered another beer.

One by one the farmers departed. Gance excused himself as well, leaving Delmas alone with his drink. Soon that, too, was gone.

That's when the monster made his approach.

"Monsieur," the monster said, sliding a pint of ale in front of Delmas' downcast face.

Delmas looked up. "*Merci*," he said solemnly.

The beast nodded. "*Homo homini lupus.*"

Delmas cocked his head, raised a brow. "Sorry?"

"It's a Latin proverb," the monster said. "It means, 'Man is a wolf to man.'"

Delmas nodded. "That certainly seems the case."

The monster half-smiled, a long canine biting into his lower lip. "May I join you?"

Delmas gestured to a chair.

"My name is Alec," the monster said, extending a hand, "Alec Moreau. Forgive my eavesdropping, but the War has hurt us all. Still, I imagine the impact upon our patriot farmers and their families has been especially distressing."

Delmas took Moreau's hand and introduced himself. Plied with beer, he began talking. He talked late into the night, and then talked some more. He told the monster about his troubles, his mill. He told the monster about Gance's revocation of the easement. He told him how he left his wife and child alone during his excursions to the City. He told the monster everything.

Finally, the monster Moreau asked Delmas a question: "What would you say if I told you I might be able to help?"

Delmas was all ears.

"I will purchase both of your calves for one-hundred *livres parisis* apiece if you'll allow."

"Two-hundred livres? That's more than the salary of a huntsman. Why on earth would you do that?"

"I was once a lot like you, a farmer and a father too. Before that, though, I was a soldier, and I was called back into service during the Seven Years War." Moreau looked past Delmas, focusing on something beyond the walls of the tavern. He stared into space and recalled his tour of duty. "My company was sent to protect the settlement of Saint-Louis in Senegal. The trip took forty days. We lost half our number to malaria and wild animals, creatures I'd never seen before. When we arrived, we were two weeks too late. The post had been lost to the British. We retreated to Gorée, but we had lost our colonies in Gambia too.

Our holdings in Africa sacked, we returned north to join the front. We fought the Prussians. We fought the Duke of Brunswick. We fought the Germans. We fought everyone. For six years I bled in the name of the King. In the end, all of our fighting, all of the lives lost, meant nothing. The King capitulated, signed the Treaty of Paris, and I returned to France. I arrived at my house and found it was no longer my home. Strangers lived there. My wife and son were missing. The police had kidnapped them years earlier. Like the families of many soldiers, they were loaded onto boats and sent to colonize the Americas."

Delmas winced. "I'm sorry."

"So, unlike you, I care very much about the possibility of revolution. I care very much about a tomorrow without a crown."

Delmas listened, chin in hand.

"The loss of my wife and son gave me new purpose: question authority, undermine the system, create chaos through design."

"Chaos through design?"

Moreau asked Delmas if he ever read Voltaire.

Delmas went blank.

"*Candide?*"

It didn't register with the peasant. It shouldn't have. The Administrators of Paris banned *Candide* for its criticism of church and state, and Voltaire himself all but disowned it out of fear of persecution.

"It's an adventure, but it's the subtext that has people buzzing. Is Voltaire criticizing Leibniz's theory of Optimism? Is he elevating Pessimism? Or is he sympathizing with Meliorism?"

Delmas frowned. He was lost.

Moreau didn't care. He continued, almost to himself. "The answer: it's not about 'isms' at all. *Candide* is about chaos. Not randomness or chance, but about chaos as order in a system. It's about the complexity and unpredictability of life. It's about how small changes to a cycle can have significant consequences, building and amplifying like a stone cast into a pond."

"Ripples on the water," Delmas said.

"*Exactement.*"

Delmas smiled. "That sounds nice in theory, but I'm afraid the idea of being a ripple is a little too grand for my family. We don't know Monsieur Voltaire."

Moreau chuckled. "Pierre, even the smallest of pebbles can have an impact. I'm but just one stone produced by the system, and I fully intend to create more. For instance, what would you do with two-hundred livres?"

"That's easy. I'd put my son in school," Delmas said.

The monster smiled. "There is nothing more radical than an education."

Delmas grinned.

So it was settled. The-monster-that-called-himself-Moreau gave the man one hundred livres and the promise of another hundred in one week's time. Delmas need only bring his calves back to this very address. The innkeeper would hold the calves for the monster and the funds for Delmas. Moreau even paid for a room in advance so Delmas need not travel home in the pitch.

Delmas dutifully returned a week later. The exchange was made.

❖❖❖

Now he sleeps deeply in the best bed L'Abattus Agneau can offer, his belly full of lamb and beer, his pockets full of gold, and his head full of dreams. Now he sleeps unaware that his alleged benefactor has transformed into a creature molded in the forges of hell . . . and that this creature awaits just outside the door of his home.

After the embers of the fireplace have died down and the house is dark, the monster enters. He passes the boy's bed in the front room, moves to the rear of the mill. Madam Delmas sleeps in a small chamber behind the kitchen. He bends down and slides through the doorway, his massive shoulders and head pressing the frame. There's a creak of oak grinding against oak. She wakes, screams at the silhouette of the thing filling the casing. The monster is on her in a beat, her arterial blood pulsing down his gullet the next.

He sways as he gulps hard from her throat. His eyes roll back into his skull. He's lost in the richness, the pleasure of the kill. He almost doesn't hear the front door open, the boy running through the snow.

Almost.

The hunt is on.

The next morning, the monster walks the stream north. He picks his teeth with a cattail. He stops to drink at a swirling pool devoid of ice and stares for a moment at his reflection. Despite his human form, he sees nothing but the Beast staring back. His broad, rounded forehead, high cheekbones, wide nose, and narrow chin are covered in meat and mess, bits of what once was the son of Delmas.

The monster shrugs. Creating revolutionaries is a bloody business.

Now it's off to the north. North to a farm owned by the youngest of six sons, north to his next victim. Tonight, the monster will play equalizer. Tonight he will fertilize the fields with Gance's blood.

At least Delmas will no longer need to worry about easements in the years to come.

Chaos works in mysterious ways.

# Track Two: Apron Strings

*Indianapolis, Indiana. 2 September 2001.*

Theresa Gerig says she already told the cops everything. Anyway, the Cinnabon will be busy soon. The dinner crowd hits City Center Mall in half an hour.

The masked man thanks her, promises that his questions are few. He'll be out of her hair in ten minutes, probably less.

"I don't know," she says, biting her lip.

He says he needs her help. He's read the Indianapolis Metropolitan Police Department's report. He calls it a "shoddy" piece of police work. "Something's missing, some detail glossed over by witnesses or neglected entirely by the IMPD."

He's tanned and unshaven. She fixates on a faded red tattoo, the number 38, on his neck.

"Murder investigations deserve more effort," he says. "Hade's flames, murders deserve an opportunity to be solved." A hand balls into a fist. He looks straight into her eyes. "And you just might be the key."

She's nodding. OMG. He. Is. So. Intense. Her face goes flush. "Um, okay, I'll try to help." After all, how many people can claim to have been interviewed by a gladiator?

He corrects her. "Centurion."

She doesn't know there's a difference, apologizes. "A centurion."

"No. *The* Centurion." His voice is like gravel. "And I can't quantify that. My guess: probably not very many."

He's angst-y and older, a loner, probably a bad boy. He smells a little of stale beer. He'd drive her mother crazy. She leans in. "Okay, Mr. Centurion," she says, popping her gum, "So what do you want to know?"

His eyes narrow. "Everything."

"Everything?" she asks.

"Yes. Everything you know about John Hooper and the night of

August 6th, the night he died."

"I don't know much about John personally." She tells him that Hooper went to school with her brother. He never mentioned him much. She doesn't think Hooper had many friends. She can't think of any enemies.

"But we know there was at least one," the armored man says. John Hooper was garroted in the elevator thirty feet from the food court four weeks ago. He was just 17. "Please, continue."

Her account mirrors her police statement. At around 6 p.m. Hooper ordered a pretzel. He grabbed a table near the Pizza Hut. He sat alone. He was still there at about 9 p.m. when her shift ended.

When she finishes telling her story, the man tells her he wants to "shake the needle from the groove." He asks her if she knows the story of Perseus.

She doesn't.

"He's a hero from mythology," the man begins.

A week from now, she'll recall Centurion's story over cosmos with her friend Marisol between episodes of *Sex and the City*. "So Perseus was this dude from olden times who wore a toga and trainers with wings on them. He wanted to kill this monster, some woman with snakes for hair, to save his squeeze. But there was a problem: this monster was so ugly she could turn you to stone if you looked at her. Yes, uglier than Carrie Bradshaw. Don't be mean. My mom likes Carrie. Wait, I forgot a part. It's important. He also carries around a mirror in his shield, which is weird because they didn't have cameras back then, did they? No, I'm pretty sure they didn't. I think they did have all of those artists and sculptors named after ninja turtles, though. So he probably carried it in case someone wanted to paint him, and who wants to be immortalized with hair out of place? So he's checking his look when all of the sudden Medusa—wait, that's the monster's name—comes and tries to turn him into stone. But because he sees her in the mirror, he doesn't get frozen. So guess what he does? He lops off her head with his sword. Chop. And do you know what the lesson is? No, it's not about pretty people being better than ugly people. No, you're not better than me. Funny, bitch. No, it's about . . . shit, now you made me forget. Anyway,

I deserved better than a C in ancient history last semester, don't you think?"

What he really says is that the direct approach may not always be the best. "Sometimes problems can be solved just by looking at them differently, like Perseus using the reflection in his shield."

"Okay," she says.

With that, he pulls a satchel from his side. He sets it gently on the countertop and flips open the leather top so she can see the contents.

"Oh, my God," she exclaims looking upon the broken body of a sparrow. "It's Mr. Piccolo."

Her story is about to change . . . and dramatically so.

Gerig named the bird after the sound of his song, after the flute her niece plays in marching band. She forgot about the bird until this moment. She last saw it the night Hooper was murdered.

He says something about memory errors being typical, that memories are inherently unreliable. Memories are more of a reconstruction than a recording. "We can only perceive so much of our world, and our brains fill in the blanks. Our brains take a lot of shortcuts. We borrow from what we've learned or from other memories entirely. Sometimes we need a trigger to get things right."

"A trigger?" she asks, before answering her own question. "Like Mr. Piccolo."

He nods. "Right."

Gerig says it's not unusual for animals to get into the mall. It's rare, but not unusual. Once in a blue moon, a critter follows an unaware shopper through a revolving door or disability entrance. Squirrels and rats are easily captured with traps and destroyed. Birds, however, are another matter. Catching them is a spectacle.

The mall gave up on capturing them about a year ago. Some upset kindergarteners on a fieldtrip witnessed some "bad men trying to hurt the birds." That, at least, is what the barrage of letters that they mailed to the Mayor said. The letters featured rough crayon drawings of keystone custodians running about with ladders, swinging away at the sky with mops, tripping over shoppers and each other. They begged the Mayor to save their "feathered friends." The Mayor's staff immediately met with the building's management company. After a brief conversation about permit issues and potential fines, the practice was halted and the mall declared an avian sanctuary. The Mayor introduced a resolution recognizing the children as "heroes," and they received a standing ovation at a City-County Council hearing.

Gerig didn't have to tell Centurion all of this. He knew the story. He tells her he read it on microfiche at the library when researching the mall, an article in the Indianapolis Business Journal. "The title was 'Crying Fowl,'" he says. "Icarus' feathers. Only Comus"—the Greek God of mirth—"would find amusement in a homonym like that. Journalists."

She nods. She has no idea what he just said.

"I've seen a lot of birds here."

She says a dozen or more make the mall their home. They soar among the rafters of the Artsgarden, a seven-story glass enclosure that links the mall to the hotels. Food is plentiful, predators absent, and their heads always protected from the elements. "They've got it pretty good," Gerig says. Then she frowns. "So what happened to Mr. Piccolo?"

"I'm not sure," he says, and he isn't, although he's certain he's somehow connected to the events of August 6th. He carefully closes the bag and lets it hang at his side. "Did Mr. Hooper know this bird?"

"Sure. Jonathon used to stop by and feed the birds a couple times a week," she says. "Mr. Piccolo was his favorite. He always made time for a conversation with Mr. Piccolo."

Centurion raises a brow. "He talked to the bird?"

Gerig laughs. "No, they *conversed*. They talked to each other."

"Birds of a feather," he says with a sniff. "Anyone else ever join their . . . discussions?"

She shakes her head.

He asks again. "You sure?"

"No one."

He asks her once more for good measure.

"No . . . just his girlfriend."

"Girlfriend?" He leans in. He tells her he didn't read about a girlfriend in the police report. It's another fact never before offered, solicited, or recorded.

She says she didn't think it was important.

"That's the problem with investigations." He says that witnesses focus too much on what they think has importance, what they think the interviewer wants to hear. They ignore the value of minutia. The path to solving a crime, he continues, is usually meandering. "Hades hides and bides his time in the thicket of details."

"Okay," she says slowly, her face a blank.

"So please continue." His invitation comes off more like a demand.

"Well, at least I think it was his girlfriend," she says, back-peddling. "She used to come in and feed the birds with him. She'd talk to Mr. Piccolo too, but Jonathan would have to translate." She hesitates.

"Tell me more."

There's a pang of pain in Gerig's expression, a hint of jealousy. "Well, she wasn't just any girl. She was exotic. She looked like a super-model, and walked like one too. I mean this girl prowled." She notices a change in Centurion's countenance, something close to a nod of recognition. "Do you know her?"

"Maybe," he says. He tells Gerig that he can't provide a description though. Doing so would risk implanting thoughts and could contaminate her memory of events. He's come so far, too far, to undermine his investigation by taking shortcuts now.

She finally understands just how serious he is about the murder. "Honestly, I've never seen a girl so pretty, at least not in person. And never in Indianapolis."

"Pretty," Centurion repeats. He goes silent. He waits for her to fill the vacuum.

"She was a black girl. Really skinny, really tall. Kind of like Naomi Campbell, but with a smile."

He pulls a piece of paper from beneath his tunic and unfolds it. It's a series of pictures, yearbook photos, and one of them is circled. "Is this her?"

Gerig nods. "Hey, that's her."

"How long were they together?" he asks in a burst, his nonchalance giving way to a rare giddiness.

"A month or two, I guess . . ."

He inhales deep, collecting himself. "Do you know where she is now?" he asks, his voice even and measured.

She shakes her head. "No, I haven't seen her since that night."

He doesn't immediately respond. He looks lost in thought. He's working out a puzzle. She imagines the border sections as complete, but she can tell he's frustrated by a handful of missing jigsaw pieces in the middle.

"Was I able to help?" she asks.

"Do you know where the security office is?" Centurion asks abruptly. He's fidgeting, like he has somewhere else to be.

"Sure," she says with a slight confused tilt of the head. She gestures beyond him. "It's over by the Nieman Marcus."

"Excellent," he says. "Thank you for everything."

She expects he'll ask for her phone number.

He doesn't.

Her jaw drops as he walks away. Her crush turns to annoyance. "Weirdo."

He crosses the mall. Signs indicate there are restrooms down the hallway to his left. He ducks into the corridor. He leans against the cinder block wall, makes as if he's waiting for someone in the bathroom. He's as inconspicuous as a man wearing white body armor in a public place can be. When he's certain no one is looking, he pulls the fire alarm at his side.

He makes one more stop in the shopping center: the security booth, where he'll find a copy of the security tape from the night of August 6, 2001. It's the final task before he buries Mr. Piccolo, the bird that tried, and failed, to save John Hooper. Heroes and friends of Mars deserve a proper burial.

Then he'll drink heavily. Again.

❖❖❖

*Chicago, Illinois.*

"That's the last of it," Chee's father says with a huff. He drops a medium-sized moving box to the floor.

"Dad, be careful," she says from the edge of her bed. "You might break something."

Her father leans against the frame of the door, crosses his arms.

Massive tomes are stacked big to small on top of an imposing oak desk. Opposite it, a mahogany dresser and a full-size bed anchor the room. A samurai sword hangs over the carved headboard. The only thing belying the fact that this is a teen's room is the cardboard filing box at his feet. It's simply marked, "Chee's," and, "Personal: Keep Out." What her handwriting lacks in detail it makes up for in flair. The words are written in incredibly slanted cursive letters that could never be contained by the horizontal lines of a composition pad. The markings remind him of his wife's penmanship.

"It's not marked 'Fragile,'" he says.

She sighs. "When you move as much as we do, labeling boxes just seems like a waste of ink."

*Touché.* She shares her mother's wit as well.

He stands there for a beat before she rises. She grabs the box, trudges to the corner of the room like a Soviet-era laborer, and stacks it with six others. She returns and slumps back on her bed.

Another second passes. "Well, aren't you going to start unpacking?"

She stares at her shoes.

"You know, if you start unpacking, you just might begin to feel a little better."

She glares at him. Her eyes don't look like those of a seventeen year-old, at least not today. Today, they're glassy, dark pools. Her anger can't mask the fact that she's been crying again. "What's the point?" she asks. "I'll just have to pack again in a couple weeks. Maybe less."

He has no response, no fatherly advice to offer. What can he say? They've spent the last month in a hotel, and he too has yet to put away two suitcases of clothes packed three moves ago. Instead, he grunts, points out the obvious. "Well, Tuesday's a big day. I'll leave you to it." With that, he nods out of the room.

He spends a few hours organizing his study. He grabs the next box.

*Marcus Jacobs—1950 N. Larrabee—Chicago, IL—60657—Study—Files—*

*2 of 6.* The ink is black, his print capitalized and neat. He studies the label for a moment before cutting the tape with an envelope opener.

When he returns later to tell her that he's ordered takeout, he finds her still fully clothed and asleep on top of the comforter. He flicks the light switch off, and the room goes black. He goes to the side of her bed, folds the bedspread around her lean body. He kisses her lightly on the cheek.

He takes a moment to survey the darkened room. The boxes have all been opened, her clothes and décor mostly unpacked and put in order. Her collection of Mold-a-Ramas—hollow molded plastic dinosaurs and jungle creatures—mingle on her dresser. The elephant from Lowry Park Zoo high-fives a green gorilla from the Lincoln Park Zoo with its trunk while a Field Museum T. Rex looks on. Her Hello Kitty figurines, on the other hand, are arranged by age. She's even hung her bulletin board over her desk. He turns to Chee to make sure she's still sleeping, and sneaks over for a closer look.

The board is illuminated by a streetlamp outside of her window. It's a collage of stickers, buttons, and pictures. One photo is of a beautiful African woman smiling in front of the Washington Monument. He extends his hand, touches it tenderly. His gaze moves to another picture, Chee with him outside the gates at SeaWorld San Antonio. That was about two years ago. Below that Kodak print is a Polaroid: Chee and a skinny boy with glasses. The boy smiles with his lips closed. They're arm in arm. A bird sits on her shoulder.

Marcus closes his eyes, covers the lower half of his face with his right hand. He breathes deep, his eyes rolling to stare at the ceiling. He sighs. "Sorry, baby girl." He tugs at the Polaroid, and it pops from its pinned moorings. He folds and stuffs it into his back pocket.

The streetlamp exposes the space on the bulletin board where the photo used to reside like a spotlight. He shifts to the small, second floor window to draw the curtains. He hesitates, peers out on the street below.

A black Taurus is parked out front. To the casual passerby, the car looks empty, just another darkened passenger vehicle. Chee's dad knows differently. As if on cue, a figure appears. A man nods from the driver's seat. Then he disappears again, going as suddenly as he materialized.

*Smith.*

Marcus slides the curtains closed.

A few miles away, headphones funnel the plaintive crooning of Nigel Crown into Astrid's ears. She lies on her belly on her queen-size bed, her geometry homework spread before her. Her legs kick behind her as she sings along to *Apron Strings*. Crown apes *Frankly Mr. Shankly*-era Morrissey.

> *She strangles you with apron strings*
> *Clips the tips of your fledgling wings*
> *You'll never fly high and wild*
> *No, mother and child*

Astrid joins in, her voice cracking and straining to match Crown's falsetto. She closes her eyes, nods her head. She keeps time with the music, striking the eraser-end of her pencil on her textbook.

> *She bounces every girl you meet*
> *Smirks at you as she cuts your meat*
> *She'll never allow you to beguile*
> *No, mother and child*

She returns to her geometry homework, flips to the next page full of triangles and equations. She hums through the chorus while reviewing Pythagorean theorem.

> *Cause a castle can't be a home*
> *Jealous matriarch on a throne*
> *You're drowning, in a manner of speaking*
> *You're going down, your ship's sinking*

Triangles and word problems bleed into the next. She yawns, closes the book. She stretches, the heel of her hand pushing the text and her notes off the edge of her bed. They fall to the floor, landing on her backpack. She rolls over, crawls under her comforter. She claps her hands, and the desk lamp goes dark. She doesn't remove her head-phones.

> *She says goodnight with poison lips*
> *Gives you one last succubus kiss*
> *But goodnight's goodbye for now and all while*
> *Yeah, mother and child*

She murmurs the lyrics as she starts to fade from consciousness.

> *So run, run, run, run, run, run, run . . . run*
> *from you mum, son*

She's asleep. Her room grows cold.

> *Run, run, run . . .*

She's darting across the sky in another place, another time. She flies over foreign woodlands and highways. She descends in a slow arc. Soon, she's twenty feet above the roof of a house. It's a small white house that sits thirty feet above a silvery lake. She floats over the back porch, across the short yard, and down the slope to the water's edge. Her feet brush the tips of the reeds. They tickle her, and she giggles. Insects—bees— make way for her. She lands, finding herself on a boardwalk facing the water.

She knows this place. It's her family's summer home on Round Lake, an hour plus northwest of Chicago by car or rail.

Grey clouds pass rapidly overhead, their shapes reflected in the water. Gusts of wind create goose bump-like ripples. A man stands at the end of the edge of the dock, a fishing rod extended over the lake.

She skips across the short boardwalk to the dock, takes three steps down to join him.

"A storm's coming," he says as she arrives at his side, his voice deep but touched with a gentle Kentucky twang. He slowly reels in the line.

"Charlie," Astrid says. She smiles.

"But you knew that, didn't you, Chickadee." Her grandfather always calls her Chickadee.

"Yes," she says, "but I wish I didn't know. I wish it wasn't coming."

"There's no point in wishing that." He casts his line again. The lure hits the water's surface twenty feet away with a *kerplop*. "You might as well wish for the seasons to stop changing. It's that futile." The reel clicks as he leisurely brings the line in. "Anyway, we all need a change of seasons. You'll never know how much you love the sunshine on your face in summer without a freeze in winter. It's those highs and lows that make us who we are. They shape us, inform our destinies."

"Destiny," she scoffs. "I'm only sixteen."

"You still have a destiny," he says, turning to face her for the first time, smiling. "Yours is greater than most. Don't be afraid of it. Embrace it."

"It sounds daunting."

"Don't be scared," he says. "I'm around to lend a hand."

She nods to herself. "Charlie, can I ask you something?"

"Sure, Chickadee."

"Are you a ghost? I mean, in the technical sense?"

He chuckles. "I could just be an expression of your unconscious mind, 'an ocean full of dangerous currents and strange monsters,' as Freud calls it. Carl Sagan might say I'm nothing more than 'memory fragments stitched onto a fabric' of your mind. Or I'm as Carl Jung would say, just the 'exteriorization' of your 'nerve force,' maybe some bizarre product of your sex drive."

"Gross."

"Or maybe you're suffering from oxygen deficiency. Carbon monoxide poisoning?"

Astrid folds her arms. "Come on, Grandpa," she says with a sigh.

He laughs hard. "Oh, don't call me that. It makes me feel old." A honeybee alights on his shoulder. It twitches, runs down his sleeve. Another lands briefly, before both take flight. They circle Astrid and her grandfather in a long, lazy arc.

"You're not old," she says. "You're timeless."

More bees now buzz past.

"Aren't you the charmer?" He chuckles. "Fine. Yes, I'm a spirit. Kind of like a ghost. How else do you think I would know about Freud and Jung? I didn't read about them in auto shop. That's knowledge you come by once you've severed your silver cord. There are a lot of smart people on this side of mortality. Death is certainly enlightening."

"I knew it," she says, hugging him. She buries her face into his chest, smells a hint of cologne, *Canoe*. "I wish I could have met you when you were alive."

Hundreds of bees encircle them, humming and rising. Others join them. The insects form a swirling cloud above their heads, a vortex that stretches further and further into the heavens.

"Me too," he says, arms wrapped around her, patting her shoulder. He puts his chin on her head. "Me too."

# Track Three: Making Plans for Nigel

*The Seelbach Hilton Hotel, Louisville, Kentucky. 3 September 2001.*

At 3:15 AM, the Ouija board comes to life.

That's how it always starts, the Ouija board at 3:15.

Nigel Crown hears the planchette vibrating. He watches it quake from his bed.

"Please stop," he begs for the thousandth time.

The shaking intensifies. Soon the planchette and board are bouncing, hopping about the coffee table, tapping away like some wartime telegraph.

"Please." He covers his eyes. He knows what comes next.

The board suddenly comes to rest.

He sucks air, his chest heaving. He listens. All's quiet. Perhaps the hex bag worked. He peaks between his fingers.

Then the planchette slides.

Crown's lower lip quivers.

The small, heart-shaped piece of wood moves slowly. It halts on a word. *No.* A beat later, it makes a small, counter-clockwise circle. It stops again. *No.* It changes direction, halts. *No.* It makes a figure eight. *No.* Another two circles. *No.* Soon, the planchette is twisting, corkscrewing about on the board's face. Its speed increases, its movement growing faster, more erratic and wild. *No. No. No.*

Crown exhales. His breath turns cold and takes shape like an apparition before him. He pulls the blankets up just below his nose. The red beeswax candles on the nightstand flicker, struggle to stay lit. His defensive magic failing, he fingers the crucifix hanging at his neck.

The room groans and gasps, like it's taking a deep inward breath. The framed lake prints shudder, pull away from the walls. The wire on their backs goes taught, leashing the suspended frames to the finishing nails. The furniture—couches, dressers, bed—all pull away from the walls of the room. They are dragged to the center by some unseen vortex, drawn in by some great inhalation, sucked towards the movement of Ouija board.

He winces and tucks his chin to his chest, preparing for the burst of anger and energy that will toss him from his bed, shatter the windows and television, and explode cushions and pillows. He squeezes his eyes closed and counts.

One.

Two.

Three.

The explosion does not come. Only silence.

He opens an eye, peers over the edge of the comforter. The planchette is still.

He sits up, slides from the bed. He adjusts his black silk pajamas and shuffles to the spirit board. The faint smell of cologne permeates the room. He hears a low rumble, like the buzz of an insect.

The planchette hovers over "Hello."

"Hi," he says. His greeting sounds like a question.

The indicator moves, but not with starts and stops as it had earlier. Rather, it progresses unhurriedly, almost with assurance. W. Up to O. Across to U. Back to L. Up to D.

"Would . . . "

Down to the right. Up to the left. Over to the right.

". . . you . . ."

Middle left, upper right, right two spaces, upper middle.

" . . . like . . . "

Over three characters, back to E, down and to the right.

" . . . her . . . " He gulps.

The planchette continues to move. Two more letters.

" . . . to . . . "

The last word is built from letters on the same line between O and T.

" . . . stop."

The device freezes, waiting for a response.

"Would I like her to stop?"

The planchette waits for an answer.

"Yes, of course. But—"

The planchette stirs again. It hovers on the D. Then the O.

Crown tracks it. "Do?"

The pointer moves to the letter N.

"Don?"

The planchette moves with purpose now, it's lines direct and angular. T. Y. O. U.

"Don't? Don't you."

W. A. N. T. T. O. L. E. A. V. E. A. H. O. T. E. L. J. U. S. T. O. N. C. E. W. I. T. H. O. U. T. P. A. Y. I. N. G. F. O. R. D. A. M. A. G. E. S.

The device pauses.

"Don't I want to leave a hotel without paying for damages for once?" Crown cups his cheek with a trembling hand. His breathe catches in his lungs. "Cheeky, aren't you?" he squeaks.

The planchette remains still.

"Yes. I'd like to get a full night of sleep. It's been ages."

The wooden device moves south to the number 7.

"Seven. Seven years? Has it been that long?"

The planchette travels the length of the board, north to the word, "Yes."

"Can you really close the door?"

The pointer circles and returns. "Yes," comes the reply again.

"I'd give my soul for a night's rest," Crown says. He then backtracks. "Wait is that what you want, my soul?" He fingers his lower lip and chin. "Are you the devil?"

A hum steadily builds in the room, like electricity running through a dying fluorescent tube. Crown looks about for the source, but the lights are not flickering, the clock radio and TV are off. Still, the droning intensifies. Suddenly, there's the sound of a "plunk." Then another. Then another. Then more. The sounds aren't emanating from his room. They're coming from somewhere beyond it, somewhere . . . outside. He eyes the closed curtains.

*Plunk. Plunk.*

He shifts from his bed. He glances once more at the Ouija board, then shuffles towards the hidden window, his heart racing.

*Plunk, plunk, plunk, plunk, plunkity-plunk-plunk-plunkity.* The drumming and the humming grow louder, more urgent.

He stands before the windows, his back now to the board. He extends his arms, firmly grasps the two drapes where they come together in the middle. He exhales hard, steals himself. He closes his eyes tight. "Now." He opens his eyes and tears the curtains open.

A thousand buzzing bees greet him. The insects dance on the pane and on each other. They're two, three layers deep, competing for his attention on the other side of the glass.

"What the hell?" he whispers. The planchette comes alive again, and he spins to meet it.

The device moves quickly, agitated, and the drone of the bees, the sandpaper-like sound of their exoskeletons sliding against each other, becomes deafening. "There . . . are . . . things . . . worse . . . than . . . the . . . devil . . . and . . . Hell . . . here."

"What do you—"

The bugs suddenly go silent, still, just a motionless mass of thoraxes, abdomens, legs, wings, and antennae.

"—want?" Crown exclaims. The sound of his trembling voice against the sudden void catches him off guard. He swallows with difficulty. "Want," he says again, trying to gain composure.

"Wrap . . . the . . . board . . . in . . . blanket . . . with . . . salt . . . and . . . bury . . . it . . . at . . . church."

Crown gulps. "And then what?"

"Wait . . . for . . . instruction."

"What instructions?" Crown asks.

The planchette doesn't move.

"What do you want from me?"

Still nothing.

He spins, seeking a response from the bugs . . . but they are gone.

The next afternoon, the day manager of the Seelbach, trailed by two bellboys, knocks on Crown's door. He's missed his checkout time. He's failed to answer the phone. There's no response, so he pounds on the door again.

"Get ready to call 911," the manager says. He doesn't know what type of destruction to expect. One of the Wahlbergs lit the carpet on fire on the ninth floor back in 1991 after a New Kids concert, but that, apparently, is nothing compared to the legendary destructionary force known as Nigel Crown. He slips his master keycard into the door with a *blip*. It pops, and the manager gives the door a gentle push.

They are greeted by darkness.

"Mr. Crown?" the manager calls. He tiptoes into Crown's room and flips on the light. The bellboys follow him in single file, each craning for a view over his shoulders. The manager gasps.

There are no broken bottles of alcohol, no drug paraphernalia, no dead hookers. The room is immaculate and clean.

"Did he even sleep here last night?" a bellboy with "Wayne" on his nametag asks.

"I don't know," the manager says.

"He must have," the second bellboy says. "The blanket at the end of the bed is missing."

The hotel runs his credit card for the room and applicable taxes. The manager consults a price list and directs the desk clerk to charge Crown another $75.12 for the cost of the blanket.

They fail, however, to notice and charge the rocker for a missing ice bucket.

Unknown to them, ice buckets and their lids make for excellent digging and scraping tools in a pinch. A few blocks away, Crown buries the blanket and its dark contents behind a bush near a cathedral. When he's done, he tosses his makeshift shovels into a nearby dumpster marked "Property of St. Luis Bertrand Catholic Church." His tour bus pulls up beside him. He enters, and they depart.

*Indianapolis, Indiana.*

By Bacchus' thyrsus, Centurion's head is pounding. It's as if the Maenads themselves are dancing on his skull, moshing about to the beat of Dionysian drums. He adjusts the visor of his galea, shielding his eyes from the harsh morning sun, before taking another sip of his mocha frappe.

He pauses for a few long seconds, surveying the McDonald's parking lot. Where did he park again? Ah, yes, there. The Chariot is just thirty feet away. Still, the rising heat conspires with his condition. The parking lot is as expansive as the Tyrrhenian Sea. He slaps his leg with a clutch of newspapers, spurring himself forward.

The Chariot does not look like much. It shouldn't. It's a '94 Dodge Caravan, the perfect camouflage for a mobile lair-slash-crime lab-slash-command center. The Chariot is home base for Centurion and his Superhero Club (trademark pending).

He pops the tailgate. An empty can of Busch Light drops from the minivan and clatters to the blacktop. It bounces once, twice, and then is partially crushed under Centurion's reinforced sandal. He stomps it again, nearly flattening it.

*Reflexes like Mercury.* In days past, this self-praise would have brought a satisfied grin to his grizzled face. Instead, he scowls.

He half considers leaving the can on the blacktop where it rests. Instead, he picks up the former beverage container, groaning as he bends. He tosses the can into the van. It lands on a pile of like aluminum near the passenger seat. These ex-cans will be recycled.

Despite these dark and lawless days, Centurion dares not litter. If a hero's duty, *his* duty, is to "clean up the streets," then he must do so literally and figuratively. Even the smallest gestures, like dropping aluminum cans into a bin, carry import. He is convinced that order, even on the smallest scale, promotes the greater good.

Plus, he'll get a bit of money for the metal that he can use for gas . . . and another six-pack. *It's win-win, Citizens.*

He pushes aside a blanket and drool-stained pillow to make room for today's press. He spreads them—a *USA Today*, a dozen pages of the metro section of the *Indy Star*, and a ketchup stained *IBJ*—across his makeshift bed. He reads aloud, drawing a thick and dirty finger across the word strings. He struggles to pronounce foreign places he will never go, economic terms that will never affect him. After all, poor is poor. Nothing the Fed says about the meltdown in Argentina or global contamination will ever change that. He pokes his temple, closes his eyes.

This didn't used to be his job. No, gathering intelligence was always

Kid Caper's domain. The Kid would sit on Centurion's stoop and tear into the *Tampa Express*. He'd scan it for signs of perpetrators, signs of monsters preying on the good citizens of Florida.

*Citizens.*

It's a term Centurion applies loosely now. It applies to both domestic and foreign born alike, to people of all creeds and colors. As Kid Caper used to say, "If justice is blind, then violence and hatred must be blind too." *Fuck, the Kid had a way with words. He was a modern day Euripides.*

Now Centurion is left to study the chronicles for clues alone.

There's an article about the cleaning of Lady Victory, a revered statue that sits atop a memorial for soldiers. *Godspeed.* There's another concerning twelve cases of food poisoning resulting from some bad fried mayo at the Indiana State Fair. *You are what you eat.* And then there's a piece about the city-county council, Republicans and Democrats fighting over the budget, over everything. *Different city, same story.*

He doesn't know what he's looking for in these pages. Something out of the ordinary. Something weird. Something that sets his senses ablaze. Something like the story of a bizarre murder that led him to Indianapolis in the first place. But he does know this: he'll recognize it when he sees it.

As for today? Absolutely nothing. Again. Aside from his conversation with Gerig and the security tape, his week in Indy has been nothing but frustrating.

"Shit!" he curses. Then he amends himself. The Kid loathed swearing. "Shazam." He rips at the periodicals before him. "Shazam, Shazam, a thousand Shazams!"

When Centurion regains his composure, there are shreds of newsprint scattered before him. He puts his hands to his face and sighs, leaving ink smudges on his tanned cheeks. He starts to clean up the van. Then . . .

A torn headline grabs his attention. *Labor Day Parking Meter Holiday.* Free parking. But of course! How could he have been so thick? He tears the headline from the paper. *Thank Gaea and Fucking A.* The Furies are with him today.

Careful not to strike the horsehair plum that bursts forth from his helmet, he climbs through the minivan to the driver's seat. He pulls a roll of scotch tape from the glove compartment. The chair reclines with a jolt as he brings himself to stare at the ceiling. He's an amateur Michelangelo working on his own Sistine Chapel. This ceiling, though, is covered in newspaper, a collage of yellowing tape, black and white photos, and newsprint.

*Local Kid Solves Caper; Busts Robbery Ring.* Beneath the headline, there's a faded photo of a Cuban kid standing proud, hands on hips, smile wide. Despite his zigzag incisors, it's a grin that could slay a gorgon. There's a caption. It reads, "Henry Famosa led police to cell phone thieves."

*Memories.* Centurion unspools tape.

He posts the ragged headline concerning free parking between two other articles, *Comic Giant Wins Infringement Suit* and *Superhero Club Renamed 'Superhero Club.'* But his eyes linger on another piece. He frowns.

*Superhero Sidekick Dies in Tragic Zoo Accident.* It too features a photo, this one of Centurion with his hand on the shoulder of a youth wearing a cowl . . . and an unmistakable crooked smile. It's dated March 15, 2001. The byline has been defaced with red pen, the names barely legible. It's cowritten. The main author is no one special. The second is a self-proclaimed expert, a big-time anchor in Chicago. The byline reads, "John Franks with Holly Rodriguez."

"Bitch." A single tear slaloms across Centurion's wrinkled cheek, cutting a crooked line through the newspaper ink that has darkened his sun-damaged skin. The tear jumps from his earlobe, landing on the tattooed 38 on his neck.

He grits his teeth. He swears yet again to any god who will listen that he will avenge his youthful ward.

A visit to the local high school is in order.

❖ ❖ ❖

People aren't born evil. Evil is a disease, a pathogen introduced by one's environment. It develops slowly, like the proliferation of a parasite, turning the soul black as it spreads. Once it has metastasized, there's very little that can be done to reverse its course, especially in a so-called correctional facility. Still, jail can serve a purpose. Like zombies, the infected must be cordoned off lest they contaminate others.

The best course of action? Preventative measures, an ounce of love. Even so, the effects of a poor upbringing, if caught and treated early enough with a little extra kindness, can be mitigated.

Centurion's seen it first hand. In a prior life, a time stolen by lawyers and reporters, he helped put kids on a better path.

Still, against better judgment, Centurion sometimes finds himself strolling through the mangrove tunnels to Al Palonias Park. He likes to watch kids at play. He studies them as long as he can, until their parents or teachers shuttle them away. He wonders how far these apples have fallen from their parental trees. He can identify those that will take root and grow into strong members of society. He knows which require nurturing. And he can spot the rotten apples doomed for failure.

He details their interactions, every action and reaction.

These observations have led him to a number of conclusions, or "truths." These truths are heuristics, shortcuts that he's adopted to help him combat evil in its various forms, whether seed, root, or vine.

He can immediately identify the kids born to be politicians, the children destined to suck the life force from their fellow humans. He can read the cheats. He knows the sociopaths. But he also knows the marginalized, the powerless seeking escape. He can pick out the kids who will embrace drugs despite all of the Surgeon General's warnings. He knows addicts. He knows abusers. He knows burnouts.

Potheads universally don't like school. They'd rather cut class and smoke weed from dawn until dusk.

That's a truth.

Except when school's out of session. For some unknown reason, stoners are drawn to school on days there's no class. They usually loiter near the parking lot or under the bleachers.

Another truth.

It's a weird dichotomy. Maybe it's a subconscious attempt by these kids to belong. Maybe it's the only place they can go to toke in privacy during the holidays when their siblings and parents are home too. Maybe they're just too lazy to find somewhere else to go. Centurion doesn't try to square it. He doesn't really care about the psychology behind it. All he knows is that delinquents only like hanging out at school when school's out.

Like days when parking meters are free, days like Labor Day.

Centurion pulls the Chariot into the empty parking lot at Belzer Middle School next to a sign that says, "Welcome Back Bruins!" Today there won't be teachers or principals to contend with. There won't be security to shoo him away.

He just needs to find some punks to interview.

Tokers make for the best interviewees. They act like they don't care about the world around them, yet they're methodical in capturing useless information and cataloging it.

*Dolphins only sleep with one eye closed and for five minutes at a time.*

*Leaches have, like, 29 brains.*

*Eating polar bear liver will kill you. Too much vitamin A.*

*Abalones have five butts.*

*Nero used to burn Christians for a nightlight in his garden.*

*Henry Ford used cannabis and wheat straw to make plastics for his cars.*

*Dude, The Declaration of Independence was written on hemp.*

*Parachutes were made from hashish in WWII.*

(Unfortunately, conversations with drug users usually devolve quickly into musings about the many practical and not-so-practical uses of Mary Jane)

The collection of factoids may be a sign that chiba chiefs really do care. Or, it could be a side effect, like an obsessive-compulsive need to clean when someone's high. Or, possibly, the compilation of data helps fuel conspiracy theories and conversation. Again, Centurion couldn't give two shits from a hydra.

More truth.

He doesn't search long. There's a group of kids dressed in black on the stairs at the rear of the school. There are four of them. They're smoking, of course. The skinny one is passing a joint when Centurion strides forth. A kid with tufts of ginger hair bursting from beneath a ski cap doesn't care. He takes it between his fingers and takes a long drag, his hooded eyes staring icily at Centurion as he does so.

"Check out Spartacus," says a fat one, chuckling and pointing at the guy in a white helmet, breastplate, pauldrons, and legion skirt. The kid's skinny jeans are a size too small, and his girth billows over the waistline. The girl under his arm giggles too. "What the fuck are you dressed up for?" he asks.

"Hello, young citizen," the hero says, cape flapping gently in the wind behind him. "My name is Centurion. What's yours?"

Skinny jeans cackles. "You got to be kidding me."

The kid's girlfriend tells him to play along.

Sure, he will. "My name is Mark. So what's it to you?"

"Well, Mark, I'm trying to get some answers to some very important questions, answers that may have life or death consequences. I'm hoping you and your friends can help." Centurion unfolds a page from a yearbook and passes it to Mark. "Do you know her?"

The kid looks at the page. It's covered in photos of students from Blake High in Tampa. There are ten rows of five photos, fifty pictures on the page. One of them is circled, an African American girl. Her hair is loose, and something like a Clovis point hangs on a chain around her neck. Mark's right eyebrow shoots up, and he passes it on and they examine it in turn. They look at each other in unison, like they're privy to a secret. "Don't answer," one of them says suddenly, staring at Centurion and handing the page back to Mark. "Don't say nothing."

"For Mnemosyne's sake, a fucking double negative," he mumbles, referencing the creator of language. *What are they teaching these kids?*

"Yeah, why should we talk to you?" Mark crumbles the photo and throws it at Centurion. It bounces off of his forearm and into a bush. "Ha, nice reflexes."

"Look, I'm really trying here," Centurion says. "I need to find that girl."

"How's that my problem?" Mark asks.

Truth: the disaffected are justified in their feelings. They may have issues with trust. They may have been oppressed. Perhaps they just feel, well, different. These feelings can lead to frustration. Kids like these are often angry and frequently are paranoid.

Truth: Centurion can't judge Mark. He was a kid like this once. He knows just how to talk to kids like this, how to communicate in a language they will understand. He knows how to build trust.

Truth: the process for building trust can take weeks, potentially even months.

Centurion does not have that kind of time. It's time for Plan B.

He leans in, grimacing, poking Mark's chest hard with an extended index finger. "You sure are full of questions, aren't you Mark?" He rasps like a rake over dry leaves. "You're not helping me, and you're not helping yourself either." He gives the fatty the skinny: he's looking for a declarative response. "The next time you ask me a question, Question Mark, I guarantee you won't like my response. So let's try this again. Do you know that girl?"

Mark's girlfriend leans away from him, her eyebrows twisting. "Just answer the guy. Tell him what he wants to know so he'll leave."

But Mark's confused. His eyes go wide. In a world where parents can't spank, teachers are beholden to helicopter parents, and kids get trophies for coming in fourth place, Mark's unfamiliar with shows of authority. "What?" he says to Centurion.

Centurion inhales through clenched teeth. "Wrong answer, Question Mark." With that, he delivers an exclamation point. He spins and kicks the kid hard and square in the stomach. It knocks the air out of Question Mark, doubling him over. He rolls off the steps, arms around his belly, groaning.

His friends don't make a move. Their reflexes and senses are dulled. They don't understand what's happening. They are in shock . . . until Mark's gal starts shrieking.

Centurion points at her, roars, "Shut up!"

Her hands go to her mouth. She immediately complies.

"I'm usually very nice, but this guy," Centurion says, pointing to the kid rolling about at his feet, "he tested me." He steps over Question Mark and gets inches from the face of the ginger. "He made the mistake of tapping into my very own sense of powerlessness, you know, Red?" He leans back slightly. "Now, I need information, Bruins. Who is going to correct Mark's mistake?"

The redhead nods. He's trembling, his freckles bouncing about his face like flakes in a snow globe. He's not the hotshot he pretended to be.

"What's your name?"

"Lyle Daley," he whimpers.

"So here's the deal, Daley. Tell me what you know about this girl. Don't delay."

Daley doesn't dilly-dally. He spills his guts. As do his friends in turn.

She moved to Indianapolis about four or five months ago. They agree on that. Before that she might have lived in Florida or San Antonio.

"Florida," Centurion acknowledges.

She didn't have many friends. Just Hooper, the kid everyone remembers for keeping snakes, hamsters, ferrets, and other creatures in his coat pockets, the kid that got murdered at the Mall.

The delinquents also agree that she was "hot" and "really smart for a hot chick." She made National Honors Society, liked Godzilla movies, and was the only girl in the computer club.

They disagree, however, as to why she left town.

Mark's girlfriend says, "I heard her dad's in a witness protection program so they move around a lot."

"I heard she got a modeling contract," Daley says.

"I thought she graduated early," Mark croaks.

"Where'd she go?" Centurion asks.

One says Iowa. Another Minnesota. The consensus is probably Chicago.

Chicago it is. But that will wait until tomorrow. He's on edge. He's got beer to drink tonight.

Finally, he asks them to confirm her full name. It's Amachi Jacobs, just as the yearbook photo states.

But everyone at school just called her Chee.

# Track Four: Ugly American Girl

*Chicago, Illinois. 4 September 2001.*

On the street outside a row of turn-of-the-century homes, a man named Smith sits in a navy Corolla. Yesterday it was a grey Malibu. Two days ago, a black Taurus. Tomorrow it will be a Buick. The vehicles are always different, an ever-changing variety of makes, colors, and plates.

Like his cars, Smith is oddly nondescript, totally unmemorable. He could be in his late twenties, his thirties, or even early forties. His hair might be brown, or possibly blonde. In police reports he is alternately described as heavy and tall, of medium build and height, and skinny and small in stature. When he's allowed himself to be seen, witnesses have even conveyed multiple and disparate descriptions in a single statement.

Today his uniform is a white button-up and khakis. It's urban camouflage, a buttress to his ability to disappear. Smith's paid for his gifts. One of them is to not be noticed.

He's also paid to monitor a dot on his laptop using global positioning, infrared mapping, and audio feeds. He plugs in a silver flash drive shaped like a bullet.

Chee exits the brownstone where she lives and hurries up Larrabee Street towards Armitage Avenue.

The blinking dot on Smith's computer moves with her.

Smith starts his car and follows her the six blocks to Lincoln Park High School.

He watches her stop, move, turn, and move again through the halls of the school. He listens through an earpiece to the mind-numbing inter-period banter, the instruction of the classroom. The dot, though, remains quiet. That is, unless it's apologizing. The dot often apologizes for getting in the way of some other, less important dot. The dot doesn't realize that the other dots are meaningless.

It's a pattern that repeats every school day, regardless of school's location.

The patterns are not themselves special. Rather, it's the interruptions in pattern, the breaks from ritual and precedent, which matter. Smith looks for Chee to veer from her usual path. He listens for her to do something more than engage in Socratic method or banal gossip.

Another bell. Smith tracks the dot as it goes to lunch. He blows hard and reminds himself that this tedium will eventually have its payoff. Sooner or later, he'll get the call to use his second gift. Sure, anyone can commit murder, but only the best can do it repeatedly and get away with it.

Sometimes, the reward for his work comes sooner.

"Check out the new girl," Astrid says to Kim.

Although Astrid can't see Kim's face beneath her trademark hoodie, she knows that Kim is scoffing.

Under the florescent lights of the lunchroom, the kids are a bright blur, everyone hurrying to their fourth period destinations . . . everyone except the new girl. She's perfectly still amongst the chaos, a snapshot taken with a long exposure.

"The poor dear is terrified," Astrid continues.

Still nothing from Kim.

"Just terrified," she repeats a bit louder.

Kim's busy drawing hearts on the rubber of her Chuck Taylors. "Really," she says, engaging Astrid without so much as a glance. "How do you know that?"

"Look at her tray," Astrid says.

Kim sighs, complies. "Looks like chocolate milk and a cookie. Wait. No pizza? That's pretty strange."

"Exactly. It's Pizza Day. Everyone loves Pizza Day. So she's shy."

"How's that?"

"She didn't want to trouble Kielbasa or Pierogi," Astrid says, referring to their nicknames for the two Polish lunch ladies. "She grabbed what was within easy reach and bolted."

"Pierogi can be intimidating. That single eyebrow creeps me out."

Kim's now invested. She leans in, elbows on the table. "Tell me more."

The new girl bites her lip. She looks from side to side as if trying to figure out her next move.

"Look at the way she carries her tray," Astrid explains. "She's holding it out in front of her, defensive, like a shield. She's using it to put space between her and her environment."

Kim agrees. "She's got that 'new meat in prison' look about her."

"She shouldn't have confidence issues, though, should she?" This girl is tall, lean. She's of African descent. Her skirt looks a little like a school uniform, and it shows a bit of leg. "She's got great stems, a pretty face," Astrid says.

"She's kind of pretty, I guess," Kim admits. "What else are you picking up?"

"Honestly? Nothing." Astrid's perplexed. She can't see her aura, her head spewing out rainbows of colors like every other person in the room. "Fascinating."

Kim grunts. "How could a girl like that not have confidence?"

It's a good question. "Something must have happened to her, something to make her less secure. Something traumatized this girl. I wonder."

So does Kim. "She's got a secret," Kim says.

"*Everyone's* got secrets," Astrid says, raising an eyebrow and nudging Kim with her shoulder.

"Yes, I guess we do," Kim says. She switches into a faux British accent and says, "Your powers of deduction do astound me sometimes, Holmes." Her intonation comes off more New Delhi than Newcastle. Her impressions have been off-shored.

"Why, my dear Watson, it's elementary." Astrid's accent is bang on, more St. John's Wood, less Baliwood.

"We should invite her over," Kim says with a laugh, "discover her secrets and make her our bitch." She's back to drawing on her shoes, this time she's making little skulls.

Astrid needs to know what makes this newbie tick. "That's a great idea."

"Hold on, I was just—"

"Hey!" Astrid shouts from their table.

"—kidding. Oh, no," Kim mutters. "What are you doing?"

"Hey," Astrid yells again. "Hey, new kid!"

That gets the new girl's attention. She looks at the pair before looking side to side. She looks at Astrid again. "Me?" she mouths, pointing to herself.

"Yes, you," Astrid says, nodding. "Come sit with us."

The new girl hesitates. A Goth and a tomboy have just asked her to sit with them. Astrid suddenly worries that this girl might reject them, might spin and run from the lunchroom and never come back. She begins to question the wisdom of the invitation and the coming rejection until . . .

The new girl smiles broadly and nods.

"Crap," Kim says. "Here she comes. Nice one."

"Kim," Astrid says, "Be nice. And get rid of that whisker before she gets here. You're not focusing."

A thick hair protrudes from Kim's right cheek. It's straight and long like a cat's whisker. Kim's hand goes to her face. She feels it. She's mortified. She turns away.

"Don't pluck it," Astrid says. "Just do your thing."

"No time," Kim says, plucking it quickly. "Ouch."

The kid approaches the table, a smile carved in her face like some insane jack-o-lantern. She can barely contain her joy. "Hi," she says a little too loud.

"Well, hi," Astrid replies. "Grab some bench."

"Thanks!" Her smile dissipates somewhat when she notices Kim rubbing her cheek, scowling. "Is it okay if I sit with you?" she asks, deferring to her.

Kim doesn't answer.

"Kim." Astrid says her name like she's a bad dog. "Introduce yourself."

She glares at Astrid a moment and then relents. "Hi. I'm Kim." She extends a clenched fist over the table, knuckles first.

The new girl looks confused.

"Fist bump?" Kim asks to the neophyte, before withdrawing her hand. "Never mind."

"Nice to meet you," the new girl says. Her features are sharp, Nubian. She wears a feather in her braided hair and a small spear tip from a chain around her neck. "My name is Amachi. But my friends called me Chee."

The Chee dot has engaged two others in the lunchroom. The pattern has never broken this quickly. It usually takes weeks, sometimes months. Smith calls it in to Mansfield.

"Astrid? That's so pretty," Chee says. "Does it mean anything?"

Astrid doesn't actually know. Her mother is Filipino, but she doubts it means anything in Tagalog. Even if it did, her mother is too Americanized to know. She was a child of the sixties counterculture. "Yes, it means my mom was a hippie."

Chee chuckles. "Is she still?"

Astrid's mom runs a pretty popular hot yoga studio. She makes money doing something she loves, but that cuts against her neo-hippie cred. "She has moments of existential crisis. Dad's trying to talk her off the ledge all of the time."

Chee laughs.

"How about your parents?" Kim asks.

"Mom passed away. Dad's in the NSA, so we travel a lot."

"Sorry," Astrid says.

"No, that's okay. I didn't really know her. She left us right after I was born."

"The NSA? Wow, your dad's, like, an astronaut?" Kim asks.

Astrid puts a hand to her face, shakes her head. "You'll have to forgive my friend. A space cadet should know the difference between NASA and the NSA. She doesn't pay much attention to current events."

"Whatever," Kim replies with a huff. "I'm going to kick your ass. How's that for a current event?"

"Such a kidder," Astrid says, blowing Kim's remark off. "Still, Chicago seems like a weird city for a National Security Administration assignment."

"We move all over," Chee sighs. "I've lived everywhere." She goes through a short list. Cincinnati, San Antonio, Denver, Tampa, Indianapolis, etcetera. "But that's okay. I'm usually ready for a change, even a cold one."

"The weather here does suck," Kim says. "But we do have a decent football team."

"But more importantly," Astrid adds, "we have the Mag Mile."

"I love shopping," Chee confesses.

"We need to take you then," Astrid says.

"That would be great."

"We'll go after school."

"Wait, don't you have a report to give in World History tomorrow?" Kim asks.

Astrid waves her off. "Yes, on religious repression in Seventeenth and Eighteenth Century France. I finished that, like, two weeks ago. So how about Water Tower Place tonight?"

Kim groans. "I can't go. I have to write a stupid poem tonight."

"Wasn't the assignment to write a haiku?" Astrid asks.

"Yeah."

"You should be able to write a haiku in your sleep," Astrid admonishes. "It's only seventeen syllables; five on the first line, seven on the next, and five again on the last."

"Actually," Chee says, "haikus use 'moras' or tonal beats instead of syllables. So the average Japanese haiku is just eleven syllables, not seventeen."

Kim and Astrid stare at Chee in stunned silence.

Chee winces. "You know, I'm sorry. That was awkward. I'm kind of a fan of Japanese culture. Manga, Samurai, Hello Kitty, that kind of thing."

"What?" Astrid asks. "Oh my God, don't apologize. I love that you're a geek."

Chee's panic gives way to the beginnings of a grin. "Then I've got a poem for you, Kim, a true American haiku."

"Really? Hit me."

Chee speaks slowly. "Everything taught . . . to me concerning haikus . . . is totally wrong."

There's a pause while Kim counts the syllables on her fingers. She counts them again, out loud, and then once more before saying, "F'n awesome."

"So you're coming with us tonight, Chee? We won't take, 'No,' for an answer."

"Well," Chee says, "I'd have to check in with my dad first."

Astrid provides the details. Chee should meet them by the south entrance after school. They'll stop by her home first to drop off her books, then they'll grab the Red line and hop off at the Chicago stop.

The bell signals the end of the period.

"Did you get all of that?" Smith asks.

"Yes," a man says in Smith's earpiece. "Engage."

"Field trip time," Smith says. "What about daddy?"

"I'll take care of Marcus," Mansfield says. "Just get into position." The line goes dead.

"I'm always in position," Smith scoffs. He puts the car into drive. He's got to exchange the vehicle and fast. He's going shopping.

Marcus holds his temple between two fingers. "I'm not comfortable with this."

"And why's that?" a man's voice on the other end of the phone says.

"For one, we don't have complete intelligence," Marcus replies. "We need to log more time in the field. We need to monitor the targets further. When have we ever struck without confirmation?"

"Smith says he has all he needs."

"How can he say that? It's been a matter of hours."

"I guess he trusts Chee's abilities."

There's too much emphasis on the pronoun *he* for Marcus' liking. Still, he won't take the bait. Marcus knows his daughter better than anyone. They don't yet understand all of the variables, Smith being the biggest question mark in Marcus' estimation. "I'm not comfortable with Smith's involvement."

"Smith is a professional," Mansfield says with a rasp. "He's one of the best. In some ways, his skills rival Hélène's."

It's a low blow. "Sir?"

"I'm sorry, Marcus. I'm not trying to offend. Of course, your wife's abilities were unparalleled, but Smith has his own . . . gifts."

"He's unburdened by conscience," Marcus says, shaking his head.

There's a break before the voice engages again. "Yes, but I was referring to anonymity."

"What if they're innocents?"

"Chances are they're not," the voice says.

"But what if they are? What if they're just normal kids? Wrong place, wrong time?" Marcus' words are intended to sting, to highlight failures in the days before Chee was activated. There were a lot of people who died needlessly. You can only use the term "collateral damage" so much before it loses meaning. You can only lie to yourself so long before people call those deaths what they really were: fucking mistakes.

There's a sigh. "Let's be clear," the disembodied voice says, "this call, like all of our calls, is made in observance of decorum. Nothing more, nothing less. I am not asking for your permission. I'm calling because I need you to be a cheerleader."

Marcus remains silent.

Mansfield continues, offering a more conciliatory tone. "Look, I admit that I'm no stranger to . . . accidents. My hands are stained red with blood. One day, I expect, I'll have to reckon with our Maker for my deeds. But when I do, remember this: He'll know I've acted in His interests and the greater good. He'll know I've tried to protect the sanctity of this country, of this earth. And, if we remain pious, he'll absolve us all. Do you understand?"

"Yes," Marcus says flatly. It's the best impression of a team player he can muster.

"Good," the man on the phone says. "You know, your daughter has an opportunity today to accomplish something I never dreamed possible."

"And what's that, Mansfield?" Marcus asks, rubbing his temple.

"Deliver two demons at once," the voice says. There's a slight but audible pop. It's a wet sound, the sound of lips separating from gum and teeth. Marcus can actually hear Mansfield's smile over the line. "Hélène and her ancestors were never able to do that."

Marcus says a bird in the hand is worth two in the bush.

The man laughs. "These birds are as well as on the plate. Tell your daughter to have fun at the mall."

*Two hours north of Indianapolis on Interstate 65.*

Radio sucks. Once you're outside Marion County, Indianapolis proper, radio sucks more. Among the cornfields, its either Top 40 or country. Centurion tries to tune out *Bye, Bye, Bye.* He considers what he learned at Belzer Middle School.

John Hooper. The consensus: decent student, average athlete. Generally scored Bs and while never picked first in gym, he was rarely picked last. An all around regular kid, if not a bit of a loner.

Loner. That bit piqued Centurion's interest. Centurion suspected it wasn't purposeful. Hooper wasn't necessarily trying to fly under the radar. He just wasn't *on* the radar. That is, human radar.

Animals were another story. They were clearly attracted to Hooper. The schoolyard kids each had a story to tell.

Question Mark told Centurion about the pigeons that would line up on the telephone wires during recess. They'd ogle Hooper the whole time, their necks craning to track his movements. "Freaky, Hitchcock shit," the kid said.

"Crows too," his girlfriend added.

Red agreed. "Ever notice," he said, "how the fish in Ms. Smart's biology class would stop swimming around whenever he walked into class? They'd press their fishy faces against the glass and stare at him. They wouldn't move again until the bell rang. Once he left, they'd return to swimming around the tank."

The skinny kid offered the most valuable information. Hooper owned a veritable menagerie, including a python, a Siamese cat, a handful of fish, a cockapoo, and a cockatoo named Keith. Somehow, this recipe for chaos never devolved into anything more than a crowd of critters at Hooper's feet. "It was a food chain," the kid said, "a tangle of paws, wings, and tails. But they never attacked or tried to eat each other. Weird."

And then there was Mr. Piccolo.

On the radio the boy band has stopped whining. A DJ cuts in. "Well, he did it again, folks. Nigel Crown destroyed yet another hotel room after performing in Cincinnati last week. At least that's what the owners of Le Grand are alleging."

Another radio personality chimes in. "Yo, Jo Jo. They're saying he did more than ten-thousand-dollars in damage this time. By my calculation, that brings his tally in damages on the Lullaby Tour to almost thirty-thousand-dollars."

"Frankie, I can't wait to see what he does in Chicago on the seventh," Jo Jo says. "I hope the Aragon Ballroom has insurance. The promoters can't be too happy."

"They've declined to comment," Radio Frankie says.

"Sure they did."

"But I'll comment, Jo Jo. Nigel, my friend: just buy yourself a house in each of the cities you're playing. It will be much cheaper in the end."

The DJs laugh.

"Well, Frankie, it's not like he needs help paying his bills. He's got that new movie out."

"Yes, *Dark as Pitch*. It's getting some mixed reviews."

"What's it about?"

"It's about a soccer player who sells his soul to the devil for fame and fortune."

"Soccer popular in the United States? Well, that's a tall order, even for the devil."

Radio Frankie laughs. "Nigel should stick to music. His latest is climbing the charts."

"Great segue, Frankie."

"Here it is, *Lullaby for an Heiress*."

Pulsing synth beats fade-in. Skittering drums herald Nigel Crown's crooning.

*Little filly seen your Churchill Downs*
*Little tiara more like a Triple Crown*
*Jockeys crop you, Miss Thoroughly Bred*
*Jockeys ride you hard, put you away wet . . .*

Centurion groans. The song received a lot of buzz because of its subject matter, Paris Hilton and her contemporaries. But he has no idea who she is. He doesn't really care to find out. He hates this modern shit.

*Listen listen clear the fog from your mind*
*There's a lesson here for you and all your kind*
*Listen listen dear to your lullaby*
*There's a lesson here that money cannot buy*

"Ugh," he groans, "this is like Style Council all over again." What happened to the Nigel Crown of the 80s? The Nigel Crown who led the sonic assault of Panic Attack, the seminal one-chord wonders? What happened to punk? He bemoans the loss of Crown, Paul Weller, and their ilk to Top 40 radio.

*Paparazzi expose you on TV*
*For making films your papa shouldn't see*
*Films made by boys who said they understood*
*Films sold by boys who said they never would*

Centurion leans over, starts pulling cassettes from a shoebox on the passenger seat. "Riff Raft" is at the top of the pile. It's Panic Attack's first album. The faded cover features the four band members dressed like the crew paddling away from a sinking ocean liner on a lifeboat shaped like a giant guitar.

*This ain't no card game*
*And Trump doesn't win*
*This ain't no disco*

*You can't buy your way in*
*This ain't no trial*
*The drugs aren't your friend's*
*This ain't no sentence*
*Any period can put to end*

"Enough already." He slides the cassette into the player, presses play. The radio goes quiet. A tinny voice resonates over the speakers a few seconds later. The vocalist is supported by a lonely piano.

*In Paris, when we parted,*
*You left me broke in heart and wallet,*
*Kicking rocks along the Champs-Élysées*
*With nothing more for us to say . . .*
*Except . . .*

There's a two second break, then . . .

A wall of sound hits Centurion, crunching guitar, the trademark of Johnny Moon. "Yes." *Crown and Moon, the greatest songwriting collaboration ever.* He reaches behind the passenger seat, one hand still on the steering wheel, and grabs a road beer from the cooler. He cracks it with one hand, takes a deep swig. His face sours. It's warm. He takes another mouthful. It will do. The guitar pauses, just for a beat, before being joined by Nigel Crown's wailing.

*You took my love like a cheap souvenir*
*Ugly American Girl*
*A bit reminder of your stay here*
*Ugly American Girl*
*You took a photo to remember my face*
*Ugly American Girl*
*Another memory for you to misplace*
*Ugly American Girl!*

Finally some thinking music.

*Ugly American*
*Ugly American*
*Ugly American Girl*

Hooper had a gift, a special ability. He was the resident Doctor Doolittle of Indy . . . minus the medical degree. He could walk with the animals, talk to the animals, grunt and squeak and squawk with the animals. And they, apparently, could squeak and squawk and speak and talk to him. It was an ability very different from the Kid's, but it was a power—no, a *superpower*—nonetheless.

*You shop like rue St. Honore will fold*
*Ugly American Girl*
*Snatching up hearts like designer clothes*
*Ugly American Girl*
*Wear them once your haute couture*
*Ugly American Girl*
*Today's fashion's on tomorrow's floor*
*Ugly American Girl*

So there were at least two kids, superheroes, murdered in a year, both with ties to the same woman. Death is in Chicago, but Centurion's on to her.

*So grab your bags and make your plane*
*Ugly American Girl*
*Don't show your pretty face here again*
*Ugly American Girl*

He couldn't save the Kid. He was too late for Hooper. He prays to the Furies he'll stop her in the City of the Big Shoulders. He prays he'll find Chee before she kills again.

His foot feels heavy. He presses the accelerator. The needle on the speedometer cruises past 80 miles per hour. He'll be in Chicago in hours. He'll find a Circuit City or a Best Buy with VHS player where he can watch the security tape. Then it's off to the nearest Kinko's to freak out some customers and buy as many fliers as $37.27 will allow (leaving a few bucks for a six pack, of course).

# Track Five: Sensoria

*Lincoln Park High School. Chicago, Illinois.*

"So, at first blush, *Candide* seems like a linear adventure, just a series of stories linked by the novel's namesake. Voltaire begins each tale with Candide full of hope, but by the end of each episode, he's left desperate. It's a loop, and each adventure is informed by the last. Pretty simple, right?"

Nobody in the classroom says a word; nobody even glances up from his or her desk to acknowledge the question. They've been lulled to sleep by Mr. Siegal's monotone.

"Wrong," Mr. Siegal says, correcting no one. "Voltaire was really tackling something greater. Hidden in the seemingly linear nature of *Candide* is a very non-linear progression with darker and darker recursions. Voltaire imbues his stories with different levels of detail. He plays with the notion of cause and effect, with actions having a disproportionate impact as the story progresses."

Mr. Siegal hasn't so much lost Chee as never found her. She fingers the assegai spear tip, a gift from her mother, hanging from her necklace.

*Driving down Lakeshore Drive, Smith clutches his ear. She's grabbed the microphone again. The reverb is almost too much. "Damn it," he says. "When they're done with you, I can't wait to put you down."*

It's not that she isn't fascinated by literature. She's an avid reader. On most days she'd be psyched to learn something more about Voltaire than the kick-you-in-the-face simplicity of his themes. She just has more interesting things to think about, like the girls she met at lunch. Astrid and Kim seem so much more fascinating than the musings of some long dead exiled author who suffered from an identity crisis.

"It's a repetitive tale full of unpredictability, changing patterns and tempo. In the repetition we find an argument for determinism. Still, the characters are imbued with free will. Knowing that, who here thinks the utopia we find at the end of the book is really the end? Anyone?"

*Smith guffaws. "Utopia? Utopia is a fallacy. Education is a fallacy. Free will is a fallacy. Everything you are learning is a lie. Your life is a lie."*

None of the students raise their hands. The closest thing to a re-action Siegal gets is a kind of shrug from one of the students in the front row. Unfortunately, it may as easily have been a stifled belch, the ghost of consumed cafeteria pizza making its presence known.

Chee writes in her notebook. "Is it too early to make new friends? Should I even try anymore?"

"Who thinks Candide's paradise is illusory, and, based on recurring patterns, likely to fail?" Siegal asks.

*Smith raises his hand exaggeratedly, almost touching the ceiling of the Corolla. "Ooh, ooh, pick me," he says, laughing.*

There are a few listless, expressionless nods. Kyle McCormack scratches "U2 Rocks" into the top of his desk with his pen. It's all an-gles, and to the kid sitting at this desk next period it will look more like "VZ ROCK5."

Siegal spies McCormack destroying school property. He doesn't once think to stop him. Instead, he simply sighs. "Okay, my little Eloi, here's a freebie. This is going to be on your quiz Friday."

The class, save for Kyle, suddenly pops to attention, eager to finally be spoon-fed. Notebooks pop open, pens come out. Kyle keeps carving.

"A question on the quiz will be: 'In *Candide*, how does Voltaire apply chaos theory to the idea of determinism?' One acceptable answer is: 'Voltaire is telling us free will and determinism can be reconciled by chaos theory. Even outcomes that seem assured are impacted by the decisions we make, and we remain accountable for those decisions.' Got it?"

Someone asks him to repeat what he said, but more slowly.

Siegal complies. "Extra credit if you can work probability theory into your answer."

Chee drops her necklace. It swings and bounces against her chest.

*The speaker in Smith's ear cracks and pops. He sneers.*

She writes down the question and the answer word for word. In Siegal's query, she finds an answer to her own psychological dilemma. She nods and smiles. She writes, "Go for it," just below her internal query and nods approvingly.

Siegal sees what he thinks is the light go on in Chee's brain. He grins to himself, content in his mistaken belief that Voltaire may have touched at least one kid since the Eighteenth Century.

The next bell rings, and the kids jump from their seats. Chee's reservations about making new friends depart like the class of exiting students, the lessons of the past lost on them all.

"Don't forget your assignment for tomorrow," Mr. Siegal calls over the clamor of kids leaving. "Chapter Two of *A Canticle for Leibowitz.*"

*The dot is on the move again. "Not long now."*

*Jane Adams High School, Chicago.*

Centurion staples a handbill to a light pole. He secures the flier with eight staples, three across the top, then three across the bottom, before popping two in the middle for the hell of it.

Posting bills is not an exact science. It's boring, barely worth the prowess of a superhero . . . or someone who pretends to be one. He amuses himself by being creative in his stapling and taping, individualizing how he secures each flier. Fifteen feet away, he's fastened a flier using eleven staples, all around the circumference of the page. Five feet further, he's attached a page using a zigzag pattern of staples, something like a sideways "M." At the entrance of Jane Adams School about thirty feet away, the sheets are hung three across by six high on the cement wall. They're held fixed by wide strips of tape.

He called Chicago Public Schools first. He asked them about Amachi Jacobs, but CPS wouldn't even confirm she was a student, let alone release her information. He knew it was a long shot, a Hail Mary dependent upon getting hold of someone with rich access but poor discretion. But he was directed to a breakdown of the CPS schools and their various enrollment processes. This feeds his backup plan, what cops call old-fashioned canvassing.

Canvassing is tedious. It is boring. As such, it's often an ignored investigative tool. But the neighborhood canvass is also the most pro-

ductive method of obtaining leads. Centurion's learned this from reading countless procedural manuals. So he will play the role of the
gumshoe, the flatfoot, surveying in a systemic fashion. He'll make contacts and detect clues, hoping he'll uncover that one nugget, that gem
of information that helps him locate Kid Caper's killer.

First, he eliminates the military academies and vocational schools.
Both the academies and vocational schools require too much commitment and specific skills for a transfer student like Jacobs. Unfortunately,
these institutions only account for about forty of the more than one
hundred high schools in Chicago.

For similar reasons, he strikes specialty schools devoted to arts and
agriculture from his agenda as well.

He moves on, excluding selective enrollment schools next. Merit
schools are the crème de la crème. Entrance is based on past performance, standardized testing, and an entrance exam. Competition for admittance in a selective enrollment school is fierce. Based on her student
performance, Amachi Jacobs would be an excellent candidate for one
of these institutions. The enrollment process, however, takes months,
even years. If Jacobs is in Chicago, she's only been here for a few weeks.
There's no need to visit Whitney Young, Walter Payton College Prep,
Lane Tech, Northside College Prep, or any of the others. He crosses
these dozen or so schools off his list.

That leaves the neighborhood schools. He'll work his way north,
then back south, postering the neighborhoods. If he doesn't get a hit
quick, he'll need to scratch some money together fast. There are about
ninety of these schools. This could take days, possibly weeks.

A girl, maybe sixteen years old or so, watches Centurion as he goes
about his work. "Is someone running for president of student council
or something?" she asks.

"No," Centurion says. He hands her a page.

The teen takes it cautiously and studies it.

The leaflet is one of hundreds of dark photocopies featuring an
enlarged black and white photo of a girl's face. Although heavily pixi-
lated, the girl looks to be between seventeen and twenty. At the top, a
handwritten query asks, "Have you seen this girl?" Under the photo,

he's scribbled, "Amachi 'Chee' Jacobs." The bottom of the page asks anyone with information to contact "Centurion" and lists a phone number to an answering machine in Tampa.

The girl shakes her head. "Sorry, no. Who is she?"

"Trouble," he says.

She starts to hand it back, but he waves her off.

"No, please keep it. Share it with your friends."

She nods and turns. He watches her for about ten seconds as she makes her way down Union Avenue. Then it's back to posting.

Nearly five miles away, Chee runs into her house, drops her book bag in the vestibule. "Hi, Dad!" she calls, taking the stairs up to her bedroom two at a time.

"Hi, honey," her father calls back from the study. "How was school?"

There's no answer. He hears her above him, opening and closing closet doors and dresser drawers. "Where are they?" she says to no one at all.

Thirty seconds later his daughter comes bounding down the steps. He's surprised. For a girl so thin, so light, she makes a racket. She turns the corner and bounces into his study.

"Did they help you find what you were looking for?" he asks, not looking up from his work.

"Who?" she asks.

"The family of bigfoot making all that noise," he looks up, pushes his glasses so that they rest higher on the bridge of his nose.

"Funny, Dad. Yes, I found my jeans."

"Good," he responds, returning to his work. He says no more, but counts off in his head. Three. Two. One.

"Dad, can I go to the mall with some friends?"

"When?" he asks.

"Now. They're actually waiting out front."

"Do I know these friends?" he asks, raising a brow.

"No, but they're really nice. I met them today at lunch."

Marcus sighs. "Have you finished your homework?"

"Of course." She looks at him like he's grown an extra head. "Wait, don't you want to know their names?"

"Oh, sure."

"Astrid and Kim," Chee says.

"Well, okay then. Astrid and Kim." He says their names like they're foreign, like they're constituted of syllables he's never pronounced before.

She cocks her head.

*She knows something's up.* He usually comes off like the Spanish Inquisition, gathering as much data as he can. He needs to be more authoritarian. "Be back by 7 PM. It's a school night," he demands. It's better to be thought of as being disconnected from teenage life than having ulterior motives.

His ploy works. "That's so early," Chee moans, unaware she's being manipulated. "How about eight?"

"Fine. Eight and not one minute later."

"Thanks so much, Daddy!" Chee exclaims. She rarely calls him "Daddy" anymore. She takes him by surprise, leaping to the side of his desk to give him a hug. He barely has time to close his files.

"Have fun, baby." He kisses her cheek. "And be safe." He emphasizes the final word.

"I will." Then she's off like a bolt, through the door and down to her waiting friends.

He walks to his office window.. Two smiling young women wait for her at the curb. The teen with a hoodie raises her hand, high-fives her. *Kim Monfort.*

The other is slimmer and has jet-black hair. She says something to Chee. Then her head suddenly tilts, like she's just heard a noise from the house. Her neck twists, her gaze rising to rest directly on him.

He almost steps away from the window, almost flees into the darkness of the study to hide behind the glare of the glass. Instead, he holds his position, smiles weakly and waves.

The girl waves back and offers her own awkward smile.

*Astrid Dunst. What does she see when she looks at me?*

He knows the answer. He's interrogated several mentalists, asking them that very question. Their reply is always the same. "Black." It's the color of liars and cons, the color of murderers . . . and worse.

The girl in the hoodie throws her arms over both Chee's and Astrid's shoulders. She spins Astrid, pulls her tight, and escorts her across the street. The embrace doesn't stop Astrid from looking back over her shoulder. She gives the second floor window where he stands one more puzzled glance.

He nods, waves again. *Yes, black.*

The girls stroll away.

He can still see them when he makes the phone call. "They're on their way." He hangs up and curses the day he ever met his so-called handlers.

*Water Tower Place.*

Astrid takes a bite of cookie. "Yummy," she says as the teens pass a movie poster.

The advertisement is for a film called *Dark as Pitch*. An older man, eyes glowing and red, offers a soccer ball with an extended hand and a smile. His other hand is hidden behind his back. It holds a black pitchfork that extends over the man's shoulder. The tagline says: "Your Soul is His Goal."

"I hope you're talking about your Mrs. Fields," Kim says.

Astrid shakes her head, her mouth full. She holds up her right hand and extends her index finger. She has something to say, and she's intent on saying it shortly.

"Gross," Kim says looking at the poster. "Nigel Crown is old enough to be your father. Probably older."

Astrid continues chewing, her left hand now covering her mouth.

"Nigel Crown? The rock star?" Chee asks.

Astrid finally swallows. "The one and only. My dad saw him play at the Metro in the eighties when he fronted Panic Attack. He's a dream."

"Nightmares are dreams too," Kim says.

Astrid pushes her cookie into Kim's hand and walks over to the poster case. She places her hands on either side of the frame. She leans in and gives the display a kiss, right over Nigel Crown's life size face. It's long and deep. She pulls away with a smack leaving a full lip balm imprint on the glass.

"Gross."

"You said that already," Astrid says, spinning away from the display. Her eyelids flutter dramatically. Her hands go to her heart. She sighs heavily.

The girls laugh.

"Would you do him?" Kim asks Chee.

"I, no, I don't think so, no," she stammers, stuffing her hands into her pockets.

"Me neither," Kim says. She takes a big bite of Astrid's cookie.

"That's because Kim only likes douchebags," Astrid says. She shakes her head, catches movement behind Kim and Chee. "Oh, no. Speak of the devil."

"What?" Kim says, spinning and spitting cookie particles.

Two boys descend on the escalator. The taller is wearing his Oakley sunglasses backwards, like he has an upside down face on the back of his head, and a bright red Hollister shirt. The shorter is wearing a yellow tee with a giant blue stripe, probably Banana Republic. His sunglasses hang by a temple tip from the corner of his mouth.

To Astrid, though, these teens are just muddy brown blotches, dirty magnetic fields.

"Who are they?" Chee asks.

Astrid smirks. She could say they're the most popular assholes in school. Instead, she provides their birth names. "Brody Rooney and Kyle McCormack."

"Hi, Brody!" Kim calls. She raises her hand high and waves. Cookie crumbs land in her hair.

Astrid grabs Kim by the shoulders, turns her, and tells her to cool it. She's too eager and threatens to make a mockery of herself. And more importantly, she's changing. Right. Now. "And pull your hoodie up. Fast."

Kim's eyes go wide in horror. She quickly pulls the hood over her head, but not before Chee notices an odd protrusion, like a flap of hairy skin folded over Kim's ear. Kim runs past Astrid towards a bench near the J. Crew.

The taller boy, Brody, frowns, shakes his head. "Freaks," he says. Kyle laughs, says something like, "Good one, bro." The two of them walk into Abercrombie past a couple of models in various states of undress.

Astrid asks Chee if she would mind giving Kim and her a quick moment alone.

"Sure," Chee says, her head tilting slightly. "No problem. I've got to head to the bathroom anyway. I'll be back in a few minutes."

"Great."

Chee marches away, her expression a mix of confusion and suspicion, while Astrid leaves to comfort her friend.

Smith spies the girls go their separate ways from a bamboo seat inside the Teavana. The Jam plays over ceiling mounted speakers.

*Go to church do the people from the area, all shapes and classes sit and pray together . . .*

He wipes his mouth with a napkin.

*For here they are all one, for God created all men equal . . .*

He stands, slips into the galleria, and . . . disappears.

Kim sits on the bench, hugs her knees. "God, I'm so embarrassed," she says as Astrid approaches.

"You're being a little hard on yourself, aren't you?"

Kim shakes her head without making eye contact. "Why can't I control it?"

"You just need to concentrate. You're getting better every day. Remember how it was when we first met?"

Kim's head dips slightly in recognition. There's truth in Astrid's words. During their first sleepover, Kim woke to find her face replaced with that of a bulldog, a tail protruding from her pajama bottoms.

"Anyway, trust me, you don't want anything to do with those guys,"

Astrid says, taking a seat next to her friend. "Their auric eggs are just disgusting. They're selfish and angry. I think they're dangerous too. Vandals, maybe."

Kim looks up. "Really?" she says, her eyes full of mock hope.

"At some point, we need to talk about your daddy issues," Astrid says.

"Let's not bring that deadbeat into this."

"Sorry," Astrid says, "but you know the divorce wasn't your fault, right? You need to stop blaming eight-year-old Kim for his move to Wisconsin. You have to recognize that it's okay to be upset."

Kim crosses her arms. "Okay, Doctor Phil."

"I'm serious," Astrid says. "It's a classic pattern, and I don't want you to sabotage your happiness by dating some loser. You deserve healthy relationships." She glances towards the Abercrombie & Fitch store. "God, I feel like I need a shower after seeing those guys."

Kim allows a hint of a smile. She sniffs and wipes her nose with a sleeve. "How do I look?"

Astrid bends and looks under Kim's hoodie. "All good. Back to normal."

"Whatever that is," Kim says.

"Let's go find—" Astrid halts mid-sentence. Her body goes stiff. Her eyes roll into the back of her head. She starts to tremble.

"Astrid!" Kim says, taking her friend's head and guiding it to her lap. She places a hand across Astrid's jaw and neck, feels her pulse building, her chest heaving.

"Chee," Astrid manages between spurts of breath. Her eyes open. "Help her," she says, her eyes pleading before her lids close tight again.

"Astrid!" Kim calls again.

But Astrid does not answer. She can't. She's no longer there.

Her doctors call these episodes seizures. They've debated the cause, scanned her brain, and searched for clues and tumors. Most have come down on the side of epilepsy. They've prescribed her everything from Tegretol to Zarntin, medicines she's never once touched.

Mentalists might call it clairvoyance or remote viewing. But there's one problem: Astrid has never meditated, never visualized, never tried to connect to the aetheric plane. She's never surrounded herself with silence or comfort, never concentrated on or visualized another world. She simply drops through a trap door in reality. It's as easy as falling.

Kim's voice fades away into the darkness. She's moving through the lowest frequencies of the astral world, transporting to another place. New sounds, strained and warbled, develop. Haunting echoes build and reverberate. They sound like cries underwater or encased in glass. The blackness begins to yield, a slow fade in bathed in blue light. With the light comes sound. A projected version of Astrid finds herself facing a locked metal door.

"Help!" It's Chee's voice. It comes from behind her.

Astrid spins slowly, hovering in space. A growing azure glow paints the corners of a small, tiled room. A bathroom. Her eyes pass over the stalls, then to the sinks directly opposite the entry. A man has his arms wrapped around Chee. He holds a blade to her neck, ready to pull it across her jugular. His other arm is around her waist, prepared to twist her like a mantis as he cuts.

"Astrid?" Chee says, her face a knot of bewilderment. She starts to writhe and struggle.

Astrid's eyebrows convulse. *Chee can see me? She can see my astral body?*

"What?" Smith says, eyes darting, pulling her tighter to him. "Where is she?"

"Astrid," Chee says again, her eyes tearing.

"Where is the bitch?" Smith says to Chee. Then he yells, "Show yourself, witch!"

A web work of energy builds in Astrid, blue electric links firing across her chest to her hands, her navel, head and feet. Her hair stands on end, her body arches. She floats, blue lightening flashing and wisps of aether wrapping around her slight body.

Chee's jaw drops.

A cloud of light builds at Astrid's midsection. It grows and stretches, rising to her chest. The energy begins to concentrate about her breastbone and grows in intensity. She exhales smoke, filling the room with mist. The aether surges, pulsating with each breath, becoming brighter and brighter. Astrid collects the energy in a ball in her hands, pushes it away from her chest.

Chee shields her eyes. "You should let go of me," she says matter-of-factly to the man.

"Show yourself," Smith says, "I'll kill her. I promise."

Chee goes limp, almost slipping out of the man's grasp.

Astrid's levitating body convulses, her arms thrusting, firing the ball of electricity. The aether, her envoy, rockets from her body, hammering the man in pulsating waves. It slams into him, overpowering him and burying his knife into his left pectoral muscle.

His hands clutch at the wound. He drops Chee, and she rolls. He gropes for her with his right hand, misses as she crawls under the counter.

He draws the knife from his chest with a growl. Huffing, teeth bared, he kneels. He grabs one of Chee's kicking feet. "You're dead girl. I don't care who you are."

That's when the door bursts open, almost coming off its hinges. A thing, hairy and wide, knuckle-walks into the room. It stares directly at Smith, its eyes black as coals. It's brow furrows. It raises its apelike head and bays from a snout equal parts wolf and hog. It beats its chest with gorilla fists.

"What the—" Smith doesn't have time to finish his question.

The fiend swats him with a massive uppercut. Smith flies, bounces off the ceiling into the mirrors above the faucets. He lands on the marble countertop, his face in a sink, glass raining down on him.

Smith groans, turns his torn face towards his attacker. "No," he mutters.

A clawed hand grabs Smith about his neck and shoulders. The beast picks him up, raising him to the sky and through the ceiling tiles. The creature screams—

"No," he says again.

—Before pounding him into the counter. Porcelain and marble snap as the man bounces with a bang and falls to the floor. The counter slumps forward, pipes bursting. A fountain of water jets across the room. A pool develops on the floor about Smith's still body.

The creature steps towards him, crushing Smith's fallen earpiece beneath its hoof. It huffs heavily, its great chest rising and expanding. It raises a heel, intent on crushing the man.

"No," he squeaks once more.

The monster starts to apply its weight, then stops, halted by its own reflection in the broken mirrors. It steps over the man. The creature bends to inspect its horrible visage more closely. Its claws go to its face, touching its snout and the beginnings of antlers at the sides of its skull. It raises is giant hands, rotates them before its muzzle. Its nails are broad and sharp like daggers, its palms leathery, cracked, and dark. Thick fur runs up its fingers and the back of its hand. It groans and starts to . . . cry.

*Chink, chink chink, chink.* Glass falls from the man's shoulders. He's crawled to the entry and stands next to the broken door. He hovers near the convex impression of a fist in the metal. Blood pours from his cheek, mixing with the water spray dotting his face and soaking his shirt. He takes a step forward and quickly limps away.

The monster moves to give chase, beats its fists on the floor. It is halted by a question.

"Kim?" a soaked Chee says, scooting out from under the mangled counter.

A beast straight from Hell regards her. A phantom floats behind the beast's shoulder over the ruins of the restroom.

Chee runs straight at the monster and hugs it, grinning. She buries her head in the fur for a full moment before pulling away and asking, "Just who are you girls?"

❖❖❖

The police scanner comes to life.

*Eleven-Forty-Two . . . are you available? There are reports of an explosion at 835 N. Michigan.*

*Ten-Four. On our way. That's Water Tower Place. Correct, Dispatch?*

*Affirmative, Eleven-Forty-Two. The mezzanine level bathrooms. Northwest corner.*

There's some encrypted gibberish, then . . .

*Eleven-Forty-Two, what's your ETA?*

*Five minutes, Dispatch.*

The police will beat him there. Centurion is at least fifteen minutes away. Still, he has an advantage. If this mall incident is somehow related to Chee, like the horrifying event at the mall in Indianapolis, the cops don't know that. They won't be able to find what they don't know to look for. They don't have a clue. Not like him.

He slams the Chariot into drive and floors it. He steers with his knees as he spreads a map over the top of the steering wheel. He weaves through traffic, the Caravan rocking. He digs into the map, flipping it over and then back. He just misses a bike messenger. The bicyclist gives him the bird and shouts Doppler-effected obscenities.

Centurion doesn't drive directly to the mall. If this is Amachi, she'll be on foot. So he locates the nearest CTA station on the map and speeds there. He turns on State Street, flies across the Bataan-Corregidor Memorial Bridge. He blows the red light at Kinzie, then another. He starts to run a third, then realizes where he is. He locks up the brakes, nearly causing the Chariot to spin. He pulls the steering wheel hard. The Caravan comes to a screeching halt against the yellow-painted curb at Chicago Avenue.

He jumps out of the car and runs to the corner. He looks left, across the street, and then right.

*Orion's light, where are they?*

As if on command, three girls step from the dark into the glow of a streetlamp. They huddle around a payphone. The shortest of the girls hands over some change.

The tallest looks like she was caught in a downpour. Despite the reflection on her dark skin, she's instantly recognizable. She is Amachi Jacobs—Chee—and she is his quarry.

# Track Six: Disguises

*Pompeyrac, France. 6 July 1765.*

A burly man in a darned Agincourt jacket tacks a "wanted" poster on the wall of the church. A group of villagers crowd for a view.

"They're going up all over Auvergne and Gévaudan," someone says.

There's a reward of 12,000 livres that will be paid to anyone who kills "La Bête." The poster describes the monster as being the size of a donkey, reddish brown with a dark ridged strip down the back.

A parishioner nods in the direction of the man in the Agincourt coat. He's returned to the company of other hunters in the service of the King's Chief Wolfcatcher. There are a dozen of them on horseback, another two-dozen dragoons on foot. The man steps into the stirrup, places a hand on the swell, and pulls himself into the saddle with a single, fluid motion that belies his heft. They hold four riderless horses and wait outside the rectory for their companions. Inside, the hunters interview three women who were attacked just yesterday.

"Think they'll catch it?" he says to anyone who will listen.

Someone responds. Today he's just a curious onlooker, but in the past he's been a farmer, a husband, a father, and a soldier. He's been both a benefactor and a taker. He's been a killer. His name is Moreau. "No, I don't, friend," he says with a smirk.

"Why's that?" the parishioner asks.

"They're wolfers," Moreau says, "but they aren't looking for a wolf."

"What should they be looking for?"

Moreau shrugs. The form of the monster could vary by day, by hour, by whim. Yesterday he offered to escort the three women currently giving testimony beyond the wall through the woods near Favart. They refused, and he half-heartedly swiped at one with a fur-covered panther claw. They cried and fled. He let them escape. He was in a merciful mood then. Tomorrow he may—or may not—be so lenient. He's an agent of chaos. He's a capricious *faucheuse*. "Something more," he says.

He's hunting less at night now and more in the daylight. He fears neither pagan nor Christian. His attacks now coincide with their holidays. He killed three peasants celebrating the witches Sabbath by bonfire light in June. He made a meal of some children on Christmas. He especially enjoys being known as "an instrument of the devil," scaring churchgoers on their way to Mass. Recently he's even developed a taste for clerics. He mocks all gods, but he excels at ridiculing the King's God and his Catholic Church.

"Do you know what this says?" the parishioner asks, pointing to a passage on the poster above a sketch of a fierce beast. It is an odd creature seemingly pieced together from a menagerie of animals. Its eyes are wild, its tongue long and hanging unnaturally from the side of a mouth full of sharp teeth. Strewn about its claws are the remains of children, bloody and disembodied heads and limbs piled high.

His question is as perverse as the monster's mission. The villager can't read. Most peasants can't. Yet the King communicates almost exclusively through words his constituents can't decipher, let alone understand. It's just exemplifies the King's detachment from his rural subjects.

"Yes," the monster says. He runs his finger along the words as he reads them so the villager can follow. "The creature resembles a wolf/hyena/baboon with long gaping jaws, claws, upright ears, and a supple, furry tail."

"What's a baboon?" a parishioner asks.

"It's like a large, tailless monkey," the Beast says.

"And a hyena?"

"A predator, I think," Moreau says. His voice is full of mock but credible uncertainty. He's a master thespian.

Of course Moreau knows what a hyena is. He's seen them, and not just in zoos. He's seen them in their natural habitat, the veldt of Africa. He's heard their whoops and laughs, witnessed them rip zebras apart in the darkness with unrestrained glee.

His troop kept the brutes at bay at with torches. At night, the soldiers slept in circles, protected by the glow of small campfires. Still, the animals' lows and giggles dogged their sleep.

One night, an exhausted soldier named Bachand had enough. "Cowards," he yelled into the night, challenging the creatures.

The carnivores hooted in response, mocking him from the shadows.

"I wish these bastards would face us," he said, turning away from the darkness and towards his compatriots positioned about the fire. "I would gut each and every one of them."

"Monsieur, it is not good to chide them," an African guide named Nsonowa said. He inched closer to the flames.

"*Mon Dieu*," Bachand said, "and just why not?"

The guide gulped and said, "Because, they are bewitched, Monsieur."

Another escort agreed. "Yes, they take children in the night. They disrespect the dead."

This last reference, Moreau assumed, was to the hyena's penchant for eating carrion, robbing graves of their occupants. In war, there was perhaps nothing more horrifying than an enemy that desecrated the dead. But at least human enemies had souls. Before he could chime in, however, another guide raised the ante.

This aborigine told of a hyena that killed a man and thirty-five of his family members in Chicaualacuala, payback for stealing land from a witch. Witches used hyenas to do their bidding in Mozambique, sometimes even using them as mounts and riding them across the night sky when the moon was full.

Another man—his name was Abidemi—trumped them all. "That's all nonsense," he said to the guides, shaking his finger. "You know not of what you speak."

"Thank you," Bachand said.

"No, Monsieur," Abidemi said, "you do not understand. These creatures are worse than my fellow Africans would lead you to believe. They are not animals of this earth. They are jinns."

"Bah," Bachand said, strolling to and lingering along the edge of light that guarded them. "Utter nonsense."

Abidemi at least had Moreau's attention. "Go on."

When God made humans and angels of clay and light, he also crafted jinns of fire. Jinns are genies, elementals. While invisible to man, they can take physical form. Their chosen vessel: hyenas. "Please talk of them no more," Abidemi said. "They are quick to punish when they have been discounted."

Bachand laughed. "Tales told by old women to scare children," he said over his shoulder. "That's all these stories are." He knelt and grabbed a stone. He hurled it into the blackness. The hyenas chortled.

"Let us go," Abidemi said to the other guides. "We tempt fate by remaining here." He rolled up his blanket. The other Africans followed suit, departing with him without speaking a word.

"Go," Bachand said, "that just leaves more of these dogs for me to kill."

"Enough, Bachand," one of the weary soldiers said, "or we'll go with them and leave you by yourself." The other soldiers, Moreau included, nodded their agreement.

Bachand grumbled but said no more. An hour later, all eight of the remaining French were asleep. That is, all except one.

When they woke, Bachand was gone. "Where is he?" a soldier asked. Another joked he was "probably off fighting jinn." "Or fairies," a third said. They laughed, Moreau remaining silent, until they heard the screams.

"Come on," Moreau said, running in the direction of the cries, returning to the scene of his crime.

They found what was left of Bachand about a hundred feet away, down a slope, beyond a line of trees. His body was spread along the edge of a stream, his limbs torn from his trunk. The children who discovered him bawled. Abidemi tried to comfort them.

They reasoned that Bachand had awoken in the early morning hours and left the protection of the fire to relieve himself. A beast took him by complete surprise, its tracks hidden (and the blood of the kill washed away) by the creek.

No one spoke ill of the hyenas again after that night. No one dared disrespect the jinn.

It was Moreau's first attempt to imitate a hyena. It took him about a month more to perfect his emulation of the hyena's jaws, including the bone-crushing premolars and sharp carnassial teeth. Frankly, he considered his design an improvement upon God's. After all, his jaws could hold 42 teeth; a hyena's maw could only hold a mere 34.

Someone shouts orders, and the parishioner directs his attention back towards the King's hunting party. Four more hooded hunters exit the rectory and stride to their mounts. Three are broad and lanky. They defer to the passage of the fourth. The fourth is leaner and taller still. He is led to a pitch-black horse sans saddle. He bends at the knee and jumps. With a single bound he lands upon the steed's back. He takes the horse by the mane and clicks his tongue against his teeth. The horse circles in place. He's about ready to address the hunters when, suddenly, his head whips in the direction of the parishioner and Moreau. The parishioner feels the eyes on him.

The hunter pulls back his hood to reveal . . . a woman's face. The werewolf hunter is not a "he" at all. The hunter is a woman, and an African woman at that. Her features are broad and dark. A pile of red hair shadows her forehead and cheeks. She stares at them for a full two seconds before pulling her hood forward again. She shifts her grasp, and the horse rotates. It canters briefly before launching into a full gallop. The party follows, the horses and men speeding past the group assembled around the poster.

"Did you see that woman?" the parishioner exclaims. "What do you make of that?" He turns to receive Moreau's response.

But no response is to be had. The monster has disappeared.

# Track Seven: Sound of Thunder

*A CTA Station, Chicago, Illinois. 4 September 2001.*

"Dad," Chee says, "would it be okay if I stayed over at Astrid's tonight?" She's standing at a payphone outside of the Red Head Bar, talking into the mouthpiece. Astrid hovers near her while Kim looks about nervously a few feet away.

"Tell him that he can call my parents if he'd like," Astrid says. "They'll be fine with it."

Chee nods, listens to her father.

A drunk approaches Kim. "Hey, you coming in, baby?" he says, his thumb pointing towards the bar. "Come on, I'll buy you a drink."

"Get bent," Kim says, hurrying to her friends.

"Byaatch," the man yells, venting bourbon. He pivots dramatically and stumbles into the pub.

"That?" Chee says into the phone. "That was nothing, Dad. Just the TV."

Astrid gives her a thumbs-up as if to say, "Quick thinking."

"I know it's late notice," Chee continues, "but I think she can really help me get ready for that Trig quiz."

Kim laughs. "Astrid's still in Geometry."

Chee and Astrid glare at her.

"Sorry," she mumbles under her breath.

"Yes," Chee lies, "the quiz is tomorrow."

Astrid's eyebrows arch. *So?*

"Uh huh. Yes. Sure. Uh huh. Yes."

Kim exhales. *Come on.*

"Okay. I love you too, Dad. Thanks. Bye." She hangs up. "He bought it."

Astrid and Kim cheer. "Sweet," Astrid says. "Let's go."

❖❖❖

Chee's father clicks the receiver and sets the cordless phone down. He leans back, reclining full into his chair. The options play out in his head.

*Smith has been delayed.*

*Smith lost his targets.*

*Smith, himself, is in fact lost.*

No. In an event of delay, Smith or Mansfield would have called Marcus by now with additional instructions. That leaves just two possible options.

*Smith is hurt.*

*Smith is dead.*

Marcus Jacobs puts his feet on his desk. He'd trade a thousand of his daughter's white lies for that news. For the first time in a long time, he allows himself a smile . . . and a prayer. He asks God to deliver the more permanent of the two possibilities.

*A lab somewhere outside Chicago.*

"Help me."

Doctor Desmond Kane looks up from his paperwork. "Oh, my God."

Smith stands before the doctor, his white button-up shirt red with blood. He clutches his cheek with his left hand. His fingers barely contain the ragged bits of flesh that hang from his skull. With his right, he steadies himself against the open steel doorframe near three bio-containment suits.

Kane rushes to Smith. He inspects his face. "What happened to you?"

"Girl," Smith manages, eyes rolling with pain. The word comes like a whisper, the force of his utterance made weak from the air escaping the tear in his cheek.

Kane takes Smith by the elbow. He escorts him into the room. Walking backwards, eyes focused on Smith's damaged face, Kane leads Smith to the exam table in the middle of the octagon-shaped chamber. "Which?" he asks. "The Monfort girl?"

Smith nods.

Kane tells Smith to lay back. "Let's see what we're working with here." He flips on a small recorder clipped to the front chest pocket of his lab coat.

Smith let's go of his face, slowly pulls his hand away.

Kane freezes. His mouth goes slightly agape.

Smith registers Kane's shock. He wheezes, "What's up, Doc?" It's followed by a feeble yet shrill cackle.

Kane shakes his head, regains his composure. He tells Smith to not speak, to not move. He pulls an overhead lamp towards Smith's face and begins to inspect the wound. "This might hurt," he says, his rubber-gloved fingers pressing against Smith's face. *Who is he kidding?* "This is going to hurt. Probably a lot too."

He watches Smith's jaw clench tight through the tattered hole in his face.

Doctor Kane lets loose a trembling breath before launching into his observations. "White male exhibits severe trauma to his face. There are one . . . two . . . three deep dermal lacerations, the longest being six, no, seven inches long. They penetrate . . . deep into the subcutaneous tissue." Smith groans as Kane pulls the flaps of skin on either side of the deepest cut away from each other. "There's extensive damage to the superficial musculoaponeurotic system, specifically the inferior or-bital, nasolabial, medial, and middle fat compartments, as well as the orbicularis retaining ligaments and the massateric ligaments. Some of the mimetic muscles are shredded: the orbital part of the orbicularis occuli, the zygomatici, and . . . yes, the orbicularis oris. The parotid duct and facial nerve have been compromised. The buccal and zygomatic branches have been severed. The muscles have been torn partially from the masseter and nasalis attachments." He pushes the operating lamp away. He says that X-rays will be required to determine the extent of damage to the skull, specifically to the cheekbone, zygomatic bone, and zygomatic process of the maxilla. "The arteries appear to be intact though."

Smith struggles to say, "Bottom line?"

Kane snaps off his gloves. "You'll heal. Eventually, you might get some of your sensation back, maybe even smile again." He pauses, the absurdity of the last sentence coming home. "Not that you smile. But first we need to get you to an ER. Stat."

"Not an option," Smith growls, blood pulsing and filling the chasm in his cheek. "Fix me."

"You need medical attention," Kane says.

"Then give it to me."

"I'm not a reconstructive surgeon."

"Now," Smith says.

"Smith—"

A voice over the intercom interrupts Kane. "Desmond, sew him up."

Kane looks up and towards the window above him. Two men look down on them. "Sew him up? Mansfield, look at him."

"I see him," Mansfield says. "Good to see you, Smith."

Smith lifts a few fingers from the flat of the table, returning the greeting.

"He doesn't look so bad, Desmond," Mansfield continues. "A few stitches and some bandages, and he'll be as good as new."

Doctor Kane's not satisfied. He raises concerns, fears about nerve damage, infection, and chronic pain.

"I don't care," Smith says, seething. "I need to finish this."

"There you have it, Doctor," Mansfield says through the P.A. system. "He's an informed patient and a good soldier. As far as the infection and pain," Mansfield gestures to his right, "we've got our good friend from Davis Pharmaceuticals here."

"But—"

Mansfield turns off the microphone, silencing the doctor. "I hope I didn't oversell your company, Martin."

"It's hard to say," a balding man in angular glasses says.

"Let's begin," Mansfield says, changing the subject.

"Please roll up your sleeve."

Mansfield complies.

Martin swabs Mansfield's arm with alcohol. He draws a syringe from a steel attaché case, checks the dosage. "You'll feel a slight prick."

"You don't have to warn me about that anymore."

"Oh, right," Martin says. He finds a vein in the crook of Mansfield's elbow, presses the needle against the aging skin. The epidermis provides a moment of resistance before the needle pierces it and slips in. He injects Mansfield with a clear, thick fluid.

Mansfield's emotionless. "You were saying, about Smith?"

"So, yes, we've got something new, an anti-inflammatory slash neuro-blocker. Tests show that it can successfully suppress pain. We developed it to address polytrauma in troops. The idea was to create a drug that would allow a soldier with severe to maximal injuries to multiple body regions—you know, potentially lethal injuries to the head, neck, spine, and abdomen—to complete their military objectives. These soldiers would, of course, be nothing more than walking corpses, zombies programmed to complete their assignments before dying." The plunger fully depressed, Martin slides the needle out and wipes the ingress point with gauze.

Mansfield flexes, bending his arm up and down. "Perfect," he says with a half smile. He rolls down his sleeve.

"But there are a couple of, well, complications."

Mansfield's eyes roll. "There are always complications. So?"

Martin shrugs his shoulders. "I think in the interests of full disclosure . . . "

Mansfield sighs. "Go on."

"The medication acts like a nerve block. So it will be difficult for the patient to really feel anything. I don't know if that block will last a few days or a week or more. Consequently, we won't know when to administer short-acting medications like a hyrdocodone or hydromorphone. We'd usually prescribe them to avoid a pretty intense pain spike. I'd also recommend an ongoing regimen of valium to help manage anxiety and muscle spasms." He packs up the syringe. He adds, almost matter-of-factly, "We've witnessed some psychiatric issues in rats."

"Rats?"

"That's the second complication," Martin says. "We haven't completed human trials yet."

"I see. Where are you with them?"

"Technically, we haven't started them. Herculovir is a prototype.

We're awaiting FDA approval for the demonstration cycle."

"Herculovir," Mansfield says with a chuckle. "That's quaint."

"Nick Davis' idea, Mr. Smith-Cumming. You don't say, 'No,' to the president of the company."

"Well, we didn't get FDA approval to start testing this either," Mansfield says, pointing to the injection point on his arm.

Martin nods. "Yes, but that's a mitotic prohibitor. The risks are different."

"Still, the same rules apply, whether drugs are designed to relieve pain or," he says, pausing to look at his arm, "for chemotherapy, do they not?"

"Well, yes."

"Then I think we can start human testing on Smith tonight," Mansfield concludes. "What else?"

"We just need Nick's approval."

"Get him on the phone. I'll get it."

"Right away," Martin says.

Mansfield stares through the window at Kane toiling below. "I can be very convincing," he says to no one in particular. Kane's piecing Smith's face together, but, like a board game from a thrift shop, pieces are missing. He does the best he can with what he has. He moves on and starts working on the knife wound in Smith's pectoral muscle.

When Kane finishes, he inspects the results of his efforts. It's not pretty, but it will do. For now.

That's when he notices the clump of thick hair hanging from Smith's fist, hair torn from his monstrous attacker. Kane bends down. There's still some flesh attached to the follicles. He's overcome with emotion. He hasn't felt joy like this since he was a kid on Christmas morning, before he was told there's no such thing as Santa. There are such things as shapeshifters, and proof exists in Kane's balled hand. For that knowledge Kane will trade a million revelations about St. Nick, the Easter Bunny, and God.

❖❖❖

A subway ride and thirty minutes later, the girls are sequestered in Astrid's bedroom. Astrid offers them dry clothes.

"So, should I order some food?" Astrid says. She walks over to her chest of drawers, opens one, and pulls out a menu.

"I'm starving," Kim says, jumping up and down on Astrid's bed. She's always hyper after a big change. Hyper and hungry. "How about pizza?"

"We just had pizza for lunch," Astrid says.

"So?"

"Fine. Giordano's or Pizza Capri?"

"Giordano's. Stuffed." She pauses. "With spinach."

"Cool. You'll love this, Chee. Nothing beats Chicago pizza." Astrid walks over to her desk, starts to pick up her phone.

"Wait," Chee says. Her hand covers Astrid's, forcing the phone back on the receiver. She looks up at Astrid from the desk chair. "Aren't we going to talk about what happened tonight?"

Silence.

She turns to Kim.

Kim stops bouncing. She folds at her knees, collapsing on the bed. She stares at the ceiling and exhales. "Fine," she says, finally sitting up on her elbows. But only after we eat. And you tell us what that guy wanted."

"And you tell us how you knew that animal was Kim," Astrid chimes in, crossing her arms.

"Yeah, and how you knew Astrid was even there. I didn't see her." She says dejected, "I've never seen her when she's projecting."

Chee nods. "Deal."

❖❖❖

1933. That's the year etched in the limestone at the base of the building. Centurion can read it from the street. The building is well lit, making the direct approach—the front stairs to the porch—untenable. He backtracks, counting homes as he goes. *Seven*. At mid-block he turns at the corner. He makes his way up the alley behind the homes on Eddy

Avenue. He counts to seven again, locates his target. He moves through the darkened gangway that separates the narrow greystones. When he reaches the shadow of the porch, he scales the side, careful to remain hidden by the silhouette of a great oak. He swings his body over the rock balustrade and creeps to the mailbox. Kneeling, he opens it. He cringes as the metal groans with rust and age. He sticks a hand in. *Eureka.* They forgot to collect the mail today. He may not need to go dumpster diving tonight. He gathers several magazines and letters. He slides back into the darkness and begins sorting through the post.

*An electric bill for Travis Dunst.*

*A TCF bank statement for Travis Dunst.*

*A ValPak mailer full of coupons for the Dunst Family or Current Resident.*

*A homecoming flier for Lincoln Park High School.* He folds and tucks the mailer into his breastplate.

*Discover magazine. Travis Dunst.*

*A Victoria's Secret catalog for Christina Dunst.* Centurion quickly flips through the bra selections before setting it aside.

*Spin Magazine.* A grinning Nigel Crown is on the cover. He's shirtless and wearing a crown of thorns. The title: "The Persecution of Nigel Crown."

Centurion groans. "Dolos' work, no doubt," he says, mentioning the Greek god of trickery. He moves to toss it aside, but catches a different name on the address label. *Astrid Dunst, 1220 W. Eddy, Chicago, IL 60657.*

*Astrid.* He tears the label from the magazine. He slides the ripped music magazine and the rest of the mail towards the post box with his sandal.

He climbs off the porch back into the gangway. He slinks mid-way in, stops, and looks up. He watches the windows and listens.

There are shadows moving in the forward-most window. There's giggling.

He moves to the front of the house, towards the laughter. "Let's see what I can find out about you, Astrid Dunst." He palms the rough cut stone on either side of the passage with calloused hands. He pushes, lifts his legs. He lodges his feet about two feet off the ground, pressing them into the buildings on either side. He releases with his hands, stands, and presses again. This time, he pulls his feet three feet higher before securing them. Spider-climbing, it takes him just a minute before he's twenty feet above the pavement.

He's about three feet from the window. He cannot see in, but the voices inside are clear. He smells pizza, and his stomach growls. It's been almost a day since he's had anything to eat. There's a flash. Five seconds later, there's a thunderclap. At least the sound of thunder will mask the sounds of his revolting stomach.

He repositions himself, turning and stretching his legs so that his back is wedged against Astrid's house. He adjusts his hips, finding a flat piece of stone to rest his lumbar region against.

*I can do this all night.*

There's another flash of lightning, this one chased by the immediate rumble of thunder. The rain begins . . . in torrents.

❖❖❖

"This is good," Chee says, wiping her mouth.

"I wouldn't steer you wrong, kid," Kim replies. "I'm glad I got to bust your cherry."

"Kim, I'm eating," Astrid says, her lips curling.

"Whatever," Kim says with a wave. "So, who spills first?"

They're sitting in a circle on the bed, the pizza between them. No one volunteers.

Kim continues, "Well, someone better offer to go first—"

Flash, the peal of thunder.

"—before I kick you out into the rain."

"Hey, this is my house," Astrid says to Kim. She gets up, goes to the window. She looks out, her face just inches from Centurion's roost. The rain beats hard on the pane. "And I'd never kick you out in this weather. I can't see a thing; it's coming down hard."

There's a single, weak cough.

Astrid mistakenly attributes the noise to Chee or Kim. "I think we have lozenges. Need one?" Astrid says, returning to the bed.

Chee and Kim look at each other, confused. "No, thanks," they say in near unison.

"Okay." Astrid props up on a pillow. "I guess I can go first. Long or short version?"

"Short," Kim says.

Astrid's eyes narrow. "Okay, long story short . . . for Kim. To put it simply, the psychisms started when I was six years old."

"Psychisms?"

"Yes, the basic stuff. A little precog. Some telekinesis. Astral projection. Talking to Charlie. That kind of thing."

"Charlie?"

"Her grandpa," Kim says, leaning in.

"Got it," Chee says.

"No," Kim corrects, "I don't think you do. Charlie's dead. He died twenty years ago."

Chee's mouth goes slack. "Oh," she musters. Her immediate thought: "Do your parents know?"

"Yes. They're pretty cool with it actually. Dad always asks me how grandpa is doing. Mom tells me she's happy he's in my life."

"Travis and Christina are pretty cool that way," Kim says, referring to Mr. and Ms. Dunst.

"Do your parents know about your gift?" Chee asks Kim.

"Ha," Kim laughs, "if they know, they certainly don't care. And I wouldn't call this a gift. It's an annoyance."

"You don't talk about it?" Chee asks.

"Let's just say they're not really that engaged in my development on a day-to-day basis. Mom works, Dad is God knows where. Plus, it's pretty easy to hide this." Kim extends her arm in front of her, pulls up her sleeve. Her skin starts to change colors, yellow and black hair grows. Her fingers shrink, widen into dark paws, her nails pulling back into claws. "Cheetah," Kim says. "I'm not sure how it works, but I can turn into pretty much anything."

Cellular epigenetic codes are fixed, held tight by methyl groups and coiling proteins. The methyl groups attach to genes, masking them from DNA transcription. The coiling proteins spool around the DNA, tightening and hiding other genes. These fail safes keep someone from waking up with a heart or a kidney where his or her brain should be.

But Kim is free from most epigenetic rules. She changes at will.

Her cellular ribosomes go into overdrive, sucking in amino acids, spitting out unique protein strands. The peptide chains rearrange the methyl molecules and cause the spools to relax, revealing genes not usually exposed. Switches running along the double helix start flipping. Now activated, Kim's cells hulk out.

Her arm elongates, the hair turning white and long, her fingers coming together, combining, merging, to form a hoof. Before Chee can guess, "Goat," Kim's arm is changing again. A flash of lightening later, her arm and hand resemble an orangutan's, the hair thick and auburn. A moment later, her arm is smooth and green, her fingers ending in bulbous tree frog-like caps. Her arm is like putty, stretching and compressing, the form changing over and over. Zebra stripes, hairless pink wrinkles, thick black fur, feathers, scales, talons, paws, and claws.

"Anything?" Chee asks.

"Pretty much," Kim says, rolling her sleeve down.

"Once she's seen an animal, she can transform her body into portions of what she's seen. It doesn't matter if it's a reptile, bird, amphibian, or mammal. It's amazing." Astrid takes another bite of pizza.

Chee's eyes are wide as she turns back to Kim. "When did it start?"

"Believe it or not, puberty. Double whammy. I got my period *and* grew six tits on the same day."

Chee chuckles, catches herself. She apologizes.

"Don't worry about it," Kim says. "I've pretty much got it under control now."

"Except," Astrid amends, "when her mind wanders. Then she loses some of that control."

"So that's what's up with the hoodie?" Chee asks.

Kim touches her nose, points to Chee with a slight nod.

"Wow. Just, wow," Chee says. "Does it hurt?"

"Nope." But Kim should be in agony. As the pain impulses shoot from her nerve cells to her spinal cord, the pituitary gland begins spewing endorphins like a morphine drip. They fill Kim's pain receptors and prevent nerve cells from releasing any further pain signals. She is shielded from pain during these transitional periods.

"Okay," Astrid says, "it's our turn to ask a few questions."

"Okay," Chee says. "Shoot."

"So," Astrid says, glancing at Kim. "Why weren't you freaked out by us at the mall today? Why aren't you freaked out now?"

Chee shrugs. "Honestly, I don't know. I mean, you both just seem really nice."

"And?" Astrid demands.

"Well, I've always had friends with cool abilities."

"Other friends—"Astrid begins.

"With cool abilities?" Kim finishes.

"Sure."

Kim and Astrid eye each other.

Chee misinterprets their concern for jealousy. "Don't get me wrong, nothing as cool as what you can do."

"Like what kind of abilities?" Astrid asks.

"All kinds."

"Give us details," Kim says.

"Well, my friend John could talk to animals. Henry could predict things. My ex, Marta, could create fire just by thinking of it. Tony could hold his breath a super long time."

"What?" Astrid and Kim say, stunned.

"I timed him once. He stayed under water for fifteen minutes on a single breath."

"No," Astrid says, "I wasn't questioning you about Tony."

"Your ex was named Marta?" a puzzled Kim says.

Astrid ignores her. "I was questioning their very existence."

"You didn't think there were other people like you out there?" Chee asks. "Well, not *like you* in the sense they're capable of doing the same things you can do, but like you in the sense that they have skills that I don't have."

"But you're talking *Firestarter*-type stuff," Kim says.

"Pet psychic-type stuff," Astrid says.

"Nostradamus-type stuff," Kim continues.

"Yes, I knew people who could do that," Chee says.

Astrid tilts her head. "Wait, you said, 'knew' and 'could.' Past tense."

Chee nods, her eyes closing tight. She starts to choke up.

"What happened to them?"

Chee settles herself before saying, "They died."

# Track Eight: They Said Tomorrow

Centurion's mind races. *Henry. Kid Caper. She mentioned the Kid by name.*

He starts to descend. The rock is slick, and it takes nearly twice as long for his feet to find earth as it did to make the climb. Once his feet are about eight feet off the ground, he let's himself drop.

He lands, a little off balance, hears a pop and feels a tweak in his ankle. He mutters something under his breath about coming up lame, about Hephaestus' foot.

He hurts. He's soaked. He's cold. He's hungry. He's tired. But most of all, Centurion's pissed.

He resolves to get the Chariot and return.

Tomorrow. He'll wait for Chee to leave Astrid's.

Tomorrow. He'll intercept her at the high school.

Tomorrow. He'll rectify things his way.

Tomorrow, Centurion tells himself, he will avenge Kid Caper. Finally.

"That's why we've moved so much," Chee says, wiping a tear. "My dad thinks it will help deal with loss, but I'm not so sure it's working."

Astrid slides over, puts a consoling arm over Chee's shoulder. "It's okay, don't cry."

Chee buries her head in her hands.

"How'd they die?" Kim asks, wrinkling her nose.

"Kim." Astrid's eyes shoot daggers. "Not now."

"Seriously, aren't you the slightest bit concerned?"

"I'm concerned about our friend," Astrid retorts.

Kim squints. She sucks the insides of her cheeks. "Don't you find it a little odd that everyone she knows is dead?"

Astrid stiffens her back slightly. Her eyes bat. "Well, I'm sure they all died in accidents. People with special abilities tend to take more risks."

Kim turns to Chee. "Is that how they died?"

Chee looks up from her hands, her mascara running across her cheeks. She nods. "Yes . . . "

"See," Astrid says.

" . . . mostly," Chee finishes.

"What does 'mostly' mean?" Kim demands.

"Take it easy, Kim," Astrid says.

"No, what does 'mostly' mean?"

"The police in Indianapolis ruled John's death a homicide."

"He was murdered?" Kim asks incredulously.

"Yes."

Kim's eyes go big, her brows cartoonish and nearly leaping off her face. "Astrid, can I talk to you in private for a moment."

"Now?"

"Yes, right now."

"Chee," Astrid says, "we'll be right back."

"I should just go home," Chee says. "I don't want to cause any problems." She starts to stand.

Kim agrees. "We'll see you in school."

"No," Astrid says, staying Chee with a hand on her shoulder. "I won't hear of it. We'll be right back."

With that, Astrid and Kim exit the room. Astrid gives Chee one more smile before slowly shutting the bedroom door.

"You've got to be fucking out of your—"

Astrid shushes Kim. "Not here." She marches quickly down the hallway, motioning for Kim to follow. Around the corner, in a landing for the stairs, they converge. Astrid says, "Okay. What?"

"Astrid, this chick isn't right. She's hiding something?"

Astrid's hands are on her hips. "We're all hiding something Kim. Why should she be any different?"

"No, our cards are on the table."

"Okay, what on earth could she possibly be hiding?"

"I don't know. She could be a psychopath, like *Friday the 13th* or something."

"You watch too many movies."

"Is that so hard to believe?"

Astrid's response is terse. "Yes."

"We don't know anything about her."

"We know that she needs a friend. . .or two."

"No," Kim says, "we know some guy was trying to kill her today."

"He was trying to rob her," Astrid says.

"Yet he didn't take anything, did he?"

"Honestly, I don't know."

Kim blows air through her nose. "Okay, I've got a question for you. What color is her aura?"

Astrid takes a half step back. She doesn't answer.

"Aha! You can't see her aura, can you?"

Astrid looks down at her socks. "Well, not really."

"And you don't think that's weird?"

"Yes. I mean, no. Maybe. Look, it could as easily be a problem with me as with her."

"Astrid, we didn't even know she was a lesbian."

Astrid's lips twist. "She might be bisexual."

"But we don't know that, do we?" Kim says. "You're making my point for me. There's a stranger sitting in your bedroom right now, a stranger with a body count."

"Come on, I can't just kick her out into the night."

Kim crosses her arms. "It's her or me."

"Don't make me."

Kim starts to tap her foot. "Make your decision."

"Stop being a bully."

"What will it be?" Kim says.

"Fine," Astrid says. "Maybe you should go home if you're so concerned."

Kim looks hurt. "Maybe I should go then."

"Maybe you should," Astrid parrots, her hands clenched at her sides.

"Fine." Kim sneers.

"Fine."

"Fine." Kim spins and stomps down the stairs. She opens the front door.

"Don't slam—" Astrid begins.

The door slams thunderously.

"—the door." Astrid shakes her head. She shuffles back down the hallway to comfort her new friend.

"She hates me, doesn't she?" Chee says, her eyes welling.

"No," Astrid says. "She really likes you."

"She has a funny way of showing it," Chee says, wiping her nose with a sleeve.

"She has a hard time making friends." Astrid hands her a box tissues. "Do you want to know how I met Kim?"

Chee blows her noses, her head nodding.

"Seventh grade. She was late to class. The only open chair was next to me. About halfway through the class, our professor told us to pair up with a lab partner. I asked her to be mine."

"So you guys became lab partners?" Chee asks, sniffing.

"No."

"No?"

"Kim told me she'd rather stuff a lit Bunsen burner up her ass than work with a Goth like me. Which is funny, because I don't like Bauhaus or the Cure or Marilyn Manson or anything dark. I can wear black and still like Christina Aguilera."

Chee giggles, rubs the tears from her cheeks.

"But I digress. We've been best friends ever since," Astrid continues, chuckling.

They talk and giggle like this for another hour. Finally they fall asleep. Astrid's slumber is fitful, though, haunted by Chee's attacker. Try as she might, she cannot form a picture of him in her head. She can't seem to describe him. All she recalls of him is what he did . . . and what he said, things that cause her to question Chee's identity, as well as her own.

In times like these, times when Astrid is full of queries and doubt, she turns to her grandfather for advice. Tonight, he does not disappoint.

"Charlie!"

"Hi, Chickadee," her grandfather says. He's standing over her bed.

"Well this is different," she says. He almost never visits her at home, and never when she has guests. Usually, he waits for her by the lake in the aether.

"I'm afraid it's not a social visit," he says, his expression shifting. Lines form across his brow, the corners of his mouth dipping.

Astrid says, "You're worrying me. What's wrong?"

"You tell me."

"My friend Chee was attacked today—"

"I know," he says. Then he corrects himself. "I knew."

"You knew?"

"Yes."

Her head tilts. "And you didn't try to help?"

"I couldn't."

"Couldn't or wouldn't?"

He sighs. "I'm not always going to be around for you, Chickadee," he says, taking a seat next to her on the bed. "It's a dangerous world out there. You need to be able to handle it yourself."

She's quiet for a moment. Then: "That wasn't a robbery, was it?"

He says, "What do you think?"

"I think it's like Kim said. I don't think he was trying to take anything. He said he 'didn't care who she was.' That's not something a purse thief says."

Charlie doesn't respond.

"And something else," Astrid says suddenly. "He called me a witch."

"And you reacted," he says.

"Yes, he was going to hurt my friend."

Charlie nods quietly. "Sounds like he did take something."

"What?"

"Information about you and Kim."

"It was a set-up?"

"I don't know," he says, scratching his chin. "I haven't been able to put all of the pieces together yet, but I promise you I'm working on it."

"Well, what do we do?" she asks.

"*You* need to work on protecting yourself, and I'm going to do my best to provide you the tools to do so."

"When do we start?"

"Now," Charlie says. He proceeds to tell her how.

"During World War II, we took a Japanese pilot prisoner after he ditched his Zero in Manila Bay. He wouldn't reveal his rank or details about his mission. The most we could get out of him after a week of continuous interrogation was his name: Shin. Our camp wasn't really set up to handle POWs, so we kept him in the tank, a small group of cells the MPs used to hold prisoners until they could be transferred to New Zealand."

"You've never talked about the War before," Astrid says.

"And to be honest, Chickadee, I'd prefer not to, but there's a lesson here."

She leans in.

"Well, I wouldn't necessarily say that Shin and I became friends during our time together on Corregidor, but I did come to view him as something more than an enemy." Charlie crosses his arms, extends his hand to touch his chin. His head tilts back as he reminisces. "His English was pretty good, better than some of the kids fresh out of high school to be honest. Still, he wanted to practice. So we would occasionally talk. He'd tell me a little about him, and I'd tell him some things about me. The conditions weren't the best; they never were in internment camps, especially temporary ones. I snuck him food. Rice, mostly. In return, he promised me I wouldn't be harmed when he escaped."

"He told you about his escape plan?" Astrid asks, incredulous.

"Yes. You think you're surprised, imagine how I felt. I would just smile. It was such a funny thing, Shin thinking he had the upper hand. He was so certain he would escape to freedom. I was certain he wouldn't."

"Did he escape?" she asks.

"Oh, yes. One morning he went missing. His cell was empty, the bars pried impossibly wide. He had hightailed it into the jungle."

"How?"

"I struggled to figure it out. Never did, at least in my lifetime. But I bumped into Shin on the other side—you come across a lot of people from your past in the aether, usually for a very good reason. *Synchrodestiny,* they call it. Anyway, I asked him about his great escape. Like most Japanese, Shin practiced a mix of Shinto and Buddhism. Part of his particular belief system was in the tarupa, derivative of the Tibetan tulpa, a magical creature created by thought. He told me he meditated for hours every night, focusing on making a mind-made entity."

"Like meditation?"

"Exactly. In the Zen tradition, it is known as 'turning the eye inward.'

"Wow," she says, blinking, "and you think he got help from this tulpa?"

"I know he did. Witnesses say that they heard something howling that night. I think it was the thoughtform. We tracked Shin by following the monstrous footprints. They were three-toed and clawed, at least three feet long. Along the path, we found thick trees had been uprooted, volcanic boulders split in half."

Astrid's eyes are huge. She's hanging on Charlie's every word.

"I think if you concentrate and visualize hard enough, you can create a thoughtform yourself."

She turns away and snorts. "Me?"

"Sure, why not?"

"Because I'm too small."

"Stature has nothing to do with it. The inferior in size are as likely as anyone else to be superior in mind."

She needs more convincing.

"Just try for me?" he says.

Her shoulders slump as she sighs. "Okay, grandpa."

"Let's try focusing on collecting and moving matter," Charlie says.

She gives it a go. Her face scrunches up like she's squatting twice her weight. She groans as her left nostril twitches. A little burst of aether appears before her briefly then dissipates. It breaks apart in grey wisps and floats away.

"It takes focus, not physical strength. It takes concentration, not sweat." He encourages her to try again. "Try harder, but also try less hard."

"What does that even mean?" she says.

He shrugs.

"Fine." She tries again. And again. And yet again.

He watches her fail . . . over and over and over.

# Track Nine: My Death

*Mount Mouchet, France. 18 June 1767.*

Mount Mouchet will become famous for hosting the Maquis du Mont Mouchet, French Resistance fighters during World War II. They will harass the German troops, delaying their movement and preventing thousands from joining the defense of Normandy against Allied forces. The Nazis will attempt to flush the Maquis from the forests of the region. They will fail.

Nearly two hundred years earlier, though, before the attacks on the Nazis and the search for the *maquisards*, a very different hunt for a very different dissident takes place in these mountains.

The wanted posters in the weeks following Moreau's flight from Pompeyrac changed significantly. The descriptions of the beast varied as he did, the latest warning of something "much higher than a wolf . . . his feet are armed with talons . . . his ears are small and straight . . . his breast is wide and grey . . . his back streaked with black . . . his large mouth provided with sharp teeth." The reports were finally starting to get it right, capturing the truth that he was something other—something more—than a wolf, tiger, or hyena. The *Paris Gazette* referred to him as a "mongrel," a monstrosity constructed from bits and pieces of all of the initial suspects.

More importantly, the fliers began featuring sketches of the monster in his mostly human form. At first, the likenesses were rough. The three women that he spared at Favart had each provided differing accounts of him, their memories twisted and their reports exaggerated by fear. Rather than tear these fliers down, Moreau left them alone. They were reminders of his superiority, of his ability to stay one step ahead of the expanding cadre of hunters. Rumors spread that the Crown had recruited witch-smellers and other experts to hunt the Beast. Pompeyrac, Moreau told himself, would be as close as they get.

But in the two years since Favart, his body count grew. So too did the number of witnesses.

His pattern changed, evolving with his hubris. His attacks became even more brazen. He didn't just consume loners. He no longer attacked under the veil of night. He often transformed in front of his victims, allowing them to see his human form prior to striking. While he devoured more than a hundred, all told he was responsible for more than 200 attacks. There were more survivors than victims, and each provided eyewitness accounts to the King's cavalry.

The caricatures quickly became more convincing, the resemblance to his human form now uncanny. More and more, they portrayed his wide set eyes, the broadness of his forehead, and the bluntness of his nose. He pulled the posters from the walls at first, but they were quickly replaced. For every one he destroyed, four more were posted.

He needed to take a different tact. He went about modifying his appearance. He let his hair grow long. He grew a thick beard. He rubbed dirt into his cheeks. Sometimes he took to wearing an eye patch.

He became unrecognizable to himself, less because of his masked appearance, and more for the horror he creates.

He took stock of his life. He's often alone. Streets are empty. Whole villages have been abandoned. The laughter of children is gone. Still, the King maintains an iron grip on his throne.

Moreau returns to Auvergne, to Haute-Loire, to L'Abattus Agneau. He enters the bar and orders a beer.

"Here," the bartender says, setting a goblet in front of Moreau. He takes two quick steps back, eyes him with suspicion. "Have we met before?"

"*Non.* I don't think so."

"No, I'm sure I remember you, Monsieur," the bartender says, his eyes narrowing, the lines in his forehead deepening.

"I just have one of those faces," Moreau says with a shrug. He sips his beer without looking up. "It's quiet here." He's the only customer.

"It's like this now all of the time," the barkeep says. "My only customers are passersby. Everyone's left because of that damn wolf."

Moreau smiles to himself. "I'm sure it will get better once the King is gone."

"Gone? I hope not. The King's why I'm moving to Paris."

"Moving to Paris?" the monster says. "Why?"

"There's no living to be had here anymore. Everyone is going to Paris. It's protected by the King."

"If Louis can't protect you here, what makes you think he can in Paris?"

"Honestly, I don't know if he can," the bartender says, rubbing his chin, "but I know he'll try. That's good enough for me."

"Why settle for good enough? Why not hope for something better?"

The barkeep tilts his head. "Wait, I remember you. You filled Pierre's head with all that talk of revolution. You paid me in advance for his room and to keep the calves for you. You never collected them."

Moreau doesn't say a word. He just takes another drink.

"Well, you can't have them now," the bartender says. "I sold them."

Moreau waves him off. "*D'accord.* That's fine. I hope you gave the money to Delmas."

"No, I did not."

"And why is that?" the monster asks, his stare icy.

"How could I? Shortly after Pierre buried his wife and son, he killed himself."

Moreau sets his goblet down. "Killed himself?"

"Yes, his guilt consumed him. He blamed himself for their deaths. After their funeral, he set fire to the mill . . . from the inside. He burned with it."

"*Vraiment?*" *Really?*

"To be honest, there wasn't much to bury," the bartender says. "I know he would have wanted to be near his family though."

Moreau's mouth goes slack. His eyes glaze over.

"I'm sorry," the bartender says. "I assumed you knew."

Moreau takes another drink from his beer, this one deep. He polishes off the pint in a few gulps. "Another," he says, setting the vessel on the bar.

Another. Another. Another. He drinks four witbiers in silence. He stares at the wall behind the bar.

It's getting late when the bartender asks, "Are you okay?"

"Chaos," Moreau says.

"What?"

"Chaos."

"I don't understand."

Moreau laughs. "I've become a king."

"What?" the barkeep asks.

"Nothing," the Beast says with a shake of the head. "I'll settle my tab now."

"No, this is on me," the man says. "I insist."

"Merci," Moreau says.

"*De rien.*" *It's nothing.* "It's obvious you cared very much for Monsieur Delmas."

Moreau guffaws and spits up his drink. He wipes beer from his chin with a sleeve. "A life without purpose is as pointless as purpose without consequence." He stops laughing and stands, putting his palms on the bar before him. "What is your name?"

"Jean Chastel," the bartender says, wiping spittle from the counter.

"Monsieur Chastel, I'd like to do you a favor."

"That's not necessary."

Now it is Moreau's turn to insist. "Do you have a firearm?"

Chastel shakes his head. "Not here, no. Why?"

"What if I told you I know where the Beast is hiding?"

Chastel says, "Stop joking."

"No, I do. Better yet, I know where the Beast will be tomorrow."

"How did you come by that knowledge?"

Moreau begins to morph, his snout protruding from his face, his ears lengthening and migrating towards the top of his elongating head. He lets loose a blood curdling howl.

Chastel cries out. He brandishes a cheese knife and waves it wildly at the monster.

"Tomorrow," Moreau growls, "I'll be in the field south of the fork in the Becade River. Be there and be armed . . . or I will come back for you." With that, the monster pulls a cowl over his head. He spins, and in just two bounds he's out the door.

The bartender shakes violently. He can no longer hold the knife. It falls to the floor with a half-dozen *clangs*. He collects himself just enough to retreat from the tavern, fleeing from the back door. He jumps on his horse and rides an hour to the home of the Marquis d'Apcher.

Despite the time, the Marquis receives him. He reclines in a lounge chair near a fire in the great room with a dark woman. She's African, and her hair is as red as the flames in the fireplace. The Marquis introduces her as courtier Lindiwe Toure. Like her mother Mbali Toure, better known as Louis-Marie-Thérèse, who attended the Sun King, Lindiwe attends to Louis XV.

Chastel tells them about the Beast. He is willing to show them where to find the wolf.

The Marquis and Toure exchange nods. "We'll leave at sunrise," the Marquis says.

"Wait," Chastel says. He has a condition.

The Marquis sighs and fingers an eyebrow. "Yes?"

"I want credit for killing the Beast," Chastel says.

The Marquis begins to rebuff him, but Toure interjects.

"That's fine," she says. She stares directly into Chastel's face, unblinking.

Chastel gulps. His nerves are saved by the Marquis' consent.

The Marquis hastily assembles hundreds of trackers and hunters. The next morning, they fan out across the countryside, the Marquis, Toure, Chastel, and a dozen others following the river on horse.

Just past midday, they reach the fork. Here, where the stream bends, the water low and lazy. They cross it by horseback to the southern bank. Toure tells them to halt. She senses something moving in the field before them. It's a sensation she's felt before, an itch she couldn't scratch back at the church in Favart.

"I don't see anything," the Marquis says.

"It's here," she says, "just like he said." She slides a double-barreled flintlock rifle from the holster at the horse's side and extends it before her.

"Can you hit it from here?" Chastel asks.

She doesn't reply. She levels the weapon and closes her eyes. She slowly pans across the field.

Chastel gives the Marquis a puzzled glance. The Marquis purses his lips and extends an open hand in Toure's direction. *Watch.*

The rifle stops moving. "There," she says and opens her eyes. Before her is the monster. It's staring right at her. The Beast takes a step forward. He presents his chest to her, turns his face away . . . and waits.

She fires twice. Both bullets hit home, entering and exiting the Monster's heart. The creature staggers, howling piteously as its life slips away. It falls just feet from where it was stricken.

The Beast of Gévaudan is dead.

Toure jumps from her horse and pulls a blade from a scabbard. She darts through the field, cutting through the waist deep grass with the purpose of an adder. She only slows as she approaches a clearing, an area where the grass is bent under the weight of the beast.

The reeds around the body trace the creature's form and remind her of the tall walls of a sarcophagus. "Anubis," she mutters as she looks upon its jackal-like visage, "may you rest peacefully in the next life." She leans into the crater and lifts a massive hind limb. Her assegai blade is sharp and easily cuts through the fur, sinew, and bone. She separates the massive paw from the creature and drops it into a pouch at her side. The claw will serve as proof to her order of the kill . . . and more. In the years to come, her masters will attempt to use the paw, like other trophies captured by her predecessors and descendants, to unlock the secrets of the Beast and to combat the witches in their midst.

# Track Ten: Look Back in Anger

*A lab outside of Chicago. 4 September 2001.*

It's late, but Desmond Kane continues to hover over his electron microscope. "Fascinating."

"What do you have there?" Mansfield asks as he enters the lab. He's been quietly observing Kane from his glass perch above the room for the last hour, similarly studying him like a microbe on a slide. Finally, his curiosity got the better of him. He had to come down for a closer look.

Kane spins in his chair. "To the layman, these are nothing more than bits of hair and skin," he says. "Smith *retrieved* them"—Kane makes air quotes—"during Ms. Monfort's attack on him. But I'd call these specimens a bona fide medical miracle. I've never witnessed cellular reprogramming like this."

Mansfield notes that scientists have been reprogramming mature cells for years. "What makes these cells different?"

"Her cells change from human to animal without ever becoming stem cells first. There are no endodermic, ectodermic, or mesodermic barriers; her cells are totally pluripotent, only they're not stem cells. Her fibroblasts are incredibly receptive; they don't just suppress cellular expression, they amplify it. It looks like they can do about anything, and they can do it fast."

"How can that be possible?"

"Did you ever hear the tale of the twin rats? It's a study that's been replicated over and over in labs across the world." Kane explains the rats were separated. One was nurtured as a baby—it received a lot of attention from the mother—and the other was basically ignored. Even though they had identical brains, they grew up to be very different. The neglected rat was poorly adjusted. It was easily startled and was less adventurous. Unlike the rat that received motherly attention, it suffered from surges in hormones when it became stressed.

"Their individual experiences," Kane says, "shaped their particular behaviors."

"As they would," Mansfield says.

"Yes," Kane says, "as they would, but the bigger mystery is how could this occur if the brains of twin rats were exactly the same? The answer is that while our genes are fixed, our experiences can alter how the genes are expressed, which is just as powerful."

Kane continues, "Molecules attached to genes, specifically methyl groups and coiling proteins, hide certain genes while making others active. We used to think the patterns were hardwired. It turns out these switches are not etched in stone. We can actually rearrange them, physically alter which genes are exposed, and in doing so change the way our cells, even our brains, work. It can happen in the womb (think fetal alcohol syndrome, for example), during early development, or even later in life."

"I'm following," Mansfield says.

Kane says humans share genes with all living organisms. "Our cells only express about 3 to 5 percent of our genes. That leaves 95 percent unexpressed. That's why we look so different from chimps despite a very small genetic variation, just 1.2 percent to 6 percent, depending on how it's measured. Genes linked to thick body hair, long arms, and other traits consistent with chimps and or other biological descendents are suppressed." Kane's gestures are growing more and more amplified. "Ms. Monfort, I think, can express genes that were suppressed by evolution. If that's true, that means that 95 percent of her genome—the genes of wolves, lions, gorillas, antelopes, everything—is in play."

A stunned Mansfield sits down. "This surpasses everything I ever believed, all I ever hoped, about werewolves, shapeshifters, and the monsters of fairy tales," he says quietly.

Doctor Kane is still talking. "And there's no foreign DNA introduction to modify the expression, these cells are cascading through a mapped molecular event. So there's no mutation. No potential for tumors."

"What are the applications?" says Mansfield, trying to shake free of the shock.

Kane is up, waving his arms excitedly. "If we can isolate that protein, find it in others, we could change medicine as we know it. Mutating onconogenes? Gone. No more cancer, no more multiple sclerosis. Neurological degeneration? Gone. No more Alzheimer's, no more Parkinson's. Got a psychiatric disorder, like anxiety or depression? Not anymore. Transplant rejection? A thing of the past. Immune rejection? Goodbye."

"That's good, very good," Mansfield says. "Can you run it against our genome database?"

"Yes," Kane says, but his voice suddenly lacks enthusiasm. His arms drop to his side as he sits. He blows the hair that falls over his forehead.

Mansfield hates drama. "What's wrong?"

Kane holds a hand up and pinches his thumb and index finger together, his pinky finger dangling away from the others. "I really need more tissue to sufficiently analyze her," Kane says. His hand bounces with every word. "Lots more."

"You'll have it. Smith will ensure it." Mansfield departs, the possibilities of weaponizing Monfort's genetic code playing out in his mind.

He dreams of an army, *his* army, of lost souls.

❖ ❖ ❖

The phone in the study rings. *Shit.* He picks up. "Marcus Jacobs."

"There's a change in plan." It's Mansfield.

"How bad is Smith?" Chee's father asks.

"His face is ruined. He's wrapped in gauze like some wretched Egyptian crypt creature."

*Like the Invisible Man*, Marcus thinks, playing up the Universal Monster theme.

"Smith is compromised. He can't disappear. There's no way he can stay under the radar. With a face like that, he's an easy make. All of the psychic energy and make-up in the world won't be able to hide that mess."

"Too bad," Marcus says. "Tell him the folks at the office are all pulling for him."

"Sure," Mansfield says, "I'll tell him you give your best." It almost sounds like a threat.

Marcus ignores it. "I'll activate another asset tomorrow."

"No need, Marcus. We'll need to put Smith out to pasture at some point, but I'm keeping him active for now. "

"What? But you just said he's been burned?"

"We're going to have to work with the pawns and rooks on the board for the present time."

"Why?"

"There's been a lot of chatter lately. COMINT suggests some potential domestic terrorist targets. Something big is in the offing, and all of the floaters have been deployed to the FBI and CIA."

*Foreign intelligence knows about a potential threat on U.S. soil, but we don't?* Marcus doesn't give his internal question voice. He knows too much already. Better to just leave it alone.

"Anyway," Mansfield continues, "Smith's throwaway now. I'll personally sanitize after he's completed his mission."

*It's just that easy, that easy for an "is" to become a "was."* "And what is that mission now?" Marcus asks.

"Capture Kim Monfort, preferably alive. Kane is salivating like a Pavlovian dog, and I'm sure our friends at Davis Pharmaceuticals will be interested in her too." He explains that they're expecting delivery of the package tomorrow at the bottler.

*The black site.* "And what about the other? Astrid Dunst?"

"Pull your daughter out. Psis are a dime a dozen."

Psi. It's a term from parapsychology, a label Mansfield uses to describe an individual with psychic abilities. In the agency, the word blankets the range of psionics, everything from telepathy to clairvoyance. The agency's divided into two camps: those who, like Diane Hennessy Powell, believe that psychic ability is a birthright and others, like psychic detective Bevy Jaegers, who suggest both Psi-Gamma and -Kappa can be learned.

Mansfield doesn't bother with the age-old debate of genetic nature versus environmental nurture. None of it matters to him. Psychic ability, innate or learned, is the devil's thumbprint. It's easier to neutralize threats than to debate the origin of sin.

"Does she have to die?" Marcus asks. "I don't think she knows anything."

"We just can't take that risk. No one is above silencing. Miss Dunst must die."

Marcus understands this too well. Mansfield once told him how the agency's predecessor intelligence group had once even executed Michel de Nostredame, better known as Nostradamus. He had, apparently, written one too many quatrains for someone's liking. It was a murder, strangely enough, that Nostradamus himself augured on July 1, 1566.

Mansfield continues. "I'm hoping Smith can complete his mission before he succumbs to infection, pain, and/or insanity. If he can't, I'll look to you for assistance."

Marcus doesn't like it, but he says, "Understood. We'll begin preparations for our departure. Where's next?"

"Atlanta, Georgia. And Marcus?"

"Yes?"

"Drive there. You'll want to hold off on flying the friendly skies for the next couple weeks."

❖❖❖

*Chicago, Illinois. A few miles away.*

"Bitch," Kim mutters as she stomps home in the rain. "Some friend you are, Astrid." She feels lethal. Small horns protrude from her temples. Her fingernails curl and sharpen into talons. She realizes with horror that she's changing. "Kim," she says to herself, "you need to calm the fuck down." Thus begins an internal monologue.

*Calm down.*

*I can't.*

*You need to talk to someone. Mom?*

*Mom couldn't even deal with Dad. Remember how she shit the bed when he transformed into a lion when he was napping on the couch? He didn't mean to shred the leather, but she never forgave. So just exactly how is she going to help me deal with my problems?*

*Well, then, how about calling Dad?*

*That drunk asshole? Let's see him do an honest day's work first, and then I'll consider it. That's assuming he has a working phone.*

*What about yoga? That provides focus and helps manage anger, right? What type of advice would Astrid's mom give me?*

*She'd probably tell me to get into the Savasana or Child's Pose.*

*Well, I'm not doing that out here. Not in public, not soaking wet, even if it is nighttime. What else would she say?*

*She'd say to recognize and accept what you're really feeling. Don't label it, just feel it.*

*Well, I feel like I'm fucking angry.*

*Okay, just penetrate your anger so completely that you dissolve the difference between "you" and "your" feelings.*

*What the fuck does that mean?*

*I have no idea. She'd also say that being angry is natural. Recognize that and realize that anger isn't always a problem.*

*Okay, but I'm about ready to turn into a bear on the streets of Lincoln Park. That might actually be a problem. Christ, I can't believe Astrid chose a stranger over me.*

*Wait, that's another thing. She'd say, "Don't believe the story your mind is telling you about what happened. Anger distorts the truth. You just need to express your pain."*

ROARRRRR.

*Wait, not that way. Try writing in a journal. Finger paint. Knit a doily. Focus on some of the lessons learned.*

*Maybe I should go back and express my pain to Astrid personally.*

*I'm not sure that's a good idea. Just focus on something that brings you joy instead. What makes you happy?*

*Hanging out with Astrid.*

*Maybe there's someone else you'd rather hang out with?*

*No, Astrid's my only friend.*

*Let's try some breathing techniques.*

*I am breathing.*

*Yes, keep doing that. That's what Astrid's mom would say.*

*Of course she would. She wouldn't tell me to stop breathing, would she?*

*She'd say refocus. Listen to the sound of your own breathing. Try some nose breathing. The three-part breath is the most rewarding yogic breathing practice. Start by . . .*

*No thanks.*

*Maybe slow breathing is a better starting point.*

*I can't believe I left Astrid there with a potential killer.*

*Start living in the present instead of the past . . .*

*I need to go back.*

*Wait, what?*

*We—I—need to go back and make sure she's okay. I can't believe I called her a bitch.*

*You're right. Go back.*

Kim stops and turns. "I'm coming, Astrid."

That's when she feels a sting at the top of her spine. Her hand goes to the nape of her neck. Something foreign juts from her skin. She plucks it out and holds it before her. An inch long steel needle reflects the light of the street lamp. Red fibers project from the back. She stares at the dart for a moment, and the picture starts to shake.

"What the?"

She's hit by another dart, this time in her shoulder. She looks to the red plug sticking out of her collarbone, and then back to the dart in her hand. Her vision starts to blur, the light ebbing.

Her body convulses, begins changing uncontrollably. Her hands begin to transform into paws. She growls and falls. She hits the ground, rolls on her back. The water beneath her soaks into clothes, her fur. She sees a man...a man with a face covered in bandages.

"You," she growls, the darkness creeping in from the corners of her eyes.

He laughs. It's high-pitched and insane. "Nighty night, Teen Wolf."

# Track Eleven: Tall Ships

*The Atlantic Ocean (Latitude 43 degrees, 4 minutes, 7.9 seconds;*
*Longitude -38 degrees, 40 minutes, 18.75 seconds). 2 August 1777.*

The *Heureux* is scheduled to make port in New Hampshire in forty days time. She leads a contingent of merchant ships in the employ of the Portuguese company Rodrigue Hortalez et Compagnie. The flagship's cargo consists of textiles from Mairy Johnson and soybeans and cocoa from Brazil. At least that's what the bill of lading says.

But there is no merchant named Rodrigue Hortalez, no manufacturer called Mairy Johnson. They are fabrications, figments from the mind of Pierre Augustin de Caron. De Caron is recognized as a watchmaker, playwright, and courtier of Louis XVI. He is an actor, better known by his stage name Beaumarchais.

He is not known for espionage. That makes him the best kind of spy.

And the *Heureux* does not carry textiles or imported produce. None of the ships in the convoy do. Instead, they carry the implements of war. The holds of these innocuous ships contain uniforms for 25,000 soldiers, 200 cannons, thousands of firearms, and gunpowder.

The ships mark France's informal entry into the Revolutionary War a full year before a formal declaration. It was Beaumarchais' idea to fund the American revolutionaries in secret. It was his idea to set up a shell company to provide the States with arms to fight their common enemy, the British.

France couldn't finance the revolutionaries alone. Beleaguered by the debt of the Seven Years War, the King turned to Spain and the Parisian merchants to each match his loan of one million livres to the shell. The collective goal of their fraudulent enterprise? Drive the British from the colony and position themselves as the States' chief trading partners.

In the months that follow, many ships will make this journey. They will bring more weapons, additional aid, and professional soldiers to provide military strategy and train the American militias. Unlike the ships to follow in its figurative wake, the *Heureux* holds an additional secret: Lindiwe Toure.

Toure crosses the deck towards the bow. She takes a position at the fore, holds the rail. She closes her eyes. The wind blows through her fire red hair. A light spray settles on her cheeks. She tastes the salt on her lips. She tastes freedom, if but for only a single moment.

Quiet moments are rare in the service of the King. Being at sea provides Toure time for reflection.

Chastel, true to word, took credit for her work. He invented a preposterous story about the death of the Beast of Gévaudan. It always begins with him praying to God for the strength to find the monster. God, the story goes, asked Chastel to melt down a medal of the Virgin Mary and use the silver for bullets. God told him when and where he would find the monster. He followed God's instructions faithfully. As Chastel told it, he interrupted the creature as it prepared to dine on a young maiden. He engaged it in the name of the very same god, and it lunged. He fired twice. The holy bullets found their mark. The horror was dead.

He told the story countless times, taking the carcass—sans one paw—on tour around the region. Thankful farmers and merchants paid for his food and lodging. They made donations to him for his sacrifice and bravery. Once he had bled the villages dry, he traveled to Versailles to collect his reward from the King.

By the time Jean Chastel arrived at Versailles, the creature had been dead for weeks. The stench of the thing was putrid. When he asked for council with the King, his entry was barred by a pair of dragoons. They crossed their boarding axes, denying Chastel entry.

"I am here to see the King," Chastel said. "I'm here to collect my reward for killing the Beast of Gévaudan."

One of the soldiers dry-heaved. The other covered his nose, pointed at the wagon carrying what remained of the monster and the cloud of flies it attracted. "You cannot bring that rotten pile of fur and flesh in here. Be gone."

"I demand to see the King," Chastel said. "Bring me to your supe-riors."

Footfalls resounded in the corridor. Two silhouettes quickly ap-proached. "You're in luck. Here they come now," said the second guard.

"*Bien*," Chastel said, sneering. He held his chin high. His arrogance, however, soon melted as the forms came into view. The soldiers made way.

"Monsieur Chastel," said the Marquis d'Apcher, Toure at his side, "we were expecting you weeks ago."

"Well, I am here now," the barkeep said, "and I am ready to collect my 30,000 livres."

The Marquis scoffed. "You are due nothing."

"What?"

"I cannot, in good conscience, allow payment."

"How dare you," Chastel said. He leaned in and whispered, "We agreed that I would get credit for Beast's capture."

"We did," the Marquis replied, "but now you have brought us a heap of unrecognizable carrion." He regarded at Toure. "Does that, I ask, look like the Beast to you?"

She shook her head. "No. I remember the creature being much . . . bigger."

"Well, there you are," the Marquis continued. He pursed his lips and shrugged. The matter was out of his hands.

"This is not acceptable," Chastel growled.

Lindiwe Toure stepped forward. She stood, her nose just an inch from Chastel's forehead. "No, I'll tell you what's unacceptable. It is un-acceptable that you claimed the rewards offered by impoverished farm-ers and merchants. It is unacceptable that you did not pay taxes on those monies. It is unacceptable that you have treated the King's time as your own. It is unacceptable that you're demanding to get paid for a pile of refuse."

"But—"

"*Mais rien.* You have two alternatives. Leave now, and take that mag-got blanket with you. Or, stay, and you will be arrested for littering in the Palace." She exchanges glances with the Marquis. "What's the penalty for dumping rubbish on the grounds?"

"Interestingly enough, I believe it's 30,000 livres," he says with a smile.

"Yes," she says, nodding, "it is 30,000 livres . . . and death."

"But—"

"*Depechez-vous.* I've lost patience. Soon, you'll lose your head."

Chastel's cart groaned as he turned about. He looked over his shoulder as he went and stared at Toure through eyes that were barely slits.

She took two steps towards the cart.

Chastel's eyes filled with alarm. He clicked his tongue, kicked his heels, and his horse immediately cantered off, the wagon and its decaying contents in tow.

The blight of the wolf was gone. No more literal monsters to fight, Louis XV's successor turned his attentions to governing. Louis XVI sought reforms. He worked to change the caste system and abolish serfdom. He promoted religious tolerance. He sought to repeal the land tax on peasants, the *taille*.

French nobles opposed the new king at every turn, choosing instead to protect their self-interests. He received cooperation, however, in his efforts to support the fledgling U.S. democracy, mainly because the new market appealed to those same self-interests.

There were troubling rumors about dead soldiers coming back to life, rumors that the British were drawing on the power of Indian necromancers to create an army of zombies. And despite assurances from Benjamin Franklin that freemasonry was free from the influence of the occult, Beaumarchais and his spies informed the King of Franklin's participation in the satanic Hellfire Clubs in England. There, too, was speculation about Thomas Paine's interest in paganism and the resurrection of Druidism.

The King needed to keep a close eye on his investments. Toure and a handful of other witch-smellers would serve as that figurative eye. The French offered her and her kind's services to the Americans. She would help the colonists find and terminate external and internal threats, witches that might endanger the fledgling revolution.

❖❖❖

The *Heureux* will beat its scheduled arrival by ten days. The arms will ensure the survival of George Washington's forces and will help turn the tide for the Americans at Saratoga in October.

In France, despite the King's attempts, the peasants will witness little in the way of change. The French will have their own revolution soon, and Louis XVI and Marie Antoinette will be executed. The French Revolution will usher in the Reign of Terror, and more than forty thousand nobles, clergy, and peasants accused of crimes as varied as hoarding to military desertion will be executed. A third will lose their heads to the guillotine.

There will be no returning home for Lindiwe Toure. Her life in the U.S. will be one of indentured servitude. Like her, her children will make their home here and will serve the U.S. intelligence community as well, as will their children and their children's children.

America will be Toure's new master, and her descendents, including Mathilde and her granddaughter Hélène, will be born into a secret slavery.

# Track Twelve: Louis Quatorze

*Chicago Red Line. 5 September 2001.*

Centurion checks his pockets. Three dollars and seven cents, not enough for a bottle of Colt 45 and a CTA ride. Reluctantly, he uses the balance of it to purchase a return trip on the elevated train.

The Red Line travels from Addison past a half-dozen stops before it plunges underground. An electronic voice tells him when he's arrived at the Chicago stop. He steps gingerly off of the subway on to the platform. He limps through the dripping ceramic-lined tunnels, his cough echoing through the tube. At the bottom of the concrete staircase, he steps aside to let the other passengers pass. He hobbles up the steps, leaning hard on the banister. He takes them one at a time, trying not to put weight on his left foot. He winces with each step.

It's slow work. It's nearly 3 AM by the time he reaches the street, and it's still raining in sheets. He limps down the block towards State Street. The last ten feet he makes by propping himself up against a building, sliding along the stonework.

"Thank Zeus," he says, ready to slide into his Caravan.

But the Chariot is not there.

He looks up at the street signs, checks his surroundings. There is no doubt. This is the right corner. This is the place.

He considers the possibility that the vehicle was stolen, wonders how his anti-theft system—essentially a car battery sitting beneath the driver's seat that delivers an electric shock if the seat's adjusted—could have been thwarted.

That's when he sees the fire hydrant—just a foot behind a yellow strip of curb designating where parking is illegal—right where he left his Caravan.

The Chariot has been towed courtesy of the Chicago Department of Streets and Sanitation.

He pulls the mailer from beneath his breastplate and reads the address. His chin stiffens, rain cascading off his jaw and down his throat.

He begins shambling north to Lincoln Park High School.

Three city blocks from the school, Centurion's leg is dragging behind him. Fortunately, many of the yards on Burling are fenced with ornamental black wrought iron—a favorite of the Mayor. These properties offer him respite. He uses the strength of his arms and upper body to claw forward, grabbing the wet bars and climbing across hand over hand. As he nears Armitage Avenue, the posh iron gives way to the chain link of the rental properties. Here, his methods change. He uses the rickety fence as a crutch.

The school's parking lot looms closer, and, despite all of his wheezing and hacking, he hobbles forward with renewed purpose.

He's about to cross the street when the first morning bell rings. Most of the kids have already entered the building, happy to avoid the rain. The few that linger enter immediately.

He's too late to catch Astrid and Chee. He's too late to see them entering together, Chee wearing Astrid's New Order *Ceremony* t-shirt cinched at the waist with a thick leather belt.

"Damn," Centurion says, realizing his plan to intercept Chee has failed. He limps over to a crossing guard. "What time do classes end?"

She's a short girl in a Scottish print raincoat. Her coke bottle glasses magnify the fear in her eyes. Centurion would terrify anyone in this state. His pallor is ghost-white. His nostrils are bright red, his eyes bloodshot and burdened. He looks like the living dead. "Are you okay?" she asks, taking two steps back.

His head bobs up and down. He coughs up sputum, and takes an awkward step forward. "Yes," he groans.

It may as well have come out as, "Brains." She takes another step away from the potential zombie towards Lincoln Park High.

"What time?" he growls.

"Three-thirty," she calls over her shoulder as she dashes away.

Centurion eyes a row of benches near the cul-de-sac on Burling behind the school. He lurches forward and spills into the nearest seat, collapsing in a heap on his side.

❖❖❖

*Lincoln Park High School, Third Period English.*

"Even for a king, Louis XIV wielded extreme authority in France. The King made all of the key decisions in government and exerted control over his ministers. He used the Roman Catholic Church as a tool to manage the populous. He enforced religious uniformity, and used spies to do so. He seized control of the Parisian police force from the Parliament, and then he did the same in the other major cities. His system of secret police—the *haute* police, or high police—promoted his agenda and hunted down anyone who might disagree with him."

Astrid takes a breath. Second period. It's too early for a report about the Sun King, but she's almost done.

She continues, describing the King's acts of repression, his intolerance of dissent of all kinds. "He crushed protests and uprisings. He persecuted the Jansenists, a religious group that believed in predestination. He kidnapped their nuns and destroyed their convents. He went after the Quietists. They believed worshippers had a direct link to God, so the Church was unnecessary. He arrested and imprisoned the movement's leaders. He did the same with the Dutch Calvinists and the Jews. He persecuted the Huguenots, enforcing old rules that prohibited them from earning similar salaries as Catholics. He converted them by giving them cash awards.

"Louis dealt with pagans even more harshly. He issued an edict against witchcraft in 1687. He arrested fortune-tellers and alchemists and tortured them for their client lists during the Poison Affair. This led to the creation of a special 'Burning Court' and the prosecution of dozens of people, including members of the French Court, for witchcraft. Thirty-four were sentenced to death.

"But his attentions were not just on those he considered heretics and pagans. He even clashed with the Pope over property and control of the Catholic Church in France . . . and pretty much won. How often does the Pope blink first? King Louis XIV was a king who commanded unparalleled power." She taps her note cards on the podium, lining them up. "Thank you. Are there any questions?"

There's a smattering of clapping among the students, but no questions.

"Now that's what World History is all about," Professor Quesada says. He takes off his wire-rimmed glasses, wipes the lenses against his sweater. "Just one question, Astrid. We've all heard about Louis' hatred of religious pluralism and his promotion of slavery through the Code Noir. In your research, did you come across any examples of the King showing even a modicum of racial or religious tolerance?"

"There certainly weren't many," she says. Most Africans in France at the time were slaves. The King did, however, hold audiences at Versailles with Africans of influence, like entertainers, dignitaries, and traders. In fact, Versailles had a menagerie with rhinos, leopards, hyenas, and other African animals. "But the King seemed particularly fond of a prince named Aniaba."

"So, he had an African friend?" Quesada asks. "That's a paradox."

"I'm not sure I'd call him a friend," Astrid says. She provides three reasons.

First, Aniaba was a Prince from Issiny, an area west of the Ivory Coast near Ghana. That title set him apart from the slaves in the King's court and saved Louis from lowering himself to someone he deemed by law his lesser.

Second, Aniaba was educated and baptized as a Roman Catholic. He was even rumored to be the descendent of Balthazar, one of the three wise men from the Bible. The King was enthralled by Aniaba's stories about black magic, his hunts for witches and sorcerers. In Aniaba's adventures the King found parallels to his own persecution of heretics.

Third, the Prince served as a gateway for greater Roman Catholic missionary work. Through the prince, Louis XIV saw the path for conversion of the continent . . . and African colonialism.

"Excellent," Quesada says. "Thank you for a great report."

"Plus, he thought having a black friend around made him cooler."

Laughter erupts among the students. An African-American kid named Calvin says, "That's true." Brody Rooney high fives him, and more laughter follows.

Quesada doesn't laugh. "Excuse me?" he says through his frown.

"I should clarify," Astrid says. "Louis XIV didn't think he was cooler because Africans were cool. He thought he was cooler because hanging with people of color made him look whiter. The royal court took great pains to whiten their skin. They wanted to look like the marble statues that decorated Versailles. So they applied thick white make-up made from mercury and egg whites and powdered their faces."

"Nasty," Rooney says.

"Okay, thank you." It's as if Quesada knows what's going to come next.

But Astrid continues. "The only thing that could make the King and his court look even whiter was posing next to black servants . . . and princes."

There are moans in the class. Calvin says, "Whoa, that's messed up."

"Okay class, take it easy," Quesada says. "Thanks again, Astrid. You can take your seat."

There's a knocking on the door. It opens without waiting for an invitation. "Sorry to interrupt," Principal Jefferson says. He's framed by two of Chicago's finest. He looks around the class, spots Astrid standing at the front. "Astrid, these gentlemen would like to talk to you for a moment."

The students, in near harmony, exclaim, "Ooooooooooh," upon seeing the police officers.

"Now, class." Jefferson says the word with scorn, as if identifying a missing component of their collective character.

Astrid retrieves her books from her desk, her eyebrows knitting a bewildered expression.

The principal escorts her and the officers to an open room on the third floor. It's a small space composed entirely of white cinderblock walls, linoleum, and white ceiling tiles. "Please let me know if you need anything, officers," he says. "We're all very eager to cooperate."

One of the officers, short and broad like a fire hydrant, gestures for Astrid to take a chair. Principal Jefferson slowly shuts the door behind him.

Astrid remains standing. "Cooperate with what?"

The officers look at each other. The taller of the two asks Astrid when she last saw Kim Monfort.

Astrid's face goes pale. She sits down. "Is she okay?"

"She's missing," the fireplug says, crossing his arms.

Astrid starts to whimper. "It's all my fault," she manages between barely controlled sobs.

The officers give each other an alarmed glance.

"I should have never let her go home alone last night."

The troubled expressions on the men in blue soften. The taller of the two takes a seat, gives her a tissue. "There, there. We've got every sworn officer in this city looking for her. Tell us when you last saw her."

The interview lasts about an hour. When it's over, Astrid asks to go to the bathroom to fix her make-up. She jogs in, passes a couple of seniors doing their hair in the mirror, and lunges into a stall. She sits on the toilet, pulls her knees to her chest, and bawls.

"Grandpa, I need you," she said, her voice breaking.

She blubbers and begs like this for nearly thirty minutes.

He does not come.

*On Interstate 65, somewhere near Lafayette, Indiana.*

Despite the discomfort of the smallish mattress . . .

Despite the bumps in I-65 . . .

Despite the procession of passing vehicles that honk upon seeing the ten feet tall picture of Nigel Crown on the side of the tour bus . . .

Crown sleeps soundly for the second time in two days, for the second time in the better part of a decade.

He's been asleep for eight hours. He hasn't moved a muscle since his head hit the pillow. He'll sleep like that another eight hours if permitted.

But he won't be allowed. The toilet flushes in the room next door. Twenty seconds later, it flushes again. Five seconds later, again.

Crown stirs. "Use the bathroom up front, Andy," he groans.

Flush.

He lifts his head. "Andy, use the plunger. I'm trying to sleep." He drops his face into his pillow. He starts to doze off again, but stirs. He feels something like the skittering legs of an insect on his skin, a bug crawling across his neck. He swats at it blindly, the insect buzzing like a bee as it takes flight. It dances close to his cheek, the hum echoing in his ear. He twists, tired eyes blinking and defensive.

But there's nothing. No buzz, no sign of any pest.

He lies on his side for a moment. The mattress and pillow conduct noise, the sound of the buses wheels spinning, kicking pebbles at the undercarriage. The white noise threatens to rock him back to sleep. That is, until he has a realization. *The bus is moving. Andy is the driver. If Andy's in the bathroom, who is driving the bus? And if Andy is driving the bus . . .*

"Andy?" he says, rolling over, staring at the bathroom door.

"Nigel," a voice says from within, "come here. You have to see this."

Crown's eyes go wide. It's not Andy. Andy's accent is wicked Boston. This guy's voice is laced with a drawl. There's a stalker on the bus.

When you're a rockstar, stalkers come with the territory. That territory can be treacherous. It's full of symbolic sinkholes and caves, swamps, and cliffs. It's full of fans that feel they're kindred spirits, the musician's best and truest friends. Most of fanatics are women. They can be scary. There are some crazies of the male variety. They are scarier.

"Is that you Paul?" Crown says, convinced a bipolar man named Paul Scheider is on the tour bus. Scheider first introduced himself on the streets of Madison, Wisconsin, back in the early 90s. Soon, he was showing up at shows across the country, Las Vegas, Nashville, Chicago, LA. No problems there. Lots of fans travel. But when Scheider somehow tracked Crown down at the City Store in Manchester, England, and later appeared at his rented home, Crown had to get law enforcement involved. He hadn't glimpsed Scheider since.

But that doesn't necessarily mean that Scheider hadn't been glimpsing Crown.

He looks for a weapon. He grabs a Grammy from his nightstand, gets up and walks towards the door.

Flush.

He reaches for the door with one hand, raising the Grammy over his head. His nerve starts to leave him. *Am I really going to bludgeon this bloke to death like some 21ˢᵗ Century gladiator?* He takes a step backwards, considers running to the front of the bus, screaming for help.

"Don't go anywhere," the voice says.

Crown freezes. "Listen, I don't want any trouble. I've got money, lots of money, and I can get more."

"I don't want your money," says the voice. The door swings open slowly. "But you're going to want to think through that whole camel-eye of the needle conundrum at some point."

*Oh my God. He's going to kill me.* Crown inches forward.

The bathroom light is on. Someone is standing just beyond the doorway.

Flush.

Crown slinks to the edge of the doorway. He leans in.

Standing before Nigel is a man, probably in his early twenties. He's wearing tailored military fatigues. He's standing above the toilet, looking into the bowl. The faint smell of cologne permeates the room.

He flushes the toilet again. "I've always heard that objects move in a counterclockwise fashion when there's a psychic vortex present, but I would have never guessed it applied to the flow of water in a toilet." The man looks up. "It's like being in Rio."

Crown examines the man—not Scheider, thank God—and sniffs. "Just who are you, and what are you doing in my bathroom?" he demands, shaking the trophy over his head.

"Charlie," the man says, introducing himself. "Charlie Dunst."

"I don't care who you are," Crown says, stepping forward. "You . . . what?" He realizes he's stepped in something wet. He looks down, finds he's standing in a small puddle of water. "Did you piss on the floor?"

The man named Charlie laughs. "No, Nigel. That, unfortunately, is one of the byproducts of tuning, modifying my aetheric vibrations to match the frequencies of this world. Don't worry though. It's only condensation."

"You're mad," Crown says, backing up. "I'm calling the police." He turns, intent on grabbing his cell phone on the nightstand. He stops dead in his tracks.

"Sorry about the water," Charlie says. Somehow, this man is now sitting on Crown's bed.

Crown does a double take. He checks the *loo*, looks back towards the bed.

"We ghosts tend to puddle."

Crown just stares.

"Is there something wrong with how I look?" Charlie gets up, looks into a mirror. "This was the best I could do. You're getting me at my prime, right after I enlisted." He faces the rock star. "Trust me, it's much better than some of the other alternatives. You wouldn't have wanted me walking around here dripping bits of brain through a hole in the back of my skull."

"You can't be a ghost," Crown stammers. Then he notices his breath taking shape. The temperature in the room has dropped thirty degrees in less than a minute.

"Why?"

"You're solid."

Charlie pats his arms and his chest. "Heck, you're right. So I am." Contrary to popular belief, he explains, ghosts are more often felt than seen. When there's enough energy to materialize, it's pretty rare for a ghost to appear as anything other than a solid entity. "Sure there's the occasional orb, but we generally don't tend to float about translucent and glowing. We don't rattle chains. We don't moan. And, personally, I'm not prone to Shakespearian soliloquies. That's just not my style, but to each his own."

"Energy?" Nigel Crown sits on a chair on the other side of the narrow room.

"Yes. To manifest, we need energy. I pull it from wherever I can. A bit here, a bit there, but never too much from a single source. I can gather energy from the earth, from moving water, from heat. That, by the way, is why you're so cold right now." Charlie takes two steps to the bed, pulls the comforter off, and tosses it to Crown.

It lands on his lap. Crown takes a moment to process the phenomena he's just witnessed before wrapping the red duvet about his shoulders.

"Sometimes," Charlie Dunst continues, "I can even draw upon a leaky auric field. Teens in particular have a lot of unused energy. It's all that angst and sexual tension, the same vibe you tap into with your music." He sits on the edge of the bed. "You know, for your age, you actually have a surprising amount of energy, at least now that you've had some sleep."

Everything suddenly clicks. "You're the spirit that came through the Ouija board the other night."

"In the flesh," Charlie says, "so to speak. So, how have you been sleeping?"

"Better," Crown admits hesitantly, thrown off by the politeness of this intruder.

"Good." Charlie nods. "That's good. You'll be fine as long as you stay away from the occult from now on. No more séances, Tarot cards, or Ouija boards. Messing with that stuff is like ringing a dinner bell for lost spirits. You'd be better off parading yourself naked and slathered in butter in front of starving cannibals."

"Lost spirits?" Crown scratches his chin with the edge of the comforter.

"Yes." Lost spirits, Charlie explains, are anchored, stuck between this world and the next. They're usually ordinary people who (1) either died suddenly or violently, and are therefore struggling with the reality of their deaths, or (2) didn't have anyone present to guide them into the next world when they died. "They missed the off-ramp on the highway of the afterlife or missed the whole tunnel of light experience. Either way, the damned are bad news. But I don't have to tell you that, do I?"

Crown shakes his head.

"They're jealous of life. They'll do whatever they can to get you to crack the door for them. They'll lie to you. They'll trick you. Once they've pried a foot in, they'll find a way to convince you to open the door just a little wider."

Crown's elbows go to his knees. He drops his face into his palms. "Poor Lisa."

"Lisa?" Charlie asks.

He pulls his hands down his face, tugging at his tired skin and revealing the red behind his lower eyelids. "She's lost, and I couldn't help her. I failed her."

Charlie bites his lower lip. "Nigel, you didn't fail her."

Crown's right eyebrow goes up, his left eye squinting slightly. "What?"

Charlie wrings his hands. "I don't know how to tell you this delicately, so I'm just going to come out and say it. Lisa has moved on."

The left eye twitches. "Then why did she contact me?"

"The spirit you've been talking to for the last seven years isn't Lisa. In fact, it's not even a spirit."

Crown scoffs. "Of course it was Lisa. I think I'd know her."

"Let me guess. She knew things about you, things that only she'd know. She knew your deepest, darkest secrets."

"Yes."

Charlie nods his head knowingly, like a doctor diagnosing a malady. "The-Thing-Pretending-To-Be-Lisa said she dated your old roommate Travis, didn't she?"

"Yes," Nigel says, pulling the blanket up around his chest.

"You secretly held hands on a double date with her at the Tivoli Theater," Charlie says. "*Jaws 3 in 3D.*"

"Yes." The blanket rises to Nigel's throat.

"You slept with her on Round Lake. Her boyfriend Travis was sleeping in the next room."

"Yes." Nigel twists his hands into the comforter. He draws it past his chin.

"You gave her the clap."

Nigel tries to rise. He's standing on the duvet, however, and it immediately pulls him back down into his chair. "That's impossible," he exclaims, still seated. "How did you know?"

Charlie crosses the room in two steps, stays Crown by placing a hand on his shoulder. "Relax. You're not the first person to be duped by a creature from the hereafter." Thomas Edison, Mark Twain, Sir Arthur Conan Doyle, and even Plato had been taken for a psychic ride.

"You're in good company."

Crown cringes at the thought of being tricked.

"Information is the one thing that's readily available in the next world. If spirits can't get it from making contact with your world, they'll get it from other ghosts . . . or worse. I can't tell you how many of these 'nonbeings' have sidled up to me and tried to be my buddy in the afterlife." Charlie says. "It's no different from any other scam, really, and the devil is, literally, in the details."

A good confidence trick starts with knowing your mark, exploiting his or her weaknesses. There's no consistent psychological profile for victims. To work, the con need only establish trust. That trust is built in bad faith through ill-gotten information.

A surprising amount of data can be gleaned just by watching a potential target. Older people are more likely to have experienced love and loss. The experiences of minorities have been shaped by racism and prejudice. Women may feel like outsiders in the workplace, excluded by the old boys' network, or victimized by unwanted sexual advances. Even clothes—the wash and fit of one's jeans, the number of buttons on a jacket, the wear of one's shoes—provide clues.

Add verbal hints, mannerisms, speech patterns, and accents, and a fuller picture develops. Here, the reactions of the mark are key. The spirit reads into responses, the quake or excitement in one's voice, posture, or eagerness to make a connection. These reactions create a feedback—or learning—loop, further informing the specter's high-probability guesses. Connections are reinforced, inaccuracies explained away or glossed over.

The spirit will keep you talking. It will keep the conversation going by being intentionally vague, complimentary, or by preying on doubts and loss. It will endear itself through lies. It will ensure it's invited back, growing more and more powerful until invitations are no longer necessary. "Patter," Charlie says, "is the gift of the ghost as it is for any charlatan." The spirit puts forth the words and allows the mark to make the connections, providing meaning and import.

Words include names, and "naming" is an essential component of the spiritual hustle. It's also the easiest. "Did you ever see *Romper Room?*"

Charlie asks.

Nigel shakes his head.

"It was a kid's show back in the seventies, and at the end of every episode, the host would look through a 'magic mirror' and say farewell to the kids watching on TV. 'See you next time Gary, Tom, and Beth.' Kids actually believed she was talking directly to them. Turns out, she wasn't shotgunning, tossing out random names in the dark. She picked statistically common names to strengthen her link to the audience. You never heard her say, 'See you tomorrow Ani, Tatumn, and Domino.'" Charlie pauses. "Did you know that 'Lisa' was the most popular name given to babies born in the 1960s in the United States?"

He shakes his head again. "No."

Charlie nods. "It's paranormal grift. In many ways, spirits use the same deceptions as psychics: slate writing, spirit pictures, knocks, table tipping. It's kind of funny when you think of it that way: ghosts and mentalists using the same tricks of the trade."

Crown's not laughing. His eyes are red and sad. "Why do they do it?"

"Most have a single goal: getting back to earth, to this physical plane. They feed off of the living, suckling from their energy. They're psychic vampires, parasites. That thing, in particular, that tormented you? It wasn't even really the spirit of a human, at least not anymore."

"What was it then?"

Charlie hesitates to describe the dark, misshapen thing that's haunted Crown.

"I need to know."

"It's a tool of black magic, a ghoul that clings to its hosts like a barnacle. It has floated about in the astral ocean for centuries, leeching off of and draining the life force from one human after another. And believe it or not, it's not the worst thing out there. Not by a long shot. There's worse, much, much worse. I've seen them."

When someone reaches out to the aether, doors are opened for poltergeists, Gestalts, dwellers on the threshold, and all kinds of other psychic baggage to enter. They clamor and push to be the first through the portal, screaming and vying for attention.

"The portal you opened," Charlie explains, "has been closed. It should remain that way. Remember, things are out there, biding their time, just waiting for you to grow weak. They're desperate. Their souls are bitter, assuming they have anything left of a soul. Open the door to the afterlife again, and they'll be all over you. They'll ruin you for eternity."

"I won't open it again," Nigel says. "It's just . . . I put Lisa through so much, the affairs, the divorce, the scandal. I just wanted to make sure she's okay, even if it meant being miserable. I still love her you know."

"I know, and believe it or not, she does too. She doesn't blame you. She didn't take those pills because she hated you. She took them because she was sick. She wasn't able to cope like other people. This is going to sound cliché, but she's really in a better place now."

Nigel starts to sob. He weeps for a solid two minutes before wiping his nose and gathering himself. "So, Charlie," he says, "just why are you here? Are you lost too?"

"No," Charlie says, smiling slightly. "I'm here for one reason, to protect my granddaughter. I've been watching you for quite some time. You were lost, but I know the type of man you are, the type of man you're going to become. I know you can help me with my mission. Coincidentally, she's a huge fan of yours too." Charlie puts forth his right hand.

Nigel looks at Charlie's extended hand, then up to his face. He inhales, his jaw setting. He extends his hand quickly, taking Charlie's in his, and shakes firmly. "Tell me what you need."

# Track Thirteen: Nite Flights

*Outside Lincoln Park High School, Chicago.*

Centurion remains on the bench, drifting in and out of consciousness. He's awakened by the sound of a car door. He struggles to raise his head, crane his neck towards the sound. He blinks, clearing the rain from his eyes.

Twenty feet away, a man has exited a grey Acura. He's a normal looking guy, khakis, white shirt, and a black umbrella. He'd go unnoticed, save for the bandages covering half his face.

This man either hasn't seen Centurion or has assumed he's homeless. Now, though, his exposed brow furrows with concern as the armored hero struggles to rise. Centurion's pauldrons clatter against the bench each time he slips. The bandaged man remains focused on him while taking a cautious step backwards.

Centurion fights to a standing position. Using the backrest for support, he yells, "Citizen. A moment, please?"

The man turns, starts to hasten away.

"Citizen, I have some questions for you," Centurion calls. "Some questions about Amachi Jacobs."

The man's pace quickens.

Centurion hops forward. "Stop!"

The man twists, sees Centurion coming, and starts to run.

"Stop!" Centurion is now loping forward, his pain be damned.

Smith turns left on the corner of Dickens Avenue. Centurion cuts down the next gangway, bouncing off the buildings as he scampers towards Halsted Street. He falters to a knee, palms the walls to stop his fall. His fingers find purchase. He drags himself up, and pushes onward, the light at the end of the passage a beacon. He bursts forth just in time to see the man in khakis run into *Café Ba-Ba-Reeba!*

"Stop that man," he yells in vain. He lumbers across the street, cars honking and spinning. One clips him, sends him sprawling to the curb. He's up quickly, roaring like a lion, blood pouring down his forehead.

He bounces off of a garbage can in front of a group of women stepping out of *bebe*. They scream, drop their boxes and bags, and run back in. Centurion kicks and crushes their buys as he limps on. One of the shoppers says she's calling the police. She calls him "a crazy man in a costume hopped up on meth."

He runs a zigzag path down the sidewalk and slides to a stop. He bangs his shoulder against the glass entry of *Café Ba-Ba-Reeba!* It doesn't open. He tries the handle, finds the door locked. He pops it hard again, and the latch bolt shreds and tears loose of the strike plate. The door slams open against an interior wall. He leaves a spider web of cracked glass in his wake. The hostess says he can't come in. He brushes by her.

"Which way did he go?" Centurion demands.

None of the customers answers, that is, verbally. Half of them find their eyes subconsciously moving towards the rear of the establishment. Centurion follows their gaze, flipping tables and pitchers of sangria as he goes. He hits a waiter, knocking him and his tray of tapas to the floor with a clatter. The lunch crowd cries out in unison.

He stumbles through the kitchen. The chefs move out of his way, clearing the way to the exit. One of them brandishes a ladle like a weapon and shakes it in Centurion's direction. Centurion cuts right, pushing off a stove and burning his fingers on a griddle. Bellowing, he crashes through the exit to find . . .

Nothing, just an alley full of dumpsters.

He takes a few faltering steps to his right, spins on his good heel to survey the way to his left. "Shit," he says. He stumbles to the nearest dumpster, hammers it with his hands. "Shit." He sighs. "Shazam." That's when he eyes a discarded umbrella near the intersection of the alley and a gangway.

He rushes to the umbrella, picks it up, and peers into the darkness of the passage. He takes a step forward into the shadows.

"Psssst," comes a sound like a steam pipe leak above him.

Centurion looks up . . . to find Smith hanging from a downspout high above him. He drops. A knee catches Centurion in the face.

Centurion goes down. Smith lands on his feet and rushes him. He hammers Centurion with blows. Centurion tries to land an uppercut, misses, exposing his kidneys. Smith attacks. His motions are fluid as he shifts from punches to perfectly timed kicks.

The hero twists, tries to wrap up Smith like an exhausted boxer. Smith knees Centurion in the groin, but Centurion remains draped on him like an ill-fitting coat. Smith delivers elbow after elbow to Centurion's shoulders and neck. He slides out of Centurion's grasp, the hero slipping and clinging to Smith by the pockets of his pants. Smith knees Centurion again, this time in the jaw, knocking his helmet clear and sending him spiraling away. Centurion lands with a sickening *crunch*.

"That's all you have?" Smith asks to the wreck of a man lying before him. Centurion is face down in a puddle. His fists remained clenched like the mandibles of a dying ant locked in a death match. Otherwise, Centurion doesn't move.

"You're not worth killing," Smith says. "You're not worthy of my talent. You're just . . . normal." The last word drips from his lips like poison.

"Wait," Centurion wheezes.

Smith kneels down, bends to Centurion's ear. "No, you're worse. You're just a freak in a cape. You're pretending to be something you're not, something you can never be." He stands up, rears back, and kicks Centurion in the stomach. "I've seen power." He kicks him again in the ribs, and Centurion groans. "I've met heroes." Another kick. He circles Centurion. "I've met villains." This time, he kicks him in the back near the kidney. "I've conquered both. I've made them slaves." Centurion moans as he receives another blow. "You're nothing but trash," Smith says. He takes a few steps back and sprints forward. He punts the back of Centurion's head like a football. Centurion's skull rises a full foot off of the ground. He goes quiet. His eyes close.

Smith opens the nearest dumpster with a rattle and a clang. He drags Centurion's body into a seated position, heaves him up and over a shoulder. He takes a few steps and hurls Centurion's unresponsive body into the receptacle. Centurion lands with a heavy thump. Rats squeal and scurry. Smith saunters to the center of the alley and snatches the galea with a swoop of an arm. He tosses the helmet end over end in the direction of the dumpster. It strikes the lid, bounces off, and lands in the dumpster on top of the hero. The plastic lid reverberates on its hinges, the displaced weight pulling it closed. The lid slams shut, hiding the vanquished hero from the light of the world.

Business returns to normal at *Café Ba-Ba-Reeba!* Throughout the afternoon, kitchen staffers dump unclaimed leftovers and food past its prime into the dumpsters. They are oblivious to the man they are burying with trash.

Day gives way to dusk.

As the sun sets, the rats return in droves. They climb the drainpipes and jump to the dumpsters. They enter through holes chewed in the hinged plastic lid. The receptacle holds a treasure, remnants of salsa, octopus, and other shareable menu items. One of the vermin digs into a pile of patatas bravas. It bites into and through a potato, and into Centurion's cheek.

He stirs and cries out. His yelp echoes about the metal container. The rats flee, popping from the holes in the lid immediately one after another like belts of fur.

Centurion flips open the lid. It bounces against the brick wall of the neighboring building and comes back down on his head. *Bang.* He tries again, succeeds.

He raises his left hand to rub his head and realizes there's something in his hand, something he pulled from his attacker's pocket. It looks like a bullet. He inspects it more closely. No, it's a flash drive of some sort. After three attempts, he successfully slips it into his pocket.

He coughs violently. He goes to his knees and searches the trash for his helmet. He locates it. It's heavy to his grasp. It's full of shrimp and bay scallops, like a bowl of rancid paella. He pours it out and shakes the food free. He coughs again, tilts his head back, and closes his eyes.

When he opens them again, he's staring at the silhouette of a water tower high on top of the facing building. It looms dark and menacing over him like some alien machine from an H.G. Wells novel. Fatigue and illness feed his delirium. He imagines it tearing loose of its piers, the bolts popping from its joists. The supports are massive tentacles, and they stretch forth to take his life. The craft roars at him and prepares to focus its heat-ray and poisonous smoke upon his position.

Centurion quakes. He pulls himself from the dumpster, falling over the side with a clank to the asphalt. He scampers up, slips. His sandal slick with tomato sauce, he drops. Panicked, he struggles up again. He limps away as fast as his bum leg will allow, his hacking resonating through the canyon-like alley as he goes.

❖❖❖

*Chez Bernard.*

Nick Davis dials a number into his cell phone. "Listen to this," he says as he hands it to Holly Rodriguez.

She holds the phone to her ear. *Good evening, Davis Pharmaceuticals. How may I direct your call?* Holly crinkles her nose. "I don't understand."

"Ask for me," Davis says with a wink.

Holly puts her palm over the microphone. "But you're not *there*."

"That's okay," he waves dismissively. "Go ahead."

*Hello? Is anyone there?*

"Um, hi, yes, this is Holly Rodriguez. I'm calling for Mr. Davis."

*Hello, Ms. Rodriguez. I'll put you right through.* There's a click as the receptionist puts Rodriguez on hold.

Rodriguez attempts to pass the phone back.

"No, keep listening," he says.

She sighs, purses her lips, and puts the receiver back to her ear.

She hears music. A piano, some classical string instruments perhaps. She doesn't know. She's never been a fan. She's always been too busy for music.

Suddenly, Nick is humming. He's humming the same tune that's being piped through the receiver, and he's doing it in time. He mimes playing the piano. It's exaggerated, like a cartoon. His piano is apparently ten to twenty feet wide. He sings as he hits the giant, misshapen invisible keys. "Da-da-da-da-dum da-da-da-da-dum dum-da-da-dum-da-da-dum—"

"What are you doing?" she whispers harshly. She looks about the room to see if anyone is watching.

"—da-da-da-da-dum—"

"Nick?" she implores.

The music plods on for another five seconds before hitting a crescendo. Nick is now pantomiming the direction of an orchestra. Then there's a beep. "Hi, you've reached the desk of Nick Davis. Please leave a message after the tone." Another beep.

"Hi," Holly says. "I have no idea why I'm leaving you a message. You're sitting across from me at Chez Bernard. This is weird. Goodbye." With that she snaps the phone shut and sets it on the table in front of Nick.

"Well?" Nick implores, smiling.

"Well what?"

"Well, what did you think?"

"I think you've never played a piano in your life." She should never have agreed to a second date. She went on the first as a favor to Carlos, her producer, because Davis is an investor. It was a mess. He was an egotistical ass. She only agreed to the second outing because Carlos convinced her Davis' narcissism was just a product of nerves. He lied.

Nick laughs. "No, the music. What did you think of the music?"

"You had me call your office so I could be put on hold and listen to elevator music?"

He scoffs. "Elevator music?"

"Sorry, it was fine, I guess, if you like being put on hold."

"It's nice, right?" he says flashing an impossibly white smile.

She pours herself another glass of wine. They're already into the second bottle, and she's done most of the drinking. She takes a gulp. There is no date so awful that a bottle of Malbec can't fix . . . or erase. She nods and raises her glass to him.

"What you were just treated to was *Business as Usual*, a recording I purchased. We're going to tie it into all of Davis Pharmaceutical's promotions. Radio spots, commercials, even the Internet. That jingle will become synonymous with DP."

She almost spits her wine and wipes her lip. "DP? You realize you've reduced the name of your Fortune 500 to an abbreviation for a three-way, right? You're making porno music. You should rename the song, *Music to Shag to.*"

"Fortune 200," he says, the joke lost on him.

She laughs to herself. She can't wait to get her hands around Carlos' throat for this.

Davis smiles. "Guess who recorded that 15-second slice of sonic heaven?"

Holly shrugs and tells him she has no idea.

"Come on, guess."

"I really don't know," she says.

"Okay, are you ready?" he says, hands in front of him like she can't wait to find out, like she's about to find out what's behind door number two on some fantastic game show. He pauses for dramatic effect. "It's the Vince Guaraldi Trio."

"Mmm," she says nodding her approval. She takes another gulp of her red. *Who?*

"That's right, the band behind the Peanuts' theme, *Linus and Lucy*. Can you believe that?"

She shakes her head. "Nope."

"The estate didn't want to sell it to me at first. But I never take 'no' for an answer. Everyone has a price. Theirs was two-hundred-thousand dollars."

This time Holly does spit. She tries to hold the wine in and chokes. Red alcohol drips from her nose.

"I figure now that we've secured some big time federal contracts, it's okay to treat myself once and awhile." He finally realizes she's choking. "Are you okay?"

Coughing, she wipes her chin. "Sorry. Will you excuse me for a moment?"

"Sure," he says, standing as she leaves the table for the ladies room.

Upon entering the restroom, she's already dreading returning to the table, dreading spending another moment with a guy who drops money like peanuts on songs like, well, Peanuts.

Spider-legged drips of mascara run down her cheeks. She dabs the corner of a paper towel about her eyes and reapplies it in the mirror. She takes her time before blinking and inspecting her work.

Inspection turns to introspection. "Who are you?" she asks the woman staring back at her. "What happened to the girl from Tampa?"

"What was that?" says a woman behind her. "Did you say something?"

"No," Holly says shaking her head, her eyes white with surprise. She smiles at this interloper nervously, tells her to have a nice night. She needs to get back to the table. Another thirty minutes with Nick has to be less awkward than being caught talking to herself in the john. It has to be less painful than dwelling on her past.

"Want some desert?" Nick asks when she returns. "The tiramisu here is wonderful. Really, to die for."

She barely musters a smile. "Sure."

When they leave, Holly pushes through the revolving door first. It's raining again and noticeably colder than when they entered. Nick doesn't offer his coat, but he does offer her a ride home.

She frowns.

He says the date's been going well and can only get better. "It would be a shame to end it now." His tongue swirls about the left side of his lips, lingering on the upper lip for a moment.

Internal voices debate. A voice says, *Why the Hell not? Let him have his way with you. What's there to lose?*

But a haunted voice, a forgotten voice, provides an answer. *Just a little bit more of your soul.*

"You know, I don't think that's a good idea," Holly says. "Let's call it a night."

"Come on, baby," he says. "You have to see my new Aston Martin." He nods towards a grey Vanquish parked at a meter across the street. "Zero to 100 miles per hour in ten seconds flat."

That's when a man barrels into Davis from behind.

"What the fuck?" Davis says, spinning to confront the man.

The guy is hurrying, shielding himself from the downpour with a newspaper. He's filthy, covered in muck and stained with food. "Excuse me," the man says. It's accentuated with a cough . . . and a lone vocative. "Citizen." He stumbles away.

Holly watches him go. He's just a silhouette outlined by the street lamps, but she recognizes him immediately.

"Why don't you watch where you're going?" Nick yells at the man as he hobbles away. "I should make him pay for my dry cleaning. Damn homeless." He turns to Holly. "So how about that ride?" His eyebrows lift.

The double entendre creeps her out. "No, that's okay," she says quickly. "I have a lot of work to do. A big story. Deadlines. That kind of thing." She watches the man lumber away. "I really have to go," she says, her foot tapping.

Davis gives her a wounded pout. "Well, do you mind if I give you a call in the morning? I'd love to hear your voice."

"You have a message on your machine from me," she replies. "Listen to that." And with that, Holly Rodriguez begins trailing the man from her past.

"Bitch," Davis mutters under his breath as he watches her go.

"Wait," Rodriguez calls to the man, "Larry!" He keeps limping along. He either can't hear her over the sound of the rain or his own hacking, or is purposely ignoring her. The cobbled streets of Old Town are holding the run off, and she shuffles and hops around the edges of the widening puddles. The water is in her eyes, but she can tell the distance between them is growing. She is losing him. She pulls off her Manolo Blahnik pumps and skips through the water barefoot. Running with her heels in hand, she calls Centurion's name.

Nick Davis grabs her by the arm.

Her eyes bug. "Nick, what are you doing?"

He doesn't let go. "Come on. You're being ridiculous. Come with me."

She tries to shake him loose, but his grip grows tighter. "You're hurting me."

"Look," Nick says as he pulls her against him. He's still smiling despite being drenched. "I'm not like the other guys you've dated, Holly. I'm a man of ambition. I don't take 'no' for an answer."

"You told me that earlier," she says, pulling free.

"So," he asks, "what's your price?"

Her tongue clicks. "What?"

"Tell me what you want. A vacation in Paris? A shopping spree in Milan? Whatever you want, I can give it to you."

She shakes her head. "I don't want anything from you."

He's not listening. "Here's my offer. Come back to my suite with me. We'll make love and sleep in. In the afternoon, we'll take a trip to Jamaica. We'll spend the week licking lotion and sea salt from each other's skin."

She shudders. "Here's my counter." Holly swings her heels at Nick's face.

He blocks her swing with a forearm. "Nice. I love negotiations." He pulls her close again, grabs her by the hair, and goes to kiss her hard.

"No!" she sputters before he puts his mouth on her. She tries to scream, but can't. Davis is all over her.

One punch later, he's all over the sidewalk.

"Stay down," a masked man says in between piercing coughs.

Nick is on his back. He shifts his weight to one elbow and rubs his cheek. "Who the fuck are you?"

Lightening strikes on cue, illuminating a man in white armor. Holly stands behind him, shielded. "Centurion," the man grumbles, the thunder rumbling and emphasizing his name.

"No," Nick says. "You are a fucking dead man." He goes to his hands and knees and feels along the loose bricks for a weapon.

"Nick, please don't," Holly pleads.

Centurion turns to her. "Don't worry, Ma'am. I'll keep you—" He halts midsentence, recognizing her for the first time. His mouth tries to form words that don't exist. He looks around, searching for the purveyors of this cruel joke, the producers of this hidden camera show.

Sadness. Fear. Resentment. There's so much emotion in his eyes, lost feelings that visit her like dark blotches after staring at the sun. She needs to reach out and touch his face to confirm that it's real.

"Ms. Rodriguez?" he asks.

"Holly," she says, offering a weak but genuine smile.

He takes a step back. "Unbelievable," he says with a growl. "This day just gets better and better." He spreads his arms to the heavens, exasperated. "Thanks a lot, Zeus."

A brick strikes Centurion in the back of the head.

"Nick," she screams, as Centurion drops into her arms. She grabs him under his armpits, struggles to keep all two-hundred-twenty pounds of him from falling.

Nick doesn't answer. His lips make an "o" while his brows crawl off his forehead. "I didn't think I'd actually hit him. Is he dead?"

"I don't know," she says, grunting to pull Centurion to his feet. "I don't think so. Get an ambulance."

Nick takes a step towards her. He hesitates before spinning and taking off in a full sprint in the other direction.

"You bastard," she yells.

A half block away, Davis starts his car with a roar. It revs twice before leaping forward. He races by them, splashing them with mud and rainwater.

"Larry?" Holly says, trying to look into his face as he slips further. "Larry?"

There's no response.

"Larry?" she says, once more. "Lawrence."

Centurion's eyes flutter open slowly.

"Try to stand. We need to get you to a hospital."

He mumbles, "No hospitals. No police."

"But—"

"No hospitals, no police," he wheezes again as his eyes squeeze shut.

# Track Fourteen: A Means to an End

*St. Petersburg, Russia. 29 December 1916.*

There were many reasons to hate Gregori Rasputin, and many in the Russian Orthodox Church and Dumas did. Their loathing was not unfounded. Rasputin was intent on destroying their institutions and remaking them to serve his vision.

He argued that salvation was something the Church could not offer. Deliverance, instead, was a personal quest. The faithful could communicate more directly with God. The clergy were nothing more than an antiquated and corrupt conduit. They were superfluous.

He took exception to Russia's engagement in the War and to the strategies drawn up by the Commander-in-Chief. He called Grand Duke Nicholas' plans to engage the Germans folly, much to the chagrin of Russia's ministers and allies. Then he exerted his influence over the Romanov court. He merely whispered in the ear of the Tsar, and the Commander-in-Chief and other disagreeable generals were immediately removed. Cabinet members, many of them pro-British ministers, were turned out as well.

Rasputin hadn't been the first to try to reshape church and state. No, institutional threats had come and gone over the years. The Holy Synod and the Russian Empire largely ignored them. The challengers were eventually washed away by their own human imperfections and time.

But Rasputin was different. He would not be ignored.

So the powers that be set out to ruin him.

The Duma called him a puppeteer. Statesmen said he was in league with German spies. The Ochrana secret police followed him, faking documents that painted him as an opportunist and a fraud.

The Russian Orthodox Church called him immoral. It accused him of pagan practices and mysticism. The Holy Synod spread rumors that he was a sexual deviant, a rapist, a Khylst. Yet the harshest condemnations came from his former friends, the clerics. They called him the Antichrist.

The Russian press was eager to enter the fray. A weakened Rasputin meant a weakened dynasty, and a weakened dynasty meant less censorship. More importantly, it meant profit.

But for all of the pressure applied by the priests, politicians, and pundits, the Romanovs would not be swayed. They were forever indebted to Rasputin for curing their son, Tsarevich Alexai, of hemophilia.

The cabal set out on a different course: when character assassination fails, assassinate the man.

That's the story, at least as it will eventually be told in history books. But there's another story, the story of an agent known only by a deadly code name. Her God-given name is Mathilde Toure, but to those who interact with her, she's known simply as the Headhunter, or Hunter for short.

The code name's neither politically nor factually correct. Headhunting was a popular practice in Southeast Asia, New Guinea, and the Pacific islands, not Africa. The only documented cases of headhunting in Africa were among the Igbo of Nigeria, and Mathilde's bloodlines are to the south. The U.S. intelligence community, however, wasn't too concerned with the inaccuracies. Espionage depends on obfuscation and fear. At any rate, the nickname was accurate in one very important sense: Mathilde was lethal.

Rasputin was on the American's radar and on Headhunter's list. He had become more than a man. He was a myth, a future legend. Many said he could heal with a touch. Others said he could communicate with the deceased. Some said he could even predict the future. But most troubling was the rumor that Rasputin was immortal, incapable of dying.

An immortal man could challenge the institutions underpinning the Russian Empire. He could affect significant and volatile change. Such a man could shake the Empire into rubble and change the world order.

A man who can live forever must, simply, die.

There are few (if any) people of African descent in St. Petersburg. Safe passage depended upon the aid of the British SIS. The Secret Intelligent Service arranged for the Hunter's transport on a Norwegian frigate. British submarines escorted the ship, the *Sophia*, as she passed through the Kattegat. Once through the straights connecting the North and Baltic seas, the E9 continued to provide protection against the German Imperial Navy to Oslo.

As the ship entered the Neva, snow fell. The *Sophia* cut west, a red slash on grey waters. It passed grey wooden docks, grey fishing-boats, grey wooden homes, and low, grey squat quays. The grey gulls shrieked their fury at this ship that dared break-up their monotony. The Hunter moved to the aft of the boat.

Lieutenant Oswald Rayner and Captain Stephen Alley greet the ship as it arrives at the Admiralty Shipyard at dusk. But the Hunter is not onboard. No one matching her description appears on the manifest.

"Better radio the Americans," Captain Alley says.

When they return to their Fiat Tipo 4, a woman surprises them. She's hiding in the shadows in the backseat. She's dark and wet and wrapped in a blanket. Steam comes off her skin and her fire red hair.

"Hunter?" the Lieutenant asks. It's a stupid question. Of course this is the Headhunter.

She nods with her eyes.

"Well, I see you found us," the Captain says. He introduces himself and the Lieutenant.

"How did you get here?" The Lieutenant asks.

"I jumped ship before reaching the wharf district," she says.

"The water must be forty-five degrees," the Lieutenant exclaims.

The Hunter nods. "When do I see Rasputin?"

The Captain provides the details. "The net's been cast. The trap takes the form of an invitation from Princess Irena, the wife of Prince Felix Yusupov. Rasputin should already be held by our contacts. We have time to get you dry clothes."

"No," she says. "Take me to him. Now."

They drive the narrow stone streets to Moika Palace. The Hunter is led to a kitchen in the cellar. A bearded man with thinning, long hair is tied to a chair. He's been beaten severely, and flecks of blood and dirt appear here and there on his robe. Three men surround him: Prince Felix, Grand Duke Dmitri Pavlovich, and Vladimir Purishkevich, nobles and statesmen, men who can and will benefit from the death of Rasputin. Their heads twist and cock as the African enters the room.

"Leave us," she says to the astonished men in perfect Russian.

Mathilde and her like do not "smell" witches so much as they sense them. Although imperceptible to Rayner and Alley, the space between Mathilde and Rasputin hums, something akin to magnetic field. Magnets can attract. She's usually drawn to those with superhuman abilities. Sometimes magnets repel. Rasputin is a like charge. He's repulsive. He's a demon in human form.

She doesn't say a word to Rasputin as she goes to work.

She mixes rat poison, enough to kill five men, with water in a glass. She pulls Rasputin's head back by his hair, pours it down his throat.

Rasputin coughs and wheezes, but swallows it without effect. He scowls and curses. He says something about fucking her corpse. He curses her descendents, tells her they're cursed to be slaves. Just. Like. Her. He promises to come back from the grave to ensure it. He says he'll be the death of her line, the death of witch-smellers.

"Mithridaitism?" the Captain asks, wondering if Rasputin has inoculated himself against the effects of the poison. It's possible he conditioned himself by administering larger and larger doses.

"Perhaps," she says. "Or he's realigned the chemicals in the toxin, making them harmless."

"Changing the molecular structure of poisons?" the Captain says. "Well, that's special."

"What's next?" the Lieutenant asks.

She pulls a long chef's knife from a woodblock. She presses the point of the blade against Rasputin's chest, finding the soft spot between two ribs. She leans forward, the knife sinking into the right side of Rasputin's chest. She halts the blade's descent four inches deep. She leans back. He groans as she pulls the knife out. She moves down a rib and stabs him again. He growls. She slides the knife out, and repeats further down his chest. Rasputin's moaning gives way to chuckling, then full on laughter. He cackles, showing teeth covered in blood.

"Good God," Captain Alley cries. "How can he live through that?"

They really shouldn't be that surprised. After all, this is a man who survived being disemboweled like a *tsivilsk* pig in Pokrovskoye just two years ago. This is a man who picked his entrails off the floor, shoved them back into his gut, and punched his attacker in the face.

The Hunter wipes the knife on the side of sugar bag. She flips it, slices the bag open at the top. Sugar pours on to the tiled floor. She up-ends the cotton bag once half the contents have emptied, dumping the rest of the confection at her feet. She shakes the bag once and drapes it over Rasputin's head. He spits defiantly, the blood staining the white sack. She grabs a dishtowel from near the sink and wets it. She circles to Rasputin's back. She wraps the towel around his neck, ties a knot.

"Toss me that rolling pin," she says to Rayner.

He does, and she catches it with one hand. She places the handle be-tween the towel and Rasputin's neck. Then she begins to twist clock-wise.

The towel knots as it compresses.

They hear Rasputin's windpipe go. He spits and hacks flecks of blood into the hood. His body shakes. Then he goes quiet, slumps over.

"Is he dead?" Rayner asks.

"Fill the sink."

Rayner does so.

The Hunter lifts Rasputin from his chair without any help from the men. She carries him to the sink, and dunks his head under water. "Hold his head there."

Rayner does.

"What now?" the Captain says.

"We wait."

An hour later, she tells Rayner to pull him out. He does, with some effort, and struggles to carry the body back to the chair.

Captain Alley pulls off the hood. He places a finger on Rasputin's jugular. "No pulse." He turns to the Lieutenant. "Bring in Pavlovich."

The Lieutenant leaves and returns with the conspirators. The men form a half-circle in front of Rasputin's chair. "Rasputin," he says in accented Russian, "is no more."

That's when Rasputin opens his eyes.

Pavlovich lets out a scream. Purishkevich prays for mercy.

"Lieutenant," Captain Alley says, "use your firearm."

Rasputin stands, breaks the chair, tears free of his bonds. He rushes forward, clutching Felix Yusupov by the throat. He strangles him.

Mathilde Toure is at Rayner's side in a flash.

"Lieutenant!" the Captain orders again.

Lieutenant Rayner searches his side. His holster's empty. "Captain?"

Shots are fired. Three across Rasputin's back, one piercing his heart. Yusupov cries.

Rasputin barks like a mad dog, bloody foam dripping from his lips. He doesn't let go.

Then there's a fourth and final shot. It hits Rasputin in the back of the head, bursts through his skull and into his brain.

The bullets come from Rayner's Webley pistol, but not from his hand. The Hunter has discharged his weapon into the revenant.

Rasputin's grasp weakens, and he collapses.

"That's my pistol," Rayner says.

Without turning, Hunter thanks him and sets the weapon on the table before the Lieutenant.

Yusupov holds his throat, huffing heavily.

The men wrestle an Ottoman rug from a study. They move the kitchen table out of their way and spread the indigo carpet across the floor. They wrap Rasputin in it, rolling his body like a cannoli.

Hunter halts them. She draws her knife. "You may want to look away." With that, she slices open Rasputin's pants. Another cut, and she's removed his manhood.

The men collectively moan. "Savage," the Captain whispers.

She pays them no heed.

"Why did you do that?" Rayner asks.

"Proof," she says, wrapping the member in a dishcloth. She places it in a satchel.

When they are done, they lug Rasputin to the balcony overlooking the Neva River. With a collective heave, they toss him into the chilly waters below.

Suddenly, The Hunter is on the ledge as well. She gives Rayner a quick nod before herself disappearing into the Neva.

None of the men will ever see her again. Decades from now, Rayner will be questioned about this day. He will recollect the events precisely, but he will never mention the Headhunter or her participation. The punishment for high treason is severe, yet it is nothing compared to the vengeance of the witch-smellers' masters.

The Captain shakes his head. "I think I've seen everything now."

"Should I contact the Bureau?" Rayner asks.

"Yes, time to inform Mansfield Smith-Cumming," the Captain replies.

Mansfield takes great interest in this particular witch-smeller's deeds. It's a revelation that will change the course of his life . . . and history.

# Track Fifteen: Crazy Wisdom

*The Drake Hotel, Chicago. 6 September 2001.*

Chee answers the phone. "Hello . . . sure, okay." She covers the receiver with her hand. "It's for you."

"Thanks, honey," Marcus says. He takes the phone from her, speaks. "Yes?"

"Meet me at Coq d'Or." It's Mansfield.

"It's a little early for a drink."

"Ten minutes." *Click.*

"I've got to run out for a moment," Marcus tells Chee. "Why don't you run down and do some shopping on Michigan Avenue. Get some air." He opens his wallet and extends a credit card.

She looks at the plastic in his hand with disdain.

For a moment, he wonders if she'll tell him about the incident at Water Tower Place. She doesn't.

"I don't feel like it," she says. She hides behind a comic called *Naruto*. A kid with spiked triangular hair kicks into the air on the cover, his hands forming tiger claws. What she's really saying is, "You can't buy my love."

He grabs his sport coat. "Okay, I'll be back shortly."

"Whatever," she says. Again, this is code. The subtext: "I don't want to move again."

"Enough of the pouting. I don't like moving, but that's part of the job. We're going to Atlanta. That's final, Amachi."

Marcus rarely calls Chee by her birth name. It's a name her mother selected. It means, "What God has brought," literally, "God's gift." When they bestowed the name upon Chee as a baby it was still so full of hope. Now, he only uses her full name when he's frustrated, angry. When had he stolen the promise of her name?

He stands there a moment. He wants to tell her that things will get better. He can't bring himself to lie to her again. Frowning, he leaves the room. He walks the hallway to the elevator. Inside, he presses the lobby button.

It's not unlike Mansfield to show up unexpectedly. Old habits die hard, and surprise has been Mansfield Smith-Cumming's calling card since his days with MI6.

*Surprise.* Mansfield visited the U.S. embassy in South Africa several times in 1980, coming and going without notice like a storm on the sea. Marcus was serving as Foreign Service Officer. They were never introduced. The first words they exchanged were on Marcus' last day in the country.

Marcus was tasked with monitoring the anti-apartheid movement. He reported back to the U.S. State Department concerning the whereabouts and welfare of freedom fighters, men following in the footsteps of martyrs like Steven Biko and Solomon Mahlangu. One by one, they were imprisoned, murdered, or disappeared. Eventually, he called on his superiors to support economic sanctions against the country. Those requests fell on deaf ears. The influence of the Soviet Union in the region was first and foremost on the mind of the Ambassador, the Secretary of State, and the intelligence community.

That fear of communism was proven out in the summer of 1980 when Hélène Toure returned to South Africa, the land of her birth, after more than twenty years. A memo from the Ambassador heralded her homecoming and spoke highly of her commitment to "community outreach," code for her attempts to destabilize the Bantus. She was six feet tall and lean, and the male FSOs—there were only male FSOs at that time—were captivated. She turned their heads and as easily spurned their advances. Unlike the others, the shy Marcus kept his distance.

It was during the embassy's Christmas party—the annual excuse for spies, secretaries, and dignitaries to fraternize—that a drunken Marcus first engaged Hélène. She was holding up the wall in the shadows, watching inebriated FS-9s dance (or try to) to Billy Joel's *It's Still Rock and Roll to Me.*

"Drink?" he asked, sidling up next to her and offering her a sip of his rum and coke.

"No, thank you," she replied without so much as a glance in his direction.

"Dance?"

"No."

He nodded. Several awkward seconds passed. They were followed by an even more awkward question. "What do you do, exactly?"

"I serve our government," she replied, "just like you."

"No, what do you actually do?"

"Whatever they tell me," she said.

"That's not right," he said looking into his drink. "This isn't right at all."

Her eyes narrowed. He now had her attention. "What's not right?"

"Our policy of public outrage but private encouragement of apartheid."

"You're drunk. You're not thinking straight."

"I might not be able to walk a straight line, but I'm thinking straight, I'm shooting straight, for the first time in a long time. Bishop Desmond Tutu is right. Our engagement with South Africa's 'an abomination.' The President's ties to the Pretoria regime are immoral."

"What's your name?" Hélène asked.

"Marcus," he slurred.

"Well, Marcus, you're going to get yourself fired. Be quiet and drink your drink."

He ignored her command. "Our support of apartheid is evil," he said, his voice rising above the music. "Fuck, it's totally inconsistent with Christian tenets."

A handful of people near the bar looked in their direction, questioning the not-so seasonal sounds. The First Secretary took a step towards them. Hélène saw this and pulled a move straight from a classic Bond film. She turned towards Marcus, took his head in her hands, and kissed him full on the lips. Marcus' eyes briefly registered surprise before closing. He kissed her back, his hands going to her hips. Hélène eyed the attachés and their wives at the bar. They nodded approvingly and went back to their drinks and conversations. The First Secretary smiled and returned to the company of the revelers. Danger averted, she allowed herself for a moment to fall into the pleasure of the kiss. She pressed against him hard, the spear tip hanging from her necklace leaving an impression on both of their sternums.

Seconds later, she pulled away. His eyes were still closed, his lips puckered. "Do you have a car?" she asked.

He slowly opened his eyes. "Yes."

"Give me the keys," she said.

His hand went to his pocket. "Here you go."

"Want to get out of here?"

"Definitely." He couldn't wait. If there had been a more emphatic affirmation, he would have used it. Blondie serenades them as they leave. "Call me," Debbie Harry beckons.

That night Amachi was conceived, the girl with her mother's mannerisms and visage. That night *he* ended, and *they* started. He let go of the absolutism of self and gave into yin-yang, the complement of another. He adored every moment of the roller coaster ride, hated when Mansfield forced their car off the tracks two short years later.

Mansfield is waiting outside the bar. He nods as Marcus exits the elevator.

Mansfield loves the Coq d'Or, the Golden Rooster. It's dark and masculine, a throwback to a bygone day. The bar opened its doors in December of 1933 after the repeal of Prohibition. It reminds Mansfield of his prime, of a time when he was known simply as "C."

They pass through a wood framed door and enter a narrow hallway filled with low tables and chairs upholstered in red leather. Mansfield selects a lonely table beneath a mural of the French countryside. He orders an "executive" old fashioned. He only drinks the best. Marcus will take a beer, whatever they have on tap.

The waitress returns, handing Mansfield his cocktail. She tells Marcus that she selected a craft beer for him, an IPA from Wisconsin. They decline her offer of food.

The light is dim, but Marcus can tell something's not right about

Mansfield. He's looking older. He always looked to be in his early six-ties, frozen in a moment 100 years ago like some pickled two-headed pig. Today, he looks seventy. No, older. *Surprise.*

Within the agency, it's no secret how Mansfield halted his aging process. The former head of MI6, the British Secret Intelligence Serv-ice, was co-opted by the U.S. in 1923. In dramatic fashion, Mansfield faked his death and emigrated. His move marked the beginning of the European "brain drain." Dozens of German, Italian, and Russian op-eratives, scientists, and war criminals followed. They formed the core of the U.S. research and development fraternity. Bitter enemies now called each other friends and slapped each other's backs over libations.

The same year as Mansfield's defection, Hitler's Nazi Party at-tempted to seize power in Germany. Their coup would fail, but Hitler would not be dissuaded. The self-proclaimed "Messiah of Germany" rose to power and instigated World War II.

What followed was a race to secure occult artifacts, holy relics Hitler sought to use to dominate Europe and later the world.

Mansfield and his operatives thwarted Hitler at every turn. They beat the Nazis to the Arc of the Covenant and secreted it away to a warehouse in the States. They located and seized the stolen Ghent Al-tarpiece, complete with a map to the Holy Grail, from Hitler's hiding place in the Austrian Alps. They torpedoed U-534, sinking the German U-boat and with it the Spear of Longinus, the lance that pierced Jesus Christ. They tracked the Nazi's search for the Fountain of Youth. Mans-field destroyed both the Storm Detachment and the Fountain in a hail of fire.

But not before he took a sip.

Now, apparently, the magic's wearing off.

"When did you start aging again?" Marcus asks.

"Is it that noticeable?" Mansfield asks.

Marcus nods.

"A few months ago," Marcus' boss says. "That's when I found the first spot."

*Surprise.* "Spot? You mean cancer?"

Mansfield says, "Yes." Cellular division is complex. Three million base pairs of DNA have to be duplicated perfectly. The Fountain ensured that. Now, mistakes are happening, damaging cells, promoting aging. Further, mutations are occurring, resulting in sarcomas. "But I'm taking a Davis drug intravenously. It will slow cellular division. Unfortunately, it can't prohibit division entirely."

"I'm sorry," Marcus says. "What's the next step?"

"That depends," Mansfield says, "on what we can learn from the Monfort girl."

Marcus rubs an eyebrow with his index and middle fingers. "How does she fit into this?"

"Her DNA may show us how we can limit the division of cells, or cellular senescence," Mansfield says. She's unique. Her cells reinvent themselves, expressing certain genes and hiding others. Consequently, her enzymes and histone modifiers open regions of the genome that express senescence as opposed to cellular reproduction. Inside her may be the epigenetic key to controlling cancer and aging.

"What will you do with her?" Marcus asks, trying to remain as conversational as possible.

"Well," Mansfield says without a hint of humor or doubt, "we're going to have to cut her up."

Marcus takes a drink from his snifter. He shakes his head. "Maybe you should just retire," he half jokes. "Enjoy your final years."

"Retirement is not a luxury afforded to those in our profession," Mansfield says. "You know that."

"Yes," Marcus says, deep parallel lines materializing across his forehead, "I'm well aware." Hélène was proof of that.

For a moment, Marcus is transported away to another time and place, the day Mansfield found him hiding with his infant daughter on the dirt floor in the corner of a corrugated metal shack. Hélène was dead, hacked to death by a mob armed with machetes. She had been outed as a "witch-smeller," a woman born from a matriarchal line of witch hunters. The throng was now after Hélène's offspring, their daughter Amachi.

*Surprise.* It was Mansfield who found them in that hovel. That night, he became both their destroyer and savior. He visited them like an Old

Testament God, promising the choice of rebirth or destruction in return for their undying faith.

"God," Marcus says under his breath. That's what it takes, having
the ego and infallibility of a god, to perpetuate the ultimate double stan-
dard: using the occult to perpetuate life in the name of further waging
war against the occult. "You'd dissect that girl?"

"I'd carve up a hundred girls," Mansfield says. "A thousand."

"Just to live forever? You'd hurt her and others to become a deity?"

Mansfield winces, finally showing some emotion. "No, Marcus, I
don't want to live forever. But I do want my life's work to live on. Even
if I could live another lifetime, I'm not sure it would matter."

Marcus doesn't know what he means.

"The world of intelligence gathering, of espionage, is changing,
and changing fast, Mansfield says. "We're losing our competitive fire; it's
being bred out of the DNA of our intelligence agencies. Soon we'll be
living in a world where information is indexed, cameras are on every
corner, warrants are no longer necessary, and everyone's phone is
tapped. We'll operate under a single security administration, and our
agency, the FBI, CIA, DIA, INSCOM, OICI, and all the others will operate less like an intelligence community and more like a homogeneous
monolith that's beholden to big data." Mansfield shakes his head. "I
don't know if I want to be here when that day comes, but it is coming,
and sooner than you think. And, after all, you can't teach an old dog new
tricks."

"Don't sell yourself short," Marcus says. "You're not an old dog."

"Thank you—"

"You're a *very* old dog."

They share a half-hearted chuckle, and Marcus feels a pang of guilt
course over his shoulders and up his neck like an unwelcome draft.
While broken trusts can be mended given enough time and the right
commitment, Marcus has yet to forgive. He'll never forgive a murderer
that continues to lie.

*Surprise.*

Marcus is certain Mansfield has lied again, that his plans go further.
He can't fathom the deeper, darker designs for Kim and her DNA, but

he knows they exist.

When Marcus returns to his room, he finds Chee sitting at the edge of the bed. Her head is bent over her chest. She's been crying.

He rushes to her side, kneels and takes her hands in his. "What's wrong, honey?"

"I think I left my necklace at the apartment."

"We can get you another necklace," he says, trying to reassure her.

"No, *mom's* necklace."

"Oh." It's the spear tip she wore the night of the Christmas party so many years ago, at least a reproduction of it. "Well, we can get it in a day or two."

"Promise?"

"Sure," Marcus says. "We'll get some more clothes too."

*Gold Coast, Chicago.*

Centurion's eyes flutter. He's in an eggshell white room bathed by sunlight. He's under a snowy white comforter, in a queen-size bed wrapped in white sheets. Holly Rodriguez is sitting to his right.

"Thank God you were wearing that helmet," she says.

"Where am I?" Centurion says.

"My place." She hops up. "Hungry?"

"No," he says gruffly. His mental resistance, however, is met with sudden and fierce debate from his stomach. It growls its disapproval. "Yes."

She says she's got turkey bacon and eggs on the stove. She'll be right back.

"Okay." He regards his hands. His knuckles on his left are bandaged. Two fingers on his right hand are wrapped in gauze. He holds them before his face. They've been scrubbed clean, as have his bruised arms. When he realizes his freckled shoulders and chest are exposed, he lifts the covers. "Hey, where are my clothes?"

"In the wash," she calls from a neighboring room.

"And my armor?"

"Don't worry," she says. "Although I was surprised by how orna-mental it was."

"Ornamental?"

"Well," her voice nears the room. "Other than the helmet, it didn't do much to protect you, did it?" She walks in with a tray, a smirk firmly on her face. "You look like you got hit by a car. A big one. Like a truck. Going very fast."

Centurion just grunts. He scoots to a seated position.

Holly sets the tray across his lap. She starts to point out the items it holds. "We've got OJ, scrambled eggs . . . "

Centurion is already digging in, inhaling the bacon. He doesn't care that it's made of turkey. He holds three strips in with one hand while he mixes potatoes and eggs together with a fork in the other. Two more bites of turkey bacon, and he's shoveling the egg mix into his mouth. He follows that with a swig of orange juice that nearly empties the glass.

" . . . Wow, I guess you are hungry," Holly says. "When was the last time you had something to eat?"

Centurion shrugs, his cheeks packed like a squirrel. He drops his bacon to his plate, holds up two fingers.

"Two days?" she says incredulously.

He nods. He attempts to talk, but his mouth's full. "Praw-bowb-lee," he manages. His attention returns to what's left on the plate.

She observes him for a moment longer before saying, "I better check on the laundry. I'll be right back."

Centurion doesn't acknowledge her. His eyes are closed as he chews. He tells her this would all taste better with a Busch Light to wash it down.

She steps out and leans against a wall in the hallway just beyond the bedroom door. She listens.

He coughs loud and hard from deep in his chest. He's in a world of hurt, a very different place than her. She's no longer a lowly beat re-porter covering court calls. She takes stock of the role the man laying in her bed played in catapulting her to stardom. She recollects meeting him for the first time six years ago.

❖ ❖ ❖

He walked into the courthouse that day, his Roman breastplate, shoulder pauldrons, and legion skirt glistening. She could smell the fresh white paint as he passed near her. He wore his armor over a clean, white toga. She laughed when the Sheriff's Office made him check his sheath and sword at security. Although she had a murder trial to cover, she was compelled to follow him into the courtroom.

Holly introduced herself, asked him why he was there. He told her he was a superhero. He explained he had witnessed a hit and run. He had caught the license plates of the vehicle involved. And although no one had been hurt, he had called the police and dutifully reported it.

She asked if he had checked in with the prosecuting attorney. He told her the District Attorney had never contacted him. Instead, he produced a piece of paper, a subpoena from the driver's defense attorney.

That's when she knew the fix was in. The police had never provided his information to the prosecuting attorney. They had set this witness up to get gutted by defense council. The only thing cops hate more than criminals are vigilantes and wannabe cops. On cue, the bailiff whispered to the prosecuting attorney, "We've already got one too many Batmans in this world. Or is that Batmen?"

She sat down to watch what promised to be a slow motion train wreck. Just before lunch, someone simply known as "Centurion" was called to the stand.

After being sworn in, the defense attorney introduced himself.

*I'm Ernie George. I'm the attorney for Michael Draws, the defendant.*

"Hello," Centurion replied with a tilted nod the head.

*I'm going to ask you a few questions, okay?*

"Of course. I'll cooperate in any way I can."

*Can you state your name for the record?*

"Centurion." Centurion was oblivious to the reaction of the spectators, defendants and victims alike. Their raucous laughter brought a quick tap of the gavel, a call to order from the judge. Holly Rodriguez scribbled furiously.

*I'm sorry. Let me clarify. What is the name on your birth certificate? You know, the name of your "alter ego?"*

"You mean my true identity?"

*Yes, that's it.*

"Revealing that could jeopardize those close to me, maybe even my ability to effectively fight crime."

*Your "ability to fight crime." By that, do mean your special brand of vigilante justice?*

"I guess you could put it that way. Sure." People snickered from the aisles.

*Well, I'm afraid I still need you to answer it. I'd hate to ask the judge to hold you in contempt of veritas et aeuquitas, truth and equity.*

"Veritas? She was the Roman goddess of truth, the daughter of Saturn."

*I never would have guessed.*

Centurion smiled as the room laughed again. The poor guy didn't have a clue.

*How about this, we'll keep it our little secret, just the people in this room. What do you say?*

"Well, I wouldn't want to be in contempt of the law. And if it's going to be a secret . . . My real name is Lawrence. Lawrence Schultz. But you can call me Centurion."

*And what do you do, Lawrence, for employment, other than fight crime that is?* More laughs.

"I'm a camp councilor for the YMCA."

*So you have access to people's children?*

"Every day, especially children with disabilities," Larry replied. The laughing stopped. The courtroom gasped.

None of Centurion's testimony really mattered after that initial questioning. Not the details of the accident. Not the description of the Ford involved. Not even the plate of the vehicle, Florida tag BSG1980. Sure, it was admissible, but juries weigh evidence as they deem fit. And George effectively demonstrated that Lawrence Schultz was unfit. It was a point the attorney underscored during closing arguments.

*There aren't any witnesses. No credible ones, anyway. Lawrence Schultz is the victim of multiple personalities, violent fantasies, and delusions of grandeur. He's a modern day Sybil, but in armor . . . and with ready access to little kids . . . special little kids . . . without defenses.*

The jury found George's closing compelling. They could not find the defendant guilty beyond a reasonable doubt based on the testimony.

Centurion was beside himself. Rodriguez caught up to him as he shuffled out of the courtroom. She told him that she respected what he had done. She offered to buy him a beer.

"I don't really drink," he said.

"How about dinner?" came her reply.

He agreed, although he cautioned her he might not make good company.

They decided to meet at a little Mediterranean place on Polk Street. He showed up in full regalia. At the dinner table, he removed his helmet. They shared a bottle of wine and talked for hours. He told her about his work, his dream of creating a superhero club, and his troubles doing so. He didn't have many friends, she learned, and never had many growing up either. His father was drunk and abusive. He spent his childhood losing himself in a world of mythology.

He handled the check and then walked her to her car. They shared a polite kiss, a peck, goodnight.

Two days later, portions of their conversation appeared in the Lifestyle section of the *Tampa Express*. The article was titled *Super Zero*. It detailed Centurion's difficulties testifying at the hearing and his larger legal problems, including the Justice Legion litigation. Although less than seven hundred words, the article proved a heavy enough domino.

The administrators at the Y told Centurion/Larry that his services were no longer needed. They received hundreds of telephone calls from worried parents. Centurion pleaded, but their hands were simply tied.

He called Rodriguez. Once. Twice. Ten times. The calls went straight to her voicemail, and over two weeks he left a string of messages. He complained. He asked for her help with the Y. He cursed. He even cried. She never returned a single call.

At some point he started drinking.

Holly was contacted by WSQZ ("Tampa Bay doesn't need a hug, it needs a Squeeze") a month later. They liked her work. They hired her as a reporter. She received a nice bump in salary.

And that was just the beginning. More confounding and fortuitous events awaited Centurion and Rodriguez, respectively.

Six months after the trial, a man turned his car into a drunken missile, rocketing across the median at 110 miles per hour, through the guardrail, and into the opposing lanes of Interstate 75 just north of Valroy Road. He struck a station wagon. Witnesses said the resulting explosion could be seen all the way at River Oaks RV Resort.

The fire department worked for six hours prying charred and mangled bodies from the wreckage. There were five including the driver of the Ford. As the police prepared to open the highway to traffic again, one of emergency medical technicians heard crying.

A five-year old girl had survived. Her name was Rose. She had been sleeping in the back of the Buick Roadmaster at the time of the accident. The blast threw her through the lift gate and into the flora along the road.

Burnt and maimed, little Rose died just seven excruciating days later. She was buried next to her siblings and her mom and dad. Hundreds of people came to her funeral. Her casket, diminutive and perverse, was closed. Her features were less discernable than the burnt text of a license plate salvaged at the accident.

That plate? BSG1980.

Rodriguez lobbied her superiors. She wanted to dig deeper into the Draws story.

"Let it go," the suits said. "The man died in a fireball. People need to heal."

"No," she argued. People wanted blood. They wanted catharsis. "This is an opportunity lost."

"You're not going to draw blood from a corpse," they said, right before they said something hurtful: "Anyway, this is something we'd give to an anchor or an investigative journalist, not a beat reporter."

So, despite public interest, despite her lobbying, and despite the initially broad coverage, the story faded into obscurity.

Or would have, had Rodriguez's passion not served as symbolic defibrillator and jumpstarted the heart of the story. She did so by harnessing the power of the Internet.

Setting up the blog was easy. Getting readers was easier. Like a great lump of clay, Rodriguez nudged and pushed the story. She turned it into something with shape. She played to the public's hopes. She played to their collective fears. She did the best work of her career, and she didn't receive a single cent for it.

Her first blog: *Failing Baby Rose*. She indicted the legal system for failing to protect Rose. She questioned the court's commitment to *parens patriae* and blamed defense attorneys like Ernie George for obfuscating the truth.

Rodriguez was persuasive. She posted pictures of Rose as a baby. She recast the child as an infant. Print, radio, and televised media followed her lead. Her bosses at WSQZ were pissed but taciturn. They gave her a segment. Their ratings were never higher.

"Baby Rose" became part of popular vernacular. Three different "Baby Rose Bills" were introduced on the floor of the Florida House of Representatives, two in the Senate.

The press camped out in front of Ernie George's apartment complex. His clients abandoned him. He received hate mail. He got death threats. He saved them the time and effort. He committed suicide just six days after the first blog post, jumping from the railing of his penthouse. His legacy was summed up both by his three-word suicide note ("I'm sorry, Rose") and the splatter of blood, brain, and bone he left on Beachfront Avenue. The stain he created delayed traffic for three hours during the morning rush. His suicide further underscored his culpability. Late night TV joked that attorneys care more about their trajectory than the messes they leave in their wake.

Without a living scapegoat, attention began to wither. Holly was satisfied with her work, but her employers implored her for more. She needed to work another angle. She went after Centurion. Again.

She wrote a blog entitled, *Superhero or Supervillain?* She wondered whether Draws would have been on the road if Centurion's testimony had been more competent. Maybe, she posited, Baby Rose would still be alive today. She interviewed psychologists about Centurion's "delusional behavior." She talked to parents who condemned "grown men running around in tights."

During this period, Centurion embraced the bottle even more tightly.

Not coincidentally, superhero costume sales fell 57 percent in Tampa that Halloween.

Rodriguez succeeded in changing the narrative. The story evolved. She took a fish swimming around in the muck and gave it legs. She let it strut out onto the beach and into the sun. It ran rampant. She had created a monster.

On slow news days, she'd return to the story. She fed the story competing headlines, and it devoured them.

The honchos at WCHC in big market Chicago took notice. They were intrigued. She had the right look and name. She could draw Latinos and men in the coveted 30 to 54 year age bracket. They snapped her up, buying her out of her WSQZ contract and tripling her salary as an anchor on Channel 5.

Yes, she and Centurion had been on divergent courses. He served as her stepping-stone and, as a result, had languished because of that. She's suspected this truth for years. Now, proof is sitting in the very next room. She could no longer hide from it.

❖❖❖

She empties the dryer.

When she returns ten minutes later, Centurion is sleeping on his side. She sets his clothing on the top of the dresser, along with an empty wallet, car keys, a handful of pocket litter, and something that looks like a bullet. It's a USB flash drive. She picks up the projectile-shaped device and examines it for a moment. She spins it, regarding it from all angles. She sets it down on the folded clothes and starts to retreat from the bedroom. She takes three steps, pauses, and regards Centurion.

He's snoring. It's a sustained rumble that's punctuated by a lengthy wheeze. The thick strip of drool hanging from his lower lip quakes.

She turns, considers taking another step, but thinks better of leaving. She quickly spins and steps heel to toe, making her way back to the dresser.

Centurion snorts.

She watches him for a full three seconds before snatching the jump drive and hurrying out. She hastens through the family room to her office. She flips open her laptop, powers it up, and plugs the drive into a USB port.

Moments later, she's watching an odd dot blink on a map of Chicago.

It's time to wake Larry.

# Track Sixteen: I Liked You Better When You Were Dead

*Four Seasons Hotel, Chicago.*

"What are you doing?"

Nigel Crown jumps in his seat, his pen leaping from his hand with a clatter on the desk. He slaps the desktop with both palms and spins in his executive chair. "Damn it, Charlie, a knock would be nice."

Charlie's sitting at the foot of Nigel's bed. He leans back, legs crossed. "Like on the walls?"

"God, no. Why don't you just rattle some chains too? Just knock on the door or announce yourself in a manner less, I don't know, *ghostly*? Anyway, wall-knocking is so cliché."

Charlie chuckles. "Point taken." He stands, smoothes the folds from his uniform. He strides over to the mini-bar.

"I'd ask you to make yourself at home . . . "

"I already have," Charlie says, opening the refrigerator.

"Yes, I realize that," Nigel says.

Charlie pulls a Budweiser from the fridge. He holds it up to the light, examining the bottle from all angles. "Boy, I sure do miss the taste of beer."

"That's Bud," Nigel says, "not beer." He turns back to the composition pad on his desk. He presses his pen against his lower lip and reads his work.

"That's something no one ever tells you about the afterlife," Charlie continues, "there's no food. Worse, there's no alcohol."

"Drinking's overrated," Nigel says. He puts pen to paper. He scratches out a word, replaces it with another one.

"What are you working on," Charlie says, approaching the desk. "Let me see."

"Nothing," Nigel says, closing the marbled black and white pad and sliding it across the desk. He turns to face Charlie again.

To his surprise, Charlie is holding his composition pad in his hands and is flipping through the pages.

"What?" Nigel screws himself around in his chair and finds his work is no longer on his desk. He twists, intent on lunging at Charlie and seizing his notebook back.

But Charlie is no longer standing in front of him. Instead, he's levitating, his feet a full five feet above the floor.

"Give that back," Nigel says. He stretches his arms over his head and jumps in a futile attempt to steal his pad back from the hovering ghost.

Charlie lifts the book slightly, just beyond Nigel's grasp, and continues reading. He reads aloud.

> *You leave a mess every time you part*
> *Pulling tape from my cassette heart*
> *I'm warped by every song I've been*
> *Go ahead and spool me in*
>
> *Your diamond touch scratches vinyl skin*
> *Round and round we go again*
> *I don't want to play for no one else*
> *So take me off your dusty shelf*
>
> *This man's charms are faded*
> *Fallen trinkets from your bracelet*
> *This man's charms are dated*
> *Symbols of what he wasted*

Nigel backs away, sits down at his desk. He puts a hand to his face.

"Wow." Charlie floats back to the floor. "That's good stuff," he says, and he means it. "You've been writing about Lisa. This is a window into some real growth." He hands the booklet back to Nigel.

"Thanks," Nigel says, pulling the notebook tight to his chest and shifting from Charlie.

"Another hit, I dare say," Charlie says.

"Maybe," Nigel allows, "maybe not."

"And why wouldn't it be?" Charlie says.

Nigel sighs. He has a confession. "I am a brand. The idea of Nigel Crown is nothing but a conglomeration." He hasn't written much of his own material in the last several years. He didn't write a single song on the last album. "It's all been, if you'll forgive the expression, ghost-written. There's a team of people the label pays to write songs they think will sound like me."

"You don't need them anymore. You're next album will be big," Charlie says. "*Boogie Woogie Bugle Boy* big."

Crown chuckles. "You're dating yourself. Anyway, I'll worry about that if I make it through tonight."

"You'll be fine," Charlie says. "Trust me."

"Do I have a choice?" Nigel asks.

"I guess you don't," Charlie says. "Unless you want a return to those sleepless and haunted nights."

"No, that's fine. Thank you."

"I hate to spring this on you," Charlie says, "but I need another favor as well."

"Wait," Nigel says rising to his feet, "that wasn't part of our deal."

Charlie greets the response with silence.

"Fine. What is it?" he asks. Exasperated, he closes his eyes and slumps back down in his chair.

"It's nothing really. You can read about it on the last page of your notebook. Good luck tomorrow night."

Nigel opens his composition pad, flips to the back, and reads. His lips move as his eyes pass over the words. "You want me to give this message to your granddaughter, Astrid?"

There's no answer. Charlie's no longer in the room.

Nigel blows air through his nose. "Not a 'hello' or 'goodbye.' Well, he's consistent. I'll give him that."

❖❖❖

*Gold Coast, Chicago.*

"Where did you get that USB device?" Rodriguez asks.

Centurion wipes the sleep from his eyes. "What?"

"That bullet-shaped jump drive?"

Centurion scowls. "Where's my clothing?"

She points to the dresser.

He throws off the blankets, jumps up, totally naked.

"What are you doing?" she says, averting her eyes.

"Don't be so bashful. There's nothing here you didn't see last night when you put me into bed."

"Truth be told," she says, "I asked the cab driver to help me with that."

Centurion's face goes blank.

"It's amazing what someone will do for a big tip," Holly says matter-of-factly.

"Fantastic," Centurion says, pulling on his underwear. "You're ability to exploit me really has no bounds."

"Exploit you?" Holly says, leaning in. "I kind of made you a star."

"You made me a laughingstock," he replies, stabbing a finger into air. "You destroyed me."

"Aren't you being a little melodramatic?" She folds her arms.

"I lost my job, Ms. Rodriguez."

"It's Holly, and did you really want to be a camp councilor anyway, Larry? Perhaps I did you a favor."

"Don't call me Larry. My name's Centurion," he says.

"No, your name is Lawrence."

Centurion ignores her. "Those kids were all I had," he says, almost to himself, sitting on the edge of the bed. "For a long time, I tried to justify losing my job. After all, superheroes have enemies. Continuing to work there could have put those children at risk. It could have exposed them to the villainy of the men set upon destroying me."

She bites her lip, starts to extend a soothing hand. She pulls it back when he turns to her.

"But I can't square it in my head," he continues. "For a long time I wondered what I would say to you, what I would do, if I ever saw you again."

"And?" she says.

"I didn't deserve to lose my job. I didn't deserve to get blamed for trying to help. I didn't deserve to be labeled a de facto murderer."

There's a momentary hush between them. Holly breaks the silence. As much as she wants to tell him, "You're right," she doesn't. Instead she asks about the jump drive again. "Where did you get the USB device?"

"During a fight. I pulled it out of a man's pocket as he pummeled me. Wait, where is it?"

"Well, this is probably the wrong time to say this, but it's plugged into my laptop."

"What?"

"Follow me." She escorts him to her laptop, shows him the blinking dot on a map. "Okay, I know it was another invasion of privacy, but do you have a computer?"

Centurion frowns, shakes his head.

"Well, now you have access to one."

Centurion shrugs. "Okay. Were there any files on it that might indicate who this guy is? Who he works for?"

Holly shakes her head. "No. There aren't any files at all. It's software."

Centurion asks who manufactured it.

"There's no manufacturer identified in properties."

He slaps his leg in frustration.

"You know what that means right?"

He stares blankly at Holly. Apparently not.

"It means the jump drive is either a prototype . . . or it wasn't created privately at all."

Suddenly it registers. "We're talking government issue?"

She lowers and raises her head in exaggerated slow motion. *Exactly.*

"What else?"

"Whatever it's tracking is currently at or near 1950 N. Larrabee Street."

❖❖❖

Centurion quickly dresses and begins the arduous process of applying his armor. He's overtaken by another fit of coughing and gets winded. He asks Holly to tighten a couple of straps to help him along.

"Look," she says, "I can go with you. Just let me call my producer and tell him I'm taking today off."

"No," he says, wrapping the straps of his sandals about his calves. "This is something I need to do alone. Anyway, I'm sure you've got more important stories to write."

She's stoic as she tells him she understands. She asks him to hold on. She runs to her medicine cabinet, grabs some cough medicine and Dayquil. She drops it into a plastic grocery bag. "Here," she says, returning and handing him the medication. "The Robitussin will help with your cough. Take it every four hours."

He nods.

"So how can I get a hold of you if I need to find you?"

He shrugs. "Why would you need to find me?"

"What if the location of the person or object tracked by that drive changes?"

He cups his chin with one hand, his thumb and index finger spread across his cheeks. "I hadn't thought of that."

"How about this?" Holly says. "I'll loan you my personal phone. That way, should you need to reach me, you can call the number on my card, and I can reach you too."

"I couldn't—"

"But I insist," she says, handing him the cell phone and her card.

He agrees and says he'll call her if he needs her.

She watches him go, shuts the door behind him. She returns to the couch, sits Indian-style. She takes a sip of coffee, examines the map on her laptop.

There's a knock at the door.

"Weird," she says. She jogs to the door. "Who's there?"

"It's Centurion, Ms. Rodriguez."

She opens the door. "Holly," she corrects. "What's up,"—then, just to be mischievous, she adds—"Larry?"

"I think the Chariot was towed."

"What Chariot?"

"My car," he says.

She shakes her head. "I'll give you a ride to the auto pound."

"Thank you," he grumbles.

"Let me grab my keys." She goes to find her purse.

"Ms. Rodriguez," he calls from the doorway.

"Yes?" her reply comes from somewhere in the condo.

"Do you think I could borrow some cash to get the Chariot out?"

She snickers. "Sure."

"And I might need some gas money too?"

Thirty minutes into the ride, they still haven't said a word to each other.

"Mind if I turn on the radio," Holly says.

"No," Centurion says. His intonation is flat, almost robotic.

She clicks on the radio. Britney sings about being a slave. She changes the stations until she finds the news. Tom Kensington is delivering the weather.

*. . . We expect the rain to continue today with the possibility of thunderstorms this evening. Temperatures will climb to about 84 degrees before tempering off to about 60 degrees overnight. Tomorrow, we'll wake to 70 degrees, the low. It promises to be warm and muggy. We could hit a high of 90 degrees and 100 percent humidity. The weekend looks better though. Saturday should be cooler with clear skies, lows in the mid-sixties and a high of about 80. Chicago should see more seasonal temperatures on Sunday as a high pressure system makes its way into the City. We'll have gusts from the northwest of up to 36 miles per hour and a high closer to 72. Monday . . .*

"Sounds like it will be a beautiful weekend," Holly says.

Centurion hisses. "Weathermen are just Pseudologoi," he says.

She looks at him blankly.

"Demons," he explains, "spreading lies and deceit."

"That's a little harsh."

"Hardly. They manipulate data to their own ends. They use the extended weather forecast to influence our thoughts, our moods."

"What?" Her smirk is full of condescension.

He continues. He says that during winter months, the fifth day of a five-day forecast is, on average, predicted to be 7.5 degrees warmer than the actual temperature. "When we look at that fifth day of the forecast, we say to ourselves, 'Thank goodness it's finally going to be nice.' But that nice day never comes, at least not as predicted. Meteorologists adjust their predictions downward over the remaining four days. By doing so, they play to our cognitive biases and adjust our expectations without us ever really knowing it." In other words: miraculous weather is never more than five days away, but it's also always just five days away.

"Wow, aren't you a ray of sunshine."

Centurion huffs. "Looks like you're a weatherman now too."

"What happened to that guy who bought me goat cheese phyllo at Mirage, that guy who liked creating integrated camp activities for kids with special needs?" she says, referring to Centurion's time at the Y. Their mission was unique compared to other day programs: provide free activities integrating the skills and disabilities of all campers. Simply, that meant making sure everyone stayed involved, emotional, mental, or physical hardships be damned. "I liked that guy."

Centurion eyeballs her. "Do you remember me telling you about a kid named Jacob?"

She thinks for a moment before her head moves side to side. "No."

"Jacob had SBS."

"I'll bite. What's SBS?"

"Shaken baby syndrome. He was born colicky. Milk allergies. His birth mother couldn't take the crying. One night, she took to shaking him violently, like a dog with a stuffed toy. His brain bounced about his skull. It swelled. Fluid accumulated. His retinas hemorrhaged."

"Oh my God," she says. "That's horrible."

Centurion ignores her and continues. He tells her how Jacob suffered blindness and cerebral palsy. He was confined to a wheel chair. He couldn't speak. "He was a shell of a boy, just a shock of blond hair and orifices, intake and output valves . . . or so people thought."

"I remember you mentioning him now," she says. Centurion spent summers designing programs for disabled children, redesigning games like baseball for them to play. If a kid couldn't use his legs, Centurion would push his wheelchair around the bases. If she couldn't see, he put the ball in her hand and asked her to throw it towards his voice. There were a dozen children like this, but Jacob was his special project.

Jacob couldn't talk, but he had a gift. He had the uncanny ability to imitate sounds. Within two weeks of their meeting, Jacob and Centurion had developed a secret language. Two whistles? I'm hungry. Three clicks? Change my diaper. A hoot and a click? Rub my head. Jacob's foster parents were astonished. Centurion promised them he would teach them all Morse Code.

"Do you know what happened to him?" Centurion asks.

"No," she says.

"I don't either. Know why?" He doesn't wait for an answer. "I got fired because some reporter wrote an article about me, and I never saw that kid again. For a 'guy you liked,' you really worked me over. I'd hate to be on your shit list."

His words strike deep. She inhales and lets out a shaky breath. She readjusts her grip on the steering wheel, keeps looking dead ahead.

They drive the rest of the way in silence.

An hour later, they're at 103$^{rd}$ and Doty. She feels like a mother dropping her kid off at school. "Here's two-hundred," she says, counting off ten twenty-dollar bills. "Why don't I wait here to make sure everything goes okay."

"No," he says, "I should be fine."

"Goodbye," she says as he closes the door behind him.

There are no offices at the auto pound. Rather, the lot is served by a series of enclosed trailers. He enters the trailer marked "cashier."

Holly pulls off to the side and waits for him anyway.

Two minutes later, her Blackberry rings. "Hello?"

"Hi, it's Centurion."

"Hi, I know" she says smiling. "Everything okay?"

"Well, they say someone with insurance has to drive the Chariot off the lot."

"You're not insured?"

Silence.

"I'll be right there." She hops from her car and joins him in trailer.

Centurion hands her the keys, explains the trick about adjusting the driver's seat. "It sits back pretty far. That's intentional. Don't pull it forward. There are two car batteries daisy chained under the seat. You don't want to complete the circuit."

"You're car is booby trapped with an electric chair?"

His model is built on the *parrilla*, a favorite device used in interrogations by both oppressive governments and cartels in South America. Instead of hooking the battery cables to a metal bed frame, however, the exposed metal springs in the seat serve as a conduit. The device won't kill, generally, but it will deliver one hell of a jolt. "Yes," he says, "assuming there's still some juice left in the batteries."

"Well, that is honestly something this reporter has never heard before." With a quick shake of her head and a jingle of the keys, she's off to find the Caravan.

She passes a heavyset guy in dirty jeans watching a black and white television sitting on an old TV tray. She assumes he's security. She walks a gravel road thick with weeds deep into the pound. The newer cars—the cars most likely to be retrieved—are the most proximate to the trailer. She's beyond them after few minutes of strolling. The condition of the vehicles gets worse as she moves further into the yard: broken windshields, flattened tires, but probably still drivable. Further still, the cars can only be described as scrap: missing tires, absent doors, incomplete engines. There's a small tree growing through the rusted tan hood of a Ford Escort. She considers turning around, assumes she missed the Chariot, then spots it two cars ahead.

The side panel is held together with painted duck tape and rust. She unlocks the driver's door. It moans like a ghost as she swings it open. She climbs in, bounces once on the seat. Dust rises in clouds. She sneezes twice. "Ouch." A seat spring pokes at her thigh, and she adjusts her buttocks. She scoots to the very edge of the chair, mindful of Centurion's warning and battling the impulse to slide the seat forward.

She surveys the interior. It looks like a frat house, beer cans and garbage strewn about. There's a box of cassettes on the passenger seat. Panic Attack's *French Licks* is on the top. It features a bunch of punks/new wave kids wearing powdered wigs on the cover. One of them is holding a ceramic bust over his head, maybe of Beethoven. Maybe it's Louis XIV. She can't tell. She picks it up, turns it over. There's a playlist, songs like *Naked Part*, *SSEX*, and *Privates*, and a photo of the bust exploding on a black and white checkered floor. The tape case is a little too sticky for her liking, and she tosses it back into the box with a grimace.

The cassette lands on top of a VHS tape. It's in a black sleeve labeled, "Security Video, August 6th." She grabs it, drops it in her purse.

She turns the ignition, and, shockingly, the car starts. "Hot damn," she says. She backs it up slowly and grunts as she muscles the shifter into drive. The shocks are as bad as the road, and she bounces all the way back to the gates, her foot occasionally losing contact with the gas pedal. The security guard doesn't get up. He gives her a thumbs-up as she leaves. She meets Centurion in the parking lot and hands over his Caravan. "Goodbye again," she says, extending a hand.

"Yes," he says, allowing a rare grin. "Goodbye again." He shakes her hand.

"Friends?" she asks.

Hating someone takes effort, too much work. Still, he's unsure if he can let it all go. She's inflicted too much damage. "I don't know," he says. He starts to get into the car.

"It would be nice if we could see each other again. Maybe grab some dinner and catch up?"

Centurion grunts, his eyes avoiding hers. "Thanks again. I better be off." He hops into the idling Chariot. He shuts the door, gives her a half-salute-half-wave, and takes off towards I-94.

She waves with her right hand as he goes, the fingers on her left drumming on the VHS tape through the leather skin of her purse.

❖❖❖

The first thing Holly Rodriguez does when she arrives at her office is order her assistant Julie to take the tape to Roland down in Editing. She attaches a Post-It. It says, "Roland, Confidential. For Your Eyes Only. Call me, only me, once you've reviewed."

Her second instruction to her assistant: "Tell Roger I lost my cell phone. I've got information on it I need for a story. Ask him to provide GPS coordinates."

"He can do that?"

"Yes," Holly replies, "triangulation. The tech nerds can do about anything."

Julie nods, impressed.

"Now," Holly says, shooing her away, "and shut the door behind you."

Half an hour later, Julie knocks. She says Roger found her phone. "It's somewhere near Burling and Armitage."

*Not 1950 N. Larrabee?* "What's over there?"

"The Marquis Lounge is over there," Julie says. "They've got specials on imports on Thursdays. Beaumont's is across the street. They've got a great DJ on Fridays."

"Julie," Holly says with a sigh, "I'm not interested in hearing your poor man's version of *Sex in the City*. What's over there that isn't a bar or club?"

Julie apologizes. "Lincoln Park High School is over there. So is Oz Park."

"Okay, ask Roger to keep an eye on it for me. Let me know if anything changes." Holly offers a fake smile.

Julie nods.

"That means you can go. Now."

"Oh, yes." Julie scampers out of the office.

"And shut the door, Julie," Holly calls.

Julie runs back and complies. "Sorry," she says through the narrowing gap as she draws the door shut.

*Lincoln Park High School?* Rodriguez rubs her temple. She spins in her chair, looks out her office window, north across the City of Chicago. "I know where you are, Larry. I know where you're going," she says, plugging the bullet-shaped flash drive into her computer. "I just don't know why. But I'm going to find out."

# Track Seventeen: Confusion

*Outside Lincoln Park High School.*

Centurion parks the Chariot in the high school's parking lot. His best chance is to intercept Chee between here and her home.

The afternoon bell rings. Classes are released for the day. Centurion watches the kids exit the building. They buzz excitedly, a stirred swarm of bees. He struggles to find the faces of Chee and her friends in the crowd. "Where are you?" he says to himself, leaning over his steering wheel for a better vantage point. The throng starts to thin. Soon, only stragglers are exiting the building, their arms full of books. "Shazam." He starts the car intent on driving to Chee's home, Plan B. As he puts the car into drive, he sees her.

Rather, Astrid sees him . . . and she makes a beeline towards his position.

He considers driving away. Instead he turns off the ignition and waits.

She crosses the parking lot with intent, a great shining auric egg of gold before her.

He starts to roll down his window, but she doesn't approach the driver's side door. Instead, she goes straight to the passenger side. Once there, she stands, waiting, just the top of her head visible in the window.

Centurion isn't sure what to do. He fumbles with the box of cassettes, tossing it over the passenger seat. He tries to quickly tidy-up the cabin, wiping the dashboard with his sleeve, sweeping crumbs from the chair.

She knocks.

"One moment," he says, pushing empty cans under the seat. He takes a moment, regards his work. *Totally ineffective.* He leans over, unlocks the door, and pulls the handle. It pops open.

She swings the door fully open on its hinge. She eyeballs Centurion up and down. He shirks from her gaze. He's not comfortable being studied. Then she jumps in.

"I'm looking for your friend," Centurion says, turning towards her, his hands planted on the steering wheel.

"Yeah?" she replies. "So am I. I'm Astrid."

"Hi," he says.

She's asks for his name.

"Larry," he says. "Larry Schultz. But some people call me Centurion."

"Cool," she says with a nod. She doesn't immediately ask him why he's dressed like a character from Frank Miller's *300*. There are pamphlets on the floor. Astrid pushes them aside with the toe of her shoe, clearing a spot for her feet. "You're looking for Chee, aren't you?"

"Yes," Centurion says. "How did you know?"

"Her picture is on all of these fliers," she says looking down.

"Oh," he says with a quick shake of the head. His expression changes, his eyes squinting with uncertainty. "Well, if you just found out that I'm looking for her, how did you know to approach me?"

"Let's call it a vibe," she says. She's referring to vibrations, the feeling one gets when sensing another's aura. However Astrid isn't just sensing Centurion's energy field, she *seeing* it and all of its very telling components. Up close like this, she can see the individual layers of Centurion's aura, each "hoop" corresponding to a chakra.

Centurion's white armor is bathed in a sky blue light, his second body. It's like an electric mist that clings to him. A layer of brilliant orange emanates from his aetheric aura like sunshine. He's strong, but the band dips near Centurion's chest and along his throat. It's thinner and more burnt in color there than anywhere else. *Inflammation*, she thinks. *He's sick.*

His hacking cough proves out her assumption. "Sorry," he says, wiping his mouth on a sleeve.

It's the third layer, shimmering and gold that catches and holds Astrid's attention now as it did across the parking lot. The glow literally fills the cabin, shimmering beyond the remaining energy bands. This is the layer that tells her what kind of person Centurion is. This is the layer that tells her he's a protector imbued with purpose, guided by a higher good. His inner light means safety.

"So what do you want from Chee?" she asks.

"Justice," he says, although she can tell he's thinking, *revenge.*

"Justice for what?"

"Killing my friend, my sidekick, Henry." Centurion describes how he's followed Chee from Tampa. He says she's responsible for at least two deaths. "Probably more based on my research."

"My friend Kim said the same thing," Astrid says, shaking her head, "and now she's missing."

"What?" Centurion's incredulous. "When?"

"Two nights ago. She was abducted somewhere between my house and hers." Her eyes remain downcast. "I should have never let her go home that night."

"Did she leave with Chee?" he asks.

"No, Chee stayed the night. Wait, how did you know that Chee was with us?"

"I didn't," he says nervously. "Like you said, it was just a hunch. A vibe."

She can tell he's lying. An image flashes bright and momentary in her mind's eye, an image of a costumed man outside her bedroom window. She crosses her arms. "Uh huh," she says.

The pieces of the puzzle are coming together in Centurion's mind. They're beginning to form a picture. "What did Chee have to say about Kim's disappearance?"

"Nothing," Astrid says.

"Nothing?"

"No, I heard her dad pulled her out school during first period, right before the police came to talk to me." She closes her eyes. "I went to Chee's house last night to talk to her about it, but she and her dad weren't there."

"She lives at 1950 N. Larrabee, doesn't she?"

"Yes, she does. How did you know that? A vibe again?" she says raising an eyebrow.

"No," he says, starting the car. "I got that from her accomplice."

Astrid's face goes white. "Her accomplice?"

"Yes," Centurion says, "the guy who kidnapped Kim."

"Is she okay? Is she alive?" She is struck by the sudden visualization of a Centurion beaten in an alley. A bandaged man stands over him. *I've made them slaves.*

"I think so," Centurion says, "but we need to find her. To do that, we need to first find Chee. I'm going to her home to get some answers."

"Can I go with you?" she asks.

His utterance is guttural and completely noncommittal.

She takes it as a yes. "I promise I'll follow your lead and stay out of your way."

"Fine," he says,

"You won't hurt Chee, will you?" she asks.

He says that he doesn't think so. His role is not to punish. He only seeks to bring her to justice.

"Okay, good," she says. Privately, however, she's not sure she can keep the same promise. If Chee's harmed a hair, be it human or animal, on Kim's hide, she will have Hell to pay.

They drive to Chee's, Centurion confirming the address with Astrid before stopping a few doors short of the home. He parks the car across the street, just beyond the glow of a street lamp.

"What are we going to do? What's the plan?" Astrid asks.

"Stakeout," Centurion says. He reaches behind his chair and grabs a bag of Tostitos with a crunch. He rolls it open, takes out a handful. He shoves them into his mouth. Chip bits crumble and fall into his lap. He notices Astrid staring at him and tilts the bag to her. He grunts something, his mouth full.

"No thanks," she says quickly. "I don't think they're home."

He nods. He washes down the stale chips with a swig of cough medicine. "That's okay," he says, "We'll wait." He crunches down on another fistful of chips. He digs into his pocket and pulls out a cell phone. "You might want to call your parents and tell them you're spending the night at a friend's. This could take time."

❖❖❖

*The lab.*

Kim's eyelids flicker. Her eyes open for the briefest moment and then close.

*White.*

They open again, her eyeballs rolling.

She strains to register her surroundings. *White on white shapes. Vertical mostly, some horizontal.*

She doesn't know where she is. She doesn't know when it is. All she knows is that forms are crystallizing, coming into focus.

*Counters.* Steel counters with acrylic polymer tops.

Blink.

*A man in a lab coat.* He's sitting on a stool. He pushes wisps of long light blonde hair from his forehead as he leans over a microscope.

Blink.

Using tweezers, the man tugs at something red and fibrous in a small specimen jar. A bit comes loose. He deposits it on a glass slide.

The man turns to his left, away from the slide. He picks up a tube of some sort.

Blink.

It's a vial. He rolls it between his hands and removes the cap. He wipes the bottle with an alcoholic pad. He picks up a syringe. He removes the needle cap. The man pulls back on the plunger dragging air into the chamber. He slides the needle into the rubber center on the top of the vial. He forces air into the bottle. He turns the bottle upside down, holding the neck between his index and middle fingers and supporting the syringe with his thumb and ring finger. He draws back the plunger. The barrel fills. The liquid is lime green but transparent. He sets the vial down. With the needle still pointing up, he forces air out of the chamber.

Blink.

She feels sick. She tries to mouth a word, but her jaw, tongue, and cheeks plot to contain it. Heavy with fatigue, she can only think it. *Astrid.* She offers it up to the universe, hoping it will float in the aether and eventually find her friend's ears.

The thought, however, never leaves the room. The facility is masked, hidden by an electromagnetic field. The field is generated by a giant solenoidal coil, a giant spring wrapped in a Kevlar vest. It circles and buzzes around an iron rod six inches in diameter, generating fifty teslas at its peak. Mighty electric pulses flash through the solenoid, guarding the building from prying psyches. The builders have effectively protected the lab from invasive second sight and the damage that can be wrought by aggressive pyschokinesis.

Blink.

He directs the needle towards the slide and depresses the plunger. Liquid hops out and onto the slide. He puts the slide on the microscope's stage, using clips to hold it in place. He clicks on the microscope's light. He puts an eye to the eyepiece. He focuses first with the coarse adjustment knob and then sharpens the image with a smaller knob.

"Fascinating," he says.

He blurs.

Blink.

Her eyes go to the vial again. *EpiGenie.* A pharmaceutical company produces it.

The vial distorts. She refocuses. *Davis Pharmaceuticals.*

Her gaze shifts, drifts across the room and over her body. She's prone and dressed in a white medical gown. Her left arm is at her side. A piece of gauze is taped over her bicep. In the middle, a stain of dark red emanates and lightens in bands, like the rings of a tree.

She struggles to lift her head, move her arm. The attempts sap her energy.

Her eyelids flutter and close again.

This time, they do not reopen.

# Track Eighteen: Red Headed Stranger

*John T. Floore's Country Store, Helotes, Texas. 14 June 1978.*

Hélène orders a Dos Equis Lager. She has to ask twice. The bartender, a sinewy and bearded coot, is either ignoring her or is hard of hearing. Maybe both.

He serves her with a sneer. He'd rather not wait on her type, but he must. There are laws that protect minorities now, and he doesn't have any choice in the matter. Besides, despite the concert hall being full, no one has ordered a drink in the last half-hour. The crowd's been spellbound by Dirk Jennings since he took the stage.

For some reason, this colored girl isn't bewitched by the siren song like everyone else.

She slides him a five, tells him to keep the change.

"What?" he says.

She points at the money, points at him.

He nods, scoops it up, and returns to his natural state: old and ornery.

Despite the name, Floore's isn't really a store as much as it is a concert hall. The Store is synonymous with honky-tonk. It's the "birthplace" of Willie Nelson. The stages have hosted the likes of Patsy Cline, Elvis, and Jerry Lee Lewis. Now, a new crop of country western singers is coming up, and Jennings is their biggest ticket seller to date.

Yet, even on the hottest of days, Jennings' shows don't move beer. It's weird. Beer and liquor sales usually triple ticket receipts. The owners figured this aberration out about a year ago, and now they compensate by simply increasing the price of admittance by ten dollars. It's an expensive ticket for the area, but fans still come in droves.

Hélène runs the dripping bottle across her forehead. Curly red hairs stick to it. They straighten as she pulls the green bottle away from her face and fall flat against her forehead. She takes a swig.

Her eyes close as she savors the taste. The edges of her mouth hint at a smile. *I hope they have beer in South Africa.* Returning to the land of her ancestors makes her anxious, but she has no choice in the matter. Her employer needs her. They always do. Quelling rebellions for friends of state is a full-time job (and more).

Jennings will play two more songs. There will be applause and whistles. Then he'll do another three, his hits, as part of the encore. After that, the twenty-year-old will retire to his tour bus. On a typical night, he'll pick two or three women to take back with him. Sometimes he picks sisters or a mother and her daughter. He'll whisper into their ears, and they'll willingly do as he commands.

The women will do whatever he asks. They'll satisfy every one of his bizarre sexual proclivities. They'll do it without wondering why. That is, until the next morning. When they wake, and he's gone, they won't be able to look at each other. They'll feel ashamed of what they've done. They'll gather their clothes, cry, nurse their wounds, and try to get on with their lives. They'll try to keep it buried, but it is inevitable that families will be destroyed. People might even die.

It all stops tonight.

The concert finishes. A bodyguard clears a path through the fans to the bus. Jennings follows, a fourteen-year-old under each of his arms. Fans stretch to touch him. They cry and shake when he passes. He ignores them.

That is, all except one: a black woman, the only black woman, in this joint. Her back's against the rail, her elbows on the bar. She barely reacts to his presence. She just smiles gently, nods slightly.

He stops, cuts through the throngs to be next to her. He releases the young girls. He must have her, and he tells her as much. He whispers something into her ear, then says, "Come with me."

She obliges. She follows him to his bus. They enter and close the door.

❖❖❖

The police respond to a 911 call from Jennings' manager the next morning. Detective Schumer arrives about an hour after the crime scene has been cordoned off.

"What do we have here?" he asks one of the troopers as he takes a deep sip of coffee.

"A bloody mess," the cop answers.

"Murders usually involve blood," Schumer says. "Can you tell me anything more?"

"No. Only you better see for yourself, and you better have a strong stomach."

Schumer enters the bus, steps into the cabin. At first, he doesn't notice anything amiss. Then he feels something under his shoe. He takes a quick step back. It is round and diced like sushi. A little pool of congealed blood surrounds it.

"What the . . . ?"

He steps into the next room. The horror inside makes him spin and flee from the bus. He retches at the door and pukes. Coffee comes out his nose. The troopers laugh.

After he's collected himself, a trooper named Wilson tells him that they may have identified a witness, someone who saw the suspect with Jennings.

"Well, why didn't you say so earlier?" Schumer says, wiping his lip.

"Because he just showed up for his shift. His name is Clive Hamm. He was working the bar last night."

"What's his story?"

"Other than being old as time?" Wilson asks. "He's hard of hearing. That's for certain. I haven't been able to get much out of him."

Wilson leads Schumer to the old man. He's sitting at a picnic table, troopers on either side of him.

"What can you tell me about last night, Mr. Hamm?"

"What?"

Schumer repeats himself.

"Sit down so I can see your face," Clive Hamm says.

Schumer takes a seat directly across from Hamm, his face illuminated by the sun. "Tell me about last night," he says for a third time.

The codger leans in and stares. "It was a bad night for tips," he says.

The officer to Hamm's right chuckles. Schumer shakes his head. "Dirk Jennings was murdered last night."

"That's what they told me," Hamm says, his jaw working. "Probably that colored girl that had sex with him."

"What?" Schumer says.

"What?" Hamm says, his furry eyebrows bouncing as he leans forward.

"You saw Jennings having relations with the suspect?" Schumer asks.

"Hell, no," Clive says, shaking his head, "I'm no degenerate."

"Then how did you know he had sex last night?"

"I saw that Jennings boy whisper in her ear."

"Did you hear what he said?" Schumer asks. He immediately questions the wisdom of this inquiry. "Of course you didn't," he mumbles, "because you're as deaf as a post."

A moment passes. Then Hamm says, "I've never tasted chocolate before."

"Huh?"

"'I've never tasted chocolate before,'" Hamm says again. "That's what I saw him whisper."

*Saw?* Then it hits Schumer. Hamm is basically deaf. He reads lips. He's registering every movement of Schumer's face, the contact between his upper teeth and bottom lip, the twists of his tongue, everything.

"I maybe deaf," Hamm continues, "but I'm still sturdy."

"I need you to describe the suspect. Describe the woman who cut off Jennings' dick, diced it up like a tuna roll, and fed it to him until he choked."

Clive Hamm muses for a moment. "She was a lady. She was colored. Her hair was red."

Schumer flips open a notepad. "Give me more details."

The bartender struggles to come up with more. "She was black."

"What else?" Schumer asks.

Hamm says something about not noticing anything else, about "them all looking the same." "Ain't knowing she was black with red hair enough in the great state of Texas?"

Schumer sighs and flips his notebook closed. "Fuck me. Wilson, please escort Mr. Hamm from the crime scene." Once Schumer is sure Hamm's back is to him, he adds, "Go back to the Civil War, you relic."

# Track Nineteen: Don't Change

*The lab. 7 September 2001.*

Kim wakes to light flashing in her eyes.

A man pulls a pen light away from her face. "Good, you're with us. Wakey wakey eggs and bakey."

The muscles in her irises contract, her pupils shrinking. She takes in her surroundings.

The ceiling is about twenty-five feet high or more. There are eight walls, four of them of floor-to-ceiling glass. They provide a view into the stacked halls beyond. Two men stare at her from a console behind a window on the second floor of the nearest wall.

She tries to move, can't. Her hands and legs are strapped to a reclined medical chair. *What type of James Bond shit is this?* "Where am I?"

"You're in a retrovirology lab," a man in a lab coat says. He pushes strands of thin blonde hair from his forehead. "One of the best tax dollars can buy."

"And who are you? Doctor No?"

"No," he says, smiling, "I'm Doctor Kane. Not that it matters, really. In the scheme of things, I'm nothing more than an instrument to study you. What really matters is who you are, what you are."

She imagines her arms lengthening, growing long and apelike, her shoulders hunching like a bear. She pictures her face stretching, becoming flat and reptilian. But she doesn't change. She cannot. "What?"

"No need for the hocus pocus here, Ms. Monfort. We're all friends. Plus, I've given you a gene expression inhibitor, basically silencing your cellular conversion. Granted, this drug is in what Davis Pharmaceuticals would call the "test" phase. It works great stabilizing microtubules in mice. Seeing as you're our very own lab rat, it seemed a logical leap. So no more epigenetic magic . . . for now."

Kim retches. She twists her head and pukes.

"Of course, there are side effects, like mild nausea. Sorry." He jots something quickly in a notebook before wiping the edge of her mouth with a towel.

She tries to raise her head upwards, can't. Her head is strapped to the table. Still, she manages to spit at him.

The sputum lands on his chest. He walks to a nearby table, pulls a large q-tip from a glass jar. He uses it to remove most of the spit from his scrubs. He pulls open a drawer, removes a clear plastic bag. He drops the q-tip and her spit sample into it, seals it, and marks it with Sharpie. "September 7, 2001," he looks at his watch, "12:17 PM . . . subject Kim Monfort." He says the word, "Expectorant," as he writes it on the baggie.

"Gross," Kim says. "You're keeping it?"

The man laughs. "I'm gross? Spitting is not the act of a debutante, now, is it, Ms. Monfort?"

Her upper lip curls. "How do you know my name?"

He doesn't answer her question. Instead he says, "You *are* a debutante, you know. Not in the sense that we're throwing you a cotillion, although this is a bit of a coming out for you. This is your 'debut' to medical society if you will."

"What are you talking about?" She pulls against her arm restraints.

"We've been trying to obtain a specimen like you for decades. We've come close, so close, to capturing chimeras before, but we've never been able to study a live sample."

Kim gulps and winces. Her throat's sore. "There are other people like me?"

"Probably more than any of us know. Have you ever heard of the *Loup Garou*?"

"No."

"The term is French, like you. You might be more familiar with the term werewolf?" There were many legends about the Loup Garou, he says, stories about people turning into wolves by the light of the full moon, seventh sons of a seventh son, conjoined eyebrows, and the like. "Except for the commonality of lycanthropy, none of it's true. Well, that, and silver bullets. A well-placed bullet, be it silver, gold, whatever, will pretty much kill any living organism."

Kim pulls against the leather around her wrists, testing the strength of the buckles.

Doctor Kane says, "Peasants in Europe thought those bitten would change into werewolves during a full moon. The reality is that wolves are disproportionately witnessed when the moon is full because there otherwise isn't enough light. Funny how these legends take on a life of their own."

"What does this have to do with me?"

"Everything. Let me show you something," he says. He walks over to a file cabinet, opens it, and starts flipping through files. "E, F, G, Ga, Ge, ah, Gévaudan." He pulls a yellowish folder from the drawer that's about an inch thick. He hurries to Kim's side, and sets the file on her belly. He flips it open, fingers his way through the pages. "Here we go," he says, pulling out a photocopy of an etching. "It's my pleasure to introduce you to your great, great, great, great, great grandfather. Give or take a great. At least that's what the DNA says."

She struggles to view the document beyond the curve of her chest. "DNA?"

"Yes, we've amassed tons of it, pieces of everyone from Houdini to Siegmund Breitbart. People with, or are rumored to have, exceptional abilities, powers. But we're not here to talk about them. We're here to talk about this guy." He holds the page closer to her face.

Kim is staring at a monster, a beast about the size of a horse. There's definitely wolf in it, especially about the snout, maw, and ears, but there are other animals too. She detects hints of bear and panther, the latter in the thick tail. "What is it?"

"Don't see the resemblance?" He jerks the page away, seeks another from the file. "How about now?" he says, dangling another sheet inches from her face.

This, too, is a copy of an etching, but this beast looks very different than the first. It is more hyena-like, and the creature's paws resemble the talons of an eagle. The snout is that of a pig.

He reclines, holds both pages in from of him at arms length. He regards each in turn. "They don't look the same, do they?" Kane says. "Rest assured, they're the very same creature. The Beast of Gévaudan, the terror of France in the mid-1700s." He collates the sheets and drops them back into the file.

"I don't understand," she says.

He puts a finger to his lip in contemplation. "Wait, I think I've got another image that will help you understand." He flicks through the file until he comes across another image. "This might be the best of them." He presents it to her, resting the edge on her sternum.

This engraving is not of a monster at all. It is a human, a man with broad features, a rounded nose, and a circular jaw . . . like hers. His fore-head is high and his hair long. His ears sit low on his head. He's dressed in a buttoned shirt and a cloak. The only peculiarity is his hands. His arms don't end in palms and fingers. Instead, thick padded paws with long claws extend from his sleeves.

"This one," Kane says, "was harder for our researchers to come by. It's rare, reproduced from a wanted poster circulated by the King's Lieu-tenant of the Hunt. This is probably the only etching depicting Alec Moreau in mid-transition. It was the distribution of these posters that led to his eventual execution, but not before he had killed and injured hundreds."

Despite being rough, she would have recognized this man as being a relative without Kane saying a word. Her eyes glaze over. Her cheek involuntarily twitches. She's on overload.

Kane gauges her reaction. "I should start from the beginning." He does.

Werewolves, or lycanthropes, were a common element in mythol-ogy and folklore. Ancient Greeks and Romans from Herodotus and Ovid to Virgil and Gaius Petronius Arbiter wrote about shapeshifting wolves and the wolf-king of Lycaeon. Those stories were adopted and exported by the Roman Empire. The myths evolved across Europe.

In Bulgaria, werewolves were called *vrkolak*. In Iceland, they were called *varulfur*; in Latvia, *vilkacis*; in Serbia, *wurdalak*; in Slovakia, *vlkodlak*. All were based on the Greek word *vrykolaka*. But it was in the lands of the German- ("werwolf") and French-speaking ("loup garou") peoples where the creatures became associated with sorcery, the undead, and often Satan.

Pagans, like the Viking berserkers of Scandinavia and the Saxons, were vilified as werewolves. Werewolf hunting became synonymous with witch-hunts, and the accusation and persecution of suspected werewolves tracked with the rise of Christianity.

The Beast of Gévaudan was, perhaps, the most famous "loup garou" because of its undeniable death toll. It was more than just a legend used to scare kids into making their beds. Cryptozoologists agree that the monster existed, but they bicker about the creature's origins (and whether there was actually more than one monster) in part because of the variety of descriptions. This led some to conclude it was an escaped hyena. Others said it was probably a trained lion. Others still claimed the Beast was an evolutionary throwback reminiscent of Paleocene predator like a mesonychid.

All of them were wrong.

Werewolf stories didn't begin with the Beast or end with its death. In France, there had been earlier instances, like the Gilles Garnier killings in 1572, the trial of the witch Claudia Gaillard (the Wolf of Burgundy) in 1590, the conviction of Jean Grenier in 1603, and the wolf attacks in 1693 at Benais. From 1809 to 1813 and 1875 to 1879 there were additional murders in Vivarai and L'Indre, respectively. In fact, there were reports of attacks in France through the 1950s.

Eventually, the creatures arrived in the New World with colonialism. They arrived in the form of Jean Moreau, Alec Moreau's son, kidnapped along with his mother and thousands of families by the French government to settle the Americas.

"It's a legend in New France," Kane says. The journey from France to Nova Scotia was seven-weeks of horror for the indentured colonists. They endured dysentery, boils, scurvy, measles, small pox, and lice so thick they could be scraped off with a knife. They were thirsty. They were desperately hungry. When they did eat, seasickness often laid claim to their meager meals of salted meat.

Gales raged for days on end, and the storms conspired with the conditions to take their toll. The dead were thrown into the sea by the dozens. Mothers who succumbed before their children were buried at sea with their living children.

Moreau's wife died at sea, or so the story goes, just three days from port. Her son, Jean, turned into a wolf as the ship's hands seized him.

After a vicious struggle, the beast was thrown overboard with his mother. The boy clung to her body for several days, bobbing and pulling her as he swam, defending her with his claws from the monsters of the deep.

Not all of the settlers believed the boy/creature died at sea. Rumors spread that Jean Moreau had made it to shore and buried his mother. He lived alone in the wild for many years, eventually changing his surname to Monfort and reentering society.

Stories of the loup-garou spread quickly amongst the pioneers and mixed with native folklore. The First Nations tribes like the Mi'kmaq, Abenaki, and Ojibwa called the monster the "rugaru," and stories spread from Quebec to Michigan and then Wisconsin as the Franco-Indian alliance expanded its domain.

"Oddly enough," Kane says, "reports of the loup garou never died out. There are still reports of the loup garou just forty-five minutes north of here along the Wisconsin border. The Beast of Bray Road and what not."

*Wisconsin?*

"Your father lives in Wisconsin? Near Elkhorn?"

*Dad?* "I don't know," Kim says. "I haven't seen that deadbeat in years. Why don't you tell me?"

Kane eyes her a moment. He's trying to read her. Failing, he continues. "But other than their immigration to the U.S., the werewolf remains mostly a European phenomenon. I have a theory about that," Kane says. "Care to hear it?"

Kim doesn't answer.

Kane takes her silence as acquiescence. "I think shapeshifters are limited by their own knowledge and imagination." He scoots his stool closer to her medical chair and bends near her, his face just twenty inches from hers. She can smell menthol on his breath. "For instance," he says, "there are no werewolves in South America. Why is that?"

"Because there's no such thing as werewolves?"

"Cute," Kane says. "No, it's because no one in South America is familiar with *canis lupus* or *canis rufus*. Shapeshifters from those countries don't transform into wolves because they don't have a point of reference. Instead, the therianthropes turn into animals unique to their ecology. In Chili, the *chonchon* transforms into a vulture. In Brazil, the *boto* becomes a river dolphin. In Argentina, there are *kanima*, or were-jaguars—"

*Therianthrope?*

"—and if you go outside of South America, you find the same thing on other continents. In Japan, shapeshifters generally become foxes, or *kitsune*. In China and Central Asia, there are legends of races of dog-men, or cynanthropes. In Africa, you have were-panthers, were-lions, and *boudas*, the were-hyenas—"

*There's a name for what I am. A therianthrope.*

"—bearwalkers are the predator of choice in Canada. In India, you have a variant on this metamorphic theme, the ape-like *vanara* and the *naga* snake people."

*Metamorphosis.* It's a scientific term. It's a word used in her biology class to describe physical change, like a caterpillar becoming a Monarch butterfly. It's a word associated with natural wonders and marvels, not aberrations.

He drones on. "Still, the animals need not always be man-eaters. Take for instance *selkies* and the horse-like *glashtins* and *pwca*—"

"I get it," she says crossly. "What exactly is your point?"

"Familiarity defines the parameters of your gift."

"Gift?" Kim says. *Not a "curse."*

Kane presses his hands together in front of his face like he's meditating or in prayer. He rests his chin on his index fingers. "Oh, God, yes," he says, nodding. "If I were to wake up your ribosomes with a dose of EpiGenie, your genes would be free to express themselves again, and they would do so in incredible ways."

"How?"

"The act of simply viewing a complex organism may serve as the triggering experience that allows you to modify the expression of your genetic code. I intend to prove that out," he says, his eyes pointing to the bandage covering the biopsy wound on her arm. "Maybe you'll even tell me where the rest of your pack is."

"I don't have a pack."

"We'll see if you're singing that song later. People have been known to give up all kinds of secrets when operated on without anesthesia."

"If you cut me again," Kim says, "I swear I'll tear out your throat."

"So cute," Desmond Kane says, "did I say that already?" He returns to his work, giving Kim his back. "Get some rest," he says over his shoulder. "There's nothing like the healing power of sleep, and you're going to need a lot of it."

❖❖❖

*Near 1950 N. Larrabee.*

Fourteen hours of silence later, Astrid is more than bored. "Can we talk?"

"If you want to," Centurion says, his eyes still focused on the home at 1950 N. Larrabee. She flirted with sleep through the night, but he hasn't slept a wink. His lids are heavy, his eyes puffy and dark.

"So what's your story?"

Centurion gives her a sideways glance. "Story?"

"Yes, your origin story."

"I don't have a story, origin or otherwise," he says with a huff, no longer making eye contact.

"All superheroes have an origin story. You know, the story about how they gained their superpowers and used them to fight the forces of evil." She's now sitting cross-legged in the passenger seat, her body facing him. She leans in, elbows on her knees, chin in her hands.

"I'm not really a superhero. I don't have any powers."

"I'm sure you're gifted at something," she replies.

He peels off his helmet, tosses it into the back of the Chariot. His face is square, cut deep by time. "This," he says, pointing to his square jaw, "is the face of a man. Nothing more. Nothing less. Sure, I've pretended to be more, but I'm not like you. I'm not like your friend Kim. I'm not like John Hooper. I'm not like Kid Caper. I age like a man. I tire like a man. I'm on the losing end of the stick like most other men." The bags under his blue eyes, the wrinkles carved into his face, say it all.

He lets his head drop against the headrest. "Maybe worse than other men."

"Something in your past had to trigger your desire to help people though."

"There's nothing special about my past," he says, refusing to tell her about the abuse and alcoholism that plagued his childhood. He refuses to tell her about his loneliness, about the foster homes, truancy, awkwardness, and bullying. He declines to tell her about his salvation, dime-store books about Greek and Roman heroes performing heroic deeds. Theseus, Jason, and Bellerophon were his only friends, and his adventures—hiding from Nessus in a maze of corn, battling Cerberus at the gates of the Hell/barn—were born solely from his imagination.

His energy dims. There's pain in his silence. A void builds between them. Astrid fidgets, fills it. "So, is this your car?"

"No."

"Did you borrow it?"

"No, I meant it's not a car. I own it."

"Not a car?" Astrid looks around uneasily.

"It's more than a car."

"Do tell," she says, running her hands along the Dodge Caravan's dashboard.

"It's the Chariot. It's my 'Fortress of Solitude' on wheels. More or less."

She inspects her fingers. They're covered with dust. "Less more," she says, "and more less."

He frowns.

"But that's a good thing," she adds quickly. "Most superheroes tool around in pretentious vehicles. I mean, come on, the Batmobile is a monument to heroic ego. The thing screams, 'Small penis.' This, though, flies under the radar."

"It's not heroic?" Centurion asks.

She says, "It's a family car—"

The frown again.

"—And nothing is more heroic than a commitment to family."

He stops scowling, his lips returning to their natural state, a tight, thin horizontal line.

"Centurion," she says, "this car is Spartan. Anything more wouldn't suit your moniker."

He nods, but it's a gesture meant to buy him time. Astrid didn't call him Larry. She didn't call him a freak. She called him by his handle, something no one has done in the last five years or more. He's caught by surprise. He doesn't quite know what to say.

He doesn't need to say anything. Astrid starts talking again. "What are these," she says, noticing the articles taped on the ceiling of the van. She reclines, puts her index finger on one, and starts reading.

He closes his eyes. "Shazam," he says under his breath.

The articles construct a picture of Centurion's recent past. Astrid reads a bit of newsprint next to a picture of a young boy. His name is Henry Famosa. After a few minutes, she switches to another article, one entitled, *Superhero and Boy Hero Start Justice Legion.* Then she's on to a faded bit of magazine about his legal problems.

Centurion and Henry Famosa, a.k.a. Kid Caper, formed a superhero organization. They called themselves The Justice Legion . . . at least until Centurion received a cease and desist letter. Justice Legion, apparently, was just a little too akin to an organization helmed by Batman and Superman. He shouldn't have marveled that its use brought immediate legal reprisals. Although the litigation only lasted a month, the legal fees crushed Centurion. He and his sidekick settled on calling their club of superheroes, simply, "the Superhero Club."

Thirty minutes later, she's scoured every piece of print on the Chariot's dirty ceiling. The entire time, Centurion sits quietly, awaiting her judgment. He expects the indictment to be harsh. To his surprise, no criticism comes.

When Astrid does finally break the silence, she asks an innocent question: "How did you meet your sidekick, Henry?"

He feels his throat swell. He gulps. It hurts, but not as much as his memories do. "Kid Caper . . . Henry . . . was special. I first saw him on TV, the evening news. It was the Good Samaritan story they squeeze in when they've got two free minutes of programming. Henry had provided police with information about where they could find some gang bangers. They'd stolen his neighbor's Maltese from the backyard. They intended to use it as a bait dog, basically a practice animal for their abused pitbulls. Henry knew the plate, knew where they trained dogs to fight. He even provided a description of one of the bastards. The police rushed in, saved the dog and dozens of others."

"That's amazing."

"No, what's amazing is that the Kid never witnessed any of it. It all came to him in a dream. Of course, the police didn't know that. They assumed he'd seen the whole thing go down. I assumed the same . . . until I read about the cell phone bust."

Astrid points to a clipping above. "I saw that article."

"The Kid led police to a network of cell phone thieves. He was never in the proximity of the thefts. He never saw the crimes occur. Still, he knew they were working out of the back of a Thai restaurant just by passing it. That's when I knew he was special."

"How so?"

"He had visions. He could see things that happened, things that were going to happen. Temple snakes had kissed his ears."

Astrid's head tilts. "Temple snakes?"

"Sorry," he says. "It's a reference to Cassandra. She could 'hear' the future because the snakes in Apollo's temple came to her at night and cleansed her ears with their tongues. Like her, the Kid could divine things."

Centurion describes how he drove over to Henry's house intent on talking to him about his gift. He parked a few doors down and waited for the Kid to return from school. "This kid comes home, but he doesn't go inside. Rather, he walks right up to the Chariot—just like you did today—and introduces himself. He told me he knew why I was there . . . and that he was looking forward to contributing his talents to my superhero team. The Kid knew I was getting together a superhero group before I ever did."

Centurion posted fliers looking for recruits. Soon, other heroes joined their nightly patrols. "I say, 'heroes,' but these were middle-aged guys like me. They had a penchant for masks, a flair for the dramatic, and, naturally, a desire to do some good. But they weren't 'super-abled' like the Kid. And none of them were as resolute as him. When the chips were down, when the press blamed me for the deaths of Baby Rose and her family, they cut and run. All of them." He counts off names on his fingers. "Rebel Red, Dead Lift, The Crocodilian." With each name, he drops a corresponding finger. Only his index finger remains extended. "Henry alone stuck by my side. He didn't care about what Holly Rodriguez or the other reporters said." Centurion rotates his hand, drops his index finger and extends his middle finger. He directs his hand towards the ceiling, flipping off an article taped there.

"Her name's on a couple of these pieces," Astrid says.

"The byline should just say 'Bitch,'" he snorts. "*Superhero Responsible for Deaths* . . . by Bitch. *Superhero Infringes on Trademark* . . . by Bitch."

Astrid can only muster one word. "Wow."

"I know," Centurion says, "she's a real piece of work."

"No, you write your own headlines in this life. No one writes them for you."

"Really?" He scoffs. "So what should my headline be?"

"*Superhero Feels Sorry for Self, Boo Hoo* . . . an exclusive by Centurion," she mocks.

He can't look at her. "Man, I need a beer."

"No, you need a dose of reality," she says.

"And a beer."

She sniffs. "Do you hate that reporter for doing her job? Did she hurt your feelings? Did she make you doubt yourself?"

Centurion drums his thumbs on the steering wheel. "Perhaps."

"I'm jealous of your naivety," Astrid grumbles.

"That sounds weird," he says, "coming from a kid. What I'd give to see life through your eyes."

"I'm not a kid," she says curtly.

He chuckles. "Children these days. You all want to grow up so fast. Live a little." He's lit her fuse.

"Let me ask you something: when you look at a crowd of people, what do you see?"

His lips twist. "I don't understand."

"When you see a group of people, what exactly do you see?"

Centurion shrugs. "I don't know. I see people. Strangers."

"And how do they make you feel?"

"Small, I guess, like I'm an outsider. Alone."

"Because you may never know them? Because they may never know you?"

"Maybe," he says.

"You're actually very lucky," she says. "Enigma is alluring."

"How's that?"

"There's a saying, about not asking questions you don't want answered. When you see people, you see mystery. When I look at them, I get flooded with responses to unasked questions."

He doesn't follow.

"I see people for what they really are, hidden motivations, fears, and sickness. I don't see people so much as I see, for lack of a better word, their colors."

He leans back, rubs his chin. "That's an amazing gift," he says, his left brow arching.

"No," she replies. "It's a curse."

"How?"

"The Cyclops traded his eye for prescience, didn't he? Do you remember what he got?"

Centurion does. "Just the vision of his own death."

"Exactly, and my vision is skewed too, but in a different way. When I watch people, I see the truth of them. What I see is a river of filth, mostly ugly shades of grey and brown rushing past. Occasionally I'll see someone good—someone like you—caught up in the current, but finding gems in the muck is rare."

He contemplates this, puts a finger to his lip. His forehead wrinkles, his brow lifts. He turns his hand, points at her. He gets it. "You never had a chance to be a kid, I mean, really be a kid. The world was never a safe place for you. You were never protected from the reality of life. You've always seen it, known it, for what it actually is." His eyes get wider as his realization deepens. "You're overloaded with stimuli, too much depressing information. You never experienced innocence."

She nods.

"That's your origin story," he says.

"And yours," she replies, "is Holly Rodriguez."

He turns away from Astrid, reclines. His bottom lip juts forward as he ponders this new truth. He's quiet for a full minute before he turns to her slowly. "So you know some mythology after all."

"Not really. I've just seen *Krull* about a dozen times with my dad."

"Well, close enough," he says.

They talk the better part of the afternoon, time passing more quickly.

# Track Twenty: One Step Ahead

*400 N. Michigan Avenue, Holly Rodriguez' office.*

*Knock-a-knock-knock-knock.*

Holly wakes up, looks at the clock. It's nearly 2 PM. She wipes sleep from her eyes. "Come in, Julie."

"Ms. Rodriguez?" Julie says, prying open the door a foot. "I didn't know you were here. I didn't see you come in this morning. Her stare locks on Holly's jacket before swinging up to her tangle of hair. "Wait, you're wearing the same clothes you were wearing yesterday. Have you been here all night?"

She has, but she doesn't tell Julie that. She's been watching the blip on her computer, waiting for it to move again. She asks Julie what she wants.

"Roland asked me to get you."

"Is he done with the tape?" Holly says.

Julie nods. "I think so."

Holly stands, her joints cracking. She bends from side to side, stretches her arms above her head with a groan. "What did he say?" she says, rounding the desk.

"Exactly?"

"Yes, word for word."

"He said, 'Oh, my God. I can't believe what I just saw. Get Holly. Oh, my God.'"

That's more than good enough for Holly. She says, "Hold my calls," and brushes past Julie, down the hall, and to the elevator.

Two minutes later she's in Roland Murphy's basement office. Roland is bookish and in his forties. He's generally pasty, but today his skin is whiter than usual. He looks like he's seen a ghost. She tells him as much.

"That's one way to describe it," he says.

His desk is piled high with videos and film reels. He turns his monitor towards her, and it dislodges a few VHS tapes at the front of his desk. On the screen, a dark bar intermittently scrolls through a black and white image of restaurants, a food court centered between several tables on the left and a glass elevator on the right. At the bottom of the screen, there's a clock next to a date and the words, "City Center Mall —Camera 12."

Holly stoops to gather the fallen tapes.

"Don't worry about them. What you're about to see needs your attention more than those tapes." He gestures to the chair across from him. "You're going to want to sit down for this."

"What is it, Roland?"

"Please sit."

She complies.

"I'm not so sure I can describe this. You just need to watch it for yourself." He presses play. "What you're seeing now," he says, "is footage from a security camera at City Center Mall in Indianapolis from August 6th of this year."

"Okay."

He looks at his notes. "At the 17:48:07 mark, you'll see a kid go up and buy a pretzel from the Cinnabon."

The counter in the upper left of the screen reads 17:47:12. A kid enters the frame. He's tall, somewhat gangly. His eyes seemingly glow as the fluorescent lights reflect off of his glasses. He makes his way over to the shop. There's no line. A woman almost immediately serves him. There's an exchange, presumably of money for food. The boy makes his way from the counter, and a bird swoops down from the rafters to greet him. It flies in a reverse arc. It dips and rises to land on his shoulder.

"Whoa," Holly says.

"Yes," Roland says, "the bird. Wait, this gets weirder."

The kid seemingly says something to the bird. He breaks off a piece of pretzel, feeds it to the animal. The two make their way to a table in the upper left quadrant of the frame. The bird hops to the table while he sits. The boy gestures with his hand as he talks. The bird bounces and nods its head in response.

"He's talking to a bird?"

"Uh huh," Roland says. "A sparrow I think. He talks to it for more than three hours." He turns the screen slightly so she can better see it. "I'm going to fast forward to about 9:30 PM."

The movements of the people entering and leaving the cameras field suddenly are a blur. They enter the frame, order food, sit, and leave within mere seconds. The boy and the bird, however, never leave their table. Their communications, their nods and gestures, are exaggerated. At the 21:12 mark or so, the vendors begin shuttering their food stands. They wipe down the counters in seemingly hypersonic speeds. The store lights blink off on by one. First the Pizza Hut, then Taco Bell, followed by the Cinnabon. Still, the kid doesn't move. He does, however, look at his watch over and over. There is no other movement on the screen.

"He's waiting for someone," Holly says.

"Someone . . . something . . . finds him alright," Roland replies.

"What?"

"You'll see," he says. Once the video hits 9:27 PM, Roland presses play again. The zipping speed immediately slows, and the ordinary pace of things resumes. The boy stands up, tosses one last bit of pretzel to the bird. He pets it on the head. The sparrow flies off to the rafters. He shuffles over to the elevator, eyes downcast, and presses a button. An elevator ascends in a glass tube to the food court. The doors open. The boy steps in. The doors close.

"Now," Roland says, pointing at the screen.

The boy doesn't have time to select a destination floor. His hands go immediately to his throat. He's struggling.

"What's happening?" Holly asks.

The bird swoops from left to right and out of frame.

Roland doesn't answer. His finger is still pointing at the screen. He's watched the video several times now, but his other hand unconsciously moves to cover his neck.

The boys feet are in the air, he's suspended, kicking in space. A hand spasmodically slaps the glass wall. He kicks off the door, bounces off the glass window of the elevator. Then there's a fountain, a spray that jets forth from the kid's neck, covering the ceiling of the elevator.

"My God," Holly says, her hand, too, now covering her throat.

The bird enters the frame again, on a collision course with the glass wall of the elevator. It hits the window hard, splintering it. Its lifeless body spirals out of frame.

"Oh, my God," she says again.

The teen spins mid air, almost in response, his jugular shooting blood low on the glass wall facing the camera. His arms drop, swinging and hanging loose at his sides. The spurts of blood grow steadily weaker. And then, the boy's head falls off.

"Oh, my God!" she exclaims a third time.

His head hits the floor of the elevator, landing beneath his still suspended feet. A moment later, his entire body collapses to the floor like a marionette that's strings have been cut. The elevator descends out of view.

Roland pauses the tape. He rubs his eyes with his thumb and index finger. A moment of stunned silence passes between them.

She breaks it. "Did we just witness a murder?"

He sighs. "Back in the fifties, my dad was a defense attorney. Back then, there were two tests you needed to satisfy to try someone for murder: you needed both a body and a murderer. We don't have a murderer."

"There has to be a murderer," Holly says. "People's heads just don't fall off."

"No, they don't. So I enhanced the video to see what we were missing." Roland rewinds to the point where the boy enters the elevator. The pointer on the screen bounces. A menu pops up. Roland clicks on certain check boxes, removes checks from others. He first applies illumination enhancement and modifies the local contrast so that the details in dark or bright regions are revealed.

"What are you doing now?" Holly asks.

"Histogram equalization," he says.

"What's that?"

"I'm altering the spatial histogram to match a uniform distribution. I also modified the intensity to capture some of the lower frequency grays we were losing." He presses a few keys on his computer. "Here you go."

A shadow appears in the elevator as the boy enters.

"There was someone in there with him." Holly slaps the desk.

The smack startles Roland, and he lets out a yelp.

"Sorry," she says.

He holds a hand over his heart. "We can also adjust for blur. We can apply some analytics measuring light reflection. I'll submit the programs now, but this could take hours . . . potentially days of processing time."

"Okay," Holly says. "I need to go make a call."

"Hello," Centurion answers.

"Larry, what happened in Indianapolis?"

"Hi, Ms. Rodriguez, how are you?"

"Larry, cut out the 'Ms. Rodriguez' crap. It's Holly."

Centurion blows air. "What can I help you with?"

"I need to tell you something. I stole a VHS tape from your van."

"The Chariot."

"Okay, the Chariot."

"The security footage," he says.

"Yes. You knew?" she asks, her voice rising.

He chuckles. "You're as predictable as Zeus cheating on Hera."

"I have no idea what that means."

"Zeus slept with Europa, Io, Semele, and, let's see, Callisto—"

"Okay, I get it. He was a recidivist. But we need to talk. Where are you?"

"You know where I am," Centurion says. "I have your phone. Where are you?"

"I'm in my office," she says, regarding her computer screen. The bullet drive is plugged in. A dot blinks on her screen, literally fifty feet from Centurion's position as triangulated by cell towers. "Why are you there?"

"We're waiting."

"*We're?*"

"Holly, what do you want?" he says, his words drawn out and exasperated.

She pauses, collects her thoughts. "Have you seen the video?"

"Yes."

"Was that boy murdered?"

"Yes. His name was John Hooper."

"John Hooper," she repeats, writing it down on a memo pad.

"You're probably wondering if I murdered him."

"No, I'm not," she says rather matter-of-factly.

"No? Why's that?"

"Because we were able to alter the image. We can see the murderer. It's rough, but it's definitely not you." Her swallow is audible. "Just what are you involved in here?"

Centurion comes clean. He reveals his hypothesis, that Hooper's murder and the Kid's deaths are related.

"Henry died in an accident," Holly says.

"No," Centurion says. "That's not true. The cops must have bungled that investigation like they bungled Hooper's murder."

"Bungled? How?"

He tells her. The IMPD report said the Hooper's body was discovered the next morning by a security guard, and that said guard immediately called police. "The lead investigator"—a transfer from Texas named Schumer with a notoriously weak stomach—"didn't follow protocol. No evidence was collected. No photographs of the scene were taken."

"Why?"

"Because he contaminated the scene." He brushed right through the perimeter to inspect the body before the medical examiner arrived. Cutting the jugular is messy business. Blood soaked deep into the carpet. It covered the windows, walls, and buttons of the elevator. With the mall closed for the night, the air conditioning had only just resumed working upon Schumer's arrival. The smell of death permeated the hot house of an elevator. The doors opened, and the stench hit him like a wall. He retched, looked down to find Hooper's severed head staring from the floor, his mouth frozen in a silent cry. "He projectile vomited. It covered everything." With the video so inconclusive, there really wasn't much of a chance of cracking the case after that.

"You found that in the police report?"

"No," Centurion replies. "I contacted *Clean Break*. They're the only company in Indianapolis compliant with the Federal Health and Safety Codes and Medical Waste Management Act. They've got a monopoly on disinfecting trauma scenes there. I got a copy of their bill to the City Center Mall. The itemization included blood, tissue, *and* bile removal. That got me asking questions."

"Wow," Holly says. "Have you ever thought about being an investigative reporter?"

He ignores her question. "More importantly, there was one critical piece of evidence that the detectives failed to inventory. They didn't notice the dead bird resting in the center of a bush at the base of the elevator shaft. That failure led to mistaken conclusions."

"I saw a bird on the tape. Like what?"

"The elevator pane was cracked in a circular spider web. The police chalked it up to a struggle. They posited that Hooper fought back against his assailant, forcing his killer back against the glass."

Yet they found no blood or hair, no traces of DNA, to help them justify this conclusion. They were at a loss as to why.

Centurion knows why, and he thanks Apollo for his clarity. "Hooper didn't fight back." He died too quickly. The splintered glass was not in fact the result of a blow from inside the car. Rather, it came from an *outside* strike, a diving swoop from Mr. Piccolo. The bird saw Hooper, its friend, struggling. The poor animal died in a vain attempt to save the teen. It died instantly, heroically, as it slammed against the lift, its neck broken.

"The bird tried to save him?" There's emphasis on "bird," Holly's incredulity coming across the line.

"Hooper was a superhero, a real superhero just like the Kid. He didn't dress up like one, but he had superpowers. Someone knew and killed him for it . . . just like the Kid."

Holly says she doesn't know what to think. "Kids with superpowers? Psychos that can walk through walls?"

"Hade's helm. He's not a ghost," Centurion chides. "He's just not visible."

"An invisible man?"

"Technically, I don't think he's *invisible*."

Holly tells Centurion he isn't making sense.

"I think the murderer might be masking his presence by creating mirages." In other words, Centurion explains, it may be as simple as the killer possessing the ability to bend light, allowing him to hide in plain sight. The bending of electromagnetic radiation, like light, could give the appearance that he's not there at all, especially if combined with psychic influence.

Light waves are fast, but their speed is dependent upon the matter they're traveling through. As light moves from one medium to another, it slows or speeds up. When this happens, light bends, especially when there is a rapid shift in air density.

A uniform and sharp shift in density levels would create multiple mediums for light to pass through. This could be accomplished by heating or cooling air or by changing its chemical make-up. Light bouncing off the killer would bend as it passes through multiple mediums. The brain, assuming light travels in straight lines, would work to fill in the informational gaps caused by refraction, potentially erasing the killer's existence.

"Like a cloaking device on *Star Trek*," Astrid says.

"Who was that?" Holly asks.

Centurion doesn't answer. He continues, "But I think the murderer's ability may have been compromised."

"How do you know that?"

"Because I think I've seen him," he says.

"You've seen him?"

"The guy that beat me up. Something was wrong with his face. It was bandaged up. Maybe that damage restricts him from changing the density or make-up of the space near him." Or, maybe his body's not providing the necessary feedback to his brain, like a feedback loop that allows the brain's motor control center to correct and adjust signals to the muscles. "Maybe he can't register the changes he needs to project because he can't feel or see, at least not like he used too."

The blip on Holly's display suddenly moves. It's slight, but it's definitely movement. "Centurion," she interjects, "the blip is moving. Now."

"Holly, I've got to let you go." Centurion hangs up. "Damn. They're in the house. They came in through the back."

He doesn't hear Holly repeating his name. He doesn't hear her tell him to be careful.

# Track Twenty-One: The Endless Sea

"Go," Centurion says.

They bolt from the Chariot, crossing the street and using the trees in the parkway as cover. Centurion favors his left foot and winces as he gallops forward, but he still beats Astrid to the foot of the stairs. There, he kneels and waits for her to join him. He beckons her with a wave. She arrives and grabs her knees, panting hard. Centurion puts a finger to his lips. Astrid nods, doesn't say a word. He points to the door.

It's cracked slightly. The light in the vestibule is on. A shadow flickers across the opening, someone standing just beyond the door.

"Chee," they hear a voice calling from inside the house, "hurry up, kiddo."

Centurion extends his finger, points to the spot where Astrid squats. He bobs his head in her direction, his eyes narrowing. "Stay," the gestures command.

He goes to all fours like a sprinter at the gate and bursts forth at the imaginary sound of a non-existent starter pistol. He's up the concrete stairs in three steps, taking two and three stairs at a time, and then across the porch in a blink. He growls as he rams the door. It bounces open as Centurion enters, slams against the wall. It bounces and shuts behind him, but not before Astrid catches a glimpse of him tackling the shape of a man.

There's a ruckus, the sound of furniture breaking.

Astrid disobeys. "Screw this." She hurries up the stairs.

"Dad?" Chee calls from inside, somewhere distant and above the hallway.

Astrid slips, skins her knee. She doesn't care. She's up in a beat and moving again, racing towards the commotion beyond the wooden door. She hits the door, puts her weight behind it while twisting the doorknob. It creaks open.

She hesitates in the frame. She's frozen. She's staring down a hallway. On one side, a battered console table rests on its back, two of its legs snapped off. The mirror above where the console stood hangs at a Dali-esque angle. It is cracked and veined. Pieces of reflective glass mix like confetti with bits of pottery on the oak floor.

Framing the opposite side of the hall, a staircase descends. Chee stands four stairs above them, above the landing. "Dad!" she screams. She doesn't know what to do with her hands. They reflexively cover her chest and neck. She regards Astrid. Her face contorts, her head cocking.

Framed by the wall and the stairs, Centurion and Marcus are engaged in battle. Marcus delivers a kidney shot, then another. The blows make Centurion wince, clutch his back. He blocks Marcus' fist and hammers him with an elbow. He brings it down between Marcus' neck and left shoulder again. Marcus staggers, and Centurion is on him. He swings Marcus around by his arm, shoving his elbow into his shoulder and bouncing him off the wall, face first. This time the mirror falls. Shards fly. Marcus stumbles, his hands outstretched, searching for support. Centurion spins him by the collar of his shirt and uses the momentum to his advantage. Grabbing Marcus by the shoulder, he rams him through the rails of the stairway. Chee hops away from the banister, backwards and up a step, as her father's head and chest crash through. Marcus' torso now occupies the space where she once stood.

Centurion takes an awkward step backwards. He blows hard. He grabs his knees.

Marcus blinks slowly, trying to assess the damage to his body. He's got something left in his tank. He works to free himself from the balustrades.

Centurion's not done. "Where do you think you're going?" Snarling, he delivers a furious kick to Marcus's ribs just above his hips. The heavy sandal connects, shoving Marcus down the stairs. Rails snap one after the other as he rolls to the landing. He tears through the decorative handrail at the bottom of the steps. The banister crashes down on him.

"Daddy!" Chee screams again.

Marcus moans.

Astrid can't help but simply stare. She's working through the image before her, trying to process what she's seeing.

Marcus is prone, his face pressed against the floor in the corner of the landing. One leg hangs off the first stair, his other bends behind him and up the staircase. His arms start to twitch, then move more deliberately. He paddles slowly on the floor like a turtle making its way through cold sand. He doesn't move anywhere. He simply pushes the broken rungs and debris about his sides.

"Astrid," Centurion says, catching her attention, snapping her out of her daze. "Step away from him."

She does. She gives Marcus a wide birth.

"Daddy," Chee sobs. She edges down the stairs.

Centurion extends his arm, grabs her by the ankle.

Chee loses her balance, almost trips down the stairs. Her arms windmill, spinning at her sides. She rocks forward, then back. Forward again and back. She bends at the knee to lower her center of gravity but can't regain her equilibrium. She crumples like paper, landing on her ass, her leg still firmly in Centurion's grasp.

Marcus moans again. He struggles to turnover.

Astrid looks at Centurion as if to say, *"What now?"*

Centurion responds with a furrowed brow. *"This."*

He seizes Chee with his second hand and pulls her towards him. He picks her up, wraps his arms around her waist. He sets her down before him, her back to her father.

"Let me go," she says, her hands pushing against his forearms, trying to break his hold. Her neck cranes over her right shoulder for a view of her father.

Centurion just pulls her tighter against him.

She looks to the left, finds Astrid there. Her eyes plead. "Help me," she says.

Astrid shakes her head and looks away.

Marcus has managed to turn himself over. He tries to bring himself to a sitting position. His hands can't find purchase. He rocks himself forward, bending at his midsection, to his hands and knees. "Please." He raises his head. "Don't hurt her."

Centurion spins Chee around to face Marcus. Her head rests in the crook of his elbow. He flexes, and it cuts off her breathing. Her hands tear at Centurion's forearm, her eyes start to bulge.

"Centurion," Astrid says, "you're going to hurt her." She says this despite knowing that Centurion has no such intent. Although his face is full of fury, his aura remains fixed.

He releases his grip slightly, and Chee gasps for air. Tears stream down her face.

"Daddy," she pleads.

"Please," Marcus says, rising to a knee, "you can have anything."

"We're not here to rob you," Astrid says, her left eye squinting and her hands shifting to her hips.

Centurion ignores the man. He shakes Chee. "Why did you do it?" he bellows at her. "Why did you kill Hooper? Why did you kill Henry?"

Chee weeps, her breath coming in great gulps. "I don't understand."

"Where's Kim?" Astrid shouts.

"Kim?" Chee's eyes are questioning. "I don't know. What's going on? Please let me go."

"Liar!" Centurion roars into her ear. He flexes again, crushing her against his armor.

She groans. She slaps at his arm weakly, kicks her legs.

"Centurion," Astrid says, "I don't think she knows."

"She knows!" he yells. "I'm going to squeeze the life out of her."

He could do it, too, Astrid considers. Still, there's no darkening of his aura. He's bluffing, hoping to force Chee's hand. Instead he forces Marcus'.

"She doesn't know anything!" Marcus cries. He's on his knees, exposing his palms to Centurion. "Please, let her go."

"She talks or she dies," Centurion says.

There are sixteen psychological approaches to interrogation. Marcus' handlers trained him to recognize and resist their various combinations. They exposed him to the elements, deprived him of sleep, beat him, and left him disoriented. He never broke, never cracked. None of his interrogators, however, ever dangled his daughter's life immediately in front of his face before. All of his training goes out the window. "She doesn't know anything. Please, I'll tell you everything you need to know."

Centurion doesn't immediately relax his death grip. He turns to

Astrid first. She nods, and Centurion shoves Chee to Astrid's feet.

Marcus fights to stand. "Thank you. Thank you for—"

Centurion grabs Marcus by the throat. He lifts him and slams him against the wall and twists his head to the side.

"No," Chee wheezes. She tries to crawl to her father, but Astrid holds her fixed.

"Tell me who you are," Centurion says. "Tell me who you work for."

"Chee," Marcus wheezes, "go into the other room. It will be okay."

Astrid bends down to lift Chee to her feet, intent upon removing her from the room.

"No," Centurion orders. "She stays. She deserves to hear this."

Marcus nods reluctantly.

"Astrid, get me something to tie him up with."

Chee sobs.

"And her too."

❖❖❖

"You killed John Hooper?" Centurion says.

"Yes." Marcus leans forward slightly over the kitchen table. His hands are bound behind his back with two broad leather belts; his feet are tied together with an extension cord. He looks across the table directly into his daughter's face as he says it, his left eye starting to swell.

"Oh, Daddy," Chee says, tears welling in her eyes.

"You killed Henry Famosa?" Centurion continues.

"Yes," Marcus says, breaking eye contact with Chee.

She sobs.

Centurion exhales, rubs his downcast eyes. "Why?"

"We hunt witches. We have for centuries, all the way back to the high police of 18th Century France."

"Did you say, 'witches?'" Centurion asks.

"Yes. Set aside the quaint notion of hags on Hallmark cards stirring cauldrons and flying around on brooms. Forget about Wiccans. In the widest sense of the word, witches are people like you and me, but with one major difference: they have supernatural powers, and we don't."

*Supernatural powers?* "Liar. You expect me to believe this? You expect us to buy into this conspiracy theory? Tell me what really happened."

"Centurion," Astrid says with hesitation. "I think he's telling the truth."

"How can you tell?"

She tilts her head as if to say, "Really?"

"You can tell that?"

Her eyebrows lift. She nods.

Centurion tells Marcus to continue.

"While outwardly witches might appear normal, they are anything but. They make Halloween look tame. They're the stuff of nightmares . . ."

Centurion slaps the table, points a finger at Marcus. "But these were children."

" . . . or will *become* the stuff of nightmares."

"You can't know that," Centurion says. "These were good kids."

"Maybe, maybe not. An ounce of prevention is worth a pound of cure. We're catching them before they can do serious damage. If you could go back and kill Hitler as a child, would you? And what if there were two kids named Adolf Hitler in the same room, and you couldn't tell which would become the Nazi and which would become a cobbler? You'd kill them both to save countless others, right?"

"Theory," Astrid says, shaking her head, "it's nothing but fantasy."

"But it's not," Marcus says. "They'll do harm. It might be innocent. It might be as an agent co-opted by a foreign government. We know this. We've seen the pattern play out countless times before."

"Witches," Centurion spits. "It's a label you've created to distance yourself from what you're doing, company man. You're murdering people. You're killing superheroes."

"Yes. The Bible says, 'Never suffer a witch.' It doesn't make a distinction for good witches."

"You're murdering her friends," he says, now pointing at Chee.

"Yes," Marcus says, his head bowing.

Chee snivels and closes her eyes. Her chest heaves and bounces as she cries.

"How is she involved in this? What's her roll?"

Marcus details Chee's secret and unknowing participation. His agency has relied upon and exploited African women, women with the ability to "smell" witches. He provides a lineage, starting with Mbali and Lindiwe Toure that runs through Mathilde Toure, her daughter Marie, and her granddaughter Hélène. The family line ends with Hélène and Marcus' daughter Chee. "It's a euphemism, really. Witch-smellers don't really sniff out witches like pigs hunting for truffles. But they are attracted to those with extra-abilities."

"She's your bait worm," Centurion says.

Marcus doesn't give voice to a response. He looks away. His shame is answer enough.

"No," Chee cries. "How could you? I hate you. I hate you!"

Marcus winces. "I'm sorry, honey. Please, you have to know, I did it all for you."

Astrid fidgets. "Ask him about Kim," she says.

"Where is she?" Centurion demands.

"She's at the lab," Marcus says.

"She's alive?" Astrid exclaims.

"I don't know."

"Let's go," Centurion says, standing so fast his chair flips. "You're going to take us there."

"What? Are you crazy? That's a suicide mission. There are soldiers there."

"Okay," Centurion says.

"Armed soldiers. Soldiers with guns."

Centurion asks Astrid to untie Marcus' feet.

"I'm going too." She kneels and begins unraveling the power cord.

"No, don't," Marcus says. "Smith has orders to kill you."

"Smith," Centurion repeats. "That's the name of the 'invisible' man?" He uses air quotes.

"You know about Smith?"

"Yes," he says, unconsciously touching a bruised cheek, "and I'm looking forward to getting reacquainted. Astrid, are you sure you're up for it?"

"Definitely," she says without looking up from her task.

"I'd like to help too," Chee says, sniffling.

"No, honey, you can't do that," Marcus says.

"You can't tell me what I can and can't do anymore," she says. "You don't own me."

Marcus tells them their plan is insane. None of them know what they're doing.

"Can I help?" Chee asks Astrid.

Astrid's unsure. She looks to Centurion for guidance.

He nods, his eyes closing slowly.

"Fine," Astrid replies. "Hold on, Kim," she whispers. "We're coming. We're coming."

❖❖❖

"Go get the Chariot," Centurion says, tossing Astrid the keys. "But don't adjust the seat forward."

"Why not?" she asks.

"Just don't."

"But I don't have my license yet." She stares at the keys in her palm like they're poisonous snakes ready to strike.

It's not up for negotiation. They can't risk parading Chee and Marcus to the Chariot in bondage for all of the neighbors to see. "The right pedal is go. Left is stop. Turn the wheel where you want to go. Bring it around to the back of the house, to the alley."

"Okay," she says. She scans the block before exiting through the front door.

Their hands tied behind their backs, Centurion leads Chee and Marcus to the enclosed porch at the rear.

He takes an extension cord and ties it around Marcus' neck. He measures three feet, and then begins to tie the cord around Chee's neck. "Why did you do it?" he asks Marcus.

"Slaves are not masters of their destiny," Marcus answers as he regards the cable that runs between him and his daughter.

Centurion knots the cord around Chee's throat. She trembles as his hands touch her shoulders. His stomach turns. He's sickened by his handiwork, by its structural reminiscence to the yokes, steel collars, and neck chains used to enslave Africans in America's south. "This isn't right," he says. He needs to erase this etching from his mind. He unravels the cord. "Chee," he says to the teen, "I'm going to untie you. Swear you won't try to run?"

She nods.

"Thank you," Marcus says.

Centurion unwraps the cord around her wrists. He moves to Marcus. "You'll help us, right?"

"Yes."

Centurion goes to work releasing him. "You know, I'll kill your daughter if you try any funny business."

Marcus smiles. "No, you won't."

Centurion's head ticks to the side, an impression of a puzzled shelter dog. "I won't?"

"No," Marcus says. "It didn't hit me until a moment ago, but you were never going to hurt her. Sure, you scared the heck out of her, but you didn't intend to hurt her. Your young friend, Astrid, gave it away. The mere idea of seeing someone killed would horrify most. But it never affected her because she knew what your intentions were all along."

"I didn't tell her a thing."

"You didn't have to. She's a mentalist. She saw your aim, and she remained calm."

Centurion grunts an acknowledgment. "She's special. Please don't make me regret this," he says.

"I won't. I promise."

He unties Marcus, letting the cables drop to the floor.

Marcus rubs his wrists and thanks Centurion again.

Centurion steps away and opens the porch door. He spots the Chariot. Its headlamps zigzag down the alley. Astrid almost hits a dumpster. The vehicle stutters forward as she rides the brake. He waves to her and she pulls just short of the house. "Good enough."

"Why don't you go ahead," Centurion says to Chee. "You're dad and I will be out soon."

Chee doesn't look to her father for permission.

"Wait," Marcus calls to her. He takes a step towards his daughter, gives the necklace a quick tug. The clasp gives easily, the chain falling from her shoulder and chest and draping over his hand.

Chee looks at him in horror.

"This wasn't your mother's," he says. "It's a replica, a beacon. It's how they track you." He tosses the chain into the hallway behind him. It lands with a clunk, skittering across the oak floor into the darkness. "Your mother's is in a lockbox."

"Is nothing true?" she asks, glaring.

"I love you," he says. "That's the truth."

She fumes and darts out the door. She bounds down the steps to the waiting car. She enters and slams the car door behind her.

"Why did you involve your daughter? I don't understand."

"Hélène, Chee's mother, quit the service. She was tired of the killing. She just couldn't do it anymore after Chee was born." Marcus pauses. "Unfortunately, you don't just quit the service."

"They murdered her?"

"Yes, her boss, my boss. Mansfield leaked that she was a witch-smeller to a tribal leader. He told the chieftain that my wife suspected him of witchcraft. In South Africa, that's a death sentence. The man acted first, rallying a mob. They hunted Hélène. They found her, and they hacked her to death. Then they came for Chee. I couldn't let her die so I made a pact. I sold my soul to the U.S. government, enlisting Chee without her knowledge."

"Why enlist her at all?"

"With Hélène gone, finding witches became very difficult." He describes why.

Contrary to popular belief, people with superpowers don't advertise their super-strength, spider senses, teleporting power, or control of electrical appliances. They're not buff or hot; they look like the rest of us.

The super-abled are not aliens. They aren't members of secret and ancient civilizations. They aren't raised in exotic locales. They don't congregate in Gotham, Metropolis, New York City, or big cities in general. They're usually from the 'burbs.

They lack pretentious names. Their first and surnames are rarely alliterative (à la Reed Richards, Peter Parker, or Bruce Banner). They don't have alter egos like Power Dude or Smarty Girl. They don't name themselves after animals.

They don't inherit wealth like the comic book superheroes. They don't use their powers to steal money like supervillains. Their parents are usually middle class. Typically, those parents are both loving and living, rarely the victims of criminal action or heroic inaction. If the parents have passed on, it's usually due to natural causes.

They might have besties or siblings, but they don't have sidekicks, henchmen, or minions. Marcus says, "The easiest way to determine someone isn't a superhero is by how they dress. Superheroes don't wear tights or capes. They don't dress up and parade around like second-rate Avengers." His eyes linger on Centurion's armor as he says this. "Sorry."

Centurion grimaces. "No problem."

In short, superpowers are difficult to discern. "There can be lot of guesswork, and guesswork generates collateral damage," Marcus says. "Before Chee started school, it was a bad time to be incredibly lucky. Anyone who won the lottery more than once, weathermen who were particularly accurate, and motorcyclists with perfect driving records, among others, were targeted."

"Why them?"

"Psychic ability. Any pattern of statistical significance was chalked up to telepathy, mind-control, memory manipulation, clairvoyance, illusion, elemental control, or luck manipulation."

Centurion calls that a wide net.

"Yes. For six years, it was the Wild West. Lots of death, lots of cover stories about gang violence and the drug war. When Chee was activated, though, the contracts with the bounty hunters, sometimes even the hunters themselves, were terminated. She kept friendly fire to a minimum."

"Bounty hunters?" Centurion says he now wishes he had a gun.

"The bottom left hand drawer of my desk has a false bottom. There's a steel briefcase under it."

"Let's get it," Centurion says.

❖❖❖

Marcus true to his word doesn't struggle as Centurion leads him out of the house. They join the girls. Centurion hands the briefcase to Astrid in the passenger seat. "Careful with that," he says.

Marcus sits in the back of the Chariot with Chee in the darkness. He holds a catalog envelope. "When you hit 90-94, head north," he says to Centurion.

Centurion makes a right on North Avenue towards the expressway.

"What's that?" Chee asks, glancing at the envelope.

Marcus extends it to her.

She hesitates, eying him with suspicion, before taking it firmly with one hand. She continues to watch him while she opens it. Inside are pictures, photos of her and her lost friends, like Tony, Jonathan, Henry, and . . .

"Marta," Chee says, holding a Polaroid of the two of them in front of a Christmas tree display at the Alamo. Her eyes well, a tear threatens to escape. She sniffs as she draws a sleeve across her face. "I knew we didn't lose these in the moves." Her voice is flat with disappointment. Another sniffle. "Why did you take them?"

"I saw how their deaths weighed on you. I thought it would be best for you to forget."

"Are you sure you didn't remove them because you were embarrassed of me, of my abilities?" she says. "Were you judging me by my company?"

"No," he says, "I realize now why I really hid them. I concealed them because they defined me—my mission—more than they ever defined you. Their eyes, their smiles, haunted me. They still do. I hid them because I couldn't bear to look at their faces."

Chee nods. Headlights dance across her face. "I know the feeling," she says, turning away from her father as the shadows shroud her again.

Centurion pulls over at a gas station on the way. He borrows some money from Chee's father, and goes in to pay. He comes out with several bottles of Orangina, a bag of white t-shirts, a gas can, and some lighters. He fills both the tank and the can, and they hit the road.

# Track Twenty-Two: What Goes On

*San Antonio, Texas. 5 January 2000.*

Marta shifts her weight from leg to leg, her only company this evening the barren live oaks. Silhouetted against the glow of the Alamo, the trees look deformed and treacherous. A cold wind blows, and the bent and fractured limbs shudder. Their shadows stretch and claw at her.

She shivers, looks at her Casio. 10:15 PM. Chee was supposed to meet her more than an hour ago. She takes a final drag from her cigarette, the ember burning the filter. "Fuck this," she says, dropping the butt to the ground. She steps on it, grinding it beneath her penny loafer. She exhales a puff of smoke.

The breeze builds again, rustling the branches. On it comes a whispered response, words from the darkness. "Fuck this."

Marta spins towards the west, towards the voice and the plaza. She squints into the darkness. "Who's there?"

There's no reply, no movement. Nothing.

She adjusts her backpack and scowls. "I'm out of here." She steps over a barrier chain, cuts over the lawn to East Crockett Street. She hurries across the street and into the Rivercenter Mall. Her footfalls echo throughout the empty atrium as she descends a staircase to the lower level. Passing the entrance to the Marriott, a lonely doorman gives her a wave. She returns a half smile, her teeth dark and eroded. She continues through the mall to the exit. Outside, the lagoon marks the beginning of the Paseo del Rio, the River Walk.

Constructed in the 1930s and 40s, the San Antonio River Walk is a network of walkways and bridges. Red, green, and blue umbrellas provide shade for the customers of the bars, restaurants, and hotels lining the canal. Bald cypress trees, most thirty feet tall or more, grow from the banks of River Walk. They shadow both the cars crossing the bridges and boats that pass beneath.

Tonight however, there are no cars or boats. The paths and sidewalks are empty, as is the river itself. The river was drained three days ago. It's emptied every January by the Parks and Recreation Department for cleaning and maintenance.

Where there was once a river, there is only a pit, a canal filled with mud and the debris of tourism. Here and there, lost cameras, silverware from the neighboring taverns, and forgotten sunglasses protrude from the sludge.

The filth is uneven, sloping downward from the walls of the embankment. Pools of water collect in areas where the mud thins. The trench emits a stench. Marta hastens and averts her nose. Still, she slows near the statue of St. Anthony de Padua, the patron saint of all things lost, including love, and says a quick prayer.

She veers west, past the Commerce Street Bridge and towards the footbridge east of Alamo Street. Here, in the shadow of the viaduct, is where she and Chee first held hands. And there, against the wall of limestone, is where she first took Chee into her arms. Marta enters the mouth of the underpass. And here, cloaked in the shadows, is where they first furtively kissed.

That was in November, when they were virtually inseparable. Those happy early days seem like a lifetime ago. She hasn't seen Chee outside the hallways of school in more than a week. Time crawls for the heartbroken.

At first she blamed Chee's dad for their parting. He was proper and conservative, just what one would expect of a federal official. She knew he frowned upon their relationship—on any of Chee's relationships—and was certain he was preventing Chee from seeing her. Over time, her initial confidence had turned to doubt. Maybe it was Chee who got cold feet, maybe it was she who wanted to break things off. Her fears paralyzed her. She couldn't eat or sleep. That is, until she received the note, an invitation from Chee to meet. At last she would get answers to her questions. She would at best rekindle a flame and at worst get closure.

But Chee was a no show. "What the hell, Chee?" Marta mutters, her voice echoing in the chamber under the bridge. "Where were you tonight?"

As if in response, a bottle drops from the walkway above. It lands directly in her path. Green splinters of a Heineken explode in an ellipsis, a long shard sliding across the cement and bouncing off the front of her foot.

She gasps, puts a hand to her mouth. "Holy shit. That scared the fuck out of me."

From above no one says a word. Not an, "Oops," "Shit," or an offer of apology.

Her initial shock turns to irritation. She stomps towards and past the impact point. "You could kill someone like that," she yells. "Somebody better come down here to clean up this mess." She looks up to confront the litterer, but no one returns her gaze. She sniffs and sneers. "Tourists."

A voice whispers in her ear, "I *am* here to clean up a mess."

She jumps, twisting to her side. She expects to find someone inches from her face, but again, no one. She does a one-eighty and quickly backtracks under the bridge. Glass crunches under her feet as she hastens into the shadows. "Who are you?" she cries. "Why are you following me?" She looks to her right, picks up the four-inch dagger of glass that struck the toe of her loafer. She stands and brandishes it before her like a weapon. She points it to the left, then to the right. "I swear to God I'll fuck you up."

Someone chuckles from somewhere in front of her. It's half high-pitched giggle, half menacing hiss.

"I swear to God," she says again, "so help me."

"I'm your god," the voice says, "and there's no help for you."

"I warned you, motherfucker," Marta says. Her hands clench into fists and drop to her sides. A belch works its way up her chest. Her eyes close, her jaw drops.

Other than the dragons of lore, there is only one creature capable of spitting fire. Her name is Marta.

Her mucous membranes go into overdrive, secreting a viscous glycoprotein and water. The mucus protects the epithelial cells that line her throat and lungs. In normal humans, mucus protects against external threats like viruses and bacteria. Marta, however, represents an evolutionary step. Her mucous membranes produce antiseptic enzymes and mucins to protect her respiratory system and mouth from an internal danger—flaming toxin.

Two baseball-sized glands positioned above Marta's lungs churn.

Bits of food making their way to her stomach have been captured by tubules in her esophagus. As the food accumulates, the glands extract glucose. Some of the food rots and feeds a symbiotic community of yeast and bacteria. The yeasts devour the sugar and produce ethanol. The bacteria live off the hydrogen sulfide produced by the waste and excrete sulfuric acid. The acid mixes with the ethanol in these glandular combustion chambers. Together, the chemicals produce an extremely flammable compound: diethyl ether.

The interaction does not come entirely without consequence to Marta. The chemicals invoke an immune response, and this response, over the years, has generated scarring and pulmonary calcification. The calcified deposits at the mouth of the glands squeeze together when her muscles contract. They strike and spark, providing the flint necessary to create an explosive stream of fire.

Fire erupts from Marta's mouth, the diethyl ether generating massive flames. Powered by vapor, the blaze projects twenty feet from her lips and illuminates the underpass in vibrant blue. Blood drips from her clasp, the shard cutting deep. The firestorm continues, azure fire lapping the sidewalk, the walls, and the bridge above.

She opens her eyes, rotates her head from side to side, up and down, sanitizing everything before her. Her lips start to sting, the barrier of mucus breaking down. Still, she takes five steps forward, walking to the edge of the egress. She counts three to be certain she's incinerated anything in her path.

She swallows. The flames cease. She drops her impromptu weapon and inspects her injured hand. With her other hand, she rubs her jaw, opening and closing her mouth. She licks her lips, tastes venom and blood.

Smoke lingers, filling the tunnel. She winces, struggling to see beyond the mouth of the walkway. As she emerges, the damage becomes evident. The bushes and earth beyond are scorched. The walk is blackened. Fifteen feet away, the branches of young cypress burn. Her antagonist has, apparently, hightailed it. She wipes sweat from her brow, and allows herself a rare, full smile.

That's when she's bumped from behind.

The man roars as he shoves her forward, beyond the bend of the sidewalk. He grabs her by her hair and jacket, puts his chest into her back. She's off balance, and his force combined with her momentum propels her through the shrubs and over the bank. They both go over the edge, and he rides her as they plummet. She extends her arms, vainly attempting to stop their descent.

Together they fall, six feet to the muck. They land with a splat, his weight forcing her deep into the mud. She's on an incline, her feet thirty degrees higher than her head. She can't see anything, can't breathe. Splayed out, she tries to push against the filth. It offers no resistance, pulls her deeper. She arches her back hard. Her face pulls free from the sludge with a sucking sound. She gulps hard and blinks wildly. "Help!"

She feels her attacker adjust his weight, his knees going to either side of her hips, an elbow into her shoulder. He lets go of her hair, moves his hand to the top of her skull. He palms her head like a basketball, starts to push.

"No!" she cries as his weight forces her face back into the mire.

"Quiet now," he says, "it will all be over soon." He finds leverage. Both hands are now on the back of her head. He leans in.

She tries to say, "Please," but the word's cut off. She tries to kick, tries to roll over, but she's held fast.

A minute later, her body goes limp. He plunges a hand in the mud, grabs her by the left shirtsleeve. She's sinking. He has to work fast. He pulls with ferocity and frees her hand. From his coat, he removes a knife. He cuts. He drops her hand into a bag at his side. Then it's on to the right hand. Repeat.

One hand is for the authorities, the other for the scientists. The rest of Marta is for the archeologists of a future century.

He steadies himself, rises to a stance. He shuffles down her back to her shoulders. He presses her arms deep into the muck with a loafer. Then he puts his weight on her head. The ooze eagerly swallows her. He walks up her spine, and she sinks. He steps onto her thighs, then her calves. Once the blackness has claimed her feet and heels, he launches himself towards the canal wall. He takes hold of the lip with a hand and elbow and swings himself up and over the edge.

He draws a triangle in chalk at the base of the pedestal of the statue of Saint Anthony. He takes Marta's hand and uses it to anoint the statue with blood. He places the hand in the center of this demonic triangle. On the wall behind and just to the left of the figure he draws an "A" in a circle. It's a symbol typically associated with anarchy, but, for occultists, it's the mark for human sacrifice. On the right, he writes, "For Holy Death, My Lady, Mistress of Darkness and Coldness. Protect me from my enemies." He lights a few black candles and pours a bottle of tequila at the foot of the saint to complete the picture.

Tomorrow the police and news agencies will blame the death of Marta Garcia on a dark variant of Santa Muerte, a cult popular amongst drug traffickers and devotees of El Mochaorejas. They will assume she's the victim of a ritualistic sacrifice. The police might involve the FBI, but neither will look for her body. Victims of the "holy death" are rarely found, and when they are, they're usually not alone. Capo de la Droga keep their sacrifices hidden, stacked like cordwood, in barns and cellars throughout Texas and northern Mexico. They just leave pieces as offerings and warnings.

The man whistles and nods as he admires his work. Smith loves his job.

# Track Twenty-Three: The Naked Part

*Aragon Ballroom, West Lawrence Avenue, Chicago. 7 September 2001.*

"Let's do this," Nigel Crown says to Stuart, the stage manager, as he walks out of the greenroom.

"Right now?" Stuart says, scratching his mop of hair. "Your opening act just finished a few minutes ago."

Nigel takes a swig of Evian and hands it off to the man. "So?"

"Well, you usually like to knock down a few between sets."

"Not tonight. Not anymore." He turns to his band. "Let's go."

Stuart steps in front of Nigel, impeding his way to the stage. "Wait, the techs are still out there, tuning guitars. The drum kit and keyboards haven't even been set up yet."

"We'll use the opener's drums. We can play without the keyboards tonight."

The manager looks puzzled. "But your set list?" Stuart says, referring to the eight electronic songs from the new album peppered amongst the classics and fan favorites.

"Screw it. Lads," Crown says, turning to his band, "how would you feel about a little improvisation tonight? David, are you okay playing some percussion tonight instead of the synth?"

"Hell yeah," David says. "Whatever you need, Nigel." The three rockers trailing Crown smile and agree excitedly.

"Well, there you have it," Crown says to the stage manager.

"But the lights?" the manager says.

"Give me an occasional spot. Or leave it bright. Frankly, I can't be bothered."

"And the tuning?" comes Stuart's reply. He gestures towards a technician who is about to walk out on stage with Crown's guitar.

"Fuck it," Nigel says, seizing his guitar from the kid. "We'll do it ourselves."

This elicits a "Yes!" from the drummer.

"Just like the old days," Nigel says, grabbing two of the band members by the shoulders.

Despite not being around in the old days, the band cheers. "Fucking right," the bassist says.

"Well grab your gear, boys," Nigel says. "We'll give this place a show unlike any since Green Day in 1994." He struts past Stuart.

"This is really happening?" the stage manager says to himself.

"This is happening!" Nigel yells over his shoulder.

Nigel Crown and the band walk out onto the bright stage. The roadies scurry off. It takes the fans several seconds to realize what's going on. There's a scream, then more, as the fans begin to understand that Crown is standing before them. The whistling and clapping begin.

Nigel swaggers to the mic at the middle front of the stage. He puts a hand to his forehead and looks out upon the audience. "It's bright up here," he says as the band mills about behind him. The stage lights dims slightly in response. "Ah, that's better," he says. "I want to see your smiling faces."

He pans left to right, over the Moorish architecture meant to mimic the square of a Spanish village. Those who left the floor to grab beer, visit the merch booth, or hit the bathroom start streaming in. Eighteen thousand fans scream and applaud as Crown's eyes pass over them.

"Hell, there's a lot of you out there . . . and my, are you a sexy crowd."

They go wild. A girl holds up a sign designed to mimic an Ouija Board. It says, "I'LL LOVE YOU EVEN IN THE AFTERLIFE NIGEL."

Crown points at her, "I love you too, darling, but I'm not into that occult business anymore. Don't play around with those spirit boards, promise?"

She nods, beaming. As she drops the poster, her hands move to her chest and cover her heart.

"Good girl," he says with a wink. He looks out towards the balconies. "So, before we kick things off, I hope you don't mind if we go through a quick sound check."

The crowd goes crazy.

"Great. I promise it won't be too painful." He keeps to his word.

They move through the sound check quickly, Crown telling stories as his band readies itself. "Want to hear a secret?"

YES.

"If you're good boys and girls tonight, I'll let you know where we're partying after the show. Deal?"

Another emphatic YES.

The guitarist walks over, whispers in Crown's ear. Crown nods. "Looks like we're ready, Brawlroom. Remember, no fighting . . . and tip the waitresses and bar staff." He turns to the band and says a few words. They nod. "We're going to play some Panic Attack tonight. I hope no one has a problem with that."

The crowd's in a frenzy.

"Good, good. This song's called *The Naked Part*. One, two, three, four." It's one of Panic Attack's early hits. The drums come in, and Crown howls like a wolf on the moors. The guitars join him as he launches into his lyrics.

> *I'm no history buff*
> *Got no love for the past*
> *Dates and all that stuff*
> *Never built to last*

He prowls the stage like a caged panther to the corner mic. His guitar joins the lead's lament. He points to a girl in the audience. Her eyes roll. She faints, falling into the arms of those behind her.

> *But when you ring again*
> *My heart skips a beat*
> *You come like a boomerang*
> *Cuz history . . . repeats*

The audience is in full roar, singing along.

> *I find, I find*
> *Conversation's a lost art*

*So lose it and lose your clothes*
*And let's get . . . to the naked part*

"Naked part" echoes throughout the ballroom. Crown feigns like he's going to unbutton his shirt, and the fans scream.

*I can't, I can't*
*Take all the stops and starts*
*So take off or take it off*
*And get to the naked part*

The guitarist steps forward. It's solo time. He and Crown go back to back, Crown playing rhythm. The guitarist nods his approval at Nigel, and Nigel smiles wide. As the solo approaches its climax, Crown's mouth forms the shape of an "O" and he shakes a hand like it's wet, emphasizing how nasty the instrumentation is. The solo ends and they separate. Crown points to the guitarist and makes an early introduction. "Give it up for Rex Paige on guitar." The crowd does. Paige grins, then Crown's back in the spotlight singing the chorus.

*You run your mouth*
*About all your foreign walks*
*A photo's worth a thousand words*
*And it doesn't need to talk*

Crown, no, the *room* is on to the next verse.

*You're as pretty*
*As a tropical postcard*
*So let me behold what I wanna hold*
*And get on to the naked part!*

The song ends with a four hard guitar strums and a drum flourish. Crown takes a bow, gestures towards the band. "Yes," Crown shouts into the mic. "Thank you, Chicago!"

The audience is of one mind, and they are collectively losing it.

Crown and his band play for another two hours. It's what many will call the greatest concert of their lives. People will lie about being at this show. It will be mentioned in the same sentence as Woodstock. It will become a part of rock history.

At the end of five—yes, five—encores, Crown asks the crowd if they'd like to hear some more.

The applause and screams suggest they would. They really, really would.

"Well, we're done here, but how about joining me at an afterhours?" They will.

He gives them an address, a warehouse just north of the City. "Just pull on in," he says. "Don't bother knocking." His elbows high in the air, he blows exaggerated kisses, and then quickly exits stage.

He doesn't bother to stop in the green room. He heads straight for his bus. He gives Andy the address as provided by Charlie. He tells Andy to drive there. Fast.

Within minutes, a caravan of fans is making its way up 90/94 following in Crown's wake.

*Park City, Illinois.*

Centurion exits I-94 on Belvidere Road. He heads east on 120 per Marcus' instructions. They pass Skokie Highway and enter Park City.

Park City is a manufactured community. The residents live in mobile homes just north of Belvidere. The trailers are uniform in size and shape, generally 16 feet across and 66 feet long. They occupy half the plots and form neat little rows like books on a shelf. To the South lies the industrial district, the Chariot's destination.

"Here," Marcus says.

Centurion takes a right and turns off the headlamps. He slows the Chariot to a crawl.

"Astrid, why don't you and Marcus switch places?"

Astrid climbs into the back of the minivan. She crawls to the rear near the lift gate. Marcus slides between the seats and takes her spot up front.

"Take this to Eighth, take a right, then take another right on Chestnut," he says.

Centurion complies. They drive a block, turn, drive another block, and turn again. On their left there's a Coca-Cola bottling plant. Semis emblazoned with red swishes line up outside.

"Take a left up there," Marcus says.

"Into the plant?" Centurion asks.

"No, around the back."

Centurion nods. The Caravan rounds the back of the second of two windowless warehouses made of concrete block. "Where's the security?"

"It's coming. Stay near the tree line. Follow it to the back of the parking lot."

In the back, Astrid bites her lip and frowns. She leans against the wheel well of the car. Her stomach turns, the muscles in her back constrict. She rubs her neck with one hand. Cold sweat builds on her back and forehead. She tries to swallow and can't. Her mouth is too dry. She closes her eyes, blows.

In the darkness beyond her eyelids, a bright spot of light dances and flickers in the distance. It moves from right to left, rising and falling, growing in size. A buzz resonates in her ears. A steady hum builds in her fingers and toes, pinpricks that signal her grandfather's arrival.

A great white bee, its eyes large and exaggerated, flutters forth. She extends her hand, and it lands on her index finger. Eyes still closed, she turns her hand slowly. The insect moves with her, crawling around the base of her finger towards the middle of her palm. She cups the pale creature tenderly.

"Charlie?" she says. Her mouth does not move, but her question is still audible.

"Hi, Chickadee."

"Where have you been?"

"Unfortunately, I've been really busy. I'm sorry we haven't spoken lately."

"Why do you look like a weird bee?"

"Turns out this is my totem animal," he says with a shake of his wings. "What do you think?" He scampers up the pad of her thumb.

Astrid giggles. "That tickles."

"Did you know that ancient civilizations believed that the souls of the dead inhabited honeybees?"

"No," Astrid says. "But why become a bug now?"

"It takes a lot less energy to manifest in this form," he says, "and there's so much to do tonight. We'll need to pull out all the stops to save your friend."

"She's here?"

"Yes."

Astrid wrinkles her nose. "I'm scared."

"I know," the Charlie bug says. "Don't be ashamed of that. Fear is a good thing. Fear warns you, telling you to be careful and to stay on your toes. Fear lets you know you're doing something worthwhile. There's no bravery without fear."

She nods. "Okay."

"Now listen. We don't have a lot of time. I need you to wait to enter the building until I give you a signal."

"What signal?"

"You'll know when you see it. Remember, though, don't enter the facility until I signal."

The Chariot creeps deep into the parking lot.

"Turn into the brush here," Marcus says, pointing towards a thin patch in the undergrowth, "and follow the maintenance trail to the left."

Centurion pulls the vehicle over and into the foliage.

"Follow this for thirty feet . . . okay, cut left again here towards the lot . . . and . . . stop."

Centurion puts the car in park, turns off the ignition.

"There," Marcus says, with a nod of his head forward. "That's the guard tower."

At the top of northernmost warehouse, thirty feet up, a structure sits on stilts.

"It's a water tower," Centurion says.

"It *was* a water tower," Marcus corrects. "See the slits along the top of the tank, just below the soffit?"

Centurion squints. "Yes, I think so."

"Those are windows. There are cameras behind them. They're providing a live feed to the guards inside."

"How many guards?" Centurion's question sounds ridiculous, and he knows it. They have no plan, one gun, and two children in tow.

"Two in the tower," Marcus replies, "and they're armed."

*Of course they are.* "So, what do we do? Go up to the front door and knock?"

"We'll need a diversion if we're going to make it to the loading docks between the buildings . . . "

Chee sniffs the air. "Do you smell cologne," Chee says, turning to talk to Astrid. She finds her with her arm extended, hand open, eyes closed.

"Astrid," she asks tentatively. "Are you okay?"

Suddenly, Astrid opens her eyes. "No," she exclaims.

Centurion and Marcus both turn. "Everything okay back there?" Centurion asks.

"We need to wait," Astrid says.

"We should do this now," Marcus says, "before we're discovered."

"No," Astrid says again, her eyes imploring Centurion. "Not yet. We need to wait."

"For what?" he says.

"A sign."

"A sign?" Marcus says. "What type of sign?"

"I don't know," she says, "but we'll know when we see it."

"We could be waiting here all night," Marcus says, "and while we wait, God knows what they're doing to your friend in there."

"Centurion," Astrid says, "you have to trust me on this."

Centurion sighs. "Okay."

Marcus is stunned. "What?"

"We wait," Centurion says, "until Astrid says."

Marcus starts to object.

"And that's final," Centurion says.

The four crowd near the windshield. They watch. They wait.

They don't wait long. Twenty minutes later, headlights illuminate the other side of the parking lot. A tour bus pulls from behind the southern warehouse and into the middle of the lot. A door opens, and a man steps out on to the pavement. He turns, says something to the driver. The folding doors shut. There's the sound of compressed gas, and the bus bounces forward and loops back. It exits the lot, leaving the man standing alone.

"What the hell?" Marcus says.

Astrid strains to make out the figure. "Oh, my God."

Centurion says, "What?"

"I think that's Nigel Crown."

"Impossible," Centurion says, "that can't be Nigel Crown."

"I totally forgot. He had a show tonight at the Aragon," Astrid says. "What's he doing here?"

"That *is* Nigel Crown," Centurion exclaims. "Holy shit."

"You're a fan too?" Astrid asks.

"Didn't you see my collection of cassettes back there?" Centurion exclaims. "I've got all his stuff. The Panic Attack albums, his solo stuff, his single with the Zou Zou Sisters."

"No way," she says.

Marcus interrupts them. "Whoever this guy is, he's about to get himself killed. Look at the water tower."

There's activity in the tank. A spotlight comes to life inside. It bounces once before suddenly locking on Crown from above like some UFO abduction in progress. One of the men exits the tower, climbing down the rungs of a ladder to the roof of the warehouse. He makes his way to the corner of the building, kneels. He brandishes a machine gun.

"They're going to kill him," Chee says. "We have to do something!"

"Get out!" Centurion says, yelling the first thing that comes to mind. He turns the ignition, throws on the headlights. "Now!"

Marcus jumps out and opens up the sliding door. He yanks the girls out and grabs the pistol case.

Centurion checks over his right shoulder to make sure they're clear, then he gases it. The headlights come to life as the Chariot ploughs through the brush. He slams his fist on the center of the steering column and honks the horn like crazy.

"Get down girls," Marcus commands as he pushes them to their bellies. "There," he says, pointing to a wide oak. They crawl on their hands and knees to the cover of the tree.

That's when the shooting starts.

*Chunka-chunka-chunk. Chunka-chunka-chunka-chunk.*

The spotlight pinpoints the Chariot. The man on the roof fires, three and four round bursts exploding from his M16A2. The first rain of bullets ricochets off the asphalt just before the Chariot. The second barrage makes contact with the vehicle, a tight cluster that shatters the windshield and pierces the roof. The Chariot comes to a screeching halt, glass dust rising in the light.

"Centurion!" Astrid screams.

"Quiet," Marcus says, wrapping his hand over her mouth.

The spot holds on the Caravan for three seconds before swinging back to where Crown stood. Crown, though, is gone. The light skips about, searching fruitlessly for the man. He's no longer to be found in the parking lot. Abruptly, it turns on the clearing from where the Chariot came.

"Stay down girls," Marcus says as the beam passes over their hiding place. He opens the briefcase, pulls out the Beretta and slides in a magazine. He tucks a second clip into his back pocket.

"I don't see him," Astrid says. "I don't see either of them." She's not referring to what's visible to her two eyes. She's referring to the blindness of her third eye. She can't see their auras. They've totally disappeared. Something is interfering with her extrasensory perception. She's convinced: "Kim must be somewhere in that facility, hidden by some sort of shield."

"When you hear the sirens, run due north from here until you hit the expressway," Marcus says. "Head east towards the suburbs. You got it?"

"We're not leaving you," Chee says.

"This is not up for negotiation. They will kill your friend," he says, eyeballing Astrid, "if they catch her—"

"Shhh," Astrid says. "Listen."

There's a hum, like the pulsing of electrical lines. It's low and rumbles across the blacktop.

"What is that?" Chee asks.

"Thunder?" Marcus guesses.

"No," Astrid says, smiling. She aims a finger at the sky. "It's wings." A cloud of insects, their wing beats rapidly vibrating, descends with a drone. Thousands of bees, thousands of souls as her grandfather would say, approach. They swarm fifty feet above the blacktop, speeding towards the buildings.

This is her signal.

# Track Twenty-Four: Talk about the Past

The searchlight swivels towards the sound, towards the sky. And then the screaming starts. The machine gunner swats at his arms, his neck, and face. In a moment, he's a blur. He's covered head to toe in a writhing mass of bugs. He staggers, tries to make his way to the ladder and the safety of the tower. He can't. He drops to his knees, shrieking, before falling prostate. He squirms for a moment before he goes quiet.

Marcus has no idea what he's watching. "What the—"

The spot bounces, its beam twisting, diving, and soaring. It shakes then holds, the beacon frozen and pointing towards the heavens. A moment later, the operator jumps through the hatch. He drops ten feet and struggles to stand. He, too, is covered, swarmed by the insects. He covers his face and runs—

"Turn away," Marcus says to Chee and Astrid.

—right off the roof of the warehouse. His scream is almost immediately silenced, cut short by the sickening thud of his impact.

"Stay here," Marcus says.

"I'm going with you," Astrid says.

"Chee stay—"

But Chee is already running to the Chariot. Astrid pursues.

"—Damn." Marcus pulls himself up. He sprints across the pavement, zigzagging like a running back. He keeps his head up, the aim of his weapon tracking with the movement of his eyes. He scans the rooflines. The fog of bees has moved on, down to the loading docks between the buildings.

Suddenly, there's screaming from the delivery bays.

Chee arrives at the Chariot first. She prepares herself for the worst and swings open the driver's side door. There's smoke, fractured plastic, and shattered glass, but the driver and passenger seats are otherwise empty. "He's not here."

Astrid dashes to the passenger side. With a grunt she yanks open the sliding door. She looks across to Chee near the driver side door. "He's not back here either."

She feels a hand grip her leg. She squeals and kicks.

"Ouch!" someone exclaims from underneath the minivan.

Astrid drops to her knees. "Centurion?"

Nigel Crown crawls out from beneath the vehicle, brushing himself off as he stands. "You must be Astrid," he says, extending a hand.

"Yes," she says, blushing. "How did you know that?"

"Let's just say we have mutual friends," he says. He adds, "Chickadee."

"Charlie sent you?"

Nigel nods. "That he did."

"Have you seen Centurion?"

"Here," Centurion says, rounding the back of the Chariot.

Astrid springs forward. She envelops him in a hug, burying her face in his armor.

Centurion thinks he hears her whimper. He freezes then pats her on the back. "There, there," he says, allowing himself a half smile.

"Hello again," Nigel Crown says to Centurion.

Chee comes around the front of the van. "Do you know each other?"

"No," Nigel says, "not formally, but we did recently bump into each other under a car."

Astrid releases Centurion, and he takes a delicate step towards Crown. They shake hands, and he stammers through an introduction. "I'm a big fan, Mr. Crown."

"Centurion is it? Well, don't you look the part? Always good to meet a fan," Crown says.

"My favorite song is *Puppy Love*," Centurion blurts.

Crown starts to sign the lyrics.

*This puppy love don't scratch or bite*

Astrid says, "I love that one." She chimes in.

*This puppy love won't bark at night*

Centurion joins in, his voice rough and off-key.

*This puppy love won't whine or beg*
*This puppy love won't hump your leg*

They stop and laugh, Crown slapping Centurion on the shoulder. "You know," he says, "I can't take full credit for that song. I stole that idea over drinks with Iggy Pop."

"The Godfather of Punk?" Centurion says. "You're kidding."

"No, it's true," Crown says. "I'm not sure he ever forgave me. I might owe him an apology in fact. Or I can just let him record a version of his own. He and Bowie were always recording each other's material after all, so why not?"

Marcus has joined the group, and he's had enough of the banter. "Quiet," he orders. "At some point, I'll find out why we're all here and just what's going on with the insects. But for now, let's just remember that this is a rescue mission."

"You're right. So sorry," Crown says.

Centurion nods his agreement. "Sorry."

"Where's your driver?" Marcus says leaning towards Crown.

"I told him to park at the front of the complex," Crown says. "He'll run interference until I call him." He holds up his cell phone.

"Okay, listen closely," Marcus says. "We don't have much time." He describes the semblance of a plan. They'll hightail it to the loading dock first. They may encounter facility staff on a smoke break, and they'll need to deal with them. After entering the facility, they'll split up. Kim should be in the main lab. "While it's only a Biohazard Level 1 facility, I expect the entry to be secure."

"Biohazard?" Crown says, his cheek momentarily spasming.

"I'll deal with any administrators on the upper level," Marcus continues. "I'll make my way to the control room and manually override the door locks. You'll need to distract the guards on the first floor to buy time to enter the lab. You'll have to deal with any technicians on duty. There will be at least one, probably a doctor named Kane. Think you can handle him?" Marcus asks.

"Yes," Centurion says, balling up a fist and striking a cupped hand.

Crown feeds off of this confidence. "Sure," he says, his voice squeaking.

Astrid nods.

"Good," Marcus says.

"What about me?" Chee says.

"Your job is critical," Marcus says, "You'll watch over the car while we're inside. From that row of trees back there."

Chee glances at the tree line behind her. She turns back to Marcus. "No. I'm going too."

"Chee, don't argue with me."

She sucks in her cheeks. "You can't stop me. Anyway, I need to do this," Chee implores. "I need to fix what I've done."

Marcus sighs. He looks first to Centurion, then to Crown. "You'll watch her?" he says.

"I'll guard her with my life," Centurion says.

"Okay," Marcus says. "You're with Centurion. Astrid, you're with the singer."

They don't have much time to prepare. Centurion and Chee empty three four-packs of Orangina. Centurion says the baseball-shaped bottles make for the best Molotov cocktails. "Easy to throw," he says, miming a pitch. He directs Astrid to fill the twelve bottles three-quarters with gasoline. She passes them to Crown who stuffs each with ripped pieces of cotton.

"Like this?" he asks Centurion.

Centurion nods. "Good."

He pulls a backpack and a grocery bag from the Chariot. He fills both with the explosives, keeping the zipper on the pack partially open for easy access. He hands out Bic lighters and makes the party test them. The Bics flicker to life one by one. They stand for a moment, regarding each other like mourners at a memorial. The flames tremble with their hands.

Marcus gulps. "Let's go," he says.

They move single file near the base of the building like a train of rodents, Marcus in the lead and Centurion at the rear.

"Heads up," Marcus says as they turn the corner and approach the docks.

Crown says, "Where?" Then he sees the three bodies in lab coats in their path, all victims of Charlie's swarm. Their faces are marked with pustules, their eyes and throats swollen from the venom. He halts. "Jesus," he whispers, "those men are dead."

Marcus says it's still not too late to back out.

"No, I made a promise."

Marcus doesn't reply. He keeps moving, and the others follow.

They climb a short flight of steps. There are two more corpses on the dock just outside the nearest door. Further down the platform, there's a second door. "I'll go this way," Marcus says, his thumb jerking towards the closest entry. "You'll go in through the next door."

Centurion says, "Okay." He offers Marcus a bag of Orangina bombs.

Marcus declines. "You take them. I've got this," he says, holding up his pistol.

"Good luck," Centurion says.

"You too." He ushers them away with wave of the hand. He grabs the handle, twists it, and it gives. He opens the door slowly, hidden behind it. He peers beyond the free edge of the door. Apparently finding no one, he enters, weapon drawn before him. He leans against the interior of the slab, and it slowly closes behind him as he makes his way in. It shuts with a soft *tchick*.

Centurion guides the others to the entrance further away. They scamper dozens of feet and then stop. Centurion moves beyond the door and checks the handle. Unlike the first, this one is locked and served by a security keypad. "Shazam," he says with a shake of his head.

"Maybe we should just start entering codes?" Crown suggests, his fingers lingering over the touchpad.

Centurion slaps his hand. "No."

"Ouch," Nigel Crown says, yanking his hand away.

"Sorry, but there could be an escalation protocol, a shutdown, for miskeyed codes," Centurion says. "I think all we probably need is a little elbow grease." He takes several steps back and prepares to ram the door.

"Wait," Chee says, spying through the door's lite, "there's someone coming." She backs away from the small window.

"Quick," Astrid says, "everyone under the dock."

Save for Centurion, they comply. Astrid and Chee jump from the edge first. They help Nigel as he makes the same leap. They steady him as he lands three feet below and pull him to a squatting position. Centurion hurries to the wall adjacent to the door's hinges. He removes his helmet and flattens himself as best his armor will allow.

The door opens.

Centurion grabs the handle as it reaches the peak of its swing.

A man strides out. He searches the pockets of his white lab coat for his cell phone. He flips it open and begins dialing.

Centurion flicks the bolt switch on the reverse side of the door to prevent it from closing and locking. It extends with a loud *clack*.

The man rotates. "It's *you*." Nick Davis stands three feet away and stares at Centurion like he has two heads.

Centurion twists his head like a dog trying to comprehend a new command. "You," he apes.

Davis' eyes narrow. "Get out of my way," he says, stepping forward.

Centurion draws his fist back and releases. He lands a right hook, connecting with Davis' temple and sending him sprawling. Davis lands on his back and flips off the platform. He falls with a *splat* to the asphalt below. His phone skitters to Centurion's feet.

Centurion picks up the device, holds it to his ear. It completes dialing. Someone's line rings. He holds the phone away from his face and examines the contact information. His eye twitches.

Davis has just called Holly Rodriguez.

Centurion begins to flip the cell phone closed. He hesitates. He raises the receiver to his ear.

Holly answers. "Hello?" she says. "Hello? Davis? Is that you? Listen, you little fucker, I told you to never call me again. Hello? Davis?"

Centurion hangs up and grins. He drops the phone to the floor and crushes it beneath a sandal. When he looks up, he finds Crown, Chee, and Astrid all peering at him, peeking above the dock. Almost in unison, they turn to look at the unconscious Davis, then back towards Centurion.

"Let's go," he says. "Let's figure out why that 'little fucker' is here."

They funnel in after him. The corridor widens beyond the door and connects to a series of rooms.

"How are we supposed to know which is the door to the lab?" Nigel asks.

"By opening them," Centurion says. He pushes the first door open slightly and peers in. There are a number of lockers here, and hanging along a wall are freshly laundered lab coats. "Jackpot," he mutters. He ushers the others into the room. "Let's change."

His helmet on the dock, Centurion opts to keep the remainder of his armor on. He hides it, however, under a long white laboratory coat. He rummages through a number of lockers and locates IDs. "Maybe these will help us get around," he says, examining the magnetic strip on one of the cards. He distributes them like magician performing a card trick to the others.

"Lokelani Keihanaikukauakahi?" Astrid says with a smirk as she inspects the ID.

"Try saying that again," Crown says. "I dare you."

"No thanks," she replies.

"Time to go, doctors," Centurion says. "Stat."

❖ ❖ ❖

Marcus makes his way through a corridor and up a flight of stairs, his M9 extended before him. It seems they've taken the facility by surprise. But he, more than anyone, knows that looks can be deceiving.

The second floor houses space for administrative and executive staff. The lights are off, the desks empty. He moves through the space, a giant open floor plan, towards the center of the building and his goal: Mansfield.

Marcus moves through the long lines of desks quietly and quickly. As he nears the hub, the command center of the main lab, he hears something like a patter. There's another, and then silence. *Footfalls?* He pauses, counts to fifteen.

Nothing.

He continues onward. Before him in the distance stands a glass wall. There is a dark room beyond it lit only by the glow of computers and communication terminals. Blue, red, and gold blinking lights dance and reflect off the pane. The chamber's comprised of two levels, almost like stadium seating, allowing the operators on both balconies to observe the lab in full.

No one sits on the upper level immediately before him. *Damn.*

He creeps forward, towards the glass door. He cranes his neck for a view down the stairs to the lower level. There's no movement, but there is the unmistakable form of a man silhouetted by the stark Kubrickian whiteness of the laboratory. He's seated and gazes into the lab below.

*Mansfield.*

Marcus holsters his weapon and opens the glass door. There's a slight *swoosh*, the sound of escaping air as the pressure changes.

Mansfield doesn't turn to greet his arrival.

Marcus takes three steps and begins his descent down a small flight of the stairs. He surveys the view, his focus alternating between Mansfield and the lab work beneath them. The room below radiates white, every instrument and fixture gleaming.

When he sees Kim, the cinematic serenity disappears, replaced, instead, by stark horror.

She is strapped down on a hydraulic operating table, covered with a surgical blanket. There's a growing red stain in the middle of her stomach. Blood seeps from a six-inch incision. The audio in the lab isn't on, but her screams still seem vaguely audible. Kane hasn't administered any anesthesia.

"He's cut through the skin," Mansfield says. "He'll verify the integrity of the specimen's abdominal wall, and then he'll continue. He'll start with the removal of her appendix and other non-essential organs first."

Marcus continues to the window, ignoring Mansfield. "Kane didn't put her under."

"No," Mansfield says, watching the scene below. "He said the advancement of medicine sometimes depends on straying from convention, or something to that effect."

"Medical ethics was never his strong suit."

"I don't concern myself with those details," Mansfield says, his seat spinning to face Marcus.

Spotting Marcus, Kim screams, something approximating, "Help me." Her pleas resonate in his head if not in his ears.

"There was a time you cared about the welfare of others," Marcus says.

"You're referring to the Nazis," Mansfield says with a sigh. "Well, that was different. Their testing benefitted the German military. They used their research to build weapons, test drugs, and develop new surgical techniques to treat their soldiers."

"And advance the notion that the Nazis were racially superior," Marcus adds.

"Sure," Mansfield says, "but to be honest, I was less concerned about that. We were fighting a war after all. Much like the war we're fighting now."

Marcus watches as Kane removes blood from Kim's wound with a suction device. "What he's doing is unconscionable. He's turned the Hippocratic Oath into the oath of a hypocrite."

"He's advancing science for the preservation of our collective way of life. Further, she's a non-person."

"That's exactly what the Nazis called the Jews," Marcus says.

"Tomato, Tomahto," Mansfield says. "So, what brings you here tonight?"

"Oh," Marcus says without a hint of inflection, "I almost forgot." He pulls his gun from his shoulder holster and points it at Mansfield's face. "I'm here to kill you."

"Now, let's not be rash, Marcus."

"Tell Kane to stop."

"I can't do that."

Marcus' aim shifts, almost imperceptibly. He fires. The bullet streaks by Mansfield's head, missing his earlobe by just a centimeter.

Kane's head jerks up and stares, startled, at the booth from the floor.

Mansfield groans. His hand goes to his ear. He grimaces as he checks his fingers for blood. "You could make someone deaf like that."

Marcus strides forward and puts the pistol to Mansfield's forehead. "Perhaps I just need to speak louder."

Mansfield puts both of his hands in the air and closes his eyes. He nods. "Okay, I'll tell Kane to stop." Marcus takes a step back as Mansfield speaks into a microphone. "Doctor," he says.

Kane's frozen.

"Doctor," Mansfield repeats.

Kane nods, his eyes saucers.

"Let's take a break."

"Tell him to move away from her," Marcus says. "Tell him to open the doors and move into the hallway."

"Kane, did you catch that?" Mansfield asks.

Kane nods again. He jogs over to the secured door, keys in a code. He pops the hatch and flees.

"I won't let you do to Chee what you did to her mother," Marcus says, extending the pistol. "Goodbye."

"You knew how much she meant to us."

"Until she decided to leave the agency."

"She didn't give us a choice," Mansfield says, his voice lilting.

"I know," Marcus says, lowering his weapon slightly.

"You do?" Mansfield leans in.

"Yes," Marcus replies, his eyes downcast.

Mansfield spies the steel and glass emergency cabinet hanging on the wall just inches beyond where Marcus stands. He fixates on the fire axe inside.

Marcus talks, almost to himself. "She enjoyed this life, at least for a time. It's taken me a long time to understand that. She knew the consequences."

"Good," Mansfield soothes, his weight shifting forward.

"But Chee never had that choice."

"Of course not," Mansfield says. "She had no control over the family she was born into. None of us do. But at least she was born to a family of privilege, a family that gained influence and wealth. Like her mother and her mother and her mother before her, she is a witch-smeller. And like her ancestors, she has helped us find"—he eyes Kim on the table below, his voice becoming a hiss—"and kill these monsters. It's what she was destined to do."

The gun grows heavy in Marcus' grasp. It falls to his side. His eyes thin and his eyebrows wilt as he continues to stare at the floor.

"There are many worse things than being a patriot." Mansfield rises to his feet. The fire axe in the emergency wall box is just three feet away. He starts to pivot on his heels, slowly turning Marcus to edge past him.

"No," Marcus says, his chin rising off of his chest. "Heredity is a copout. We made all of the decisions. We're the ones who condemned her."

"Come, now. Don't you think you're being a bit harsh?"

"We did," Marcus says, his full attention returning to Mansfield. The gun is suddenly up in front of him again, pointing directly into his employer's chest.

Mansfield is just eighteen inches from the cabinet. "I still remember when I found you," he says in an attempt to appeal to Marcus' compassionate side, "you and Amachi in the dirt, hiding in the corner of a rusted metal shack. Do you remember?"

"I remember," Marcus says.

Mansfield takes a half step forward, still showing his palms. "Then you remember she would have died if I hadn't helped her escape."

"From the very mob that you unleashed on her mother."

Mansfield shrugs.

"Did you know the police couldn't find enough of Hélène's body to justify a burial?" Marcus asks. "Those maniacs hacked my wife to pieces with machetes. They ate her flesh thinking they could obtain her power. I wonder where they got that idea?"

"No," Mansfield lies. "I didn't know that." He inches closer to glass panel that protects the axe.

"Stop," Marcus says. "I will kill you."

"No. You won't. As soon as I learned you were coming tonight, I took precautions."

"You knew I was coming?"

"Yes," Mansfield says.

*Shit.*

A hyena giggles from above them.

# Track Twenty-Five: Show of Strength

They move single file through the halls. Centurion's girth fills the middle while the others follow in his shadow. His broad frame shields Chee, Astrid, and Nigel in that order.

The corridor intersects another hall. They have a decision to make.

"It's got to be left," Centurion says.

"But I can't get a read on Kim in that direction," Astrid says.

"Can you get a read on her in any direction?" he asks.

"No," she admits, dejected.

"Don't worry," Crown says. "We'll find her."

"Maybe we should split up," Chee says.

"Maybe," Centurion says as he checks each hallway.

"Okay," Crown says, "You two"—he indicates Centurion and Chee—"go left. We'll take the right."

"Here," Centurion says, handing the backpack to Crown. "Take these. Make sure you throw them after you light them."

"Good advice."

Without a further sound, they go their separate ways.

Centurion and Chee don't speak as they move through the warehouse, opening doors and examining corridors. Chee finally breaks the quiet.

"I'm sorry," she says suddenly. "I'm sorry about Henry."

The words halt Centurion in his steps. "You don't need to apologize," he says. "It wasn't your fault."

Silence again. Then she says, "I know he loved you very much."

Centurion grunts and nods. He pushes a door open and peers in. Just boxes full of medical supplies. He turns back to Chee. "He talked about me?"

"Some," Chee says. "For instance, he told me about the game you played, coming up with names for groups of science fiction and horror creatures."

Centurion chuckles. "That was fun. We created some cool terminology." He brightens up. "What do you call a bunch of Skeksis?"

"Like Chamberlain and the reptile-birds from the *Dark Crystal*?" she asks.

"Those are the ones." She passed a minor test, an initial assessment of her nerd cred.

"I don't think you need a group name. Skeksis is both plural and singular."

His eyes glaze over. He has failed his own test. "Oh, right," he says.

"Give me another," Chee says, eager for a new challenge.

"Later," he replies half-heartedly. Then, "Listen." The clap of shoes against the linoleum echoes from further down the hall.

Doctor Kane rounds the corner twenty feet away. He jogs right to them.

"Doctor," Kane calls to Centurion as he approaches. He lurches to a stop. He catches his breath, grabs his hips and leans over. He breathes hard. "Doctor," he says to Chee looking up at her. A puzzled expression crosses his face as he scrutinizes her, his eyes traveling up and down, from her torso to her head and back. They lock on to her All-Stars. "Wait, you're no doctor."

"No," Centurion says, grabbing Kane's lab coat near his throat. "We're not doctors." He spins him around and presses him hard against a concrete wall. "And that's really too bad too, because you're going to need one."

Kane tries to cover his face with his hands. "Don't hurt me. I was just taking orders."

"Where is she?" Centurion demands, his voice rumbling like summer thunder. "Where's Kim Monfort?"

"She's in the lab, just around the corner."

Centurion shakes Kane violently. "What's the entry code?" he brays.

"It's open," the doctor says, his legs going weak.

Centurion bounces him off the wall one last time. "Come on," he says to Chee.

Doctor Kane slides down the wall and draws his knees to his chest. He shakes, too terrified to move.

A glass wall confronts them as they fly around the corner. Centurion cups his hands against the window and peers in. "Someone's in there," he says. He slaps the glass. "Hey!" he yells. "She's not moving."

"Look," Chee says, hopping and pointing, "there's the entrance. It is open."

They follow the line of glass wall and sprint down the passageway.

"We're coming, Kim!" Chee cries.

They hear a yelp, a plea for help, and Centurion runs harder.

They enter the lab through the portal like door. Chee rushes to Kim's side. Centurion, though, pauses to survey the room. Above them, Marcus is talking to two men in a booth, the apparent control room. Guns are drawn. Centurion races to the operating table. He sets his bag of Molotovs on the floor and helps. She's already unbuckling the straps at Kim's ankles. He moves to her hands.

"She's bleeding," Chee says.

"Don't move her yet," Centurion says. "We need to close that wound somehow."

Kim groans. "It's not as bad as it looks," she says.

❖❖❖

"So," Nigel Crown says, "you talk to ghosts. That's got to make you the most popular kid during show-and-tell."

"Actually," Astrid says, "it kind of makes me the school freak. But I'll really be popular once I tell everyone I met you."

They come to another junction point. "Which way now," Crown says.

"Mmm, that way," Astrid says, indicating the corridor to the left with a wave of her hand.

"Works for me."

They take two steps, just two, before they're halted.

"Hey," a guard calls from behind them.

Crown and Astrid turn like the neighboring gears of a watch with a dying battery.

A guard in black military garb greets them as they complete their slow revolution. "I need to see your badges," the soldier says. The muzzle of an assault rifle peeks over his shoulder, a pistol bulges at his hip.

❖❖❖

Centurion tears open a drawer on a nearby counter. *Nothing.* He tries another, then a third. *Bingo.* "Here," he says, pawing a roll of gauze followed by a spool of surgical tape. "Apply this," he says, handing over the gauze, "then wrap the tape around her waist several times."

"Got it," Chee says. "Can you sit up?"

Kim flinches as she lifts herself. "Yes. Yes, I can." Her face suddenly distorts, her lips twisting to expose an incisor.

"Is it the pain?" Chee asks.

"No," Kim whispers. "It's just . . . well, I'm naked under this blanket."

Centurion pulls off his lab coat revealing the white armor beneath. "Here," he says, handing the coat to Kim and turning his back. She takes it with one hand while using the other to hold the blanket to her chest.

"Almost done," Chee says as she wraps the tape under the blanket and around Kim's midriff again.

Kim stares at Centurion and his armor. She sniggers. "Aren't you a little tall to be a stormtrooper?"

"What? Oh, the armor," he says, without turning. "I'm Centurion." He gives her a little wave over his shoulder. "I'm here to rescue you."

"You're who?"

"We're here to rescue you. We have Astrid with us." His attention returns to the booth looming above them.

"Astrid is here? Where is she?"

"Hurry," Centurion says to Chee.

"This is like a scene from *Star Wars*," Chee says beaming. Then she catches Centurion staring into the control room, and her nerdy delight turns to horror. "What's up there?" she says. "Oh my God. Dad?"

❖❖❖

Marcus twists and targets the entrance.

Smith laughs again. "Take it easy," he says from the doorframe. His weapon is directed at Marcus' heart. "You look like shit."

Marcus rubs his face, feels the cuts and soreness from bruising. "I met my better tonight," Marcus says. "What's your excuse, Tutankhamen?"

Mansfield interrupts. "Smith called me from your house earlier. He was very concerned about your well-being."

"You sent him to kill us?" Marcus asks Mansfield, his eyes still affixed on Smith.

"No," Mansfield says, shaking his head. "That was simply Smith taking initiative. He was looking for the Dunst girl. And we'd never harm Chee, would we, Smith?"

"Sure," Smith says. Bits of spit spray through his torn smile.

"When he found Chee's necklace and your place in shambles, I suspected you'd want to tie things up."

"Don't trust him," Marcus says. "Once I'm dead, Mansfield's going to kill you next."

Outwardly, Smith scoffs. His eyes, though, convey the truth of his worry. They bounce immediately to Mansfield, pleading for a response.

"It's true," Marcus says. "What do you think you're worth to them now? How valuable is an assassin who can't hide? An assassin who draws attention? You're compromised."

His mask of bandages can't hide Smith's expression. He now looks both emotionally and physically wounded. He asks Mansfield if it's true.

"Of course not," Mansfield replies, backing up. He feels resistance, the emergency cabinet against his back. "Take him out. Now."

Smith hesitates.

"Just leave," Marcus says. "Walk away. Let me finish my business."

Smith doesn't have time to consider his options. He spots movement on the floor of the lab. "They're freeing her," he snarls.

Marcus and Mansfield both twist towards the laboratory. Kim is leaning against Chee, her arm thrown over her shoulder. They are shuffling towards the exit. Centurion, however, stands directly before them, defiant. Something smokes in his fist.

Marcus faces Smith. Smith trains his firearm on the teens. "Stop!" Marcus yells. He rushes into the line of fire.

Centurion bends, grips a petrol bomb in either hand. He steps in front of the teens. "Chee, you need to get out of here."

"But what about my dad?"

"I'll take care of Marcus. Now move!"

Kim's dressed. She scoots off the table towards Chee. "Grab those vials on that counter. And those syringes," she says.

Chee doesn't move. Her focus is on her father.

"We've got to get out of here," Kim says, grabbing Amachi by the shoulders.

Chee blinks. Her head bounces up and down. "Okay." She's off, scooping up a dozen vials and a handful of syringes and needles in her arms. She returns to Kim, and they stuff the materials into the deep pockets of her lab coat.

Kim tosses her arm over Chee's neck. "Move." They hobble towards the door.

The sound of muted gunfire resonates from above and behind. Muzzle flashes light up the booth and the laboratory.

"Daddy!" Chee cries. She tries to reverse course, but Kim won't let her. She holds her tight and uses her weight to prod her forward.

"Come on," Kim says as she shoves Chee through the exit.

They wouldn't have had much to go back to anyway.

Centurion lights the homemade grenades . . . and firebombs the place.

The first bomb strikes the wall next to the booth.

The second Molotov's directed at the other side of the room, an interior wall. It takes out the wing's electrical grid. With it goes the electromagnetic field generated about the facility.

"Run," Crown says, and Astrid does. They scatter at the next junction, him peeling left, and her to the right. They hunker down on either side of the hallway. Crown slips off the backpack, grabs a couple of home-made grenades. He slides the bag across the hall to Astrid.

The guard is on his radio.

"He's calling for help," Astrid says.

There's an explosion from somewhere in the facility. Then another.

"Great minds," Crown murmurs to himself. He stands and holds an Orangina bottle before him. "Here goes," he says. The lighter sparks. He brings his hands together, and the cotton wick lights. He holds the bomb away from his body as he peers around the corner.

The guard approaches, his steps cautious and measured and his handgun extended before him at a forty-five degree angle. He's only fifteen feet away. "Halt," the man says as he levels the weapon on Crown. He lets a bullet fly, and it strikes the concrete corner block at eye level and ricochets down the corridor.

Bits of cement strike Crown in the temple as he yanks his head in. "Wanker." He takes three deep breaths, and leaps forth into the hall. He pirouettes, burning bottle in hand. He grunts as he hurls the bomb at the guard's feet. It lands short, exploding and sending burning fuel through the passage. The soldier's pants leg ignites. He falls backwards, screaming and slapping the flames wildly. Crown allows a grin, but it's short-lived. Beyond the flames, he spots three more sentries in fatigues entering the fray. He frowns. "We've got company," he tells Astrid. He scurries to safety.

Astrid regards him as if he's a stranger, like she's meeting him for the first time.

"What's wrong?" he says.

A pink cone emanates from his chest, spiraling and floating two feet above him. She can see his aura. "Whatever was blocking my vision is gone," she says. She's immediately overwhelmed by the sense of Kim. She can feel her, detect her. She's in the building. She sighs and shakes her head. "We went the wrong way," she says.

"What of the others?"

Other auric entities are near her, one of them golden. "I think they're with Kim," Astrid says, her tone even with relief.

"Good. Let's buy them some time," Crown says. He leans over, lights another Molotov. He counts to three and whips it around the corner without looking.

There's a blast followed by a shriek. The resulting heat is intense. It forces him to inch away from the hallway. The guards spray machine gun fire in his direction. Bullets throw mortar and bounce throughout the corridor.

"Get back," Crown says to Astrid. "Cover your eyes!" He slides down the wall, making himself smaller.

She hears Crown, but his voice is fading, replaced by another voice from somewhere deep inside of her ear canal. She trembles. She's losing consciousness.

The sprinklers kick on. "Damn it," Crown says.

Astrid's eyes shut. Her grandfather whispers, "Hello, Chickadee." He instructs her, commands her to do something she doesn't think she's capable of doing.

Her head bobbles from left to right and back. "Impossible," she says to him.

"You're communicating with a dead man right now," his disembodied voice says. "Don't talk to me about what's possible and what isn't. Use your imagination. Conjure."

"Astrid, are you okay?" Crown calls, but she can no longer hear him. His words and the sounds of gunfire have faded away into the abyss of time space.

The trance is deep. She stands alone on white plane in a white void. A dark beam, the absence of light projects towards her. The energy is black and pure, the color of discord and confusion. The ray enters her head and expands. It fills her. Her hands ball into fists, her face twitches. She strains. The dark mass contracts and pools near the base of her spine. Her fingers extend, her hands spring forth, and the black ball projects from her. It's packed tight and dense, and shrinks to the size of a basketball.

She begins molding the matter, shaping her thoughtform. She gives it talons, fangs, and wings. She allows it to buckle and grow. It's four feet, no, now eight feet tall. It's massive, and strains against her influence. She leashes it, holds it fast with tendrils from her mind. Stayed, she infuses the creature with her will, programs it to do her bidding. She gives it design. She whispers one last command to it before releasing her Id Monster, hurling the beast into the void above her.

Astrid's eyes pop open. She blinks away the rain spitting from the fire suppression system. She turns to Crown. "Nigel?"

"Thank God," he says, barely audible over the gunfire. "You're alive and with us again. You had me worried."

A blood-chilling screech reverberates through the facility. The roar is somehow both synthetic and natural, the bastardization of a moog stretched to its limits, the moan of a blue whale, and bellow of a grizzly. The foundations quake, the walls tremble.

Crown's hands go to his ears. "What the hell was that?" He starts to stand, prepares to run.

The firing stops. The screaming begins.

"No," Astrid says, "stay."

Her eyes mean business. Crown doesn't move. He just lets the water drip off his face and listens as the monster howls again. Soldiers cry for their mothers. Bones snap. Bodies are pounded into pulp. The remains of a soldier hurtle past them. What's left of him lands grotesquely with a wet *slap*. It rolls to a stop somewhere beyond their field of view. There's crashing, the sound of concrete crumbling and falling. It's the sound of the devil breaking loose from his chains and releasing hell on earth.

A moment later, there is silence.

"Okay," Astrid says, droplets bouncing off her face. "I think it's safe for us now."

They enter the carnage of the hall. The ceiling has partially collapsed, there's exposed electrical. Water pours from ruptured sprinkler lines. A giant hole leads to the second floor. Blood covers the walls and pools with water on the floor. Concrete debris litters the passage, pulled from the walls by giant parallel gouges. The claw marks run uninterrupted for fifteen feet, exposing the cores of the cinder blocks.

Crown steps over a soaked and headless body. "Just what did you do?"

Astrid shakes. Her chest heaves. Tears mix with the water pouring down her face. "I don't know," she says. "I—" Her sentiment is cut off as she begins to retch.

Crown collects her with an arm around her waist. "It's okay," he says. "Let's go." He escorts her through the structural and human wreckage.

❖❖❖

Smoke fills the lab, masking the command room. Centurion calls for Marcus and chokes. There's no answer from above. He spins blindly before locating an illuminated "Exit" sign. He lurches toward it.

A fog of soot billows from the chamber and into the halls. The emergency lights do little to illuminate his path. He limps onward. He tries to inhale, to call for Chee and Kim. He coughs violently instead.

His eyes water. He puts his head down and stumbles forward, knocking Chee and Kim to the ground. They land in a heap with a collective groan.

"You need to get out of here," Centurion groans.

"That's what we were doing," Kim says, clutching her stomach.

"Where's Dad?" Chee says.

"I'll find him," Centurion says. "Find Astrid and get to the Chariot."

"The Chariot?" Kim asks.

"The Dodge Caravan in the lot," Centurion says. "Go."

"Follow me," Chee says. They move.

Centurion crawls on his hands and knees in the other direction. As he creeps along, the smoke starts to dissipate. He gets to his feet, stooping below the artificial ceiling created by the smog.

Soon, he arrives at a staircase, the very steps that Marcus ascended earlier. They may lead to death. He follows them up.

❖❖❖

Marcus rolls, glass and bits of ceiling tile cascading off his back. It takes him a moment to understand where he is, to recollect the twin explosions. The first Molotov landed high and to the right of the control room. It clearly wasn't intended to kill. Rather, it was meant to do the opposite. Buy Marcus time.

The pain is sudden and piercing. Marcus groans, coughs blood. He touches his chest. It is warm and wet with arterial blood. He feels it pulse and spill.

He stares at what's left of the ceiling through the thick smoke. He can barely see anything beyond it and the flames.

The second bomb was directed away from his position, a shock and awe diversion. It was also a lucky shot. It sheered the conduit carrying electricity to most of the wing. The emergency lamps flash with the beat of Marcus' heart. The room alternates between washes of orange and red.

Glass breaks, followed by the clang of metal against the tile. There's the slow shuffle of feet scattering debris. Something drags behind.

He's not alone. "Smith," Marcus croaks.

"No," Mansfield says, shambling forth.

Marcus wheezes. "Seems nothing can kill you."

Mansfield hacks. "No," he says, "I will die, an eventuality made more likely now that Ms. Monfort is gone."

"Where should I send the flowers?" Marcus rasps.

"We will find her again. If it's not me, it will be someone else. It's just a matter of time."

"So this isn't about you," Marcus says. "Tell me what it's really about."

"It's about military might," Mansfield says, stepping from the shroud of smoke. He's just a silhouette of a nightmare, axe in hand. "That's what it's always and ever about. Us beating them to the punch."

"The punch?"

"The perfect soldier."

"A myth," Marcus says. "You've been reading too many Captain America comics."

"No, it can be a reality," Mansfield says. He creeps forward. His face is red and insane. "Imagine a soldier who can heal his wounds in the trenches of battle without any medical attention. Imagine a soldier with the strength to lift a tank. Imagine a warrior who can change into a monster, a dog soldier, or a were-bore. Now imagine an army of them."

"You're mad."

"'There is no great genius without a mixture of madness.' Aristotle."

"At least Aristotle had the good sense to die. I should have killed you when I had a chance," Marcus says. He struggles with the words, his strength waning.

"I know why you waited. I know why you didn't kill me immediately. You've had a death wish, an unconscious desire to die. It's guilt. Well, I'm happy to be your genie and grant you that wish."

"Do it," Marcus says, staring Mansfield in the eyes.

Mansfield raises the axe above his head.

❖ ❖ ❖

"Wait," Kim says. She digs into her pockets. "Help me with these vials. Find one that says EpiGenie."

Chee fingers the bottles, turns them before her face. "Here." She holds a glass container of greenish liquid before her.

Kim instructs Chee to open a syringe and fill it with the chemical. "Okay, now push up on the plunger to remove the excess air."

"Like this?"

"Yes, perfect. Now, inject me with it."

"Chee's eyes grow large. "I don't think—"

"Stick me," Kim says. "In my upper arm."

Chee's lips pucker.

"Now," Kim demands.

Chee does as she's told, pulling the lab coat back to reveal Kim's bare shoulder. She presses the needle against Kim's skin. The needle pokes, creating a slight indentation, before slipping through the epidermis. She takes a deep breath before depressing the plunger.

Kim's shoulder grows warm. The drug works through her arm, courses through her body. It wraps her in the heat of a blanket. Her head lolls to the side.

"Kim!" Chee yells, certain her friend has overdosed.

Kim snaps to attention. "Don't yell," she says. Her senses come alive. She sniffs the air and grins. *Menthol.*

"Are you okay?"

Kim's brow furrows. "Find Astrid."

"But—"

"I'm fine," she says. "I'll be right behind you."

"Where are you going?"

Kim's eyes narrow. She sneers, her lip pulling back to reveal a fang. "To keep a pledge."

❖❖❖

Mansfield lowers the axe.

"Do it," Marcus says.

Mansfield leers from above him. He tosses the axe to the side.

"I knew you didn't have the guts," Marcus says.

"It's not a matter of guts," Mansfield says, the flames encroaching on them. "It's a matter of poetic justice. I'm going to let you burn like all of those witches you've condemned." He laughs hard.

His cackling is interrupted. An insane supernatural roar resonates throughout the floor. The flames ebb momentarily as if somehow giving deference to the entity behind the ungodly howl.

Mansfield doesn't say the words, but his expression shouts, "What the hell was that?" He looks about, his mouth wide with worry, and disappears behind the curtain of smoke. His rapid footfalls on the stairs expose his fear.

❖❖❖

Kim stops, and sniffs the air again. She twists her head and snorts deeper. *There.*

Before her is a door marked, "Janitor's Closet."

Scents mix with the mint on Kane's breath. She smells his sweat, sniffs the lactic acid and urea. His apocrine glands aren't producing the sweat of a man who has exercised. They're producing pheromones of someone anxious, someone terrified.

"Doctor Kane," she sings, "I smell your fear."

She walks, her bare feet barely making a sound, to the entry. She turns the knob, and the latch releases. She draws the door open a crack.

The room is dark. Her eyes adjust, changing and turning yellow. A wolf-like membrane between the retina and lens develops, reflecting light back to the retina. This, and the high concentration of rods in the retina near the optic nerves, increases her eyes' sensitivity to low light.

Kane sits in the corner, his trademark tendrils of blonde hair plastered to his sweaty head. He holds a quivering broomstick before him as protection.

Still, even if she couldn't smell him, even if she lacked night vision, Kim would know he's here. She hears his desperate and shallow pants. He lets out a little yelp as the door swings wide.

"Doctor Kane," Kim says, remaining in the light of the hall, "I've got a surprise for you." Her muscles twitch. Her bones crack and groan. Her body lengthens, and her shoulders broaden. Muscle develops in her calves, chest, and arms. Her eyes deepen, her forehead widens, and her hairline pulls back. Her lips thin, and her cheekbones rise.

"Bonsoir," Kim's impression is for once in her lifetime impeccable. "What do you think?" she continues, her accent masculine and French. She displays a cat-that-ate-the-canary-like grin, a grin very similar to the one Alec Moreau displayed hundreds of times to hundreds of victims.

Kane shrieks. His legs kick, as if he believes he might be able to slide deeper into the closet and escape, as if he might be able to crawl through the wall that contains him.

Standing before Kane is a wanted poster from another time. Standing before him is Alec Moreau, Kim's ancestor.

"You were right," the Kim-Moreau creature says. "There really is no limit to what I can do."

He alternates between cries for help and mercy.

"You asked about my dad earlier," the thing that was Kim says. "I do remember one thing, some advice he gave at the dinner table when

I was little, when he still lived with us. He used to say, 'Don't play with your food.' I think he'd scold me for my behavior if he could see me now.'"

Her body snaps and pops. Fur grows in thick tufts about her neck and chest. Her ears stretch above her head. Fangs protrude from her jaw, claws burst from her paws. She becomes a creature from lore. She is the demon feared by Henri Boguet and the very first witch-hunters of France. She is the *loup garou*.

And like all good monsters, she has returned to destroy the creator who made her so.

❖❖❖

"Andy," Nigel Crown says into his cell phone, "now would be a fantastic time to meet us in the parking lot."

More soldiers are coming. There could be a dozen, possibly more. Their true numbers are masked by the narrowness of the hall.

"How many fans? Really, that many? That's well nice. It's critical that they follow you, understand? No stragglers." He slides the phone into his pocket.

"This way," Astrid says.

"One moment," he says. He lights another bomb and drops it into the backpack.

"Oh. My. God," Astrid says. She takes flight.

"I'm right behind you," Crown says. Rather than heaving the bag of explosives at the soldiers, he swings it over his head and slams it into the floor six feet away.

The lit grenade ignites the other Orangina bottles. There's a flash and a *kaboom*. The floor melts. The ceiling catches fire. Smoke billows through the halls.

Presto. When the soldiers finally clear the flames, the intruders are nowhere to be found.

❖❖❖

Mansfield runs as fast as his ancient body will allow him.

The thoughtform gives chase, its screams resonating and shaking the timbers of the second floor. It throws desks and tables clear as it gallops towards him.

Mansfield enters a narrow stairwell and slams the door behind him. He hops down a handful of steps and holds his side. He sucks air. He leans against the wall like a man who thinks he's safe, like a man confident the monster can't touch him. He stares at the landing above him. Whatever it is, it surely can't open doors. Whatever it is, it must be too massive for the frame. Whatever it is, it can't reach him here.

He's wrong.

Astrid's Id Monster knocks the steel door off its hinges. It squeezes its massive head through the opening, bursting the metal frame. The thing levels its horrendous gaze upon Mansfield. It roars, exposing row after row of shark-like teeth. It rattles its head furiously, its mane tossed to and fro, its massive tusks scraping the concrete floor. The casing pops, and the wall gives with it. Studs snap. Structural supports fail. The creature threatens to bring the roof down with it. Mansfield blubbers and flees. He runs down the stairs, around a corner, and down a long hall.

Davis has come to. He struggles to his feet, rubs his face. He yawns to test his jaw. Sluggish, he makes his way up to the platform and to the entry.

Mansfield Smith-Cumming bursts through the exit and on to the dock. He slams into an unsteady Davis. He skips down the stairs in two bounds, and flies around the side of the building. He heads for the cornfields.

Davis again sails off the platform, this time landing on a shoulder below. His legs go over his head as he rolls. He comes to rest on his stomach. "What the fuck, Mansfield?" Davis yells.

The exit erupts, blown open by the gargantuan thoughtform. The corrugated metal siding blossoms, the header and jambs splintering. The heavy door, still in its frame, soars towards Davis. Nick rolls in the nick of time, barely escaping becoming even more of a stain.

Something heavy thunders across the platform. It howls as it leaps from the stairs. The creature lands fifteen feet clear of the loading dock. It shakes the earth and sends bits of bitumen flying. It continues to chase Mansfield, its electrical grunts fading off into the distance. Moments later in the distance, Davis hears a sharp wail, the cry of a man in agony. Then there's nothing.

"What the fuck?" Davis says again, his mouth agape and quivering.

That's when a tour bus enters the parking lot. It's followed by hundreds of vehicles. They park, and the parking lot floods with Nigel Crown's fans.

Davis decides it's time for him to leave.

❖❖❖

As Centurion nears the top of the flight, Smith steps into the landing.

Smith says, "Shit."

Centurion says, "Round two."

Smith lunges at him, his teeth bared like a jackal. He catches Centurion near the shoulders, and the two roll end-over-end down the stairs.

# Track Twenty-Six: Hero

*Lowry Park Zoo, Tampa. 14 March 2001.*

"Go ahead," Henry Famosa says.

"You don't think it's stupid?" Chee asks.

They are sitting on a bench in a gazebo in the Ituri Forest, a dozen light pink flamingoes sunning themselves in the pond behind them.

"I know a lot of adults who collect toys," he says. Heck, his uncle has been stockpiling *Star Wars* figures since the Hasbro years. Uncle Juan gets peeved whenever Henry calls them "dolls," tells him how they're going to be worth a ton of money in Henry's lifetime. Henry doubts it. "Go for it."

"They're not toys," she says, her hands on her hips. "They're Mold-a-Ramas, and they're a piece of Americana."

She had only discovered the vending machines in the last few years, but she's right. Introduced during the 1964 World's Fair, the blow-molded plastic figures are featured in dozens of museums and zoos around the United States. From Florida to Texas and north to Chicago and Dearborn, Michigan, the figurines amassed a following from collectors nostalgic for the 1970s and 1980s.

He smiles. His canines are a bit too pronounced, and his incisors crooked. Still, the uneven gaps project a fearless innocence that's rare to find in kids these days. This kid is genuine.

He likes Chee a lot, so he doesn't question her need to spend two bucks on a piece of wax that probably won't even make it out of the park in one piece. "Okay, get your fix, crackhead."

Chee offers a grin in response. "Do you want one?" she asks.

"No, thanks. I don't want to go down that pathway of addiction with you," he jokes.

Chee giggles, slaps him on the shoulder. "Whatever. You're going to wish you went with me."

"I'm sure I will," he says.

"You will. Trust me." She starts to back away. "Last chance. Want one?"

"Okay, if they have a train, I'll take one."

"A train?" Chee's lips twist into a semi-frown. "I think they only sell animal molds here."

"Okay, never mind," he says. "I'm good. Hurry up though. The zoo closes in thirty minutes."

"Be right back." She heads down the path that will take her past the meerkats and giraffes to the safari lodge and gift shop

*A stand.* That's what a group of flamingoes is called. The birds take long, elegant strides across the pond, their heads tilting slowly, searching for fish to swallow. They're totally ignorant of the tortoises and pigmy hippos they share the enclosure with.

*A bale of turtles.*

*A bloat of hippos.*

Henry studies the names of animal groupings. It's a hobby. It started with birds: a flock of seagulls, a gaggle of geese, a paddling of ducks, a sord of mallards. Then it expanded to reptiles, fish, and bugs. Sometimes, the congregational names are clever: a wake of buzzards, a prickle of porcupines, an intrusion of cockroaches. Other times, they're mysterious: a smack of jellyfish, a shiver of sharks, an unkindness of ravens.

Centurion's always bugging him to tell him the names of different animals. Often, he asks about something pretty obvious.

"What do you call a group of dogs again?" he'd ask while feeding a stray.

"A pack."

"Oh, yeah."

Recently, Centurion's been asking him to generate collective nouns for fictional creatures. For example, Centurion introduced Henry to Doctor Who several months back. After watching an episode featuring Tom Baker on VHS, Centurion asked, "What do you call a bunch of Daleks?"

"Daleks." Henry replied sarcastically.

"Come on," Centurion urged.

Henry didn't hesitate. "An extermination."

"Awesome," Centurion crowed. "Just awesome."

Since, the list had included:

- The mythological. Basilisks? A sight.
- The geeky. Jawas? A crawler.
- The geekier. Wookies? A knot.
- The domestic paranormal. Wendigo? A blubber. This suggestion Henry based on an Ogden Nash poem.
- The international paranormal. Jin? A conjure. This was followed by a debate about whether Jin actually hangout in groups.
- The scary. Zombies? A shamble.
- The scarier. Clowns? A compact. This led to a follow-up from Centurion: *What about evil clowns?* Henry's response: *Is there any other type?*
- The plain weird. Molemen? A burrow. This after a Son of Sven goolie marathon.

This line of questioning has become more prevalent in recent weeks. Henry suspects it's a ploy to fill the void whenever an uncomfortable silence descends upon them.

They don't hangout like they used to, partly because of Centurion's recent bout of drinking, partly because this kid is tired of being *the* Kid. He's sick of being referred to as a sidekick. He's sick of their conversations defaulting to the same old topics, like crime fighting and the special responsibility of being a superhero.

Recently he tried to convince Henry that they needed matching tattoos, specifically, the number 38. When asked why, Centurion launched into a story about Kitty Genovese and the 38 people who, as the New York Times noted in March of 1964, "watched a killer stalk and stab a woman in three separate attacks." "It's a call to action," Centurion said, "a reaction against the 'bystander effect,'" or the idea that there's an inverse relationship between the number of witnesses to a crime and the likelihood a victim will be helped. "We are responsible for our fellow man."

"I've read *Watchmen*," Henry/the Kid replied. "There's no way Mom and Dad will let me get a tattoo."

That didn't stop Centurion though. He got "38" inked on his neck, just below his jaw. It was a scarlet number bearing as much significance as anything Nathaniel Hawthorne could dream up. Like Hester Prynne's letter, it symbolized shame. Not personal shame, but societal shame. It wasn't a sign of repentance. It was a pointed accusation, a demand that the cowards of the world step up to the plate.

Centurion's crusade is noble, but it is also exhausting.

Being with Chee is different. With her, it's not all about the drama of life, the fight for justice. She likes him for who he is at his core, and not because of his power of extrasensory perception. He can be himself around her without pretense. He can be a kid, not *The Kid*. It's effortless, and that's nice for once.

Henry leans back on the bench, puts his hands behind his head, and locks his fingers. He exhales slowly, stares out across the pool. He slowly closes his eyes, focusing on the feeling of the setting sun on his face. He listens to the cries of birds, the sound of the wind rustling the reeds and stirring the leaves in the trees.

This is contentment.

That's when his stomach starts to churn and cramp. He bends over and grabs his belly. He groans.

This is not indigestion. This is not diarrhea. Something bad is about to happen. Something so bad it clouds his second sight. Darkness obscures the angles, blurs the lines of effects and their precedent causes. He is only in the here and now. He is blind.

*Chee.*

He needs to fight through the pain. He needs to get to her. He stands, grabs hold of one of the gazebo posts, starts towards the boardwalk. He stumbles, clings to the banister, and forces himself forward.

He bumps into a ghost, something invisible.

*Cackle.*

A man titters like a hyena.

*A group of hyenas is called a cackle.*

His vision returns in a rush. He's paralyzed by foresight, by the certainty of causality.

He goes down on his knees. He feels hands tighten about his neck. They constrict his esophagus. He chokes.

He offers no resistance. He can't muster the will to defend himself against this Cyclops truth. He's consumed by melancholy, the immediate despondence that comes from the foresight of one's death. He curls up in a ball, closes his eyes and cries. He's a victim of despair, of a dissociative trauma that has yet to occur, *pre*-traumatic stress.

*Coalition.*

He senses he's being dragged across the wooden planks of the elevated walkway. He knows where.

*A group of cheetahs is called a coalition.*

He accepts his fate.

He has one last premonition.

*Centurion.* It's a dual prediction painted in reds and browns, strokes of violence and stability. Revenge and blood. Friendship and safety.

Henry Famosa smiles his last crooked smile.

Chee returns, brandishing a deep green elephant in her hands. She lifts it to her nose, inhales the smell of cast plastic, as she scans for Henry. She calls for him.

He is nowhere to be found.

She searches the Ituri Forest and Safari Africa. Then she checks again before making her way to Wallaroo Station and requesting help at the petting zoo. She's told the zoo is closing for the day. She'll need to wait at admissions and ticketing near the main entrance.

She waits an hour before a curator greets her. The keepers and volunteers have searched the zoo thoroughly. Every store, every path, and every stall of every bathroom has been combed. There's no sign of her friend.

Frantic, she calls her father. He arrives in minutes, saying he was in the neighborhood. "Don't cry. I'm sure he had a good reason for leaving." She cradles her hollow toy pachyderm in her lap as they make their way home.

The next morning, zoo hands find Henry's body in the Cheetah paddock. His neck's broken, presumably a result of the fall from the boardwalk. Unfortunately, a pair of cubs found him first. They used the encounter as an opportunity to discover their fangs and claws. They made messy work of Henry's face, neck, and chest.

❖ ❖ ❖

Chee's father sends his regrets to Henry's family. Chee can't attend the funeral at The Garden of Memories Funeral Home. Marcus has been called away again, and they must be in Indianapolis in two days. They leave the day before the services.

❖ ❖ ❖

Centurion attends the memorial service with a fistful of flowers. The Kid's casket is closed. Rather than pay their respects to the body, Henry's fellow students and their parents linger at a photo-covered poster board on an easel. From there they move on to give their condolences to Henry's parents and relatives.

Centurion stops at the poster. There are two-dozen or more pictures glued to the cardboard. Many feature Henry as an infant or toddler. A few depict him as a teen. There are a couple of photos that Centurion took with the Kid. In each, Centurion has been cropped out, either cut or folded out of existence.

He makes his way down the receiving line, but Henry's parents refuse to greet him. An uncle, Juan, steps forward and escorts the man dressed like a gladiator from the funeral parlor.

Of course, they blame Centurion's influence for the death of their son.

*They're not wrong.*

In the parking lot, he tosses the flowers on to the hot asphalt.

He vows to make good on his debt to his sidekick and friend. He vows to make someone pay.

It is as the Kid, in his final painful moments, envisioned.

# Track Twenty-Seven: Both Ends Burning

*The lab. 7 September 2001.*

Smith twists as they fall. He pulls Centurion underneath and behind him as they hit the base of the stairs. He leans back and applies a head-lock and yanks forward. He clasps his hands and squeezes, choking Centurion between his arm and chest. He laughs his hysterical high-pitched laugh.

Centurion flails, fails to make contact. He labors to breathe, gulps for air like a snared sunfish on the deck of a boat. Seconds pass, his vision tunnels. Black haze squeezes in from the fringes. He feels his body going limp. His free arm drops.

*Chee.* A promise to Marcus brings him back from the brink.

Centurion jerks his elbow in and underneath him. He uses it as leverage and rolls on his side. He swings his arm over the top of Smith's shoulder and grasps his other hand. Smith's body bends forward, and Centurion forces his forearm under his opponent's chin. He kicks his leg, lifts his butt up on to first stair, and continues to rotate away from Smith's back.

Smith slides backward, tries to prevent Centurion from moving, but the steps thwart him. He's locked in position.

Centurion rotates further until he's able to bend his leg down. He swings it, tries to catch Smith's head. It fails to find purchase, instead ripping the bandages from Smith's face. Centurion gasps at the horror beneath.

Smith cackles a maniac's laugh, ignorant of the rot that's infected his cheek. He's oblivious to the hand-sized hole that exposes his skull.

The stench makes Centurion's stomach turn. He rocks his leg forward again. This time the back of his knee connects and holds. He brings his leg down with all of his might.

Smith's grip starts to slip.

Centurion locks his legs, scissoring Smith's neck.

The madman's grasp fails.

Centurion grabs his enemy's near side arm and tugs it towards his chest. He straightens and crushes with his thighs.

Smith slaps the concrete with his hand. He continues laughing, even after it's become little more than a wheeze. The sound skips about throughout the stairwell. It bounces around in Centurion's head.

It's all the motivation he needs to bring this man's life to an end. He rolls.

Smith's neck cracks.

A single word gurgles forth from his lips as he dies. "Chaos."

Centurion kicks the corpse away and starts up the stairs again.

❖❖❖

Astrid and Crown fly around a corner. They bulldoze Chee. The three go flying.

Astrid is up first, scrambling to Chee's side and taking her by the hand. She helps her up. "Where's Kim? Where's Centurion?" she asks.

A contingent of guards comes into view. "Astrid," Crown says, his voice rising.

She sees the soldiers. "We'll talk outside," she says.

They run like mad, past a crushed stairwell and through a smashed corridor. They exit through what was once a door.

"There," Crown says from the dock, pointing towards the crowd amassing around his tour bus.

"We need to get to the Chariot first," Chee says. "That's where we'll meet Kim and Centurion. And my dad."

When the soldiers emerge from the hole in the wall, there's no sign of the trespassers.

Instead, they're greeted by a mob of hundreds, all of them cheering and chanting. "Nigel, Nigel, Nigel . . . "

A soldier radios for instructions. No one responds. Even if someone had, there are no contingencies for events like this. They stand on the platform's edge staring blankly at the expanding crowd.

Not a single one of them realizes Kim's behind their backs, her lab coat red with blood, staggering out of the facility. She backs up against the wall, and slides away. She almost trips over a gladiator helmet. She dips down quietly, and picks it up. She tiptoes away and around the side of the warehouse still unnoticed, intent on finding the Caravan. Her physical—and mental—metamorphosis is now complete.

Centurion makes his way through the ruins of the second floor. Tables are overturned and broken into pieces. The fire from the first floor leaches through a giant hole in the floor and climbs the walls like wild sprouts of ivy. He works his way to the glass wall at the far end of the room.

Marcus hears someone laboring through the wreckage. "Smith?" he asks.

"Dead," Centurion replies. He skips down the stairs to Marcus' side.

"Tell Chee I love her," Marcus says.

"Tell her yourself. I'm getting you out of here." Centurion cradles Marcus in his arms, carrying him up the stairs and through the lapping flames and destruction.

"Mansfield?"

"Don't know," Centurion says. "But it looks like someone, something, is looking for him."

Marcus grunts. "The files."

"Forget them," Centurion says. "Let them burn."

"No," Marcus moans, "we can't let this happen again." He stretches out his arm and points to one file cabinet in particular. "There."

Centurion nods. "Okay." He sets Marcus down on the nearest structurally sound table. "Do you have a key?" he asks.

Marcus looks at him as if to say, *Do you really need a key?* "Second drawer," he says.

Centurion tugs hard on the handle and works his fingers behind the front panel. He groans as he pries the cabinet open. He shakes the drawer and the cabinet fiercely, tearing the drawer off its gliders and trashing the locking mechanism. He pulls the drawer free, drops it on ground. He begins removing file after file.

"Here," Marcus says straining. "Give them to me."

Centurion moves from and to the drawer, placing five phone book-size piles of documents on Marcus' chest. Marcus wraps his arms around them. Centurion lifts him again and carries him out of the facility turned tomb.

❖❖❖

Astrid runs to greet Kim in the middle of the parking lot.

"Kim!" she says, wrapping her arms around her friend.

"Ouch," Kim says, a hand moving to the bandaged incision in her stomach.

"Sorry, I didn't mean to hurt you."

Kim's nose crinkles. "Well, I didn't say you had to stop."

They embrace again, Kim closing her eyes and letting Centurion's helmet fall to the ground.

Chee watches the two friends hug from the Chariot. She smiles and turns her attention to the tour bus on the other side of the parking lot. "There must be a thousand of them," she says.

"That's close to two-thousand," Nigel says from the back seat. "I've played enough festivals to know." He scans the lot. "Look," he says, pointing.

"Dad!" Chee cries.

Centurion strains as he carries Marcus from the burning building. His steps are slow and measured. His arms tremble.

Astrid tells everyone to stay put. "I'll help them." She hands Kim Centurion's helmet and instructs her to go to the minivan.

Centurion's arms and legs are on fire, but he ignores the pain. He brings Marcus around the side of the Chariot, out of view of the mob.

Astrid collects the files.

"Open the back of the car," Centurion says, forgetting, for once, that his car is called the Chariot. Centurion slips into the back of the vehicle and delicately supports Marcus.

Kim, Crown, and Chee exit the minivan. They circle and crowd the tailgate.

"Nigel," Centurion says, "call an ambulance."

Crown pulls out his cell phone and starts dialing.

"No," Marcus says, "it's too late for that."

"Then we'll drive to a hospital," Centurion says.

"No," Marcus says again.

Chee begins sobbing. She's frozen in place, unable to approach her father.

"You," Marcus says, grabbing Centurion by the chest plate.

Centurion tells Marcus to save his breath.

Marcus coughs blood. "No, this must be said . . . while I still can."

Centurion leans in. "Please. Don't strain yourself."

Marcus continues. "Every self-preserving impulse in your body must have screamed, 'Run.' But you didn't. You propelled yourself into the mix, risking your own life to save my daughter's . . . and mine."

Centurion shakes his head. "It was . . . nothing."

"No," Marcus says, his eyes wide, teeth clenched and stained red. "People can learn to be generous, but self-sacrifice is bred. Your brain is different—"

"Just rest," Centurion says. "Nigel, where is that ambulance?"

"—It's the structure of the septal region of your subgenual cortex. You're hard-wired for altruism. Your brain is special." Marcus coughs and spits. Flecks of blood spray Centurion's cheeks as Marcus' eyes start to roll.

"Stay with us," Centurion demands.

Chee sobs.

Marcus struggles to continue. "You're different. You're special."

"Nigel!"

"They're coming," Nigel calls.

Marcus pulls himself towards Centurion's face with a final burst of strength. His eyes bulge. "You are a hero."

"No," Centurion whispers, "I'm not."

"Teach my daughter what it's like to be a hero," Marcus says, his words labored but urgent. "Take care of her."

"No, don't," Centurion mouths, his eyes filling with tears.

Marcus slips backwards, his grip loosening on Centurion and his eyes slowly closing. He turns to his daughter as his body goes limp.

"No, don't leave me," Chee cries. She runs forward and leans into the Caravan.

His hand reaches out, caressing her face. His fingers leave trails of blood on her cheek. "I love you," he says to her.

He closes his eyes. Then he's gone.

"His heart. It's stopped," Centurion says. "Get me the car batteries from under the driver's seat!" Centurion pleas.

"No," Astrid says, reaching forward and putting a hand on his chest. "It's too late."

Chee buries her head into Marcus' chest and wails. Centurion puts his free arm over Chee's shoulder.

Kim spins away from the scene and clutches Astrid with all of her might.

"Shit," Nigel says quietly, wiping away tears that come in torrents.

Sirens sound in the distance.

Astrid decides to greet them. "Come with me, Kim."

"Don't," a voice—Charlie's voice—whispers to her.

"Why?" Astrid begins to ask before answering her own question. The coming klaxons are not those of an ambulance. It's much too soon for that. The sirens emanate from dozens, possibly hundreds, of vehicles. They're police cruisers, maybe military police.

Centurion says, "Everyone in the car . . . the Chariot." Chee jumps into the back and wraps her arms around her father. She sobs into Marcus' chest.

Astrid crawls under the liftgate and places a hand on Chee's shoulder. She turns to look for Kim and sucks air in a burst. Marcus' spirit stands just outside of the vehicle. He's watching over both his daughter and his corporeal vessel. There's an intense buzz in Astrid's ear. Suddenly, her grandfather materializes. He joins Marcus. There's a silent and brief introduction before Charlie escorts Marcus away. They walk ten feet and disappear in a flash of light.

"Chee, honey," Astrid says, whimpering. "He's gone to a better place." Her voice drops. "They both have."

Chee twists and looks Astrid in the eyes. They fall into each other's arms, sobbing. Kim climbs into the Chariot and drapes her arms about them. Nigel closes the gate.

Centurion moves to the driver's side door, Crown following him. He gets in and fires up the ignition. "Nigel, get in."

"Look, I can buy you some time," he says.

"Don't be crazy."

Nigel laughs. "This is the most sane thing I've ever done. Now if you'll excuse me, I've got some fans to incite. I'll see you soon, though." He starts to step away from the car, but hesitates when he remembers something. He pulls a piece of paper from his pocket. "This is for Astrid."

Centurion takes it. "Good luck," he says.

Crown knocks on the Chariot as it pulls away. He waves as he watches the Caravan speed around the side of the blazing building. He allows himself a satisfied smile. "Time to live up to my reputation," he says to himself. He saunters towards his bus, towards the chanting horde of life-long fans, general music enthusiasts, groupies, and glory seekers, some of Astrid and Kim's classmates among them, who just want to be able to say, "I was there when." He claps his hands together. "Things are about to get heavy."

❖❖❖

*400 N. Michigan Avenue, a conference room. 9 September 2001.*

The story is all over channels 7 and 9. It's on cable. It's in the *Trib*. It's the front-page of the *Times*. The flames, the mobs, the damage. It's all the radio hosts and callers can talk about today.

"Why didn't you get this?" Holly's producer fumes.

"Carlos, no one actually got this."

"What are you talking about?" Carlos says, pointing at the TV. "It's right there in front of our eyes."

CNN is showing scenes of Nigel Crown standing on top of his tour bus, inflaming a crowd.

*Witnesses say that the popular singer called on his fans to engage in acts of civil disobedience, asking them to riot, destroy property, and impede law enforcement in their lawful duties.*

The telecast flips to an image of two teens, Brody Rooney and Kyle McCormack from Lincoln Park High School, jumping up and down on a police car, a warehouse burning in the background. Two officers tackle one and drag him off the hood. The second teen hops off the car and out of focus. Others take their place on top of the vehicle.

*There are also reports that charges might be brought against Crown for jeopardizing the safety of minors and for making and transporting incendiary devices across state lines. The landlord of the property was unavailable for comment at this time.*

There's crude video of Crown, beaming, being ushered into a police cruiser. Fans pelt the police with bottles and rocks. Some officers lash out with batons.

*The Chicago region hasn't seen anything like this since the 1968 Democratic National Convention—*

Carlos switches off the TV with the remote. "What do you have to say for yourself?"

"That's not investigative journalism," Holly says. "That's just a bunch of video captured by kids with smart phones. That's not honest reporting."

Carlos shakes his head. "You don't get it. News is whatever people buy. It's whatever our advertisers want it to be." He adds, "Anyway, when did you start worrying about integrity? Hell, what does that word even mean?" He says the word again like it's a bug in his mouth. "Integrity?"

She doesn't reply.

"Where's the Holly Rodriguez that I hired? You know, the woman from Tampa who took no prisoners and let the chips fall as they may?"

*Prisoners? Chips?* There once was a day in the not too distant past when Holly would have replied, "How many more metaphors can he squeeze into this reprimand?" Instead she hangs her head, too tired to tease her boss. "I don't know if I'm that person anymore," Holly says.

"Well," Carlos says, "you better let me know, because that was the reporter I hired. Dismissed."

Holly leaves her producer's office and walks the long hall back to her own. She puts her head down and holds her temple, feeling a migraine coming, as she passes her secretary's desk.

"Ms. Rodriguez?" Julie says.

"Yes." Holly doubts she has the strength to deal with her secretary today.

"You got a package," Julie says. "A big one. It's on your desk."

"Thanks," Holly says without looking up.

"The delivery guy was really weird too," Julie says as she returns to work. "He was dressed like some kind of knight or something."

Holly rushes into her office, closes the door behind her. On her desk is a white cardboard file box. She bumps the desk as she tries to race around it. She stands before it, rubs her left hip. There's an envelope on top. She opens it, turns it upside down. A handwritten letter slides out. It's from Centurion. It says simply, "It is time to do some good."

She opens the box and begins flipping through the documents. There are memoranda labeled "Operation Freakshow." They're endorsed with Mansfield Smith-Cumming's trademark signature, a simple "C" in green ink. There are medical and personnel records. There are drug requisitions, orders from Davis Pharmaceuticals. Some of the folders are covered in blood.

And then there are photos. Dozens of them. Photos of dead men and women. Photos of dead children.

There is no mention of Chee or Marcus. Centurion purged any references to them from the files.

Thirty-six hours later, Holly has pieced together enough of the materials to run with an initial story. She calls Carlos. "Stop the presses," she says (she's always wanted to say that). She has an exclusive that will rock the nation, even the world.

❖ ❖ ❖

"You've got a call," the deputy sheriff says. "He says he's your attorney."

Crown stands up and shuffles towards the Sheriff's Deputy. He nearly trips on the cuff of his baggy orange jumpsuit. "My attorney?"

"Yep," the guard says. "Follow me."

He leads Crown through the cellblock. Inmates applaud and hoot, like he's some modern day Johnny Cash and this is Folsom Prison, not Lake County Jail.

*Nice one, Nigel!*

*You showed those fucking pigs!*

*Give us a song!*

They reach a room furnished only with a table, chair, and yellow phone. Crown trundles over, picks up the phone, and says, "Hello."

"Nigel Crown?" The man's accent is thick. He's from northern England. Liverpool.

"Yes."

"*The* Nigel Crown?" The question is punctuated by a slight giggle.

"Yes," Crown says, his expression quizzical.

"Don't you remember me? Has it been that long? Have the drugs taken too much of a toll? This is your mate, Johnny."

"Johnny?" Crown asks. "Johnny Moon?"

"How the hell are you, mate?"

"Good," Crown says, his face breaking into a smile. "How are you?"

"Well, I should say I'm fine," the guitarist says, "but the fuckin' truth is I'm bored out of my skull. That's retirement for you. All arthritis, hemorrhoids, and *Murder She Wrote.*"

"I always preferred *Matlock*," Crown says, laughing.

Moon chuckles. "When I saw what you pulled on the news, I thought, 'That's fuckin' punk rock.'"

Crown raises an eyebrow. "Well, yeah, I guess it was pretty punk."

"I've got to tell you, it really gave me an itch for the old days."

"Yeah?"

"Definitely," Moon says. "That brings me to a question: what would you think about jamming a little when you get out of the clink? Nothing serious, mind you. We'll just see where it goes."

Crown's psyched. "Perfect."

"Great," the guitarist says, "I'll be in L.A. in a few weeks. I'll give you a call when I'm stateside."

Crown says it sounds like a plan. "Assuming I'm out of jail by then."

"Until then," Moon says, "watch your ass in there, mate."

# Track Twenty-Eight:
# Of All the Things We've Made

*11 September 2001.*

"Are you watching?" Holly asks. "The promo will be on any second."

Centurion holds the receiver to his ear. "Channel 7, right?"

"You know it's Channel 5," she says, talking into a speakerphone at her desk.

"I know," he says. "I was kidding." He reclines on his bed. He's wrapped in a robe, "The Drake" embroidered on the lapel. The hotel stay was an unexpected gift from Holly, a thank you.

"This is big time, too. Two minute promos are rare."

"Wait, I think this is it." He turns the volume up on the television.

*Narrator: Join us tonight at 10 PM for WCHC Channel 5 exclusive brought to you by Holly Rodriguez.*

*Holly (walking in front of the burned out warehouse): Black magic and witch-hunts. I'm not talking about Salem. No, I'm talking about the here and now. Join me tonight as I reveal how a hunt that began in 18th Century France persists to this day, enslaving matriarchal witch-smellers, shaping U.S. foreign policy, and deciding Presidential elections.*

*Man in a dark room, his voice augmented, identified only as "Government Drug Contractor": It's a hunt that's as old as time, a mission bigger than the church, bigger than science, bigger than the struggle of good versus evil. They wanted to preserve the purity of mankind by any means necessary, even murder.*

"Is that Davis?" Centurion asks.

"I can't reveal my sources," Holly says. He can almost hear her smiling over the line. "Not yet, anyway."

"Well, thanks for letting me sit this one out," Centurion says. Holly is his only connection to the warehouse. The fire tied up all of the remaining loose ends, including, he hopes, the deaths of Smith, Doctor Kane, and the soldiers.

Holly sighs. "People really should know about your involvement. You really are a superhero."

"No," Centurion says. "I have people to protect. Promise me you'll never mention me."

"I promise," Holly says. "Scout's honor."

"And promise me you'll never mention Marcus or his daughter."

There's silence on the other end of the line.

"Listen, I appreciate what you did, planting the story about him being killed during a home invasion, but I need to be certain you'll leave his name and daughter alone."

"You know, your staging of the crime scene on Larrabee was pretty impeccable. Have you been watching *CSI*?"

"Just don't mess with me," Centurion says, "and don't change the subject."

She giggles. "Fine," Holly says. "I promise, Centurion."

Her use of his alter ego to address him is not lost on Centurion. "Congrats again, by the way," he says. "I'm sure your story will be great."

They say their goodbyes.

Once the plane hits the second tower of the World Trade Center two hours later, they both know the story will never air.

The station punts it a week. A week becomes two. Two become four. Then six.

President George Bush signs the Patriot Act on October 26th. The Act expands the scope of counter-terrorism initiatives and loosens the requirements for surveillance, allowing for roving wiretaps, sneak and peek warrants, Internet monitoring, and the seizure of a host of records without a judge's consent.

Six men from the National Security Agency arrive at WCHC minutes after the President's endorsement, literally in the time it takes the ink to dry, the time it takes to ride an elevator from the lobby to her floor. They seize Holly's file box of materials, her notes, and all video related to Operation Freakshow.

In the days and weeks that follow, Centurion becomes more and more certain the government is planning a response to their raid. He's sure the operatives will regroup. They will recruit more witch-smellers, more assassins. They will continue to hunt down people with special abilities. He needs to be prepared. They need to be prepared. He takes it upon himself to train his youthful wards.

Astrid's parents rent the basement of their vacation home on Round Lake to Centurion. He gives Chee the bigger of the two bedrooms for her books and massive furniture. He gets a job at the Kmart on Rollins Road, and she starts school at Round Lake High School, District 116. He pays $500 per month for rent, mows the lawn, and keeps the driveway clear of snow during the winter. Next summer he plans to make some cool modifications to the Chariot.

There's initially some argument over the name of their superhero team. They settle on Centurion's *Superhero Club*, although Astrid is still partial to *Freaks Anonymous*. She argues the club is not so much a collective of superheroes as it is a support group. Their team offers shelter from the storm of a Borg-like monoculture. Centurion's pat response is that he doesn't want to deal with another lawsuit or trademark searches. Still, he feels his commitment to his original concept shaking. It's just a matter of time before Astrid gets her way.

*What do you call a bunch of superheroes, Kid Caper? A Freak.*

*A freak of superheroes.*

The Club meets every other Saturday at the lakehouse.

Chee leads their discussions concerning training and mission objectives. She sets individual and group goals for the team to review. She's committed to performance management. Further, she helps Centurion recruit, indentifying those with abilities that they can bring into the fold and protect.

She recently dyed her hair bright red like her mother and the witch-smellers that came before her. She doesn't talk about her dad much. Centurion senses she's hiding in her work. There's always work to be done.

Astrid and Nigel have become pen pals. They write back and forth every few weeks. Astrid says there's talk of a Panic Attack reunion and a *Black as Pitch* sequel. Centurion tries to act cool when he gets these up-dates, but he's frankly giddy over the prospect of new Panic Attack ma-terial.

Astrid's having trouble sleeping. She suffers from flashbacks and anxiety attacks in the weeks that follow their rescue mission. She's racked with guilt for the deaths of the soldiers, for their families. She's haunted by recurring nightmares.

In her dreams, there's always a door. It's thick and oaken, and it ap-pears anywhere she visits as she slumbers: at school, in her house, against a tree, anywhere. As she passes the door, she hears someone on the other side scratching. It sends a shiver down Astrid's spine, like long fingernails across a chalkboard. The entity beyond the door whispers to her. It says its name is Lisa. The entity asks Astrid to open the door. Lisa wants to return, the soldiers that she killed want to return, *all of them* want to return, from the otherworld. When Astrid refuses, the pound-ing starts. Just a single fist at first. And then there are two. Soon there are dozens if not hundreds of spirits raining blows down on the door, pummeling it and screaming her name. She wakes in a cold sweat at 3:15 AM almost every morning.

Despite Centurion telling Astrid that it's normal to feel powerless and to have bad dreams, she compensates with behaviors that border on OCD. She washes her hands frequently; she counts her steps; she checks the locks five or six times a night. He worries her attempts at control are becoming a compulsion. He does his best to help her. He tells her that she shouldn't feel remorse. "They were looking for mon-sters; you only gave them what they wanted."

Still, he realizes he'll never replicate the reassuring bond she had with her grandfather. When times are particularly tough, they read Char-lie's letter together. *Hello, Chickadee* . . .

Kim, on the other hand, seems unaffected by the battle. In fact, her confidence has grown by bounds. Her wardrobe is changing too. She isn't as worried about cloaking her body in oversized clothes. Her con-trol over her power is getting better. She rarely transforms now. Cen-turion chalks it up to her improved focus.

Kim never talks about Kane's death or her torture, and that worries

Centurion deeply. He's unaware of her drug use, but he knows she's keeping a secret of some sort. Despite the lakehouse being just forty-five minutes from Elkhorn, Wisconsin, she never once mentions visiting her father.

They are most comfortable when they are together, especially at the lake. Often, their meetings devolve into debates about pop culture. Last week, they discussed the treatment of female superheroes in comics and film. The consensus:

- There are too few strong female superheroes.
- There are even fewer that represent the LGBT community.
- Those that exist on-screen rarely pass the Bechdel test.
- Among female superheroes, brunettes are underrepresented in comics. *There's like, Zatana and Wonder Woman. That's about it.*
- Wonder Woman's superpowers kind of suck. *She's got bracelets and a lasso. What is her superpower? Accessorizing? And what about the Lasso of Truth? What's a criminal going to say? "The truth is you are kinky and your superpowers suck."*
- Invisible planes aren't necessarily a plus. *What's the point of having an invisible plane if people can still see you when you're flying it? And where do you land it? Can you imagine the conversations she has with her peers?*
*Wonder Woman: "Hi, I'm here and ready to fight crime with you, Superman."*
*Superman: "We finished while you were looking for a parking spot for that stupid airplane."*
*Wonder Woman: "I'm sorry, I had to park it at O'Hare, and traffic on the Kennedy was a bitch. By the way, can I get a ride back with you? Maybe you can help me find where I parked it . . . because, you know, it's invisible."*
- The Clique song *Superman* that REM covered is probably about a stalker. *"I am Superman, and I know what's happening. If you go a mil lion miles away I'll track you down, girl."*

Sometimes Astrid and Kim chide Centurion about Holly. They haven't been on a date, but they talk a couple times a month. Centurion argues that his duties—and state of mind—would make him a poor boyfriend. More so, he quietly worries that she would be a bad girlfriend. It's not lost on him that Chee never joins the teasing. He assumes it's because she doesn't like Holly's aura.

Tonight, however, their conversation centers on superhero names . . . specifically, *their* superhero names.

Centurion has been calling Kim by the handle, "Kim Era," for the last few weeks, a play on the word "chimera." It's the perfect super identity. It's catchy, it's unique, and it describes Kim's ability to transform into multiple animals at the same time. It seems to have stuck, despite Chee's objection. She's still pushing for *Kaiju*, regardless of the inherent Gozilla inference. It's a Japanese word meaning "strange beast."

Astrid wants a cool name. "Something dark and brooding, like Nightwing," she says, alluding to Batman's former sidekick.

"How about Broken Wing?" Kim jokes.

Astrid smirks. "Ha ha. You're so funny."

It is Chee, though, who provides a possible moniker: Astrid Plane.

"Why not just Plain Astrid?" Kim cracks.

Chee ignores her. "It's a reference to the astral plane. Astrid. Astral. Get it? They're close, right?"

"I kind of like it," Astrid says without fully committing.

Centurion watches these young women interact, and he can't help but smile wide. In them he's found a family, a real family that he can depend upon, for the first time. They, in turn, can depend on him. Whether or not they know it yet, he will live and die for them.

THE END

# Monument

## A Dystopian Short Story

"Welcome. I'm Nick Davis, President and CEO of Davis Clinics, a subsidiary of Davis Pharmaceuticals."

Repetition has drilled the narration into my skull. "Wealth is truly not monetary," I say as I pull at my face, my chin coming to rest in my hands.

"Wealth is truly not monetary," the disembodied voice continues. "It shouldn't be quantified in dollars and cents. No, real fortunes are measured by wellbeing. Think of us as your trusted advisors. Our dedicated team of professionals won't gamble with your investment. We're here to serve you, and we'll ensure you get the benefit of a return, whether that be next month, next year, or five years from now."

Hidden speakers pipe the recording into the waiting room. As it concludes, a smooth jazz accompaniment of piano, drums, and bass fades in. There are four distinct movements in this looping musical wallpaper, each representing a season of the year. The selection reminds me of The Vince Guaraldi Trio's *Linus and Lucy*, save for the wintry selection. It is buoyant, never slowing to an eyes-downcast-Charlie Brown-shuffle. It never approaches a dirge.

I sigh. The keyboard bluster is almost too jaunty for someone in my condition.

The waiting room is empty, just the receptionist and me. Her name is Hillary. I know even though she's never introduced herself. She occupies herself at a desk with a piece of rectangular glass, a new tablet. I'm finding it harder to keep up with the latest gadgets, but I've seen the ads for this one. It's marketed as The Taffy® for good reason. Hillary stretches the computer from the top and it expands. She presses the sides, compacting the device, and the edges magically contract. The images elongate and realign, the patented chemical composition ensuring both the device's pliancy and the screens continued legibility. Long gone are the days of screen pinching.

We had something like this when I was a kid, albeit much less high-tech. It captured images and came in a plastic red egg. We called it Silly-Putty.

A wall-sized monitor silhouettes her, a panoramic backdrop of the French countryside living and breathing behind her. It's hyper real, begging me to enter the field and bust my nose in the process. Time marches on, the weather warming and cooling on the display, a year passing with each loop of the accompanying *Peanuts*-style backing track. I've watched winter descend upon a deer grazing and aging in this field five times now. Each time the grown buck exits stage left, only to return as a fawn from the right as the simulated snows begin to melt.

I regard the anachronism wrapped around my wrist. Doctor Winters—Rich—is late. He's always late. I don't like being on this side of the doctor-patient equation. I suck air through my teeth and do the only thing I can. I wait some more.

I search for a distraction. The end table to my right is barren. There's not a single magazine to be found. My fingers stroke and linger on the wood surface. I ask the receptionist if she remembers *Highlights*.

She allows the facsimile of a smile. It's an approximation, totally disconnected from her emotions. Her eyes are dead. Or, rather, that's how she sees me. Dead. She shakes her head, her cheek twitching and her mouth tugging slightly to the left. Of course she doesn't know anything about the children's magazine. She's all of twenty-five years of age. The only paper she knows, really anyone knows anymore, is the type used to clean buttocks.

I long for the physicality of print. I long for substance. Everything's ethereal, remote currents of data cleansed and filtered, clustered and classified, homogenized and served using this week's hottest algorithms. Information is mined. Knowledge is directed. There are no accidental discoveries, no happy coincidences. Not anymore.

"Welcome. I'm Nick Davis . . . "

Spiderlike, a shudder climbs up my spine. It spins a web, taking up residence between my shoulder blades. The message grates on me. It didn't always bug me, but Davis' discarnate voice has welcomed me on at least two-dozen occasions over the past three months.

I'm making a logical leap, of course. No one knows if I'm really listening to the real Nick Davis. More likely than not, I'm not. It's probably something synthesized and modulated, tested through countless hours of market research, to elicit a particular emotional response. If so, the researchers didn't fully complete their analysis. They didn't factor the impact of excessive plays on a hostage audience.

I'm sure they'll get the voice and message right in version 2.0. The big data geeks are always promising another super-ego breakthrough. They say they're getting closer to predicting my moves and desires. They threaten to define the entity that is me.

*Health is wealth.* Everything's calculated.

*Life is ROI. Death is bankruptcy.* Everything's cold.

" . . . and we'll ensure you get the benefit of a return . . . " And everything's pre-recorded.

But the data gurus will never fully comprehend my *sehnsucht*, my *toska*, my *saudade*. Hell, I can't define my desperation using the English language, let alone with words as foreign as the concepts they attempt to claim. A bunch of kids equipped with machine learning tools will never understand this. They're unfamiliar with the trappings of the past, the nuance of my story.

This superiority complex-slash-social reticence is exactly why Rebecca's filed for divorce. I chuckle.

The receptionist raises an eyebrow. She eyes me with disgust, like I'm some rat in her kitchen. She's not wrong. I'm a lab rodent, but a conscious one. I know I'm in a maze hunting for test cheese. I know I'm a cog wedged between turning gears of a great big pharma machine. Yet I still run. I still turn.

I regard Hillary and just shrug my shoulders. She shakes her head quickly, almost as if she might be able to shake my existence loose from her mind, from this room. She goes back to whatever she was doing on the device named after pulled candy.

I sigh aloud so she knows I'm here. She must deal with my existence.

"Stop being so negative. Stop being so cranky," Becca's voice snaps. I close my eyes and nod.

Becca still calls to me. Her echoes berate me from deep within the hallways of my memory. Sometimes I think she's a living ghost, communicating to me from far away via some telepathic portal. That's a nice thought, to think she still cares. It's also a crazy thought.

I worry that the cancer in my brain has somehow distorted my own internal voice, perversely appropriating my conscience and labeling it "Rebecca." If so, it doesn't really diminish my need to hear her. I welcome her reminders, even if they are hallucinatory.

The voice has a point. Other than this disease, I've never really faced insurmountable odds. The trials of medical school, the Boards, work, relationships, and the latter's subsequent and inevitable dissolution . . . it all pales in comparison. Admittedly, even riddled with a Bounty of mutinous cells, I still have it better than most. After all, I'm here while every other terminal Tom, Dick, and Harry is outside begging for a verdict less finite.

How is it that I was given this opportunity? Why do I get to shake this Etch-A-Sketch of a diagnosis? How did I get the chance to wipe away my death warrant as if it's scrawled on a plastic display in aluminum dust? I don't think about it much, but I'll offer a guess.

White privilege. The benefit of being a half-of-a-percenter. The networking gap. I could lie and call it luck, but probability is kind to those of my gender, those with my skin tone, those who come from money like me. My family's fortunes and genes turned the odds in my favor. Without that combination, I never would have gone to med school or met Rich.

Rich comes from a prominent family, a family of money *and* history. His is a political dynasty, one with seats in City Council and with plots in Graceland Cemetery. His dad's grave is just yards from the island where Daniel Burnham was buried. Yes, Rich opened a lot of doors for me—both personal and scientific—that would have otherwise been locked, barred, and barricaded.

"Doctor Winters will see you now."

My chin pops up from my chest. "What?"

Hillary's nostrils flare. She says it again. Slower, like I'm somehow challenged. She nods towards an open door at the far end of the room.

"Thanks." I stand and smooth the wrinkles from my pants. "I know the way," I say as if there's even the remotest possibility of her offering further instruction. I make my way down a hall to Rich Winters' office.

I knock on the doorframe, and Rich spins in his chair. "Hey, buddy," he says, his voice unusually nasally. He rises to shake my hand. I take a step towards him, but he pulls back. His eyes close, his head jerks. He sneezes violently into the crook of his elbow.

"God bless you," I say.

He grabs a tissue, blinks, and blows into it. One of his eyebrows arches over the top of the Kleenex.

"Sorry," I say. I correct myself. "*Gesundheit.*"

Rich nods, his bloodshot eyes narrowing, a smirk twisting his lips. It's an expression that lays bare his inner workings. He's giving himself a mental, "That a boy," a pat on the back for defending his atheistic non-belief system.

"When did you atheists get so darn sensitive anyway?" I say. I grab a picture frame from the top of his desk and spin it towards me. Rich is posing with his wife and daughter next to a speedboat on a dock. His daughter's holding a fishing pole. She has Rebecca's nose, her lips and chin.

He seizes the picture back from me. He sets it on his desk, this time beyond my reach. "Since *your* Christians started targeting teachers on the street."

God and science used to coexist. That accord was once realized in the forms of Einstein, Schrodinger, Pasteur and a brilliant host of others. The good ol' days. The dogmas haven't played nice in decades. Each rejects the other completely while somehow still coveting what the other has.

Science-deniers are nuts. The idea of an omnipotent, omniscient, and omnipresent divine entity is difficult to get behind. That difficulty is exacerbated when the flock ignores the very rules their shepherd has handed down.

On the other hand, scientists can be equally narrow-minded. Anyone who supports String Theory and the notion of a multiverse shouldn't find it too tough to back the possibility of a supreme deity. And if not in this world, at least in some postulated parallel universe.

It's nothing but a religious Cold War, really, lots of *post*-postmodernist saber rattling. Still, I'm not ignorant of escalating tensions. I read the *Trib* and watch CNN, despite being out of fashion. A militant Christian splinter group called the Holy Lance has executed three teachers in the last two weeks for simply discussing evolution. Two days ago they crucified a school librarian for failing to pull Mark Twain and *The Scarlet Letter* from the bookshelves.

"Those aren't Christians," I say. "Anyway, you know I'm agnostic." I take a seat without being asked.

"Always hedging your bets," Rich says.

"Why do you think I'm here?" I say.

Rich says, "Touché." It sounds like he's speaking through his nose instead of his mouth.

"You sound like Fran Drescher singing *To All the Girls I've Loved Before* in French," I say.

He laughs. "Is she still alive?"

I suddenly feel old. Well, older. "The mold and pollen counts are way up," I say, disregarding his query and addressing his symptoms. "Too much rain."

"Rain, rain, go away," Rich says with a sigh. It has rained for 237 consecutive days in Chicago, just a tenth as long as the ongoing megadrought in the southwest. Over the past few years, hundreds of square miles of Illinois prairie scrub has disappeared, the savannahs ceding ground to sugar pines and alders. Rich wipes the edge of his nose. "Yes, unfortunately for me, my allergist decided to take a leave of absence." He winks.

"You haven't been in to see Liz yet?" I say, referencing Doctor Elizabeth Rogers. "I gave you a referral two months ago."

"I haven't had time to make an appointment. I've been busy."

"You're lucky she even agreed to see you. Her dance card is full and getting fuller. She's one of the best allergists in the country." I remind Rich that she was featured in the *Journal of Science*'s "Top Forty under Forty" list for 2027. The article featured a picture of her at her desk in her office, the wall behind her a spectacle of color. A dozen framed exotic butterflies hung where most doctors would display their honoraria. Liz eschewed accolades, and I found her modesty endearing. I remind him of her groundbreaking work in immunology. "May be *the* best now."

"Now that you're out of the picture, you mean?" he says.

I hold my hands up at my sides, palms up. My head cocks as my brow arches under the brim of my USMNT World Cup Champs cap.

"You are one confident SOB, I'll give you that," Rich says. "That's probably why my sister married you."

I smile wide.

"Probably why Rebecca's divorcing you too."

My grin evaporates.

"I'll make an appointment soon." He sniffs. He feels my medical judgment weighing on him. "I promise."

"Do it soon." Allergic conditions have been on the rise, increasing thirty-fold in the last decade. There are a thousand potential factors, including the seemingly never ceasing rain, but most of these causes can be cataloged under a single rubric: the hygiene hypothesis. "We've done so much as a society to eradicate disease and improve our collective health, but maybe too much. Cities are too clean. We don't let kids play in the dirt like we did when we were young . . . "

Rich pinches the bridge of his nose between his thumb and forefinger. He's heard me spout off about the importance of micro-biodiversity countless times before.

" . . . We're not exposed to germs, fungi, or parasites. We've stunted the development of our kids' immune systems."

When I finish my rant, he says, "On behalf of mankind, I thank you for worrying about us. Now stop."

"Liz actually treated a woman the other day who developed an allergy to her own hair." I slowly repeat the last four words. "To. Her. Own. Hair." I tell him she's got to shave her arms, her legs three times each week. I hesitate. "And other bits too, plus her head. She'll wear synthetic wigs the rest of her life."

Rich laughs. "How horrible. Can you imagine having to go through life like that?"

I remove my faded cap and rub a hand over my hairless scalp.

A grimace ripples across his lips. "Of course you can," he says. "Sometimes I can be as insensitive as you. Sorry."

"No worries," I say. "I'm getting used to looking like Wooly Willy."

Rich's expression is blank.

"You know that toy? From when we were kids? The one with the magnetic wand that you use to draw whiskers and hair on the bald guy with a big red nose?"

Silence. The void is accented by a deepening wrinkle over his eyes.

I cringe. "Why do I date myself like that?"

Rich leans in. "Anyway," he says, "you need to stop worrying about the rest of the world. It's time for you to think about yourself."

I tell him that worrying about myself is all I ever do. It's all I've ever done. "Ask Becca."

He sighs. "Listen, I know you and Rebecca went through some punishing rounds. But at the end of it, you're both standing. You're a good guy. I wouldn't have introduced you to my sister if I didn't believe that. She knows it too. She may not say it, but she's pulling for you."

I gulp and stare at the ceiling for a moment before making eye contact again. "Thanks. I want the best for her too."

"So, buddy," Rich says, "it's time to get down to brass tacks. Let's talk about how this all works."

"Isn't that what we've been doing the last three months? You don't have to sell me. You've already got my money. And it's not like I have alternatives. Well, save for the obvious one, which seems more like an eventuality than a choice."

"I have to do this. Informed consent laws require it. This isn't your typical procedure."

I roll my eyes.

"Come on," he says. "Help me keep my license."

"Okay, okay." I lean back in my chair. "Shoot."

Rich walks me through the process again. Over the next hour he explains three chief steps.

First, I'll receive an injection of Davis Pharmaceuticals' gene expression stimulator. It's called EpiGenie.v.27.12. Funded by a NASA grant almost thirty years ago, the drug aimed to create the next Buck Rogers. While Martian travel ultimately failed to get the green light, Davis was able to take the research into new areas, like treating insomnia, delaying brain death due to oxygen deprivation, and, more recently, maintaining the vitals of trauma victims like lumberjacks or roughnecks miles from an ER. Those advances led to suspended animation trials three years ago.

"You're number nineteen," Richs say. Only eighteen other people have received a dose of v.27.12 through the FDA's "compassionate use" loophole. Without that approval, the drug couldn't be used outside of clinical trials.

"The drug works on the genetic level," he says. EpiGenie loosens coiling proteins spooled about DNA strands, exposing ancient genes. "We share these dormant genes with our mammalian forebears, creatures like bears and ground squirrels. To put it simply, the drug unlocks the secrets of hibernation."

Second, Davis Clinics will connect me to a drip, a neural inhibitor. That's important. This drug will keep me from dreaming. I could be asleep for months, maybe a couple of years until they find a cure. "That's a long time to be stuck in a nightmare," Rich says.

"Or with morning wood for that matter."

Rich doesn't crack a smile. "Third—"

"Third, you'll place me in the coffin."

"Don't call it a coffin," Rich says. "It's the Chrysalis. This isn't barbarism. This isn't cryonics. We're not cutting off your head and freezing it in liquid nitrogen. You're certainly no Ted Williams. Remember, I've seen you throw a ball. It's pretty pathetic."

I laugh. If I had any sense of the passing of time while in the

Chrysalis, I'd miss these conversations. I'd miss winding Rich up. "I hate that name. Chrysalis."

"Why?" Rich asks. "It's about transformation. It's inspirational. Or, if you'd rather compare your emergence to a rebirth, we could call it an artificial womb."

"I definitely don't want to think of it like that," I say.

"Great, we're sticking with the butterfly metaphor then." He passes me a pile of paperwork, setting it at the edge of his desk.

"Paper?" I say, but the weight feels good in my hands. I flip through the pages. The texture is somewhat course, a welcome change to the smoothness of an edgeless world.

"Yes, the Feds are serious about this stuff."

"Or they're just antiquated."

Rich says, "Either way, they want hard copies of the releases."

"Okay." I initial boxes on multiple forms and sign several others without reading them.

Rich collects the documents from me. "And these," he says, pushing another pile of paperwork across the desk towards me.

"What are these?"

"They're organ donor forms," he says.

"What?" I say, my voice squeaking.

"I'm kidding. They're asset disposition forms."

"Okay," I say, signing the top page. "Wait, why would I need to sign these?"

"In case you're under for a prolonged period. Or something goes wrong."

I frown.

"But nothing's going to go wrong," he adds hastily.

"That's not what I meant. I'm not divorced. Not all the way. Not yet."

Rich squints, his eyes start to water. It's not the allergies responsible for this pained look.

"I know," I say. "I will be."

"And when you are, the probate court won't recognize Rebecca as your beneficiary. You need to designate one."

As expensive as this whole process is, Davis Clinics has ensured there's at least a modicum of shared risk. At its heart, this is a contingency deal. Twenty percent of my payment remains in escrow and reverts to a beneficiary if I don't come through the other side.

I sign away and toss the pages back to him.

He shuffles the documents in his lap. He pauses, looks up at me. "You designated Rebecca as your beneficiary anyway?"

I don't respond. I avoid his gaze and act like I'm studying the dozen or so certificates on the wall. Instead, I say, "What's next?"

I don't see him smile. "Now comes the fun part."

The rest of the afternoon is spent semi-naked on an exam table in a subbasement. A parade of strangers enters and exits. These technicians prick and prod in silence, measuring and notating on their tablets in quick succession.

Finally, a man enters that I recognize. His name's Lal. Deep lines cut vertically across his forehead like the yard markers on a football field. He's actually much younger than he looks, but frown lines are a trade risk for conscientious medical professionals. Rebecca told me I looked like I was forty when we met. I was just twenty-six.

Two months ago, Lal fitted me for a stasis suit. His measurements were as exacting as a tailor on Savile Row, and for good reason. This suit will protect me from the saline soup I'll stew in. Today he carries a nylon garment bag by the hanger over his shoulder. "Let's get you dressed," he says, closing the mirrored door behind him.

Lal makes alterations to the suit while I stare into the mirror. The suit is heavy grey foamed neoprene. It is unforgiving, showing every one of the twenty-nine pounds I've added in the last sixty days drinking specially formulated Davis protein shakes. He instructs me to lift and drop my arms and legs for the next thirty minutes as he checks the fit. I date myself yet once more when I tell him I feel like a Tae Bo instructor.

He remains quiet.

"Really?" I say. "Nothing?" I let it go.

A few minutes later, he's done. "There," Lal says, "your Hiber-suit is ready." *Hiber*, as in *hibernate*, not *hyper* as used by Ridley Scott, James

Cameron, and nearly every other sci-fi movie maker since the 80s. True stasis is not hyper-sleep, it's hiber-sleep. "Are you?"

I nod.

Lal escorts me down the corridor to a massive hall lit by ambient light. Inside, there are four rows of pods, perhaps forty in all, half or more of them darkened. The instrument panels on the others flash green and occasionally yellow. A lone spotlight shines on an elongated sphere in the middle of the room, my Chrysalis. It's ten feet tall, a large round window occupying a third of the real estate of the pod's front. It reminds me of a washing machine from a decade ago. A technician rolls a platform ladder to a base of the pod. Rich stands nearby in the halo of light, his hands clasped before him.

"Good luck, Billy Blanks," Lal says, his hand extending towards my destination.

"Hey, you did get it," I say, my voice cutting the quiet hum of the room. "Nice one," I say, my voice quieter. "Take care."

He nods and turns quietly. I catch the hint of a grin as Lal spins out of view.

I pass four pods as I approach my Chrysalis. The first and the second are empty, but the third is occupied. I pause and peer through the porthole.

An occupant floats serenely in a saltwater mix. Her curves are bathed in soft blue light. Tubes rise from the regulator at her mouth, from ports on the side of her skull and the nape of her neck. The latter deliver medication and, if required, essential nutrients. Another shunt removes toxins should they happen to build-up. They shouldn't. Like a hibernating bear, she won't lose much muscle or bone mass. She doesn't eat or drink, defecate or urinate, not in this state.

The name on the tank says, "M. Norris." I lean in, the glass fogging as I breathe. I wipe the pane, and it's like touching the surface of a frozen lake. I watch her hovering in the fetal position, slowly rotating in space. She gradually twists towards me. I take a step back.

Her face is hooded in a neoprene sack. There are no lenses like one would find on a scuba mask. She's like some bagged, expressionless *Doctor Who* monster.

"Well, that's creepy," I say in a near whisper.

"Graham," Rich calls with a wave of his hand.

I am all too happy to disengage from the human aquarium. "Cancer too?" I say poking a thumb towards the pod.

"You know I can't give you details about another patient's health," he says.

"Who am I going to tell?" I say. "Come on. What's up with Monica Norris?"

His eyebrows rear up like the forelegs a defensive horse. "Her name's not Monica."

"What is it?"

Rich purses his lips.

"Fine," I say, "but realize you're no fun. My last thought before I enter stasis is going to be, 'Rich Winters is a killjoy.'"

Rich isn't fazed. He's heard it before.

He tells me more about the facility. It's totally off the grid, powered by an independent UPS and backed up by a solar drip. It's staffed around the clock, although, according to the good doctor, it need not be. The facility is self-sustaining. "The medication is produced onsite, the dosages synthesized and delivered exclusively by machine," Rich says.

The whole thing is pretty damn amazing. Yet I can't tell Rich this. It would go straight to his head. "So, is this my egg?"

Rich scratches his eyebrows with the thumb and forefinger. "*This* is your Chrysalis. Follow me."

He leads me up a dozen stairs to a landing at the top of the pod. The open hatch reminds me of something from an old submarine movie. A metal grate covers the porthole. He positions me on the platform just above the brine. The techs work quietly, checking the fittings and connecting tubes to my suit. They pull on gloves and ensure the seals. I feel a slight pinch as the epiGenie is administered through a port at the base of my neck. The shunt for the neural inhibitor hurts less. It slides into a vein near my temple with little more than a slight pop.

"It will feel cold," Rich says, "but not for long. As soon as your body temperature begins to drop, you'll go to sleep. Your metabolism with slow 90%, your heart rate reduced to just a single beat per minute. An hour from now, you'll be taking just one breath every ten minutes. Two hours from now, it will be one breath every twenty."

Most important is what goes unsaid. The process will suspend the progression of my cancer. "How will you wake me again?"

"It's natural. You'll awaken as your core warms." A technician hands him a hood with a respirator. "Ready?"

"Rich," I say. My lips quiver. I can't muster more.

He cups my face in his hands. "Don't worry. It's okay to be scared. You'll see Rebecca and me on the other side. I promise."

A tear escapes my eye. "Okay."

Rich looks to his left, over his shoulder down the aisle of pods. He looks at me again and says, "Melinda Norris. She's been brain dead for nine months. Car accident."

My lips make an audible smack as they part to reveal my smile. I run my tongue along the edges of my mouth to assuage the dryness. "Thank you."

Rich applies my hood himself, blindfolding me like an executioner. Everything goes black. There's jerking around my neck and head, fingers testing the tubes and the connections to my suit. When they're done, I feel a hand, presumably Rich's, pat my shoulder. The platform descends.

The cold works its way up from my ankles as I sink into the water. I take a few deep breaths, the respirator humming, once I'm waist deep. The pressure builds around my chest, then my neck. I'm submerged. My feet lose contact with the platform. I'm floating.

I wrap my arms around my chest, each hand clutching the triceps opposite it. My breath comes in pants now, the cold working its way through my suit. I shiver uncontrollably.

I spasm. What am I doing? I want out. My right hand leaps out searching for purchase in the sphere. There is none. I grope with my left. My feet kick, extending vainly to locate the sides. I yell and it echoes about in my cowl. I suck in air and prepare to shriek.

"Hush," Becca says.

I take a deep breath, and a state of calm passes over and through me like a breeze tickling the needles of a pine. My shoulders relax, the muscles releasing, my body curling into a fetal position. My consciousness wanes. I struggle to construct the outline of Rebecca's face. She fades.

My body succumbs to the cold, to the darkness. I knowingly exhale one last time. It's like dying.

Waking is a violent act. It's painful. It blisters one's senses like volcanic steam. It terrifies.

I gasp, my eyes going wide like a bass laboring in a jon boat's hull. I'm on my side, my left arm trapped against a slab of concrete beneath my weight. Saltwater stings my eyes; I taste droplets on my quaking lips. My lungs heave, filling and collapsing, each breath testing their capacity.

I shake. I blink wildly. Bit by bit, inky forms take shape in the gloom.

"He's not dead after all," a man says. His voice scratches like sandpaper.

"I told you," a woman says.

"And you're sure that's him?" the man says.

"The tank said G. Duncan. There can't be more than one G. Duncan here."

The man isn't convinced, so he decides to ask me. "Are you Graham Duncan?"

My body bounces with every labored breath, the stale air piercing my throat. I offer no reply.

He leans in and asks me again. His features come into focus.

His face is thin and piebald, a series of dark and light jigsaw pieces extending up from his jaw to the bridge of his nose.

I twist, straining to locate the woman as I tremble. She's behind me, standing over my shoulder, wrapped in rags.

"Mr. Graham Duncan?" she asks. Her face, like the man's, is a patchwork. Depigmented elliptical shapes surround her eyes and mouth, giving her a surprised Jack-O-Lantern expression.

My eyes and mouth go wide, an unconscious imitative response. I'm shuddering, too cold to offer anything but a single auditory droplet. "Yes," seeps forth.

"Let's get him to Mother," she says.

"What about the others? Like that one in there?" he says. He points to the tank holding Melinda Norris.

"No, Mother's instructions were clear. Just Duncan."

The man calls out to others. "It's him."

There's the shuffling of feet. I'm rolled onto my back by a collection of hands into an open blanket. One of them pulls the blanket under my head and shoulder. He clutches the cover between the sides of his hands as a seal might grab a ball between its flippers. His hands are mottled like the others' faces, but his knuckles are thick and bulbous like knots on a tree. His crippled fingers twist and break at impossible angles. He awkwardly flips the blanket around my neck. It stinks of mildew. I don't have the strength or focus to complain. I lose myself in its warmth.

Arms jostle me, sliding under me. "Lift," the woman says, and they do in unison. They carry me from the chamber up two flights of stairs and onto the streets of Chicago.

Leaves swan dive and spiral from their roosts. It's crisp. Fall has taken hold. I stare up into the sky as dusk turns to night and realize that, for the first time, I can see stars. Their radiance isn't competing with the sky glow of light pollution. Other than us, the streets are deserted. The streetlamps and offices are dark.

They haul me down State Street, under the serpentine skeleton that used to be the elevated train system. The hours pass, and I drift in and out of sleep, my dreams blurring with a new and unacceptable reality.

My stomach wakes me, growling and knotting. The smell of boiled chicken hangs in the air. I'm on my back on a futon. A floral duvet covers me. I struggle to lean forward on my elbows. I'm wearing a grey sweatshirt. A fire burns in a hearth on the far side of the room, a large cauldron of sorts sitting before it. Smoke escapes the flue, rising and snaking about the exposed rafters. The woman kneels near the pot, stirring it occasionally until she realizes I'm awake. She ladles broth into a bowl and walks it to my side. "Here," she says, cupping the bowl with her wrists, almost as one might bump a volleyball. She holds it tight with the radius and supports it with the ulna of each hand. "Eat."

Her hands show all the signs of the early onset of rheumatoid arthritis. Her thumbs are beginning to splay, her knuckles deviate and pop from joints. Her finger bones don't properly align. They curve slightly away from her thumbs and then back again. It's called swan necking. The muscles and tendons on one side of the joint are overwhelming their counterparts on the other. In a few years, her fingers will all bend like the letter S.

Worse, her skin looks irritated and red. The backs of her hands are covered in silvery scales.

I take the bowl from her with both hands and pour it down my throat without asking what it is.

"Slow down," she says. She pulls at the edge, tugging the bowl away from my face.

I'm not dissuaded. I tear the broth away from her and continue to devour it. It's full of bits of chicken and carrot. It's unseasoned, but it's delicious. When I finish, I hand it back to her. "More," I say.

She studies me for a moment before returning to the cauldron.

"What is this place?" I ask. My voice is horse, my throat scratchy.

The woman says nothing.

"Where's Doctor Winters?" I say.

She simply puts a finger to her lips. "Shhhh," she says. "Mother will answer all of your questions."

"My mother lives in Pasadena," I say.

"Not your mother," the woman says. "Our Mother." She comes to my side and presents me another bowl.

I begin to slurp, then pause. My head cocks. "What's your name? Can you tell me that? Or do we have to wait for Mom?"

"Panda," she says.

She doesn't have to tell me she's named after the inverted vitiligo blotches on her face.

"How old are you?"

"Twenty-four," she says.

I eyeball her, my jaw going slack. She has the hands of a sixty year old. "And who were those people with you last night?"

"My tribe. Puzzle, Spot, Star, Clown, Globe, Galloway, and the others. Mother sent us for you. Finish your food."

I'm all but too eager to oblige. As soon as I'm finished, I pepper her with more questions. "Now, where am I?"

The door behind me opens on cue. An elderly woman shuffles forward. Her face is not a quilt of pigment like Panda and the others. She's dressed in a long orange muumuu and is escorted by two men. They hold her beneath her arms, supporting most of her weight. They guide her beyond the threshold. "To my left," she tells them, and I realize they are blind. They glide her to the chair across from me. "Here," she says to the men. She turns to me. "'When' is probably a better question."

"When?" I say.

"It's so nice to see you again, Graham," she says.

"Do we know each other?"

"Yes, although I don't expect you to remember me. I've changed a lot since then." She lowers herself into a seat. "They call me Mother because I'm the oldest. You called me Elizabeth Rogers. It's been thirty-seven years."

"Okay, this joke isn't funny anymore. Where's Rich?"

"Rich Winters is dead. He died thirty years ago."

"What? I just saw him." I start to get up, but my body puts up a fight. I'm not going anywhere. Not yet.

"I know it feels like you were just with him, but you've been in Hiber-sleep. I know it's hard to accept, but you've been in a pod for nearly four decades."

I stare at her as she speaks. She's so much thinner, but I can see similarities in the bone structure, in her straight, once blonde hair. The room spins. "This can't be. Liz?" My colleague? "No," I whisper. "Get me a mirror," I tell Panda.

Panda looks to Mother, and Liz nods her approval. She quickly walks towards the hallway entrance that frames Liz's chair. She disappears down the corridor and returns a moment later holding a cracked handled mirror.

I struggle to pull myself to a sitting position. I prop myself up against the arm of the couch. I seize it from Panda, steel myself, and regard my reflection.

I half expect to hear Becca tell me to "take it easy," to tell me that no matter what I see "everything will be okay." The absence of her voice is thunderous.

I brace myself, preparing for a stranger's greeting. The man I see, however, looks only slightly older than the one Lal fitted in a neoprene suit before a full-length mirror. A shave and a haircut, and no one would be the wiser. I look to Liz, my face twisting with confusion.

"Congratulations," she says. "You are officially the oldest man alive on Earth. You don't look a day over sixty though."

I look in the mirror again. I pull at the skin under my eyes. "I don't understand."

"Suspended animation," Liz says. "The process not only halted the progress of your disease, it slowed your aging process."

"Pickled," I say under my breath. "Like Rip Van Winkle."

Panda's eyebrows knit. "Like who?"

"An old story," Mother says. "I'll tell it to you some night." Liz turns her attention back to me. "I have some very bad news. I asked Panda and Puzzle to wake you. Prematurely, I'm afraid. I cannot offer you a cure for your cancer. No one can."

The mirror drops to my lap. I bite my lip, taste blood.

"I can offer you something far greater," she says. "A place in history." Her smile is soft. It reveals Elizabeth's trademark gap between her central incisors. "The world has changed drastically since you walked into that clinic."

"No," I say again. A pain builds in my gut. It's something other than hunger. It's something more. It's the cramping that flows from anxiety, the nexus of the brain-gut axis. It tells me that all of this is more than just a dream. It signals that I'm trying to cope, that I've given Liz's words credence. Something catastrophic has happened. Worse, I shouldn't be here.

"It started with a bug," she says. "Staphylococcus Interfectorem.

The Grapes of Wrath."

Staph gets its name from its structure, spherical bacterium that clump like grapes hanging from a vine, what the Greeks call "staphyle."

"Clever," I mutter.

"The R-naught value was between twelve and twenty." Once infected, a person was likely to pass the pathogen on to between twelve and twenty others.

"How is that even possible?" I say.

"It was crafty. Resilient. Communicable despite the infected being asymptomatic. It went airborne in Sierra Leone. The CDC speculated that it jumped a flight to Paris. From there it globetrotted. The incubation period was between fifteen and thirty days. It was everywhere before WHO knew what it was."

Medical detachment washes over me. It's not something that can or even should be taught. It's not an ability to celebrate, the casual flip of the switch between empathy and cold calculation. I'm not sure which is "on" and which is "off," viewing bodies as humans or humans as bodies. Regardless, I'm in mechanic mode now. I've opened the hood of the corporis humani and am checking the engine. "Symptoms?" I say.

"Vomiting. Fever. Sudden loss of blood pressure. Diarrhea. Skin lesions. Death within three to seven days of showing symptoms." She says this with the conviction of a physician, shaking the last vestiges of doubt I had that she is, indeed, Doctor Elizabeth Rogers.

"The fatality rate?" I ask.

"Ninety percent. I witnessed it firsthand. I survived it. My husband and daughter did not."

"And antibiotics?"

"Useless. This outbreak wasn't just resistant. It was impervious. The thing mutated unlike anything we had ever seen. It lived and reproduced in UV light up to nine months."

"Nothing worked?"

"Nothing. Until . . . " Her voice trails off.

"Yes?"

"Until the introduction of a new class of antibiotics, a computer screened oxadiazole. Davis Pharmaceuticals went into mass production with a vaccine. They created enough to treat every remaining man, woman, and child in the first and second worlds. And they did. It worked."

"There's a 'but,' isn't there?"

"But," she says, "it worked too well."

She doesn't have to say more. I can guess. The vitiligo. The arthritis. The blindness. The aggressive psoriasis. Everything suddenly adds up. "It was the nuclear option."

Mother/Liz nods.

I can tell her the rest of the story, and I do. "We lost our old friends," I say, referring to a theory that walks hand in hand with the hygiene hypothesis.

Our immune system is a schoolyard bully. It's always itching for a fight. Typically, it's beating on the kids from the neighboring schools—bacteria, parasites, and fungi that don't look like they belong. This provides cover for our cells and the friendly bacteria that cheer on the brawling macrophages as they beat the living tar out of the jerks from the rival institution.

When our bodyguard is in danger of losing a fight, someone inevitably calls the antibiotic cops. They arrive on the scene and arrest the outsider. Then they cruise the area for several days to make sure none of the punk's hood friends come around. Unfortunately, the antibiotic police make friendly bacterial flora in our guts nervous. Some of them might disappear for a few days. Some of them might not ever come back. When they don't, our immune system turns menacing.

Our immune system—with all of its macrophages, B and T cells, complement molecules, etc.—is a bad boy. It's dark and brooding. When rivals stop showing up on the playground to fight, the system gets surly. Ask it what it's rebelling against, and like Marlon Brando the macrophages will say, "What do you got?" Before long, it's overreacting to allergens, beating our cells mercilessly for looking at it wrong, and cutting good bacteria with a switchblade under the bleachers with joyful abandon.

That is, effectively, what the new class of antibiotics had done. They permanently changed the composition of our microbial environment. The drugs turned helpful microbes and our own cells into enemies, devastated our internal biodiversity, and made us more susceptible to diseases, including autoimmune ailments like myasthenia gravis, lupus, vasculitis, MS, type 1 diabetes mellitus, Guillain-Barre, and hyperthyroidism.

These men standing on either side of Mother are blind because their immune systems have turned on the cells that makeup their optical nerves. Their vitiligo, like Panda's, is due to an aggressive immune response to melanocytes, cells that produce pigment. Their hands are misshapen and inflamed because of an immune attack on their own synovial fluid in their joints and the resulting destruction of cartilage.

"Yes, that's my theory," she says.

I nod, but something puzzles me. "If you know all of this, why wake me? It can't be for my sparkling conversation."

Liz smiles. "No. I'm banking on the fact that the process that kept you alive all of these years also preserved the diversity of microbiota in your stomach. We can bring back species of bacteria long believed extinct. We can rebuild microbial ecosystems. I've been searching for you for a decade. I would have pulled you from your pod sooner if I could have. I'm sorry."

"Chrysalis," I say. But a worm builds a cocoon, sleeps, wakes, and is transformed. I'm still just a worm. "But pod seems more appropriate now."

"No, your emergence is to be celebrated," Liz says. "You're not just a moth. You're a rare butterfly. The rarest. You're a silver studded blue. And you can save us."

The harvesting of my gut microbes, although much less arduous than it sounds, is much more disgusting. About two weeks into my stay, my stool is solid enough to collect. Liz wants to transplant my germs to others via my fecal matter.

The process actually has a name: fecal bacteriotherapy. It's something Liz is well versed in. She oversees the productizing of my excrement, cutting it and serving it to the tribe wrapped in bits of meat or vegetables. She has created test groups. Some will get just a single dose a day. Some multiple. Some will receive a course of therapy over a few days. Others several.

Like I said, it's pretty gross.

Liz isn't a good candidate. While the diversity in her stomach is broader than most, it too has been compromised by her exposure to antibiotics and advanced hygiene standards. Her attempts to improve the health of a control group using her own fecal matter failed.

I am older. The biodiversity in my guts will be broader, like an old growth woods. I've been removed from continuously improving water quality and the ubiquity of antibacterial soaps. My microbes haven't been subjected to the haphazard prescription and slipshod use of antibiotics.

I track the days, scratching them into the wall behind the couch with the tine of a fork. Panda takes care of me on most of them. Like a mother potty-training a toddler, she applauds me when my bowel movements are consistent in size, shape, and timing. She pouts when I'm bound up or my stool is too loose.

She cooks and cleans my apartment. She washes my borrowed clothes. She helps me bathe. She works with me to strengthen my muscles and build stamina. Sometimes the guards outside my door allow me to stroll the hall under their supervision, but I usually just stand and stare out the window. By day seventeen, I can remain at my perch for up to four hours before my legs begin to shake, watching buildings and parking lots erode in real-time from three-stories up.

I wonder to what end I pursue this course. Although Panda loves to hear stories about my time on Earth, I easily grow fatigued. I'm forgetful, often repeating anecdotes. She doesn't seem to care, but I do.

I have not heard Rebecca's voice since being purged from the Chrysalis. My cancer, I fear, is advancing.

I carve a line across four parallel marks, the twenty-fifth day since my awakening. I ask Panda for an audience with Liz. She visits me that very night. She asks Panda and her escorts to wait outside.

"You look well," she says once they've left the room.

"Thank you," I say. "I think I'll be able to walk out of here of my own volition soon."

Liz frowns. "I'm not sure that's such a good idea. Chicago has changed. There are wild animals out there, creatures freed from the zoo. Worse, there are even wilder people. To be fair, I don't even know if they can be called that anymore."

"I'd really like to visit my wife's grave."

She shakes her head. "I don't think you understand. When the pandemic hit, resources were stretched to the brink. The dead littered the streets, and people were buried en masse to reduce the risk of infection and disease. Her grave is certainly unmarked."

"But—"

"You're better off here," she says, "under our protection."

"Maybe I can meet the others," I say. "Perhaps sit with them during dinner?"

"I take it Panda has been poor company," Liz says.

"No, not at all, she's been great. It just gets a little lonely."

"I'll replace her immediately," Mother says, scooting to the edge of her chair. She turns to call for the guards.

"Wait," I say, "please don't do that. She's fine. Really."

Liz nods. "Good." She calls for her escorts.

"Can't you stay longer?" I ask.

She apologizes and tells me she needs to help a midwife with a delivery on the fifth floor.

"I didn't even realize there was a fifth floor," I say as her attendants pick her up. "How many floors are there?"

Liz doesn't say anything as they guide her to the door.

"You know," I say with a chuckle, "I'm beginning to feel a bit like a prisoner."

She is almost to the door when she hears this. She tells the guard to halt. She instructs them to pivot her. "I'd prefer to think of you as my guest," she says, facing me. "Our guest. Goodnight, Graham." And with that, she's off.

When Panda arrives the next morning, she's sullen and reserved.

She doesn't want to hear my stories about the lights and bustle on Michigan Avenue at Christmas. She goes about her work preparing lunch.

"Did I already tell you about the Mag Mile? I'm sorry."

"No," she says, eyes downcast.

"Then what's wrong?" I ask.

"Nothing." She skins and cuts potatoes at the table. She throws them into the iron pot, each chunk generating a soft *dong* as it strikes the bottom.

"Well, something's wrong," I say.

She suddenly stops, and drops the pot on the floor. "This is my last day with you. Mother has asked me to go back to the clinic where we found you tomorrow."

I inch forward. "What?"

"She wants us to open another pod. She wants us to wake someone else."

"Why does she want that?"

"She didn't say. All I know is that I won't be assigned to you anymore." A lone tear skips from her cheek.

"Can you ask Liz if I can talk to her again?"

Panda nods and wipes her eye.

"We'll make it better, okay?"

She nods and smiles.

I spend an hour telling her about Water Tower Place and answering questions about the holiday displays, carriage rides, and pizza.

After I eat, Panda departs. She promises she'll return with news from Mother. I stare east out the window like some gargoyle and watch the sky grow dark. The rock and steel edifices of a past culture turn pink as the sun descends somewhere behind me. I press my head against glass and look down.

That's when I notice the relief of the masonry brick, a pattern of two protruding bricks spaced every two feet vertically and horizontally. That's when I notice the canopy two floors below.

Panda does not return that night. And Mother—she is no longer Liz to me—does not visit.

That evening as I ready myself for sleep, I consider my escape.

The next morning, I wake to find a man sweeping the floor with a busted broom. Despite being short, he must bend at the waist in order to reach the floor with the broken handle. The vitiligo has formed a series of dark and white lines across his chin and cheeks.

"Who are you?" I say with alarm.

The man stops and turns to me. "Good morning, Mr. Duncan."

I repeat my question.

"I'm Zebra," he says. "I'm your new attendant."

I swing my legs off the couch and stand. "I don't want a new attendant. Where's Panda?"

"I don't know," Zebra says, his shoulders hunching.

"Go away," I say, collapsing back into the couch.

"Don't you want breakfast?" he asks.

"I'm not hungry."

He nods and hurries to the door. He gives it a quick knock, and the guards open it and allow him to exit.

"Tonight," I say to myself. Then I go back to sleep.

A clamor at the door wakes me a few hours later. "I thought I told you to go away," I say, rolling on my belly.

Panda shuts the door behind her and looks at me, perplexed.

"Sorry," I say, rubbing my eyes. "I thought you were someone else."

She rushes to my side. "You need to leave. Tonight."

I ask her why. I don't tell her about my designs to do so anyway.

"We brought another body back from the clinic this morning."

"Body?" I say.

"She didn't wake when we pulled her from the tank. She's alive, but she never woke."

*M. Norris.*

"Where is she now?"

Panda winces.

"Where?" I say.

"With Mother."

"Take me to her."

"No," Panda says. "It won't do any good."

"Why is that?"

"Because," Panda says, trying to stifle a sob, "Mother killed her."

"What?"

"She said that the woman couldn't be fed and couldn't help like you could."

"So she just killed her?"

"No," Panda says, trembling. "She cut her open first."

"Tell me how."

Panda doesn't spare me any of the graphic details. Mother cut into Melinda Norris' chest with a scalpel, first down the middle, then across the belly and below the neck. She pulled back the skin, muscle, and fat to expose her rib cage.

I imagine the flaps of tissue pinned back like the wings of a butterfly held fast to a mounting board.

Puzzle helped Mother cut the breastbone with a pipe saw. They cracked her chest plate open, and Mother removed the comatose Melinda's lungs. Bits of lung were cut away and placed on clear plates with lids.

"Petri dishes," I mumble. "She's trying to culture bacteria. She's mad. What then."

"She kept cutting until there was too much blood. The woman stopped breathing."

I shake my head. "Thank you," I say.

"I'm scared," Panda says.

"Don't be," I say, although I too am terrified. "I'll make sure you never have to do that again. Now go. Go before anyone gets suspicious."

She exits with one last look over her shoulder. The door closes.

"Goodbye," I say to no one. To everyone.

Mother and Panda have changed my plans.

❖ ❖ ❖

Once it's dark I slide the window open to the right. I step out on to the sill and crouch, my back braced against the stile, the exposed edge of the open window. I lean forward, placing my weight against the frame. I palm the inside wall with my left hand while watching my right. I stretch and my fingers touch a six by six inch protrusion of brick. I can't quite grasp the top of the edge. I close my eyes. I actually say a prayer. Then I lunge.

My palm bounces against the brick, and my fingers barely find purchase on the inch deep edge. My legs swing, the momentum pulling me. My chin scrapes the protrusion just below my handhold. My grip starts to slip, but my feet kick and find a ledge below. That moment allows me to grasp the bricks near my chest with my left hand.

I close my eyes and sigh. I'm out. Time to descend. I feel for the ledge against my chest with my right hand, and it takes hold near my left. I shift my weight to my left hand and leg, and drop my right foot as I lower my chest. My arms pump and pain shoots up from my elbow. My upper body strength is not what I thought.

My right foot finds support, and I bring my left to join it. This is how it goes, arms then legs, for the next fifteen minutes until I'm about twelve feet off the ground.

That's when my handhold erodes, the brick façade tearing loose under my nails.

I fall backwards, arms flailing. I miss the canopy. I bend forward, trying to protect my head from the rushing concrete.

The collision never comes. I land in a boxwood, my arms and lower legs hanging beyond its unkempt edges. The evergreen tears at my jeans and punctures my shirt, but it cushions my impact. I sit up and check the sting at my side. An eight-inch scratch curls across my hip and bleeds freely. I press my shirt against it and rush south.

The moonlight illuminates my path forward, highlighting the broken glass and cracked asphalt ahead. I cross my arms and thrust my hands under my armpits to keep them warm in the growing cold. I follow the river south to State Street and cross the crumbling swing bridge. In places the concrete has slipped from the rebar, exposing holes in places big enough to swallow a compact. I keep to the edge, keeping a hand on the railing. As I pass the southeast tenderhouse and its dedication to the veterans who fought in Bataan and Corregidor, I hear voices. I slip behind the disintegrating limestone. Kneeling, I peer beyond the edge of the turret.

Just twenty feet away on Wacker Drive, a dozen or more people make their way west. They carry torches and the carcasses of two deer. They laugh and celebrate their kills. Once they've reached the intersection of Dearborn, I make my way forward again.

Thirty minutes later, I arrive at the clinic. I enter through the frame of what was once a glass door. I veer right to a staircase and descend. One flight down, I grab my knees and expel air. I question my physical ability, but not my resolve. I trudge on to the subbasement's landing. Feeling my way forward, I locate a fire axe behind emergency glass. I lean into it, popping the pane. The shards fall to the ground and shatter. The crash echoes through the staircase. I hesitate and listen for a response. Hearing nothing, I pull the axe from its moorings. It's heavy, but the insulated handle ensures that it doesn't slip from my weakening grip.

The hall of Chrysalides is lit by the instrument panels of just nine functioning hiber-chambers. Some of the previously populated pods are now empty, but there's evidence that the program continued to recruit after me. Lights glow from two units in a row that were unused when I entered my sleep dozens of years ago.

Tonight it all ends.

I have no idea how to take down a UPS. I do, however, know how to unplug an aquarium. I simply need to find the power lines. Then cut.

I don't for a single moment consider what I'm about to do as murder. I reason that these deaths will be painless, like slipping away in one's sleep, but I don't view this as mercy either. It's more simplistic. I'm delivering on a contract. They mortgaged their short lives for a dream. Their dreams cannot be answered, not in this world. Keeping them in limbo is wrong. They deserve to move on.

I begin at the closest live chamber. *P. Snyder.* I press my ear against it and hear the engines whirring, water stirring and the movement of air. I circle the tank, touching the base of the pod, searching for cabling in the darkness. At the back I find a clump of tubes, tentacles that emerge from machine and complete the circuit. I position myself directly in front of it, my legs split, my feet firmly planted. I raise the axe above my head and let the weight of it do the work. It falls.

*Clank-clank-cla-clank.* The axe strikes below my target and bounces off of the cement.

I inch forward and swing again.

The axe finds its mark. Electric sparks leap forth, illuminating the area before me with a blinking, stroboscopic effect. Then everything goes dark. The instrument panel goes dead. The hum of the pod ceases . . . as does the life it contains.

I move to the subtle glow of another Chrysalis.

*A. Rodriguez.*

I address him by name. I apologize. I wish him well on his journey. Then I cut the cord that binds him to this plane.

I do this eight more times.

*P. Huggins.*

*W. Simmons.*

*R. Hawkins.*

*M. Hale.*

*A. Tipnis.*

*I. Williams.*

*M. Klein.*

*F. Hrin.*

I say each of their names.

The weight of the axe threatens to pull me to the ground and hold me fixed against the floor. It would be easy to slumber here. It would be a privilege to join these souls, these adventurers into the unknown. But I still have things to do. I drop the axe at my feet. I step over it and stagger through the darkness. I exit this lab-turned-tomb and start my journey north.

When I pass the Friendly Confines, I know I'm getting close. I took Becca to her first game here. She was bored. She complained the game lacked the pace and skill of soccer. I welcomed the downpour that came in the fourth inning, and we abandoned this shrine to futility in full sprint. We skipped through the puddles, kicking sprays of gutter water at each other. Soaked, we made our way to her apartment and spent our first night together. I grin as I shuffle past the fallen billboards, the caving parking structure, and ruined Wrigley taverns and hotels.

At Clark and Irving Park Road, I enter Graceland Cemetery through an open wrought iron gate. I veer off the once carefully manicured paths towards Lake Willowmere. Wolves call from somewhere in the distance. I can't tell if they're within the walls of this graveyard or beyond. I stoop to pick up a fragment of a tombstone. It is pointed and sharp.

Deep grass claims the headstones. Trees stretch and break forth from the mausoleums. Yet the engraved names remain legible.

*Kinzie. Clark. Pinkerton. Adler. Ebert. Field. Getty. McCormick. Burke. Ward. Daley.*

Titans of industry. Masters of design. Political giants.

I arrive at the lake's edge, interrupting a chorus of frogs. A hush descends over the water.

*Burnham. Wacker. Pullman. Harrison. Palmer. Goodman.*

Pioneers, inventors, and dreamers. From these people, civilization was born.

*Richard Winters.* Rich. His marker is less opulent than most of the vaults and monuments here, but that's of no matter. His was a life no less lived. I touch the limestone and search the weeds on either side of his grave.

A marker lies on its back. I pull it forward. I slide it back onto its marble base.

I drop the shard. I fall to my hands and knees.

*Rebecca Winters.*

They're both here. I turn to Rich's plot. "Just like you promised," I say.

My gaze returns to Becca's headstone. She died just five years after my internment. The inscription just below the lunette reads, "Loving wife of Graham Duncan."

She never divorced me.

I hug the stone and place my cheek against it. I allow myself a moment to cry, but only just a moment. There is still work to do.

I grasp the pointed rock and walk on my knees to Rich's tomb. I lift the stone and place the sharp edge against the marker, just below his name. I work the fragment up and down and from side to side. I move from left to right, carving horizontally and vertically. When I'm done, I wipe my brow.

*Melinda Norris.* She died so that others might live. Her biome will live forever in generations she'll never know. Her name belongs in this place, in this exclusive club.

I return to Becca and scratch, "Loving husband," just below my name.

I curl up amongst the weeds, directly over her casket.

"Where have you been?" she asks me. "I've missed you."

I sigh as her words caress me. "Nowhere," I say. "It doesn't matter. I'm here now."

"Will you stay?" she says.

"Forever," I say. We talk until I fall asleep.

## About the Author

Matt Darst's childhood addiction to reading took a turn for the worst when he started writing . . . for fun. His experimentation with notebooks (a classic gateway) led to dabbling with typewriters. Soon he was hitting the hard stuff: word processors.

After law school, he decided to straighten out his life. He went cold turkey. He got a responsible job, a house in Chicago, and a dog. He surrounded himself with all the trappings of a normal life. Still . . .

Pen and pad call to Matt late at night, cooing his name, telling him to take another hit of fiction. Sometimes, when he's weak, he heeds the siren call of the drug. He wakes from each blackout amid reams of freshly written pages, pages that have seemingly written themselves.

*Freaks Anon* is Matt's second novel.

## Also by Matt Darst

*Dead Things, A Novel*

## About the Charity

Cancer loots and extorts. It pilfers and defrauds, stealing from us and the ones we love. Cancer is nothing short of biological larceny.

We must face the bandit. We must fight. We must take back our bodies and our lives.

I'm hoping to make a difference, even if it's a small one. Towards that end, I'm committing all of the proceeds from *Freaks Anon* to charity. Royalties will be catalogued quarterly and donated to Stand Up To Cancer (SU2C). Progress will be charted at:

http://do.eifoundation.org/goto/mattdarst

SU2C is an initiative created to accelerate innovative cancer research that will get new therapies to patients quickly and save lives now. SU2C brings together the best and the brightest researchers and encourages collaboration instead of competition among the entire cancer community.

The charity received a grade of A- from Charity Watch in September 2015. Approximately 77% of SU2C's cash budget is spent on programs versus overhead.

Thank you for helping me stand up to cancer.

## ALSO FROM GRAND MAL PRESS

# A SHADOW CAST IN DUST
## by Ben Johnson

The ancient order of the web spinners is changing. An old friend returns brandishing a curious silver knife, and Stewart Zanderson is drawn into a strange world of wonder and deceit. The ensuing bloody scene sets Detective Clementine Figgins on his tail, and into a case she could never explain. But the boy, escaped from the dreaded warehouse, now has the knife. And running from his captors through the canyons of San Diego with his new friends and special dog, he ties everything together. People fight. Some die. The ancient order will change, but who will rise when the dust settles?

"An engaging Urban Fantasy Adventure!"

# ALSO FROM GRAND MAL PRESS

# DEAD THINGS
## by Matt Darst

Nearly two decades have passed since the fall of the United States. And the rise of the church to fill the void. Nearly twenty years since Ian Sumner lost his father. And the dead took to the streets to dine on the living. Now Ian and a lost band of survivors are trapped in the wilderness, miles from safety. Pursued by madmen and monsters, they unravel the secrets of the plague...and walk the line of heresy. Ian and this troop need to do more than just survive. More than ever, they must learn to live.

Dead Things has been called "an amalgam of Clerks and everything Crichton and Zombieland."

ISBN: 978-1-937727-10-9

**Available in paperback and all ebook formats.**

"Dead Things a first-rate triumph. Darst is taking the zombie novel in a really cool new direction."
-Joe McKinney, author of *Dead City* and *Apocalypse of the Dead*

"A first-class zombie story which takes place in a beautifully realized post-apocalyptic world. Highly recommended!" - David Moody, author of *Autumn*

# HAFTMANN'S RULES
## BY ROBERT WHITE

The first full-length novel to feature White's recurring private investigator, Thomas Haftmann! Out of jail and back on the streets, Haftmann is hired to find a missing young girl in Boston. But what he uncovers goes beyond just murder, into a world of secret societies, bloodshed, and betrayal beyond anything he has experienced before. HAFTMANN'S RULES is an exhilarating read into one man's maddening journey for truth, justice, and self destruction.

ISBN: 9780982945971

**Available in paperback and all ebook formats.**

*"Haftmann's Rules grabs you by the soul and doesn't let go!"* -Simon Wood, author of THE FALL GUY

*"White's recurring private investigator, Tom Haftmann, would do Dashiell Hammett proud!"* - Sex and Murder Magazine.

# ALSO FROM GRAND MAL PRESS

# DEAD DOG
## BY NICKOLAS COOK

It's the late 70s and Max and Little Billy are back from Vietnam trying to mind their own business when they stumble onto the murder of a local boy. With organized crime and local thugs on their trail, it's up to these two heroes to solve the murder.

ISBN: 978-1937727246

# WALKING SHADOW
## by Clifford Royal Johns

Benny tries to ignore the payment-overdue messages he keeps getting from "Forget What?," a memory removal company. Benny's a slacker, after all, and couldn't pay them even if he wanted to. Then people start trying to kill him, and his life suddenly depends on finding out what memories he has forgotten. Benny relies on his wits, latent skills, and new friends as he investigates his own past; delving deeper and deeper into the underworld of criminals, bad cops, and shady news organizations, all with their own reasons for wanting him to remain ignorant or die.

ISBN: 9781937727253

# ALSO FROM GRAND MAL PRESS

# The Summer I Died
## by Ryan C. Thomas

**ASIN: B00DUMIAQQ**

The cult thriller novel is back in this all new edition which features the original text as it was meant to be published! Dubbed one of "The Most Intense Horror Novels" ever written by many horror review sites, *The Summer I Died* is the first book in the Roger Huntington Saga and soon to be a major motion picture!

"A tense bloody ride!" - Brian Keene

"*The Summer I Died* is an endurance test. It's certainly not for everybody. But if you want to freak yourself out on your next camping trip, you can't really do any better."
- BloodyDisgusting.com

# Last Stand In A Dead Land
## by Eric S. Brown

**ISBN: 9780982945971**

A small band of survivors is on the run during the zombie apocalypse. Led by a mysterious man with an arsenal of deadly military weapons, they must work together to stay alive. In a desperate attempt to locate other survivors, they find sanctuary in a lone farmhouse, only to discover the surrounding woods hold more dangers than just bloodthirsty undead. Featuring Sasquatch, roving rotters, and even more surprises, Last Stand in a Dead Land is an explosion of cross genre action that will leave you wanting more.

# ALSO FROM GRAND MAL PRESS

## Angel Steel
### by Randy Chandler

When virgin warrior Braga learns from a cross-cult sorcerer that Fate has chosen her to steal the sword of a rogue angel, she lights out on a dangerous quest from mystical Hag Mountain to other worlds, and even into the bowels of Hell. With her soul in the balance, she and the mist-walking sorcerer encounter all manner of damned souls, demons, the living dead and noble fighters. A sweeping tale of vengeance and manipulative evil, ANGEL STEEL takes you on an intriguing trip into the dark fantastic.

ASIN: B00EDX6RUW

# DARKER THAN NOIR

When a mundane mystery needs solving, you call a private detective. But when the mystery involves ghosts, demons, zombies, monsters, mystical serial killers, and other supernatural elements, you call the detectives in this collection. They'll venture into the darkness and hopefully come back out alive. Just remember, they get paid expenses up front, and what they uncover, you might not like. Featuring tales from seasoned vets and up-and-coming talent, the game is afoot in a world that is Darker Than Noir.

ISBN: 9780982945957

For more Grand Mal Press titles
please visit us online at
www.grandmalpress.com

www.ingramcontent.com/pod-product-compliance
Lightning Source LLC
Chambersburg PA
CBHW050519110726
47899CB00005B/1514